THE DEATH AND LIFE OF IPHIGENIA

J. SUSANNE WILSON

NINE MUSES
PRESS

For my mom.
Thank you for lending me your name.

PROLOGUE

I am Iphigenia, High Priestess to Artemis, daughter of the cursed house of Atreus, and killer of lost men.

I died at the hand of my father. Mine was the first drop in a scarlet river that would flow for ten years. I, bride of golden Achilles, was the innocent gift to Artemis, who kept the sea winds caged until I came to her, my life-giving blood flowing from my throat.

You sing, Muse, of the tears that soaked my youthful cheeks, but you do not remember that I stumbled to my fate, unknowing. You do not tell how I fell to my knees, begging with silent eyes for the goddess to change my father's mind.

You do not tell of a false wedding and a desperate mother. You do not sing of a dazed victim, who wandered toward her death, unwilling and afraid.

You do not sing of exile in a barbaric land, a girl who is forced to do unthinkable things with her own clean hands. You do not tell of the fear and the longing and the triumph.

Instead, Muse, these are the tales you whisper into the ears of far-traveling bards and steady-handed painters and soft-skinned maidens in great halls: you sing the song of Agamemnon's daughter who, with courage in her beating heart, unleashed the swift winds that ushered a thousand ships from Greece to the shores of Troy, beginning the long and brutal war among men and gods.

But this is not my true song.

Listen to me now, Muse, and I will sing to you my truth. I will not omit the ugliness to shelter the gossiping maidens. I will not add noble gestures to aid the painters' hands. Nor will I replace the dusty truth with flowery phrases to please the singing bards. I give you my story, with no fear of your wrath in my heart, for you to sing to future generations so they will not forget.

The gods have silenced my ears and stolen my ability to sleep for an entire night. It is difficult for me to remember whether I ate figs or cheese for breakfast, or if I dined alone or with companions last night. But I remember my youth as clearly as you remember yours. The gods have allowed my early years to dance in my memories in full color and full sound.

Sometimes it is difficult to know whether this is a curse or a blessing.

But I do know this: the story I'm about to tell you is the truth. These fourteen years of my life that I'm about to relive for you are as real as the blue sky above your head and the cool breeze on your cheeks.

I swear this to Artemis. And, as you are about to learn, that is no small thing.

PART ONE

CHAPTER 1

I phigenia! Elektra! Hurry!" Ismene herded the two of us like lambs toward the stairs that led to our maiden room.

The horns blew again, the hollow blasts echoing off the palace walls, impossible to ignore. I squeezed Elektra's little hand as we climbed the wooden steps side by side, Ismene and my new maid, Damalis, close on our heels.

"But—" I started, turning my head to look at my former nurse. She cut me off. "Go!"

"But what about Orestes?" I managed to get all the words out on my second try.

By this point, we'd reached the top of the stairs and Ismene gently pressed between our shoulder blades to keep us moving. Her breaths were labored now, but finally she wheezed, "Your brother's nurse has kept him safe."

Just before we reached our room, five of Mother's guards rushed past us, heading back the way we came, their short white tunics fluttering behind them. They didn't acknowledge Elektra and me with bows or polite greetings. Instead, we were forced to flatten our backs against the hard wall so the guards had the room to pass unimpeded.

The third set of blasts came just as my little sister and I were stepping into the safety of the maiden room we shared. Ismene latched the heavy door behind us, muffling the last note.

"How do you know he'll be safe?" I demanded, my eyes darting from Ismene to Damalis and back.

But before either of them could answer, Elektra asked her own question. "What do those horns mean?"

I understood why she was asking. Our entire lives, those same horns had meant nothing but good things. Those very horns had sounded from the many lookout posts, where they were sounding from now, countless times before. Each time Father returned home from a journey—hunting trips, diplomatic calls to nearby cities, or visits to his brother in faraway Sparta—sentries blasted their announcing calls. But those announcements were cheerful, an exuberant display of six blasts repeated three times.

In fact, we'd seen a dozen of those long bronze horns only three weeks before, when Father led his great army out of the citadel, under the great city gate and through the winding streets toward the promise of glorious war. Twelve men flanked the palace gate, six on one side and six on the other, blasting long, triumphant notes from the gleaming horns. On that day, drums and tambourines and flutes accompanied them, of course, creating a joyous cacophony to send our men off to glory.

These four stunted blasts were new to me. How could I have known, then, that the sounds I was hearing were code for *echthros?*
Enemy.
Over and over again: *ech-thros, ech-thros.*
"The horns are telling you to run to safety, Elektra," Ismene

answered.

"But what's happening?" Elektra's dark eyes glistened with unshed tears.

"I don't know."

Our maiden room was tiny, nothing more than a space to dress, sleep, and dress again. Our two beds lined opposite walls with a wooden chest sitting at the foot of each. A small window pierced the top of the exterior wall, the wooden shutter almost always propped open, as it was on this day. The door to our room opened into the colonnaded oak corridor, but the thick stone walls and low wood ceiling swallowed any light that tried to slip its way in.

Ismene picked up the tongs and squeezed a hot coal from the jar on the floor to light the tall lamp inside the door. The bowl of oil burst into orange flames that lit the corners of our room.

Elektra and I perched on the edge of my bed, and Ismene plopped her plump body on the bed across from us, the sound of her labored breaths filling the room.

Damalis paced, twisting the hem of her tunic in both fists. She'd made only a handful of circuits around the small space before the footsteps sounded down the hall outside our door.

They were heavy, booted steps. They were men.

I wrapped my arm around Elektra's narrow shoulders and pulled her close to my side. A bead of sweat slipped down my back and my heart fluttered in my chest.

The footsteps stopped outside our closed door. Nothing happened. Nobody shattered the timber planks, nobody shouted commands for us to come out. Nobody even spoke.

Ismene, her face still red from exertion, nodded toward Damalis, who hesitated wide-eyed a good long time before shuffling toward the door.

She slowly reached for the latch, then lifted it free, knuckles white as snow. I'm certain we all held our breath.

Damalis shot a look back at us, saving a special foul glare for Ismene, then cracked the door just enough to poke her head through. I saw her shoulders sag with relief and she pulled her head back inside.

"Two guards," she said, then stepped into the corridor.

I couldn't see the guards, but I heard them as if they were standing right next to me.

"The queen sent us to protect her daughters," one of them announced. His voice was young and fresh, hints of high notes lingering every few words. "Until she finds out who the strangers are."

"Tell me what you know." Somehow, Damalis sounded calm, not as if she'd been jittery as a cornered mouse only moments before.

An older voice answered, thick and coarse. "Only that men approach from the north on horseback."

"Men? How many?"

"Don't know." The man clipped his words impatiently. "At least a dozen. And they wave King Agamemnon's banner."

"Why raise the alarm if they carry our banner?" Damalis asked.

"It may be a trick." This came from the young guard and was followed by a scuffle and a thump.

"What?" the boy pleaded. "It's the truth!"

The older guard hissed, "They're all listening. Don't put sorry ideas into the princesses' heads!"

"Did the queen send instructions for her daughters?"

The older guard answered. "They are to remain in their room. Until she sends for them."

The younger voice added, "And we'll be here to protect them the whole time."

I imagined the boy puffing his chest out with the words. Across from me, Ismene rolled her eyes to the ceiling.

I hoped Mother at least sent her high guards, and not lesser guards like these, to protect the only prince of Mycenae, my brother Orestes.

I closed my eyes, willing my thrumming heart to slow.

When Damalis came back inside the room, the calm facade she'd put on for the guards dropped like a curtain. Ismene patted the bed beside her. My maid hesitated, then perched lightly on the edge, ready to bolt at the smallest hint of danger.

Sounds poured through the open window and seeped, muffled, through the walls. Guards shouted commands across the courtyard, boots thumped the stone floors in a never-ending staccato, advisers muttered clipped phrases as they passed under our window.

We heard words like *machêtês* and *xenos* and *kataskopos*. Warrior, stranger, spy. Nobody knew who this band of men might be, though Ismene assured us that Mother would have certainly sent scouts to find out by now. The palace, she said, would prepare for this man to be friend or foe.

Each moment that passed, the air in our tiny room thickened with smoke and heat and fear. Damalis tapped both her feet in a sharp rhythm, and even Ismene's labored breaths seemed like they'd never grow easier. I wiped my sweaty palms on my tunic.

Ismene tried to distract us with the tale of Medea and her cursed sons, and I'm still not sure why she thought this would be a good time to tell the story of a witch who murdered her own children.

We fidgeted, and I strained to hear the sounds of the palace over her voice. Even Damalis, who was usually so eager to please Ismene, twirled the corner of her tunic, twisting and pulling until her fingertips turned purple.

Gradually, Ismene trailed off, leaving Damalis's tap-tap-tap the only sound in the room.

Elektra jumped and squeaked out a sob when a great boom reverberated through the walls. I squeezed her narrow shoulders to my side and Damalis's feet froze mid-tap.

We sat in silence, listening to the chaos in the palace, until my body almost itched with impatience. Before I gave myself the chance to think it through, I jumped to my feet and announced, "I'm going to find Mother. She'll tell us what to do."

Ismene grasped my wrist and yanked until I relented and sat back down on my bed.

"This is exactly what you're supposed to do right now, Iphigenia. Your mother already told you, if you hear four short blasts, you're supposed to run to your room and stay there until she calls for you. So, this is where you'll stay." She jabbed her finger toward the floor, but she wasn't done. "You won't leave until your mother, the queen, gives her permission."

I glared at my former nurse, the woman who'd raised me as if I were her own daughter until I turned thirteen last year. The woman who still raised my little sister.

Damalis cleared her throat and began to hum a flat and tuneless song.

"Shhh!" I snapped.

She clipped her last note into silence and dropped her gaze to her busy hands, twisting and twisting her fabric, the tips of her ears glowing pink.

A wave of guilt washed over me. We'd played together as little girls. She was as shy and mousy back then as she was now, and the rest of us used to make fun of her big ears. We called her *kantharos* because we thought she looked like one of those big two-handled cups. Or we called her sparrow because she was plain and brown and had wings growing from the sides of her head. She'd never shouted at us, never fought back. Instead, she'd turn to go home, silent tears sliding down her thin cheeks.

My eyes slid away from the girl. I was a princess and I would be a queen someday. Surely a good queen would never snap at a servant like that. A good queen would always act with dignity and grace.

"Sorry," I muttered, shame lodged in my throat. Then I took a breath and pulled my head high. "I would like to think in silence."

The girl nodded, still staring at her hands.

I glanced at Ismene, who beamed at me with something like pride in her eyes. Then I remembered I was angry with Ismene, so I crossed my arms over my chest and glared at her. She glowered back, the flame from the lamp dancing in her eyes.

I wasn't sure if I should admire her bravery, shooting black looks at a princess of Mycenae, or if I should scold her with my new authority as a woman with a maid instead of a little girl with a nurse.

In the end, I was the one whose eyes slid from hers, and I

sat staring at my slender hand clasping my sister's pudgy fingers, listening to the commotion in the palace.

Chapter 2

Another echoing thud came from across the courtyard, the sound bouncing toward us like a rushing beast. I threw a glance toward the window behind me. It was too high for me to see out of without dragging one of our wooden chests underneath, but I knew Ismene would never allow that kind of behavior without putting up a fight. I didn't want to waste time arguing with Ismene about whether it was proper behavior for a princess of Mycenae to haul her royal self onto a piece of furniture so she could peep from a window as if she were a spying slave.

I jumped to my feet once again, suddenly feeling like an animal, caged in this close room. This time, I avoided Ismene's eye and stepped straight toward the door. Elektra gasped as I pulled the door open.

"Iphigenia," Ismene started.

I ignored her pleading voice and stepped across the threshold. I'd been right about the guards. The younger one was barely older than me. Maybe sixteen or so. I didn't recognize him, but I did recognize his companion. I didn't know his name, but he'd been a palace guard for as long as I could remember. He was much older, at least thirty, battle scarred and pockmarked.

"Princess," the older one said in his gravelly voice, and they both bowed their heads and kept their eyes at my feet.

"I am going to see the queen. Where is she?" The tremble in my voice betrayed me and I cursed myself in my mind.

"She ordered us to keep you and the little princess safe in your room until she calls," the man said, eyes fixed on the ground.

"Is she in her chamber? I will go speak with her myself." I took one step toward the stairs.

The young guard cleared his throat, but it was the old guard who spoke. "Princess, if you leave the safety of your room, I will be forced to call more guards to fetch you and bring you back."

I paused. The image of this man hauling me back to my room like a scolded child sat cold in my mind. I clenched my jaw tight and felt my cheeks burn.

Taking a deep breath, I turned and stepped back into the room. I didn't miss the smirk that touched the guard's lips as I passed.

Possibilities bounced around my fevered mind, each one worse than the others. To calm my thoughts, I tried to work through the puzzle one step at a time.

The strangers came from the north. That meant they could have come from so many places. For the first time, I was glad I'd paid attention all those times I eavesdropped on Father's meetings with his advisers. Many great cities and tiny villages alike sat to the north of Mycenae. These visitors could have come from Thebes or Orchomenos or Athens.

Maybe they came from Delphi, Apollo's famous oracle, carrying a cryptic message from one of the god's sacred priests. They might carry a more personal message: perhaps news of Father's sister, my aunt Anaxibia, who lived in Phocis across the Gulf of Corinth.

Or maybe they came from Aulis. The thought sent a flutter through my belly.

Since the day he set out for Troy, Mycenaean messengers had streamed into the palace delivering news of Father, so we knew that he and his thousands of troops had been camped in the bay at Aulis for at least two weeks. Did something go awry? Had Father angered one of the gods? Could it be that his men rebelled against him, threatening to murder their king, Agamemnon?

The flutter grew into a squeeze.

There was still another possibility. Instead of news, the visitors might have come with malice in their hearts. A chieftain might have sent them to scout the palace, testing for weaknesses to exploit while most of the fighting men were away.

A sudden wave of anger washed through me. With the king away, and most of the able-bodied men of Mycenae with him, we were little more than fowl in a pen, exposed in our palace perched on the hill.

Sure, Father left behind guards and a handful of advisers who were able to fight if needed, but a well-organized band of young fighters might take us all.

And yes, he'd left his trusted cousin Aegisthus here to look after us, the royal children and queen, in his absence. Aegisthus had been nothing but loyal to Father since the day Father had reclaimed his throne from Aegisthus's own father. Aegisthus had sworn an oath of loyalty to Agamemnon, the new king of Mycenae, under the gaze of Zeus himself. Everyone knew an oath like that was unbreakable.

But what of the other men left behind? Could one or more of

them have organized a coup while the king was away fighting in Troy?

My father called himself many names—Agamemnon, Lord of Men; Agamemnon, Great King; Agamemnon, King of all Greece—and he complained of men who didn't appreciate his claims. Some said he was a pretender, that he was himself no more than a petty king in a stolen palace. Some even accused him of the mortal sin of hubris—unearned, extravagant pride. This, above all others, was the accusation that always threw Father into a fit of red-faced rage that sent his advisers cowering from the throne room.

These men who complained the loudest were kings in their own rights, even if their tiny realms amounted to nothing more than rocky little villages or lonesome, windswept towns.

But Father insisted on calling these petty kings *chieftains*, denying them the title of king even in their own little realms.

Did an offended chieftain send men to plot against the king while he was away at war? Or was the lesser ruler himself among these men, harboring an evil plan in his breast as he rode toward our mighty citadel?

I couldn't stop the shiver that traveled down my spine. My pacing feet stopped dead in their tracks and I stood motionless, staring at the closed door.

Damalis tried humming again, high, tentative notes that were barely perceptible above the commotion across the courtyard.

Elektra moved to sit by Ismene, who wrapped her in both heavy arms, rocking her back and forth in time to Damalis's tune. I allowed my mind to wander again.

Since he was the Lord of Men, it was my father who'd called all fighting-aged men of Greece to arms when he and his brother, my uncle Menelaus, developed an urge to invade the eastern city of Troy across the boundless sea.

Promises of unending riches, infinite glory, and innumerable women rang in the eager ears of the men and boys from each corner of Greece who answered the king's call. Most hurried straight to Aulis, the agreed bay that would launch their countless ships across the sea. But those who were nearby came pouring into Mycenae, swelling the lands around our citadel with poor farmers and rich generals, shy shepherds and trained warriors. Our halls burst with soldiers, young and old, seasoned and green.

The great palace of my ancestors, normally bustling with business and entertainment, became a raucous den of shouts and boasts and brawls. Our slave girls and women were tormented daily and nightly. Sometimes I heard happy squeals, sometimes terrified screams that made me crawl into Elektra's bed and cover her ears with my hands.

I couldn't even imagine what havoc the soldiers wreaked in the parts of the city that had the misfortune of lying outside the citadel walls. From the safety of the palace, we heard men fighting, women screaming, and dogs barking.

Father told Mother he allowed these men their pleasure because they were the chieftains of the farthest reaches of Greece. It was these men who brought their own men from the hills, the mountains, the shores, and the plains. Father had to keep these chieftains happy, he said. But I saw that it troubled him. He wore his worry in the lines between his thick eyebrows and in his clenching jaw.

I didn't see Father much in those weeks leading to the army's departure, but the times I did see him, he didn't seem like himself. In the evening hour before he joined the chieftains at their supper, we'd all gather in his private chamber—his wife and three royal children. He was irritable and had no patience for Elektra's incessant questions or Orestes's infantile cries and would inevitably command Ismene and Amalthea to take them out of the room.

Because I was silent and still, he allowed me to sit on a cushion by his feet while he and Mother talked in hushed voices. If Father was in a heated mood—which happened more and more as the days wore on—each evening was the same. They spoke of the war Father insisted on starting. Father would sling sharp words at Mother.

It's because of your sister, he would say. *Helen has played the whore, running off with a nobody prince. A prince who is less than nobody. A shepherd in royal clothing, a dishonorable breaker of the sacred laws of hospitality, of* xenia. *Your vile sister has put us in this position. We have no choice.*

Mother would say, *You always have a choice, husband. You and your brother are choosing to wage a war on a city brimming with warriors who are famous for their bravery, and you're using my sister as your excuse. Everybody knows you wouldn't muster all the men of Greece to chase after a woman, even a beautiful one. Menelaus has never cared for his wife. He can find another as easily as he can order roast lamb for dinner.*

Father would say, *Menelaus insists we bring Helen back to her rightful place by his side. She is the queen of Sparta and the mother of a princess. We swore an oath, all those years ago in Sparta, to avenge and protect your sister if anything were ever to go wrong. And now it's gone wrong.*

Mother would say, *That is a convenient excuse, husband. I, for one, doubt the truth of this oath. I think it was never spoken and has been invented only now, as a cover for your foolish war.*

On evenings when Father's nose bloomed red with too much wine, he hurled hard words at her. He accused her of calling him a liar. Mother sat tall in her enameled chair, and I held my breath, waiting to see what Father would do. He never struck her, even when I saw in his eyes that he wanted to.

And I would sit at their feet, silently soaking all the words into my thirsty mind, never able to decide whose side of the story I believed most.

ᙣᙏᙣᙏᙣᙏ

"How much longer?" Elektra pressed her ear against the panels of our door. I didn't even realize she'd joined me there.

"Hush. Come back and sit." Ismene patted the blanket next to her and Elektra obeyed, laying her head in the nurse's wide lap. "I'm sure it won't be long now."

What exactly were we waiting for? Or what was waiting for us? If this stranger was an enemy, the four of us would have no way of escaping. Were we supposed to believe these two lesser guards—one too old, the other too young—were enough to keep out whatever evil may storm the corridors?

My heart galloped and sweat slicked my palms.

"Iphigenia!" Ismene's sharp whisper pierced my thoughts, and I realized she'd been saying my name for a while now. My focus snapped to her familiar eyes and the riot of tension trickled from my body.

"Take a deep breath."

I obeyed.

"Queen Clytemnestra won't let any harm come to you girls or your brother."

My brain said, *How do you know?* But I allowed my fists to loosen their white-knuckled grip on my tunic and my heart to creep back down to a canter. I breathed the stale air deep into my lungs, three times and then four, as Ismene had taught me when I was a little girl.

Panic wouldn't solve anything, wouldn't change the identity of the approaching men. If they were enemies, they would find us whether I stood in my maiden room drenched in a cold sweat or not.

ରେରେ

The weeks leading to Father's departure had been stressful for all of us, but Elektra and I found amusement where we could. Over the years, we'd become experts at sneaking through the narrow corridors of the palace, silent on our bare feet and invisible in the gray shadows. We knew the hidden alcove near the throne room where we could crouch on the stone ledge so nobody saw our toes beneath the curtain. We spent many hours hidden in this secret place, listening to the conversations of unsuspecting men.

Father finally left, taking the boisterous chieftains and their destructive men with him. Silence filled the palace like a cool fog, creeping down the hallways, under the doors, and through the cracks in the painted stone walls.

When the strangers arrived, Father and his troops had been gone for three weeks, and the silence had never truly left.

Elektra and I sat on the edge of the bed again, and this time, when Ismene began to tell a story, Elektra listened. Ismene chose the happy tale of Eros and Psychê. I half-listened to my old nurse and kept my other ear trained on the commotion that still roiled outside the walls of our room.

Ismene had only arrived at the part of the story where jealous Aphrodite orders Eros to make Psychê fall in love with the ugliest man alive when I heard the faint footsteps. They were still distant, but I picked them out of the rest of the noise because they were clearly the footsteps of someone walking along our wood-floored, second-story hallway instead of the stone and plastered floors below us.

Ismene once again trailed off, another story unfinished.

I stood and Elektra came to stand beside me. We held our shoulders back, our chins high. I forced my breath to slow, and I heard Elektra do the same. We clasped hands.

Ismene and Damalis retreated to the corner behind us, and Ismene's shielding presence behind me made me hold my shoulders back with confidence.

The footsteps neared, light and quick. It was a woman coming, but not Mother. A cacophony of guards, advisers, and maids would have attended Mother.

No, this was a solitary woman.

She didn't speak to the two guards posted outside our door before she cracked the heavy wooden door and popped her head into our maiden room.

My breath dislodged itself from where it was wedged between my chest and my throat in a loud burst.

Ampelos, Mother's beloved maid, smiled her wide grin and her eyes gleamed black in the torchlight. Damalis squeaked and Ismene sighed, sounds I could only interpret as the overwhelming relief I felt.

Elektra dropped my hand and rushed toward the young woman as she stepped into our room, hugging her around the waist, before coming back to me red-faced. In her relief, she'd forgotten herself.

Ampelos bowed her head to me.

"Princess Iphigenia, Queen Clytemnestra has asked for you and the princess Elektra." She spoke to my feet, and I blushed. I still wasn't used to being treated like a grown woman, and it was awkward to have this maid, who was barely older than me and who had giggled and played alongside me when we were girls, now bowing her head as my subject.

"But we want news now! Who are the men on the horses?" Elektra's words came out in a high-pitched squeal.

I nudged her shoulder. "Mother will tell us the news," I said in my most adult voice. "Let's go."

Chapter 3

With Ampelos and Ismene in tow, Elektra and I marched straight through the sunny courtyard toward the other side of the palace, dodging servants and slaves whose arms were loaded with trays of food, pitchers of wine, and cushions of soft wool.

In normal times, Mother entertained the wives and daughters of visiting chieftains in the queen's chamber. She hired musicians and dancers to fill the space with joyous laughter and gossip. Once a month, she saw female Mycenaeans in this room, doling justice and helping find solutions to their various issues.

But when I stepped into the queen's chamber on this day, my feet stopped dead in their tracks. Today, the room was filled with advisers and guards. They stood in corners or perched on stools. Some paced back and forth and others leaned against the great columns.

Men weren't allowed in women's rooms.

There were no windows. The only light came from lamps, evenly spaced in small alcoves set into all four walls, burning Mother's favorite jasmine-scented oil. The spicy aroma mingled with the potent smell of too many men crammed between the walls of a woman's chamber.

Mother sat tall on her bright throne, dressed in her finest gown of gleaming white. Ampelos had twisted her curls into a dozen narrow braids that fell to the middle of her back, each braid the deepest of black and oiled until it glimmered in the light of the lamps. Her crown of beaten gold, inlaid with glowing red gems and white enamel, sat lightly on top of her head.

My breath caught and Elektra's hand tightened around mine. Her black hair and white gown contrasted with the painted wall behind her throne, an intricate fresco of blues and reds and golden swirls.

My knees threatened to betray me when I stepped over the threshold. I'd never seen Mother in her full power. She'd always lived in Father's shadow, all but unnoticed, and today she almost looked like a stranger.

I hadn't seen Mother very often in the weeks since Father left. She'd kept herself busy meeting with advisers. Elektra and I, worn out from the weeks of spying on the chieftains and soldiers who filled our palace halls, hadn't been interested in spying on Mother's meetings.

"Daughters, come here." Her voice carried an unfamiliar edge, and she clenched her jaw tight. With the wave of a hand, the advisers, guards, servants, and slaves scattered. After a couple of shuffling moments, Elektra and I were alone with our mother, Ismene and Ampelos tucked into the shadows behind us.

My heart thumped in my chest as we stepped closer. Had she called us here to tell us bad news?

"As I'm sure you know, our sentries spotted men approaching

Mycenae. My scouts tell me they're less than an hour away now." We both nodded. "Your father has been stranded in the Bay of Aulis for nearly two weeks. The gods have sent him no favorable wind to sail to Troy. I think it's a blessing, but his men disagree. They think it's a curse."

We knew this, too, of course. Almost as soon as my father and his countless men trickled into the bay, the wind had died entirely, like a pair of lungs that had squeezed out their final breath.

"My advisers tell me the men are restless, as men always are. They're eager for the glory and spoils your father promised them, and they won't stop harassing him, as men always do."

I shifted from one foot to the other, trying to keep my face blank. Elektra and I already knew all this. This wasn't the exciting news we were hoping for.

Mother continued, her voice sharp and her brows meeting between her eyes. "The men, whoever they may be, come from the direction of Aulis."

I'd already worked this out, but hearing Mother confirm it made my heart drop. Elektra grabbed my icy hand. A disaster had fallen. Father was dead or captured or transformed into a doomed beast by an angry god.

"But I'm not worried," she said, her voice returning to her familiar soft tones. "It's only a small band on the road, and they wave our flag."

Elektra and I sighed as one.

"But I still don't know who they are, or why they've come. Now that the scouts have reported the number of men, I've sent three of my advisers to discover their identities and purpose." She studied us, brows still furrowed. "You two must stay ready in your room, in case you're needed. If your father sent an emissary, I may need to show proof that my prince and princesses are safe."

I cleared my throat, nervous but determined to speak as a woman, not as a child to be ordered around. "Mother." My voice came out too weak. I cleared my throat again. "Mother, I want to stay with you. Here in this room. I want to sit beside you and learn what you're thinking. If I'm to become a queen one day—"

"You will do as I say, Iphigenia."

I flinched. Mother never interrupted me. I was her daughter, and she'd always heard my concerns, complaints, and questions before, no matter how childish. My mouth snapped shut, and any arguments refused to spill out.

For the first time since we arrived, Mother peeled her eyes from her two daughters and looked toward the servants in the shadows. "Ismene, go tell Amalthea to put Orestes in his red robe."

"Yes, my queen." Ismene bobbed her acknowledgment and turned to leave.

As an afterthought, Mother added, "And have her put his wreath of golden leaves around his head. I hope it still fits."

Her attention back on me, she said, "Have Damalis put you in your pale-blue dress. And your yellow mantle. You look beautiful in yellow and blue."

"What about me?" Elektra stepped forward, her bright face gleaming in the lamplight.

Mother smiled, her features softening. "Elektra," she said, "you will always shine above the rest, no matter what you wear."

I swallowed the jealous pang that rose in my throat. Elektra was born to be beautiful. I was not.

◎◎◎

Damalis brought folding stools into the corridor just outside our maiden room door, plopping a soft cushion on top of each one. She didn't say it, but I guessed she wanted us close enough to our room that we could dive back inside in a matter of seconds.

It was a narrow space, but here in the corridor, with its great painted columns opening into the courtyard, Damalis and Ismene could take advantage of the bright mid-day sunshine as they arranged our hair.

Damalis got straight to work combing tangles from my long hair. I'd been told since my earliest days that my hair was unruly. Instead of the thick black curls that Mother and Elektra shared, one vengeful god or other had given me straight locks that never glowed above a dull brown, even in the best light. And worse, my hair refused to stay in braids, no matter how many pins tried to trap it in place. The slick strands immediately found their way out of the elaborate twists that any maid or nurse attempted.

"Will we get to meet the visitors?" Elektra asked as Ismene's nimble fingers flew around her head, creating half a dozen cooperatively thick braids and twisting them into an intricate pinned pattern atop her scalp.

"I don't know," Ismene answered, ever patient with Elektra's unending questions. "But you need to look your best, in case your mother calls you."

"Who do you think they are? Are they enemies?"

"I don't know, Elektra. But if they were truly dangerous, we'd be doing something much different than fixing your hair right now."

"What would we be doing?"

I heard Damalis snicker behind me, probably happy she wasn't the one who always had to answer Elektra's famously never-ending questions.

Ismene didn't respond right away. "We'd be safe in the throne room, and your mother would post guards all over the citadel walls to protect us. Since they're not, then the men must be friendly."

The older guard remained motionless, but the younger boy shuffled his booted feet on the floor. Was he ashamed to be guarding the room of two mere daughters, instead of pacing the citadel walls, ready to fight any enemy who tried to breach them?

"If they're friendly, can we go watch them pass through the gates?"

I sighed. I was still sulking over Mother sending me away, and Elektra's childish questions annoyed me. "She's only guessing, Elektra." My words came out more clipped than I expected, and my sister flinched on her cushion. I tried to soften my tone. "We don't know if they truly are friendly. We know nothing."

I stood. Damalis had finished securing twists to my scalp with jewel-tipped gold pins, but she was still combing the loose hair down my back. So, she was forced to follow me the few steps into my room, trying to pull out the comb that was still stuck, mid-stroke, in my hair.

Elektra followed me. Unasked questions burned on her face.

Ismene rushed past the two guards and into the room after us, cushions and stools tucked under her arms, hands full of ivory combs, golden pins pinched between her lips. I closed the heavy door behind her and the four of us stood for a few moments, torchlight dancing across our cheeks and brightening our eyes.

"Please help us dress," I said. "Elektra and I would like to see our brother."

"You can't leave your room until the queen calls for you. You know that." Ismene was used to the two of us wanting to run around. For once, she had a valid excuse to keep us in place.

"We'll go straight to Orestes's rooms. His guards will keep us as safe as . . ." I waved a hand toward our door, "as our guards." The unexpected authority in my voice sounded more like Mother than I remembered ever sounding before.

Ismene heaved a sigh. She didn't argue with me, but I knew she wouldn't leave it be.

Ismene and Damalis helped us out of our simple tunics and into our fine dresses, wrapping our mantles around our slim bodies, belting them around our narrow waists. Damalis adjusted my yellow mantle to expose the entire front of my blue dress for admiration.

Elektra opened her wooden chest and dug her doll from the rich folds of dresses, mantles, and scarves. The wool-stuffed fabric was worn so thin in spots that stuffing oozed from the seams. Most of the painted face had flaked until only a nose, chipped dark eyes, and half a smile were left. I hadn't seen that doll in months and it surprised me to see her clinging to it now.

"Elektra, my love, we talked about this." Ismene softened her voice, as if she were talking a toddler out of a tantrum. "You've outgrown your doll. I thought you threw her out."

Elektra glared at our nurse—*her* nurse—over the doll's head.

Ismene rolled her eyes, then busied herself folding our discarded tunics.

I took my sister's hand, and she gripped her doll in the other.

"Let's go." I hoped my voice held hints of the bravery I wasn't sure I felt.

Ismene stood. When she opened her mouth, I knew she wanted to forbid us from leaving. She may once have been my nurse, but now that I was a woman and had my own maid, Ismene had naturally become my inferior. I gave her the most imperious look I could manage, and her mouth snapped shut.

I pulled the door open. Ismene spoke quietly. "Just . . . please, just remember, you're both noble princesses. Remember who your proud parents are. And, Iphigenia—" Her eyes were pleading. "Remember, you're no longer a girl."

I softened my eyes and gave her a nod, the way Mother would have done. Elektra and I swept out of the room, past the two guards. They shuffled into action behind me, and I spun to face them.

"Stay here. We're going to check on our brother and we will return shortly." I spoke in the formal tones Mother used with her servants, and both men hesitated. The boy looked at the old guard, questions written across his face.

"The queen . . ." the old man started.

"The queen is not here. I am the princess of Mycenae and I am ordering you to stay here until we return."

Elektra and I marched toward Orestes's rooms, leaving the two guards to watch over a room with only a nurse and a maid inside.

A smile spread across my face, and I didn't even try to stop it.

We walked the long interior corridors from our maiden room toward Orestes's nursery, passing servants and slaves along the way. The mood had changed from stifled panic to excited anticipation; voices turned from frightened murmurs to happy chatter.

Elektra tugged at the skirt of the dress Ismene had forced her into with mutters of *You're growing too fast, child,* and *I need to remember to let this out tomorrow.*

"Why do we have to wear these stupid costumes when Mother probably won't even let us see the visitors?" She began adjusting her red mantle now, fastened neatly at the shoulder with a long pin of hammered gold.

"Stop fussing," I snapped. "We have to be prepared for anything. We might need to meet these men." My clothes were uncomfortably tight, too, with my newly widening hips and breasts that were beginning to swell.

A slave girl of ten or eleven rounded the corner ahead of us and hurried down the corridor in our direction, arms piled with rich fabrics of reds and blues and yellows.

I touched her arm as she passed. "Who are the men approaching the palace?" My voice sounded more authoritative than I planned. I cleared my throat and my eyes darted away from hers.

The girl curtsied gracefully, keeping her bundle balanced in her arms. "I only know they've turned onto the main road and will pass through the gate soon."

The girl brushed past us, her hurried footsteps echoing off the walls.

"Let's go watch for them!" Elektra tugged at my wrist, pulling me toward the stairs that led down to the courtyard.

"But we're going to check on Orestes," I argued, planting my feet and refusing to move.

"Ismene says he's safe with Amalthea. And everyone says the visitors are friendly. Let's go!"

My heart leaped into my throat. I'd felt daring when I disobeyed Ismene and dragged Elektra toward Orestes's room. But it was another matter entirely to prowl the palace walls when our clear orders were to stay in our room. Mother would fume if she found us climbing walls like goats and mingling with guards like slaves.

A servant boy breezed past us, nodding in greeting.

Elektra danced from foot to foot, her dark eyes shining with impatience. She must have seen the curiosity on my face, because she tugged at my wrist once more. This time I followed.

We scurried across the courtyard like two mischievous mice. I knew where she was leading me. How many hours had we spent huddled atop the great stone walls, spying on the ordinary comings and goings of merchants and royal advisers, peddlers and servants? Back then, we thought nobody knew of our secret hideouts. But now with the wisdom of age, of course, I know it was no secret. We were noisy children, giggling and whispering, pretending to be invisible.

Each guard was conveniently turned away from us as we tiptoed toward our spot. When I think of it now, I realize they must have already known who the men were. No guard in his right mind would allow two of the king's three surviving children to sneak around the ramparts if there was any thought of real danger. But on that day, how my heart pounded with the thrilling danger of it all.

From our perch, Elektra and I could see what was happening outside the wall just as easily as we could see the bustle within the protected citadel. We peeked over the ridged stones, first this way and then that way and then back again, like kittens following the path of a darting lizard.

Inside the citadel walls, the air buzzed with barely controlled chaos. Men and women of every class bustled about, hauling baskets and bags, pulling carts and pushing crates. Children dashed around, scattering like sparrows at the wave of a hand or an impatient shout.

Our secret little perch was near the north gate, the gate nearest the palace, and I could see that the guards had sealed the entrance tight against the strangers. Maybe that had been the crashing sounds we'd heard earlier from our room. The bronze-clad gate doors were enormous—three times the width of a normal door and twice the height of a man. They would have sent a booming shudder through the palace when slammed closed.

They were going to make them wind their way down the road to the main gate. The one guarded by two looming lions, poised impossibly high above the heads of all who entered Mycenae. Our visitors were meant to feel small and insignificant as they passed between those terrifying petrified maws.

My heart sank when I realized we'd missed seeing the band of men make their way past the closed north gate and toward the great main entrance. They would have passed directly under us if we'd been here sooner.

"Come on!" I jumped up from my crouching position and tugged at Elektra's red sleeve. "I want to be in our spot before he gets up to the palace."

My little sister obeyed me for once, and we hurried back toward the queen's chamber.

Mother wasn't there. The room felt hollow. Our footsteps echoed off the high ceiling and wild beasts stared at us from the walls, their painted eyes accusing. We weren't supposed to be there.

"Where is she?" Elektra's whisper fell flat in the vast chamber.

Someone cleared their throat and we whirled around. Bumps rose on the flesh of my arms and my scalp tingled when I caught a flash of movement from the deep shadows behind one of the great columns.

A wide band of pale light spilled from the open door, and a small girl stepped into the cloud of dancing motes. My breath escaped in a loud, relieved puff. She was just a harmless girl about Elektra's age, a basket tucked under one arm and a cushion under the other. She bowed her head and stared at our feet.

"Where is Queen Clytemnestra?" I asked in my newfound formal tone. I hoped the tremble in my voice wasn't as obvious to the girl as it was to me.

"She's in the throne room, Princess." She kept her head bowed as she spoke, and even in the silence of the empty chamber, I had to strain to hear her.

"Thank you," I said automatically. When the girl stayed planted in her spot, I added, "You may go."

She scurried off.

Mother was in the throne room? But that was Father's room and Father wasn't here. Why would she choose to greet the stranger in the throne room instead of her own queen's chamber?

I took one look at Elektra and saw her mind had gone to the same

place as mine had.
   "We have to hurry!"

CHAPTER 4

We were winded by the time we wove our way across Mother's private garden and through the empty corridors that led to the throne room. When we arrived, it seemed as if every guard, every adviser, every servant, and every palace slave gathered in the inner courtyard and porch. Late afternoon sunshine slanted into the courtyard, leaving the porch in deep shadows.

Elektra and I crept our way around the porch perimeter, keeping our backs pressed against the cool plastered walls. Even though my heart thumped hard in my chest, I felt certain everybody was so engrossed with their own tasks and gossip that we sneaked by unnoticed.

Our favorite spot was an alcove in the wall of the vestibule just outside the throne room. Six alcoves set into the walls of the vestibule flanked the entrance to the throne room, three on each side of the wide doorway. We honored each of our family's favorite gods here, carved of dark wood and painted in vibrant colors by our ancestors: Poseidon for his might at sea, Artemis for her hunting strength, Demeter for her life-giving harvest, Zeus to beg his help in justice, Ares to bring us power in war, and Apollo to keep away plague and to protect us against our enemies.

Years before I was born—maybe even before Father was born—Poseidon, in his anger against the many sins of the house of Atreus, sent such powerful tremors through the earth, countless Mycenaean homes collapsed and thick walls tumbled. Even though the palace remained mostly unshaken, the worst damage was with these six statues. All of them tumbled from their honored perches within the walls of the vestibule, and their wooden faces and wooden limbs splintered, shattered.

The statues were repaired with loving hands, but some still showed the ancient damage: a slightly crooked finger on Ares's left hand, a hairline crack tracing its way across Artemis's forehead.

I'd always sensed the power radiating from these likenesses of the gods. Sometimes when I passed by them, their painted eyes following my movements, chilly dread coursed through my limbs; other times the gods emanated peaceful calm. On this day, I felt nothing but the thrill that coursed through my veins.

Keeping in the shadows, Elektra and I crept toward our favorite nook, a little closet next to the statue of Apollo. This closet was filled with things needed in the throne room when visitors arrived: cushions and cups, tables and trays, stools, lamps, and jars. A delicate curtain hid the clutter, and I always imagined my grandmother must have woven the fabric with skilled hands.

Elektra and I slipped into the space, now empty after preparations to entertain our unexpected visitors. We buzzed with excitement, crouching in our cramped hideout behind the long blue curtain. We didn't make a single sound, barely breathed. My hands trembled and my heart raced.

Nothing happened for what felt like hours, as if Chronos, the ageless god of time, had brought the world to a standstill.

Then, all at once, the guards scurried about, giving sharp commands. Their voices ended in a sudden silence when Aegisthus announced, "Odysseus, chieftain of Ithaca!"

My heart plummeted.

This was nobody exciting at all. Just another chieftain from a meaningless island, probably come to tell Mother exaggerated news of the ill-conceived expedition to Troy.

I wanted to grab Elektra's hand and get away from this suffocating closet. After the excitement, the questions and uncertainty, I was in no mood to listen to state business. But, of course, it was impossible to leave without being seen.

Elektra looked at me in the blue-tinted gloom, her dark eyes screaming, *Let's run for it!*

But I shook my head. Daughters of the Lord of Men and his royal-born queen could never be caught spying.

So, we waited.

Footsteps passed through the vestibule where my sister and I hid and entered the throne room, the boots hitting the plastered floor with hollow thumps.

To help time pass, I tried to imagine the scene. Did Mother dare to sit on Father's throne?

Maybe someone had carried her throne into the great room and set it up next to Father's empty seat.

While Mother and this man, Odysseus of Ithaca, exchanged formalities, I pictured her sitting tall, as she had been when Elektra and I had seen her only a few hours earlier.

"I've come with news," Odysseus said.

Slippery. That was the word Mother used to describe this man when he was in our palace weeks ago. And I heard it now, in his false tone and his exaggerated royal accents.

"I assumed as much." Mother spoke in the formal tones she used to speak to her inferiors, and she clipped her words.

"Yes, Queen, of course you did. I come with news directly from your husband."

Mother said nothing. In my mind, she sat motionless, her hazel eyes daring him to say more.

Odysseus cleared his throat. "Our great king requests your daughter's presence. Your eldest, the princess Iphigenia."

My stomach flipped at the unexpected sound of my name, almost foreign on this man's northern tongue.

The silence that followed filled the palace, heavy as a wet woolen blanket. Elektra shifted beside me, and I held a trembling finger to my lips. We couldn't risk being discovered now.

I didn't know if it was excitement or dread that coated my palms with slick sweat. Why in the name of the gods would any father, especially the king of Mycenae, call his maiden daughter to a camp full of battle-ready warriors?

When Mother's response finally came, I strained to hear her whispered word: "Why?"

She didn't bother to hide the poison in her voice.

Odysseus hesitated. His next words sounded sticky, the way a nurse might sound trying to convince a toddler to take just one more bite. "My queen, he calls his daughter for a joyous occasion, of course! Would you think otherwise of our great king?" I wasn't sure, but I thought I noted a tremble beneath his bluster.

"Please," she said, "do describe this joyous occasion, Odysseus. I cannot wait to hear it."

"My queen, what is the most joyous occasion you can imagine? What is the greatest cause for celebration among men and women alike?"

Mother didn't respond, but I knew the answer before Odysseus said it.

"A wedding, of course! The king has arranged an enviable marriage for his daughter. A marriage that will bring the highest honor to Princess Iphigenia and her parents alike."

Odysseus waited for Mother to ask the obvious next question, but she didn't.

"King Agamemnon has arranged for the beautiful princess Iphigenia to marry none other than Achilles, son of Peleus, prince of Phthia, leader of the Myrmidon troops."

Achilles? The name sounded distantly familiar, but I couldn't bring to mind any details.

I glanced at Elektra next to me in the dim alcove, and she beamed. In her mind, it seemed, this news was as great as Odysseus had promised. A royal wedding to a man who was said to bring us high honor.

But Mother still didn't respond.

Odysseus rambled. "Achilles is a golden prince, Queen Clytemnestra, the son of a goddess, a nymph of the sea. The beautiful Thetis protects and honors her son in all ways, my queen, and she will protect and honor his wife and children. He's as brave and as honorable as men twice his age, and your husband, the king, has chosen him above all men. You will be very proud—"

"Do not tell me how proud I will be, chieftain. Who are you to come here—into my lands, my city, my palace—and tell me that my beloved daughter is to wed a foreign prince who is barely a man himself?"

Odysseus cleared his throat again.

"Why would a fresh young warrior wish to marry on the eve of sailing off to battle? And to marry a girl he has never even seen?"

Odysseus had an answer ready. "The boy's father is old, my queen. Peleus wants his son to marry and produce an heir, in case the gods do not wish Achilles to return home. Please remember, Queen, this young man is goddess-born, son of Thetis. He himself is godlike. It's said Chiron, wisest of Centaurs, taught him from infancy so he would never learn the evils of man."

A long pause filled with sounds of shuffling feet.

"You came here to tell me my daughter is to marry the son of a nymph who was raised by a Centaur?"

"Queen Clytemnestra, this is a high honor. It is said his mother has made him immortal. Your grandsons will be grandsons of the goddess, under her protection until their dying days."

"How did this only now come about, Odysseus of Ithaca?" Mother didn't disguise the irony in her voice. "What was it that made Peleus realize, at this late hour, that his cherished son may not return from the fight against the dreaded Trojan warriors? Why did he not marry his son to a local bride and wait to see her belly swell before sending him off to war?"

"My queen, I cannot see into the hearts of other men." Odysseus threw Mother's unguarded irony back at her. "I can only obey the orders my king has given."

"Why did my husband send you to carry his message? If this news is so joyous and this arrangement is so honorable, why did he not come to deliver it himself? I know my husband well. He would want to see the joy on his daughter's face when she hears the wonderful news."

Odysseus answered quickly, as if he'd been expecting this question too. "Of course, my queen. That is an excellent question. King Agamemnon is very busy, keeping the men under control at camp. They are very restless, as I am sure you can imagine. We have been stranded in the windless bay at Aulis for weeks now and the men are impatient for the plunder and glory they have been promised. He cannot leave them, or the entire camp will break into turmoil."

Mother was just as quick with her response. "You are telling me that my husband is the only man in the Greek camp who can keep these men under control? What about you, clever Odysseus? What about Menelaus, the brave man who started this war in the first place?"

Mother let out a brief laugh, one that even I could hear wasn't genuine. "Ah, but of course, the great chief Menelaus cannot be expected to keep his men under control. He could not even keep his own wife at his side where she belongs."

A deep silence followed. No guard shuffled his feet now, no slave cleared her throat, no bird trilled outside the palace walls. My heartbeat thrummed in my ears, filling my personal silence with an anxious *thum-thum-thum-thum.*

"Your husband, the king, has spoken." Odysseus broke the silence softly, but the words he didn't speak hung heavy in the air:

You must obey your husband. You must obey your king. You have no choice.

Quiet fell once again, but it was a busy quiet. Mother spoke words I couldn't make out. Then came indistinct murmurs and sandals slapping the plastered floor in all directions.

I'd crouched too long in one position and I wanted to stretch my legs, but I didn't want to risk making any noise. Elektra shifted beside me, rocking from her bare toes to her heels. When had she removed her sandals?

We looked at one another in the dim light, and I shrugged.

Then, out of nowhere, a bare arm plunged around the blue curtain and into our secret space.

The hand attached to the arm grasped thin air directly in front of my nose while a second hand tore back the curtain, laying bare Clytemnestra's two shameless, spying daughters.

My face burned. We lowered ourselves from our perch, hobbling into the hallway on numb feet shot through with hot needles.

The guard who had rudely exposed us stepped aside, revealing behind him an exasperated Ismene. She shook her head, squeezed our hands a little too tight, and led us across the vestibule, away from the door to the throne room.

Ismene muttered words I won't repeat here as she tried to fix the mess she saw before her. I stole a glance at Elektra, taking in the wild hair, the crumpled dress, and the long mantle twisted almost sideways around her little shoulders.

I didn't want to imagine how I looked.

Our nurse's hands worked quickly, roughly. Then she took a step back and examined us. The frown that wrinkled her brow told me everything I needed to know: I looked like a childish mess.

"Your mother called for you," she said to me. "You're to present yourself to the honored guest. Take your brother and your sister with you."

Amalthea, whom I hadn't noticed in my shame-blinded state, thrust Orestes into my arms and he immediately wriggled his way out of my grasp. She adjusted the golden wreath circling his head before melting back into the long shadows.

"Go!" Ismene spun me around so I was facing the door to the throne room. Normally a harmless opening, it now gaped before me like the doorway to the Minotaur's labyrinth. What lay in wait for me beyond that threshold seemed, in that moment, just as terrifying as the jaws of the beastly Minotaur itself.

I inhaled incense-scented air and blew it out in a noisy puff. Grasping the hands of my brother and sister, I led them across the vestibule, the six life-sized gods glowering down on us.

When I passed into Father's cavernous chamber that afternoon, I felt smaller than I had ever felt before. The great fire blazed, its thick smoke drifting through the opening in the high ceiling.

Mother's burning eyes pierced into my living heart. She'd called on us to stand before this visitor—this chieftain Odysseus—so she could display her royal son and daughters with pride. We were to be the next King of all Greece and two queens of powerful Greek cities. We were the pride of our parents and the future of this land.

And Elektra and I looked like slave children. Worse than slave children. We weren't fit to stand within these glorious walls.

I swallowed the tears that swelled in my throat and poked my chin forward, hoping to display some sort of dignity.

Mother clenched her jaw and gestured for the three of us to stand beside her throne.

That request, at least, I could obey.

Only after I'd moved to stand beside Mother did the scene before me come into focus.

Mother did, in fact, sit on Father's throne. Her white gown seemed to glow in the sunlight that streamed through the open door and her oiled braids stood boldly against the white enameled throne. Aegisthus stood beside her, and the sight of him wearing his blue cloak, his dagger tucked in his belt, soothed me a bit. He'd become Mother's trusted adviser these past weeks, and I felt safe with him nearby.

A chill ran through me. What would Father think when he learned about this? What would he do?

But Mother held her head high, so I did the same.

Odysseus stood before us, Agamemnon's entire family in full display before him. He looked road-weary, covered in a thin layer of dust. His long beard was light brown and not oiled. His hair hung tangled below his shoulders and matted to his scalp as if he'd been wearing a cap for a very long time. But he stood tall in his dusty tunic, looking every bit as regal as my father ever looked.

"The children of the great Agamemnon," Mother announced. The pride in her voice sounded false to me. "My daughter, Iphigenia, as you can see, is only just a woman. She has only just turned fourteen. She's still too young to marry, even if her betrothed is a young man himself."

Elektra gave my hand a tiny squeeze. I gazed around the room. Advisers and guards were scattered around in what looked to be a haphazard way. But were their positions strategic? Had Mother instructed her men where to stand, what to look out for? These were the questions I needed to ask Mother, the reason I wanted to be by her side. I needed to know what she was thinking so I could make these decisions myself someday.

As I scanned the room, my eyes rested on Talthybius standing near the door. He'd been part of the army Father brought with him when he and Menelaus had come from Sparta to reclaim the throne of Mycenae. As a reward for his loyalty, Father made him his herald, the honored position many men hoped for, and he'd proudly marched out of Mycenae at Father's side just weeks earlier.

He looked just as road weary as Odysseus, and I realized he must have been part of the party Father sent to come collect me. His eyes rested on mine for a heartbeat, but the softness I was accustomed to seeing there was missing. He flicked his eyes from mine without his usual smile.

Odysseus bowed his head to us in deference, gray eyes gleaming and a grin barely concealed on his lips.

Did he laugh at us because of our disheveled appearance, or did he find something else amusing?

Orestes fidgeted beside me, and I prayed he would behave himself for just a few minutes at least.

"Your children bring honor to you and to your husband, the king," Odysseus said. "But it is not for me to decide the marriage date for your beautiful daughter. Your husband sent me here with orders to bring his eldest, the fair Iphigenia, to him in the bay of Aulis. I must follow my orders, Queen."

Mother stood abruptly, the folds of her gown releasing a breath of her jasmine-scented perfume into the still air, and her guards moved toward the door. "Very well," she said. "I will have her wedding chest ready in three days."

"But . . ." Odysseus started.

"Three days. She does not leave before then." Mother brushed past the bowing Odysseus, her gown billowing behind her.

I didn't know what to do. Odysseus stood motionless, so I took that as a signal we should follow Mother. I led the three of us in her scented wake, leaving the dusty traveler, head bowed, alone in a room full of Mother's men.

CHAPTER 5

Mother cut through the vestibule, toward a shortcut to her own chambers. All I saw was the tail of her white gown skimming the stone floor as she rounded the corner, but her perfume still hung in the air and filled my nostrils as I followed with dread in my heart.

She sat on a low stool next to the tall bronze lamp in the corner. Ampelos was carefully removing the crown from atop her braids.

With a flick of her hand, she sent Ampelos hurrying from the room, cradling the crown as if it were made of eggshells and not hammered gold.

Mother moved her head to look at me. Only me. Her hazel eyes glistened bright in her powdered face, but she kept her expression shrouded, so I couldn't guess what she felt. Disappointment? Anger? Sadness?

I placed Orestes's hand into Elektra's and nudged them out the door, wiping my hot palms on the soft fabric of my mantle.

Somehow, I knew Mother wanted to speak only to me. She wanted to lecture me about my appearance and remind me that, as a woman, I was expected to keep myself and my sister under control at all times. That it was no longer proper for me to appear before a chieftain—even the chieftain of an insignificant island—looking as if I'd been running wild in the hills beyond the citadel walls. She was going to tell me that I'd brought shame to the shades of my ancestors, the great kings and queens of the house of Atreus.

But I was wrong.

Mother's face softened into familiar lines, and her fiery eyes dimmed. She straightened her spine and sat tall on her short stool as if she still sat atop Father's gleaming throne.

"Your father has called you to join him in the bay of Aulis, where he's camped with his men. You are to be married." Her voice was thin and distant, though she looked me in the eye as she spoke.

I hoped I acted as if this were the first time I'd heard the news. "But you said I'm going to marry a prince of Pylos or Tiryns when I'm sixteen. Father said he was going to talk to the chieftains and decide which prince would be best for us."

"Your father seems to have changed his mind," she said. "And we must all obey our king." She left words unsaid, and I understood them to be important, but I couldn't grasp the missing words or their meanings.

I only sensed they were not there.

I felt neither dread nor joy at the idea of marriage. Since my earliest memories, I'd known it was my duty to one day marry as my father chose, to marry a man who would bring security, riches, and honor to Mycenae. Like my mother before me, her mother before her, and so on, back to the days of the great Titans, my role in life was to become a wife and a mother and a grandmother. My duty was to bring honor and security and riches to my parents through marriage, and to bring glory and fame to my husband through the sons I would bear him.

But none of this was supposed to happen yet.

"Will this be a good match?" I didn't know what else to ask.

"He's a young man, said to be famous for his bravery. But I've never heard of him before all of this." She waved her hand, indicating these last weeks of chaotic war preparation. "He's said to have been born of a goddess, the sea nymph Thetis. I'm told she's made him immortal by dipping his infant body into the River Styx, granting him eternal protection. He can't die."

Mother paused, staring at her hands resting in her lap, her eyes blank. When she looked at me again, her sparkling eyes had hardened and her mouth straightened to a firm line.

I tried to swallow the lump in my throat.

"I can't guess what your father is thinking, Iphigenia. But we have no choice. We must obey and submit to his . . . whims." She clipped her words and left no room for argument. "We'll leave in three days. I've bought us that much time, at least."

Bought us time for what? Why delay if this was happy news?

"You're coming with me?" My voice sounded shaky to my ears.

"Of course I'm coming with you. It's your wedding!" Her voice rang false. She was trying too hard to soothe me, as if I were a toddler and not her grown daughter. "Who else will give you away to your new husband, if not your mother?"

She motioned for me to come to her and squeezed me tight to her thumping breast. "But you must not mention this to anybody. Odysseus must not learn until the last moment that I'm coming. I don't think he wants me there."

"But why?" I asked, breathless from Mother's tight embrace.

"Why would my own mother stay behind when I'm to be married to a shining prince?"

She loosened her grip on my body, and I took a step back. She stood from her stool and looked me in the eye once again, cupping my cheeks in her warm palms. I was tall for my age and already almost of a height with her.

"I don't know."

ⱺⱥⱺ

The three days that followed were all bustle and no rest. Mother kept us busy packing my wooden wedding chest.

Not quite one year before, this large oak chest had been delivered to the palace, proudly displayed to Mother and Father in the throne room by the carpenter, whose very hands had crafted the intricate piece. I'd been standing beside Mother, and I heard her tiny gasp when the man flung away the cloth that had been hiding the chest. With a steady hand, he'd painted the planks with geometric designs of the most vivid yellows and reds and blues, and the bronze clasp glittered in the sunlight.

The day we started packing, I caught Mother gazing at the chest as it stood, open and hollow, in the middle of my maiden room, and I wondered if she was remembering the same moment.

Damalis and I followed her instructions. The first things into the chest were the gifts I would present to my new husband on our wedding day. We started with the golden *kantharos*, its two ear-like handles sending a wave of shame through me as I once again remembered taunting little Damalis all those years ago.

Then came the painted ceramic bowls, exotic sea creatures decorating the center of each. And finally, the brooches and pendants in silver and gold.

Then we chose one of my newer gowns and matching hair ribbons, which Mother said I should wear the day after my wedding. And the most important item went in last: my wedding gown.

Since we had no time to make a new gown, Mother dug through the garments in the chest at the foot of my bed. A gown of the purest white was my newest, and it had been designed with extra room for the hips and breasts that were still growing. When wrapped and belted just right, it highlighted my features very well, according to Damalis. And, to wear on top of my white dress, Mother let me choose my favorite mantle. Mother told me how the deep saffron dye played off my hazel eyes, making them shine more gold than green.

I was excited to have an opportunity to wear it again. The only time I'd worn it so far was during the Dance of Persephone, when girls and unmarried women danced in the olive grove outside the palace. On that joyful day of feasting and laughter, we called upon the maiden to abandon her winter home in the underworld and rejoin her mother, sorrowful Demeter, in the world above to usher in a fruitful spring.

Mother handed my long blue hair ribbons and matching belt to Damalis, sighing that my purple ribbons were too frayed to wear on my wedding day.

"You should have a new pair of sandals," she said, clenching her jaw as she looked through my footwear. "But your father won't give us time for that. Pack these."

She shoved my newest leather sandals toward Damalis. She seemed so angry that I couldn't have new sandals, and I didn't understand why. Did she really think Achilles would be focused on my feet? Even I knew better than that. Mother should be happy I already had a gown and mantle that did such fine work showing off what little I had.

We laid each piece on my bed before smoothing it, folding it, and then gently laying it into the chest.

Before Damalis and I clasped the flat wooden lid closed, I peeked to be sure nobody was watching, grateful that Ismene had taken Elektra from the small room because she did nothing but get in the way. Then I slipped a secret on top of my wedding dress. She was ivory, no longer than my first finger, and a great snake draped itself around her cream-colored shoulders. She raised her hands toward the sky and bared her breasts in the old way.

She was Artemis, protector of babies and girls and young women. My protector.

⌒⌒⌒⌒

Poor Ismene spent her days rushing here and there following Mother's orders, and her nights consoling Elektra and me as we shed girlish tears at the idea of our coming separation.

"Will I come home afterward?" I asked Ismene on the second night.

"That's for your husband to decide." She was removing the shining bronze pins from my hair, dropping them into the shallow ceramic bowl on the floor at her feet. Her fingers trembled as she ran them through my loosened strands. This was Damalis's job now, but Ismene had insisted on helping me prepare for bed.

"Do you think he'll want to take her with him to Troy?" Elektra sat cross-legged on her bed, waiting her turn.

Ismene let out a soft laugh. "No, he certainly will not. A battlefield is no place for a princess. He'll either send your sister to his own home to await his return, or he'll send her back to us."

"I hope he sends her back to us," Elektra said, her voice still thick with her latest round of sobbing.

"Of course. We all hope so."

Ismene dropped the last pin into the bowl. The tiny *ping* expanded itself until it filled the empty silence in our maiden room.

"Do you think he'll be kind to me, Ismene?" My voice was no more than a whisper.

Ismene turned me to face her, her thick brows meeting in the middle. She thought for a long moment, her soft brown eyes scanning my face. "He's young. That's a good sign."

"Why is that a good sign?" Elektra asked.

"Well, how do I say this?" Ismene cleared her throat. "Old men know what they want from women. And sometimes they take what they want and don't care what the woman thinks."

She paused for more questions, but neither of us knew what to ask.

"If Achilles is a young man, he may not know exactly what he wants yet. He may be kind."

I remembered the words of Odysseus the day before: *Peleus wants his son to marry and produce an heir.*

"Will he want to get me with child?" The words strained through my tear-filled throat. Of course I knew how men put babies in women's bellies and I understood how babies came into the world. Everyone knew these things.

Women scream bringing babies into the world. They pant and they moan. They weep prayers to Artemis, to Demeter, even to Athena—to any goddess who will listen.

Women die bringing babies into the world.

Ismene put her hands under my elbows and lifted me from my stool. She was shorter than me by a half a head, and I had to look down into her brown eyes. "I can think of no other reason for your father and his father to arrange such a hasty wedding."

I tried to swallow my tears, but they flowed down my cheeks, unstoppable. Ismene pulled me into an embrace, squeezing me to her breast. Her familiar lavender scent filled my nostrils and my tears turned to uncontrollable sobs.

"Shhh, little one," she whispered. "It will be all right. Everything will work out fine. I delivered four babies and stand here to tell the story. Don't be afraid."

But my tears were not only tears of fear, were they?

I had a terrible sinking feeling that something was very wrong. But I had no way of knowing why.

CHAPTER 6

A storm rolled through the night skies over Mycenae. Flashes of silver-white flickered through the cracks in our shutter and thunder boomed in the distance, sounding both faraway and ominously close. Elektra moved to my bed and wedged her little body against mine, so I was trapped between my sister and the firm wall behind my back.

As we lay listening to the rain pummel the roof, my mind drifted to another stormy day, years ago.

I was seven or eight years old. The low skies had opened and wept autumn rains, unceasing for days. Water poured in sheets from the palace roofs, cascading in thick waterfalls that spilled over the edges and splashed onto the courtyard tiles. Puddles formed in low spots, spreading into pools that crept toward the open-walled corridors lining the yard.

Ismene kept me in the nursery with Elektra, pacing back and forth while the toddler squeezed her fingers for precious balance. I must have been restless and asked too many questions, because Ismene shooed me off to the kitchen to ask for a bowl of figs or some other sweet treat to stuff into my mouth.

I padded off, slapping my bare feet into any puddle that had found its way beyond the lipped corridor threshold. The walk to the kitchen should have taken me only a couple of minutes, but I wandered, humming my favorite tune, until I realized I'd walked straight past the corner that led to the kitchen.

When I turned to retrace my steps, I noticed voices coming from the storeroom, hushed and urgent. I crept toward the cracked doorway, looking down the corridor both ways. When I saw that nobody was coming from either direction, I peeked through the crack. Two slave girls stacked cups and bowls into baskets, speaking in a near-whisper above the gentle clinks of the tableware.

Both had their backs to me. I pushed the door open just wide enough to slip my slender body through. My breath hushed in my lungs and my mind prayed to any god who might be listening that someone had recently greased the hinges.

In one smooth motion, I ducked and slid behind a wooden bench that rested along the near wall, throwing a quick and silent thank you to whichever god answered my prayer.

At first, the blood rushing in my ears was so loud that I could barely understand the girls' whispers, but after my heart slowed to something resembling a normal beat, I could hear them perfectly. I peeked around the bench.

"... but don't go getting too comfortable," the tall girl whispered. "He seems like he's kind, but he's still a king. He doesn't order daily beatings like they say some lords do. And sometimes he tells us we can have a few extra sweets. He does call women to his rooms at night—almost every night—but I've never heard of him calling anyone as young as you or me."

The smaller girl paused, a goblet in her hand. Her profile showed a stubbed nose and full cheeks, her mouth turned down. She must have been twelve or thirteen.

"Even with all that," the tall girl continued, "you shouldn't go getting too comfortable. He isn't a good man, underneath."

"How do you know?"

The tall girl turned to face her companion, widening her eyes. "My mother told me a story about him once. She said when he still lived in Sparta as an outcast from Mycenae, he chose Queen Clytemnestra as his wife. But she wasn't the queen, then, so I guess she would have been called Princess Clytemnestra. Anyway, Agamemnon picked her for his wife, but she was already married!"

The girl paused for effect, and her companion played along with a well-timed gasp.

"What did he do?"

"Well, my mother says he did the unthinkable." She paused again, and I could see that the other girl was holding her breath now.

I held mine too.

"He murdered her husband!"

The girl squealed, her little hand flying to her mouth.

"Yes! But it gets worse."

The second girl stared unblinking at the first above the hand that still clasped her mouth.

"Do you want to know what else?"

She nodded, but I shook my head. I didn't want to hear any more, but I couldn't stand up and walk out without being discovered.

"He killed her baby too! A Spartan prince. And he ran his sword straight through his little belly. Like this." Her eyes darted around and she grabbed a long ladle, making a stabbing motion toward the other girl's belly.

The younger girl backed away until her heels met the wall.

I bolted from my hiding spot, my vision blurred with hot tears. I ran through the damp corridors, heading straight for Mother's rooms.

I found her in the first place I looked, weaving in the large, airy room dedicated to just that one task. She was standing at the loom, a ball of colored thread in one hand. Her head popped up when I burst through the open door and her eyes filled with concern. Questions danced on my tongue, but when I opened my mouth to let them escape, they fell silently to the floor.

Instead, I ran into her arms, tears flowing, uncontrollable sobs squeezing from my throat.

Each time Mother asked what was wrong, I shook my head and buried my face deeper into her robes. With time, my tears slowed, and Mother held me at arm's length.

"You can tell me when you're ready," she said, smoothing my hair behind my ears.

But even then, I knew. I would never ask the dreadful question. I would never repeat those awful words.

Because if I never said them aloud, if I forced myself to forget, then the words couldn't be true.

෩෩෩෩

The next morning, after our hair was combed and braided, Elektra and I sat on our beds as Ismene packed a travel basket for me.

"When will you pack Elektra's things?" I asked. "And when will you pack your things? Mother says we're leaving just after daybreak. We're running out of time."

Ismene froze, the bundle of sweet cakes she held in her hands suspended in midair.

When she finally spoke, her voice was only a whisper. "We aren't going."

The thought of traveling outside Mycenae without my trusted nurse knotted my stomach. "Not going? But you have to go! Elektra and I need you with us!"

Ismene didn't look up from the bundle that still hung in her two hands. "Elektra isn't going either. Your mother told me yesterday."

I didn't believe my nurse's words. I was to travel abroad without my sister or my nurse for my own wedding? It didn't make sense.

Before Ismene could object, I snapped Elektra's little hand into mine, and together we marched out of our room, down the stairs, and through the long corridor. Mother's private rooms were empty, so we tried the queen's chamber. She wasn't there either.

We found her in the throne room, seated once again in Father's mighty seat. Aegisthus, Talthybius, and two guards stood before her, and the five of them spoke in whispers.

Elektra and I burst into the chamber, loud and impossible to ignore, and Mother dismissed the men with a nod.

"Well?" Her sigh sounded tired rather than impatient.

I had dragged my little sister through the palace with a single-minded mission. I'd burst into this great room with fire in my heart and spiced words on my tongue. But standing before my mother as she sat on the king's throne, my courage drained from me. She loomed above me, the powder on her face failing to conceal the worried lines that had etched her smooth skin almost as soon as Odysseus arrived in this very room.

"Mother . . . I don't understand . . ." The tears came once again, stinging my already-swollen eyes and freezing the syllables in my mouth.

I swallowed, then forced the words out. "Why can't Elektra and Ismene come with me? I want them at my wedding. I want—"

"They can't come with us, Iphigenia. The trip is too long for Elektra, and Ismene must stay back to care for her."

Mother's words rang false. "But why is Orestes coming? If he can handle the journey, then Elektra can. And I need my nurse! Who will weave the ribbons in my hair? Who will help me dress?" The words spilled from me in one panicked breath.

"Do you think I would abandon my eldest daughter on the happiest day of her life? Is it not a mother's place to dress her daughter on her wedding day? To braid ribbons into her hair?"

She stood slowly, and she looked old and small. "You don't need a nurse."

ഗ⁄ഗ⁄ഗ

That night's feast was meant to serve as a celebration of my happy news, but I couldn't enjoy myself. Servants and slaves had worked hard to convert the throne room, vestibule, and porch into a long hall for the feast. Tables stood in the middle of the vestibule, heaped with rich foods and pitchers of Mother's best wine. Couches lined the walls of the throne room, piled with thick cushions of every imaginable color. Tapestries hung on every wall, hiding the everyday painted scenes with fantastic frescoes filled with magical beasts, otherworldly heroes, and formidable gods—tapestries woven by the very hands of my mother and grandmother, aunts and cousins of old. Of course, none of my work hung from these walls. I was nothing if not a dreadful weaver.

I was allowed to dine with Mother, Odysseus, and the few lingering regional lords who'd weaseled their way out of going to fight at Troy. That alone should have been reason to celebrate. Mother was treating me as a woman.

Instead, it was a reminder that I was leaving in the morning.

I picked at my food, barely tasting the tiny bites I forced into my mouth. I didn't savor the sweet wine, or the herbed roasted lamb, or the honeyed spring fruits.

The night was mild. A light breeze drifted through the vestibule and into the throne room, making the great hearth fire appear to dance in time to the music of the flutes and lyres in the corner. Silver stars filled the heavens, glittering through the open roof of the vestibule, the storied constellations spreading in a protective arc above us.

But I couldn't enjoy any of it. I sat stiff-backed and nearly mute beside Mother, thinking only that I would part from my sister in a few hours. Mother gracefully filled the silence I created with polite talk, but I could hear the edge to her voice.

I didn't sleep that night. Elektra and I lay in each other's arms on my soft bed, each sobbing into the other's shoulder. She eventually cried herself to sleep. I didn't.

Ismene came in before dawn. I squeezed my eyes tight, a vain hope that I could force myself to slumber through what was turning into a nightmare. She sat on the edge of my bed and stroked my hair, humming my favorite song.

"I know you're awake, Iphigenia."

I opened my eyes but didn't move. Ismene's round face flickered in the orange light of the oil lamp she held, and her unshed tears glowed.

She swept me up and into her plump arms, holding me so tight I could barely breathe. I heard her sniffle, and my own tears flowed once again. She patted my back and then pulled away.

"No more tears," she said, wiping first my cheeks and then hers with the corner of her tunic. "We all must be brave. We must beg Artemis to lend us her strength today and in the days to come."

I nodded and swallowed the lump that seemed to have permanently lodged itself in my throat.

"Come. I'll fix your hair."

I sat on my stool and closed my eyes as Ismene removed yesterday's braids. She combed my loose hair, more gently than usual, and then twisted fresh braids, which she piled and pinned into a knot on top of my head, leaving a few to hang free beneath my shoulders.

She turned me on my stool and gazed at me in the flickering torchlight. "You look beautiful, my Iphigenia."

I shook my head. I knew I wasn't beautiful; I wasn't Elektra, with her shining black curls and round black eyes.

Elektra, sitting in bed, hiccupped, her poor little body worn out from a night full of crying.

Ismene nodded. "You'll be a beautiful bride, and I can only pray your husband deserves you."

She helped me dress in my traveling clothes. By then, dawn's glow was softening the sky, and Ismene pulled me into the open passageway. We looked down into the courtyard, the purples, yellows, and pinks of the spring flowers still shrouded in gray shadows. The kitchen smell of new-fired flat bread mingled with the fresh dew in the courtyard and I inhaled.

"You'll melt your mother's heart. And, if the gods are willing, your father's too." She smoothed imaginary wrinkles from my dress and pressed strands of hair that had already escaped. "Your hair will need attention when you arrive. Have Damalis fix you up before you meet your father."

"Why is Damalis going and not you?" I knew my childish whine didn't become me, but I couldn't help myself.

In answer, Ismene only shook her head.

Mother swept up the corridor toward us. "Good. You're ready. We must leave soon." Her words were dull and formal.

She moved closer, and the growing light showed red-rimmed eyes that must have matched mine. Maybe it was the abruptness of the whole affair that made an otherwise proud and joyful moment so sad and unbearable.

"Say goodbye to your sister and your nurse." She turned toward Elektra and Ismene and said, "Stay here until we're gone. We don't need a scene for people to weave into a story."

"No!" Elektra balled her hands into fists at her side, and her face glowed ruby. "Why can't I go? I want to see Iphigenia's wedding!"

"I've told you." Mother's words sounded calm, but she held her body taut as a pillar. "The trip is too long for a girl your age. And a camp of restless warriors is no place for a princess."

"But Iphigenia is a princess, and she gets to go!"

"That's not my decision, Elektra. It is your father's command. Whatever evil god has possessed him, whatever reasons he's contrived for this sudden marriage, we must obey him. Iphigenia must go. And my command is for you to stay home with your nurse."

"No!" Elektra's voice escalated to a shriek that echoed off the corridor walls. A four-year-old tantrum coming from an eight-year-old girl. "I'll never see her again. Artemis showed it to me in a dream last night. When Iphigenia leaves Mycenae, she'll never come back. I want to go with her!"

Mother moved toward Elektra, but my sister backed away, bumping into Ismene's plump belly. Ismene wrapped her arms around Elektra's shoulders, and her sobs slowed.

"Believe me, Elektra, I'll do everything I can to convince both Agamemnon and Achilles to send your sister back to us after the wedding. There will be no reason for them to deny me, her own mother."

She stepped closer to Elektra and Ismene, bending toward her youngest daughter. "I will bring your sister home."

We all believed her.

CHAPTER 7

Mother led me to Father's private rooms, where Odysseus was waiting. She sat in Father's place and together with the visitor, we ate breakfast. Odysseus had a ferocious appetite, devouring every bit of smoked fish and roast lamb, dried figs and preserved olives that were set before him. Oil dripped into his beard, which he'd already oiled for the day as it was.

Mother and I had no appetite at all. We both poked at our porridge but ate almost none of it.

"You remind me of my wife the morning I left to join your husband's cause," Odysseus said between bites.

Mother stared at the man but made no comment.

"But of course you know my wife, don't you? Penelope. I'd almost forgotten the two of you are related."

"Of course," Mother said, her eyes glued to his. "How was my cousin's health when you saw her last?"

It was Odysseus who broke eye contact, and my heart swelled seeing that my mother, who was just a woman, could make such a brawny man so uncomfortable. Maybe it was her eyes, unusually bronze in the morning light, that forced him to lower his gaze to his empty plate.

"My wife is the most beautiful woman in all of Greece. Or maybe, the second most beautiful," he blustered. "But you know that already."

Mother nodded, an almost imperceptible movement.

When Odysseus offered no more, she said, "Yes, she was very beautiful when I was with her last. Before she married you. But I asked about her health, not her beauty."

Odysseus seemed to gather a bit of resolve. He cleared his throat and his words sounded bolder, more substantial. "Penelope is the best wife a man could want. She is beautiful, as we've discussed, but also loyal and obedient. When we parted, tears fell from her eyes, but she did not protest. She did not beg me to stay, because she knew I must go. I had no choice, and her objections would only make it harder for me to leave."

"That, indeed, is the picture of a perfect wife," Mother said. Her words were flat.

"I trust her with all my heart to care for our son, born only weeks before I left."

"Motherhood is the most noble calling."

Odysseus popped a purple berry into his mouth. "Not all mothers are equal to the task."

This time, it was Mother who broke eye contact. Her ears flushed and she stood abruptly, the wooden legs of her chair scraping against the stone floor, an ugly, jarring sound. "It is time to go."

Mother sent two men to carry my wedding chest to the waiting cart, and then she dropped the surprise.

"And Aegisthus." Her voice rang clear in the morning air. "Have two of your men carry my chest to the cart as well."

Odysseus paused, his ceramic cup frozen on his lips. A glint flashed in his gray eyes, and he took a long swallow.

"I suspected you were up to something, Queen Clytemnestra." There was something slithery about his words and invisible fingers crawled across my skin. "But your husband—the *king*—sent me with strict instructions that you are not to come along. He has put your daughter's keeping in my hands, and I will not disappoint."

Mother met his gaze with a frigid stare. My blood coursed icy in my veins. "I will join my daughter on her journey. I would not miss this—how did you word it?—this *joyous occasion* for anything."

ᴏ∕ᴏ∕ᴏ

Mother and I walked side by side through the long corridors. I struggled to keep up with her pace and I was short of breath before we even stepped out into the sunshine. Servants and slaves bowed to us as we passed.

Helios's disc still hung low and white in the eastern sky when we left the palace, and a warm breeze promised a hot day to come.

We stepped through the courtyard and toward the grand staircase that joined the inside of the palace to the outside world. Soaring red columns flanked the freshly painted black stairs, holding up the high roof of the portico.

Mother and I paused at the top of the staircase between two of the tall columns. My throat constricted at the sight before me. People lined the road leading down the steep hill from the palace to the citadel walls, and when they saw their queen and their princess emerge from the shadowed portico, their voices rose to a roar.

Warmth spread from my belly to my fingers and toes. I stood tall next to my mother, the queen of Mycenae, and felt that this was where I was meant to be. As the cheers morphed into a chant, I knew someday I would stand before a different crowd and they would chant, "Queen Iphigenia!"

There were a few men, but it was mostly women and children who stood side by side, forming a narrow path for us to pass through. Since we were still safely within the citadel walls, these were all people of high rank, and I recognized many of them as older male advisers and women who'd kept Mother company before the men left for war. Bits of prayers hung in the air as I passed through the tunnel of people, blessings and hopes for my happiness.

In better days, Father would have hired musicians to send me off with fanfare, and the streets would have been congested with men instead of lined with women and children. But these weren't better days, and I had to accept what was before me.

It would have made sense for us to leave from the north gate since we'd eventually be traveling north, but we wound our way down the stone-lined path toward the main gate. Two of Mother's men led the way. Ampelos, Damalis, and Amalthea, Orestes on her hip, followed behind us. Odysseus and his men must have trailed them, but I never turned to look.

When we finally reached the main gate at the bottom of the hill, Mother paused, and so I paused too. She turned around and faced the palace, now perched high above us, its towering walls painted blue, red, and black. She raised her white hand and waved to the people who had come out of their homes to wish me well.

I raised my hand to them too.

We passed through the great gate, its opening looming high as we walked under the massive stones.

Throughout my life, I'd passed through these gates twice a year. Once to take part in the sacred Daughters of Artemis ceremony at the end of each spring, and then to make our annual early-winter pilgrimage to the sea to honor the great Poseidon. But this time I passed through the gate for me, and me alone. The thought expanded in my mind.

On the other side, I turned to look at those famed lions flanking the entrance, their massive stone heads covered in a film of shining gold and their haunches painted an impossibly vivid yellow.

Aegisthus waited for us just outside the gate. Our chests had already been loaded onto the wagon that would carry us to Aulis. Mother climbed up first, sitting on the low wooden bench that would serve as our only seat for the next many days.

I took my place next to Mother and was immediately grateful for the cushions that lined the bench; the boards felt hard even through the fluffy woolen stuffing.

"What is all this?" Odysseus's voice was light, but his glare was sharp as a blade. He stood tall, out in the open space beyond the city gates, and I wondered if he'd been trying to make himself seem hunched and small while he was inside the palace. His broad shoulders suddenly looked powerful and his gray eyes flashed.

For her part, Mother seemed as calm as the day before, and she shot her own glare back at the chieftain. "What do you mean?"

"My orders are to bring your daughter and her maid. Now you have added yourself to the party and there seems to be nothing I can do about that. But who are these women?" He waved his hand carelessly toward Ampelos and Amalthea. "And the boy. The king didn't ask for his boy."

Mother stiffened beside me. "My husband will want to see his son. His prince. Why would he not?"

Odysseus didn't respond. His nostrils flared.

"And I must have my maid, of course. And my son needs his nurse." Then, as if anticipating the man's next objection, she nodded toward Aegisthus, who stood behind the wagon, dressed in his travel clothes. "And, naturally, I want my adviser with me. As you know, Aegisthus is my husband's most trusted friend, his own cousin."

Odysseus and Mother stared at one another for what felt like an eternity, but it was the man, and not the queen, who broke contact. He spun on his heel and scanned the clump of people nearby. When he spotted Talthybius, he jerked his head, indicating the herald step away with him. They spoke for many moments. Then, without looking back at us, the two men started to clear the crowd, making way for our wagon to pass through. Our driver urged the two donkeys to move, and we lurched forward into the packed street.

We wove our way through the streets and the buildings that had, over the generations, sprouted like mushrooms against the thick citadel walls, eventually spreading out on the surrounding rocky hills. I was used to seeing these homes and shops from above, studying their flat wooden roofs from the height of the walls.

Now that I was down among the structures, I could see they were small, packed tight together, and simple. Those closest to the city walls boasted mud-brick painted in any color we might see in the palace. But as we traveled further out, headed toward the road that would take us away from Mycenae, the residents kept the buildings plain and unpainted. These must have been the homes of the poor, the less protected.

The people who lined these streets were still mostly women and children. A handful of old men dotted the roadside, along with a few injured men. All the people who gathered to watch us pass reached hands to touch our travel cloaks as they muttered prayers to Artemis and Hera, begging for marital happiness for their princess.

As we neared the north gate, my mind flipped over to Elektra. Would she watch us drive away? I knew just where to look, and she didn't disappoint. From so far below, I could only see her dark head shining in the early morning light. I raised my hand, a farewell gesture I couldn't be certain she could see. I don't know if she waved back.

A sob tried to rise in my throat, but I forced it down.

I was done with tears.

Chapter 8

Hyacinth flowers blanketed the rocky hills as we rolled further and further from home, each bloom sending its spicy-sweet aroma into the breeze. We couldn't have asked for better weather, and Ampelos guessed this must be a good omen from the gods.

But my mind was in no state to worry about omens or flowers or sunny, windless days. I sat as still as I could, my body only swaying with the wagon's movements and nothing else. My eyes watched the hills pass by, but my heart was stuck in Mycenae, with Elektra and Ismene.

After we'd been on the road for an hour, Mother took my hand in hers. With her other hand, she turned my face so our eyes met.

"Have I told you the story of your birth?"

Of course she'd told me the story of my birth. I'd heard the tale countless times my entire life. But I saw what she was trying to do. I drew a deep breath, reminding myself that a queen—a true leader—doesn't pout and dwell on sad times. She moves forward, learning and growing from hardships.

I nodded. "Please tell me again."

She sat in silence then, a private smile touching her lips. "You weren't born within the first year of my marriage to your father," she began. "Before you, another baby came, a boy who arrived in the world too easily. Too soon."

She didn't finish her thought, but I knew. He spent his only living moments silently gasping for air and his eyes never opened to see our mother's weeping face.

I gave her hand a gentle squeeze. "But I came after him, right?"

"Yes, you did. But before him there was a baby who came after only two months of marriage. The rush of blood wasn't painful so much as it was uncomfortable."

Again, she paused. I'd always known that the stabbing pain in her heart never disappeared, never even dulled, and was with her still.

She pulled a ragged breath through trembling lips. But she straightened her back, and a mask fell over her features. She smiled, and her voice seemed a little too cheery when she finished the story. "So, when you burst into the world full-sized and red-faced, I was so full of happiness and relief, I almost couldn't believe you were real. When I held you to my breast for the first time, naked and squalling, I assumed I'd be the one who chose your name. Since you were just a girl. Right away, I started thinking of you as Leda, named for my own beautiful mother. I'd even whispered the pretty syllables into the top of your fuzzy head: *Leda. My perfect little Leda.*"

But when Father saw me for the first time, and I gripped his finger in my tight fist, baby-blue eyes studying his face, his dark eyes filled with tears and he overruled Mother.

He called me Iphigenia.

Strong-born.

When my lusty wails echoed through the halls of the palace and my fat legs kicked against my swaddling, he didn't care that I wasn't the precious son he'd prayed for so passionately, the desperate heir he needed to secure his fresh new role as king of Mycenae. He cared only that I was alive, his first thriving child, born strong and undeniably healthy.

Her story worked. My thoughts no longer rested on Elektra, making room for a new thought. Why had Father truly called me to Aulis? Somehow, the idea of marrying me to a young warrior-prince, a man who was almost unknown to anyone, on the eve of battle, didn't seem quite right.

But I was Iphigenia, strong-born. I would stand solid and face whatever awaited me.

ΩΩΩ

I don't remember if I smelled or heard the camp before I saw it. I only remember the eye-watering stench of hundreds of fires mixed with roasting meats, unwashed bodies, and overfull latrines, together with the ever-rumbling thunder of men's voices, women's shrieks, clashing of bronze, and countless bellowing animals penned and tied in place.

It wasn't until we topped a high hill that I saw the army of men laid out before me, their black ships suspended, motionless in the blue waters of the bay.

It wasn't impressive.

Let me clarify: the army was impressive in number, but it was chaotic.

The bay nestled within a bowl of high rocky hills, its sandy beach stretching to the southwest, waters shimmering to the northeast.

Canvas tents filled almost every bit of beach as far as I could see. They sat in clumps with only small pathways separating each section from its neighbors. The tents themselves looked nearly identical: broad, grayish peaked rectangles with open flaps for doors. Each little grouping had one larger tent with a banner hung above the opening, the only spots of color in a sea of gray canvas.

Each little grouping, each colored banner, must have represented the different commanders and their men. My eyes scanned the scene, and I wondered which of these colorful banners represented my future husband and his men. And where was the tent for Mycenae?

Mother stood next to me and took in the sight herself. After a moment, she pointed to the right. "See that yellow banner? That's the camp of old Nestor of Pylos."

I squinted. From this distance, it was difficult to make out details, but eventually I found the banner of our trusted neighbor to the west.

"And there. The red banner to the left. That will be the Locrian Ajax from far, far to the north of us." She paused, scanning. Her brows knit together when she said, "And that's the camp of your uncle Menelaus."

We stood atop the windless hill, watching.

I'd imagined brave warriors running drills, practicing with their spears, swords, and arrows. But there was no order to it all. Men filled the few open spaces. They wrestled here, played games there, groped women near the red tents that stood on the southern edge of camp. Animals were penned near the center of camp, adding their terrified bleats and brays to the clamor.

Mother moved toward the sea and stared at the ships. I followed and couldn't believe my eyes.

A thousand ships!

How many times had Father bragged of his thousand ships? The stories of this brave expedition were already spreading through Mycenae—probably through all Greek cities and villages.

But, standing beside Mother atop that hill at Aulis, I saw nowhere near that number. I didn't have time to count, but I guessed maybe two hundred warships floated on the still waters in the bay. Two hundred fifty at most.

Even if Father included the cargo ships in his mighty count, the numbers didn't match. But surely, he didn't mean to deceive. Surely he only meant to count the ships that carried brave warriors; he couldn't have meant to count the ships that carried pack animals and wine, tents and prostitutes and barley.

The warships were fearsome, to be sure. My skin crawled just thinking of the terror in the hearts of those who saw these beaked painted ships sailing their way. They were tall and black and sleek, mighty to behold even as they bobbed peacefully in these clear blue waters.

"Do you think there are more in another bay? Maybe around those hills?" I pointed.

Mother only shook her head, disappointed.

Six men rode sturdy horses toward us as we stood looking down at the bay and the camp. Odysseus rode to meet them at a distance from the rock where Mother and I stood. They talked for a long time, one man or another casting glances at us now and then.

Aegisthus stood behind us, muscles held tense. Though we had come at my father's bidding, obeying our king's commands, we were the strangers here.

Why did these six men not bow low to their queen and congratulate their princess on her happy betrothal? Why, instead, did they stand out of earshot, clumped together like a pack of wolves, glaring at us through narrowed eyes?

Mother and I stood watching Odysseus and the men, the yellow spring sun beating down on our faces with no breeze to cool our skin. As Odysseus rode back toward us, Mother wrapped her arm around my shoulders, squeezing my body to hers for one beat of our hearts.

"The king will see you after he finishes his mid-day meal."

Mother took her arm from my shoulders and brushed past Odysseus, wordless. She spoke quietly to our maids and Amalthea, and then, holding her skirt above her ankles, she began picking her way down the goat path that outlined the steep hill. "Come, Iphigenia. We'll join your father at his table."

I followed, watching Odysseus from the corner of my eye.

"My queen." Odysseus tried to put his body before hers, but Aegisthus blocked his path.

When he spoke again, Odysseus's tone held a trace of something new. Was it panic? "My queen. The king is not ready for you. He said he will see you after his meal."

"Yes, you have already said that, Odysseus," Mother said, her voice thin with impatience.

"Your husband will not be pleased," Odysseus continued. This man was so smooth, even his cracks were difficult to distinguish.

Mother stopped short, and I nearly ran into her. When she

turned to speak to the minor king Odysseus, her face was blank and unreadable. Her cheeks were smooth and pink from the sun, her hazel eyes neutral, and her mouth, normally held in a firm line when she was irritated, showed no tension.

"I will handle my husband." She whirled around and started back down the path. Then she threw over her shoulder, "You may go now, Odysseus of Ithaca. You have done your duty to your king, and I will take it from here."

By this time, Mother and I were halfway down the hill, Aegisthus behind us.

Odysseus stood at the top of the hill. His muttered words sliced through the windless air: "You will not like what you find."

ʕ๏ʔ๏ʕ๏ʔ๏

By the time we reached the bottom of the hill, sliding and sending cascades of pebbles down the steep hillside, we'd finally been spotted. The mighty warriors of Greece hadn't detected a group of strangers hovering high above their heads, but they sure paid attention when they spied two well-dressed women picking their way down a goat path toward their stinking tents.

At first, only a handful gathered around us, but their numbers multiplied quickly. These bored men flew to us like fleas to an unlucky dog and Aegisthus shoved them away, leaving us in a circle of unwashed boys and men.

Mother and I held the edges of our cloaks over our mouths and noses in a vain attempt to filter out the eye-watering stench surrounding us.

"Which way to the king's pavilion?" Aegisthus asked the group.

"Which king?" one man shouted from the back of the crowd. "This place is riddled with them." Most of the men around us laughed.

"Agamemnon, of course. The Lord of Men. Which way?" Aegisthus's voice was more gruff than I'd ever heard it before.

"Ha!" This came from a soldier to my right. "Do you mean Agamemnon, Lord of Dogs?" Laughter erupted around us, and a few men even shouted out their own shocking insults.

I gasped and Mother stiffened beside me.

An old man stepped forward and said to Aegisthus, "Follow me." He turned to lead us deeper into the camp, and Aegisthus elbowed and shoved until a narrow path cleared before us.

I searched the men's faces, hoping my future husband would shine above the others, his golden hair glowing in the sun. But I only saw a sea of unfamiliar and unfriendly faces. Some looked younger than my fourteen years, others looked to be as old as Chronos himself. Most men wore nothing more than loincloths, though a sprinkling of them wore fine tunics, even if they were filthy.

These were the men who'd answered Father's call to arms? These were the men summoned to defend the honor of my beautiful aunt, Helen?

My head spun. This reality didn't match my imagination: honorable warriors in the tens of thousands, tall and strong in their gleaming armor, eager to retrieve Helen and return her to her rightful place by her husband's side.

Mother guided me in front of her so that, when we wound

our way through the narrow pathways between tents, I walked between Aegisthus and Mother and another guard brought up the rear. That was the best protection she could offer me. Men came out of their tents to join in the commotion, and when they saw Mother and me, most of them joined in the crowds ahead of us or behind us.

When we were deep into the camp, drab tents looming on either side of us, the suffocating air grew so hot and so foul with the miasma of unwashed men, bile rose from my belly. The hills loomed around us and I felt penned in, trapped with no visible road out of this place. The thought flicked into my mind that the old man who'd volunteered to lead us to Father's pavilion might take us somewhere else, dark ideas in his mind. My knees turned wobbly, and I grasped Aegisthus's cloak. "I must sit," I said weakly. "Where's my father? Where's my betrothed?"

He steadied me, keeping a firm hold of my shoulders. "We need to keep moving. We can't stop here."

Mother asked, "Can you keep going for a little while? Surely we're almost there."

She spoke as if she were coddling little Orestes, and shame washed through me. I was a grown woman, a princess, a future queen; I was stronger than this.

Nodding, I forced my legs to keep moving.

"Make way for your queen! Make way for your princess!" Aegisthus's voice carried a new urgency as it boomed over the heads of the massed men. The sea of bodies parted before us, and we had no choice but to walk through a column of leering and growling warriors, jostling shoulder to shoulder and tossing out insults that I won't repeat here.

Not one familiar face appeared before me. Not Father, not Achilles. Not even a familiar face of Mycenaean farmer or palace guard.

This was certainly not the welcome I had envisioned.

CHAPTER 9

We followed the old man for what seemed like too long and fresh panic rose in my belly. How would we know if this old man was taking us in the right direction? Could he be leading us into a trap?

When we finally reached Father's great pavilion, Mother and I both let out sighs of relief. Father's tent was the same grayish thick canvas as the rest, but a banner as tall as a man and half as wide hung limp above the opening, the blue, yellow, and red vivid in the colorless sea of gray.

A slave, rather than a guard, greeted us in front of the closed flaps of Father's tent.

"Queen Clytemnestra. Princess Iphigenia." The man bowed low. I recognized this slave, a wrinkled man who worked in the stables.

"I am here to see my husband." Mother held her chin high. Her dusty scarf drooped over her hair, and a few curls clung to her forehead. I touched my own scarf, and it felt limp with sweat and humidity.

The man's shoulders sagged and his mouth turned down, as if defeated, even though Mother had only made the one request.

"Excuse me, Queen." The man lowered his voice so that I had to strain to hear him. "Do you recognize me?"

Mother peered at the old man. "Do you work in the stables?"

"Yes, Queen, I do work in the stables. I was part of your dowry. I came with you from Sparta to Mycenae when you married the king." He bowed a second time.

She nodded impatiently, her eyes fixed on the tent.

The slave dropped his voice even lower, and his foul breath made me hold my own breath in my lungs. "I'm loyal to you, Queen." His quiet words hung heavy, loaded with unspoken meaning that I didn't understand. "Have you spoken with your man, Pherimos?"

I couldn't be sure in the bright sunlight, but I thought Mother's face drained of color underneath her sun-pinked skin. Her lips straightened into a tight line, and she nodded.

Who was Pherimos?

The slave paused, daring to look Mother in the eye for a heartbeat. He flicked his eyes to me, and then bowed his head and stepped aside. He pulled open one of the canvas flaps of the pavilion and gestured for Mother and me to pass through.

My pulse raced. Whether from uncertainty about what had just passed between Mother and the slave, or from the anticipation of seeing Father for the first time in weeks, I didn't know.

We passed into the great tent. The mid-day sun glowed through the fabric roof, creating a hazy light inside. The scent of roasted meat and strong wine lingered in the close space. Incense burned on a small table, but it did nothing to disguise the stale air.

Father stood at the far end of the space, dark and tall and solid. His face was a blank mask, carefully arranged in neutral lines.

In the filtered light, it was hard to tell for sure, but his fine tunic, normally white, seemed a cream color now. His uncovered head shone black and his long hair lay unbound, the curls spread over his shoulders. He hadn't oiled his beard, so the hairs stood out in dark, wild wires. In that moment, I thought he looked like a god caught unprepared, slightly disheveled, but still shining and larger than life.

Without thinking, I ran to him. He caught me in his arms, the way he used to when I was as little as Elektra. The faint smell of cedar oil lingered in his hair, even if he hadn't used it in a long time, and his arms were heavy and strong against my ribs.

I felt safe. Secure. Familiar.

"My sweetest Iphigenia," he murmured. His voice sounded thick, not exactly what I remembered.

"I've missed you, Father," I said. "You've been gone a long time."

When I pulled away, unshed tears stood in his brown eyes.

"Father! You've missed me too!"

He cleared his throat, blinked his tears away. "Of course I've missed you. Orestes and Elektra too. How were your brother and your sister when you left?"

I opened my mouth to speak, but Mother interrupted. She still stood in the tent opening, and the sun blazed behind her, a nimbus of golden light. In that moment, she looked like a great goddess, a perfect companion to my god-like father.

"Your youngest daughter is well," she said, her voice icy. "Your son is here with us now."

A loaded silence followed. Nobody moved.

"And you, wife." The cheer and warmth in his voice brimmed with irony. "I wasn't expecting you to come. Nor was I expecting you to bring my infant son—my only son—to this place. A soldiers' camp is no place for a lady or an infant."

"But this camp is a good place for your eldest daughter, an unmarried girl of fourteen? This is a safe and virtuous place for Iphigenia, princess of Mycenae, daughter of your heart?"

Father took a step toward Mother. She stood as still as a statue.

"I called Iphigenia here for a noble cause. As you know, I've arranged a great marriage for our daughter. I can't think of a better match for her or for Mycenae." He clenched and unclenched his fists by his side. "I'll keep my daughter safe from the grasping hands and prying eyes of these men. You should have stayed in the comfort of Mycenae and kept your two youngest children safe by your side."

The air in the pavilion suddenly felt thicker. I longed for a breeze, but the air, both inside and outside, hung lifeless.

"Father!" I said, hoping to distract my parents from whatever battle they were fighting. "Why didn't you meet us when we arrived? Why didn't you bring my husband to meet me?"

Father blinked, breaking his hard gaze on Mother. Confusion flashed in his eyes, but when he looked at me, his eyes softened.

"Ah, my sweet girl. I didn't expect you today. When I heard you delayed yourself to prepare for your wedding, I didn't think you would arrive before tomorrow."

I wanted to believe him. As far as I knew, he'd never lied to me before.

"But, Father! Odysseus sent a scout ahead of us. Surely, he came straight to you, letting you know when we would arrive."

He squeezed his fists at his side again. Squeeze, release. Squeeze, release.

"Daughter, my days here are very busy." He flung his arm around the tent, though nothing was there to indicate overwhelming activity. "I never have a moment to myself. The work of leading a great army of bold warriors is unending. If Odysseus sent a scout, I didn't speak with him."

Mother still stood in the opening, silent and motionless.

I was getting nowhere. I felt as if Mother and Father were in the midst of a silent conversation between themselves that only they could interpret. With glances and glares, clenched jaws and flared nostrils, they spoke a language that I couldn't hear.

I tried again to brighten the mood. "When will I meet my betrothed?" I asked, keeping my voice bright. "I'm eager to see him. He's famed for his beauty, isn't he?"

Again, Father seemed to pull himself out of a trance, tearing his eyes from Mother's. "Yes," he stammered. "Yes, Achilles is considered very fine-looking, I think. And he's quick. He's not the fastest man I've ever seen, but he's the quickest by far."

"But when will I meet him?"

"Oh, yes, of course. I've had a tent prepared for you. You should go and clean yourself up. You don't want to meet Achilles covered in dust from the road." To Mother, he said, "My man will take the two of you to Iphigenia's tent. Stay there until you're summoned."

"Don't you want to see your son? It's been an entire month, and children his age change so fast. I'm sure you wish to see him." Mother's words dripped.

"Yes, yes. Of course. I'll come to you after you've had time to wash."

He dismissed the two of us with a wave of his hand, his golden rings dull in the flat light. But before we could turn and leave, he said to Mother, "Send in Aegisthus. I'd like to speak with him."

Father's slave, the one who'd greeted us only minutes before, led us to our tent. He walked with a dramatic limp, though I saw no injury on his leg.

The walk to our tent was more of the same. Soldiers must have sensed our presence and seemed to materialize out of the ether. They followed us as we snaked our way through the narrow pathways, muttering phrases I tried very hard not to hear. I followed the limping slave—who couldn't offer us any protection if we needed it—and Mother walked behind me, but I wished Aegisthus walked behind her.

Anger bubbled in my belly. How did Father dare to send his wife and his unmarried daughter through a crowd of men like this, unprotected?

No one dared touch me, but the men's eyes, as they crawled up and down my body, felt as intrusive as groping fingers. I shivered and clenched my dusty cloak against my throat, despite the heat of the day.

Thoughts crowded my mind, but as we picked our way to our tent, one thought rose to the surface. How had Father known Aegisthus had come with us if he didn't even know we were arriving today? He'd said that he hadn't spoken to Odysseus's scout, so how could he have known his cousin stood outside the pavilion?

Our tent was identical to the others that surrounded us. Gray and moldering, its inhabitants of the past weeks disgracefully ushered from its flimsy walls. Their smell lingered and spilled out to where we stood: unwashed, unfamiliar men. For a moment, I thought it might have been more pleasant to stay in one of the red tents with the women who followed the Greek army around, but I pushed the indecent thought away, ashamed for the seconds it had played in my mind.

Mother ushered me inside, telling me I needed to get myself out of sight before one of these men got any ideas. The rest of our party was already there. It was going to be cramped with five grown women and a three-year-old. Where would we all sleep? Only two low pallets lined the walls. With a small table between them and our chests stacked in the corners, I didn't see where our maids could even lay a blanket on the sandy ground to sleep on. Maybe Mother would stay in Father's pavilion. Maybe he would even ask for Orestes to stay with them, keeping his eyes on his only son as long as possible before we went back home to Mycenae.

Mother stayed outside in the beating sun, apparently considering herself safe from the same unruly soldiers that posed such a danger to me. She and Father's slave murmured for a long time, low words I couldn't make out, no matter how close to the canvas I placed my straining ear. They stood close enough to the tent wall, their figures outlined in sharp black against the sun. They bowed their heads close together to keep their voices low, and the clamor all around was too loud for me to hear a single clear word.

Could Mother be planning a surprise for my happy day? Maybe she needed this man's help in preparing a magnificent gift to give me. Maybe, given more notice, she would have prepared my gift at home, but with such an abrupt departure, she was forced to improvise.

A smile formed on my lips. What a foolish girl I was then.

I stood, watching as Damalis and Ampelos unpacked the two chests. Damalis opened the lid to mine and glanced at me when she saw the ivory figure I'd laid on top of my wedding dress. I hadn't forgotten her, of course. No, I'd thought of her often as we jounced our way across rough Mycenaean lands, sending silent prayers that begged her to keep me safe. Now, I plucked her up and tucked her out of sight under my cloak, running my thumb across her smooth skin and sending out another prayer.

Soon, I'd become a princess of a faraway city, and someday I'd be queen of her people. When my husband returned to me, rich with Trojan gold and jewels and slaves, he'd take his young bride to his homeland, where we'd live comfortably together until Artemis chose to bless us with our children.

My sons would be sons of the great Achilles, and grandsons of Agamemnon. My daughters would be granddaughters of the clever Clytemnestra and the fearsome sea-nymph Thetis.

If Thetis truly made her son immortal by dipping him into the River Styx, could it not be true, then, that she would do the same for her grandchildren? Would her grandchildren not live into shining eternity?

A man shuffled to the tent door, a basket in one hand and a jug in the other, eyes averted as he dropped off his delivery. Bread, fruit, and watered wine.

The noises outside were becoming familiar to me, settling into the back of my mind the way the sounds of the palace faded into the background.

Mother returned, her cheeks flushed from more than the sun. She sat heavily on one of the pallets. Her eyes darted around the tent, taking in her surroundings like a penned beast, desperately seeking an escape. Her gaze finally settled on the tent opening, tied up to let in any air that dared stir outside. She pulled the basket onto her lap, snatched a dried fig, and took a bite. As she chewed, her gaze grew distant.

"Are you unhappy, Mother?" I whispered, not wanting to upset her more than she already was. "Your daughter is going to marry a splendid man. Someday I'll be queen of Phthia—wherever that is—and before then, I'll give you grandchildren. This is a happy time for me."

She dragged her eyes from the opening, blinked, and looked at me. Her face softened. She set the basket beside her and took both of my hands into hers.

"Of course I'm happy, Iphigenia."

Her words rang false in my ears, and her eyes hardened as she spoke. Why wouldn't she celebrate with me? Tears stung my eyes, and I swallowed.

"Don't cry," Mother said, and in that moment, she sounded more like Ismene than I remembered hearing her sound before. Her own eyes glowed with unshed tears.

"You're right. This is a happy time, and I should spend every moment I can with my daughter before . . ." Her words trailed and caught in her throat.

Her sadness at giving me away in marriage touched my heart. She was grieving my loss even while I still stood before her.

"You'll miss me! Of course you'll miss me. But I'll go home with you after my wedding. You said it yourself. You're going to beg Father or my new husband to send me home with you and we'll wait until this war is over. We still have time together!"

She squeezed my hands, but her smile didn't reach her glistening eyes.

"And who knows? I might bear your first grandson within your palace walls, and you can be the first to hold him."

Chapter 10

We changed into clean tunics and washed our faces, then waited for Father to come to us. But, sitting inside the airless tent, we'd sweat through our clean clothes before the sun began its slow descent to the west.

Ampelos and Damalis had unpacked and brushed the travel dust from the rest of our clothing, and my wedding clothes lay on the second bed, the saffron folds of my mantle adding a welcomed burst of brilliant color to the dismal space. My eyes roamed to gaze at the rich color over and over again.

We were all growing restless. Damalis and Ampelos busied themselves straightening the fabrics that lay on top of our closed chests, and then straightening them again.

Mother paced before the tent opening, back and forth, only three steps in each direction.

When Orestes woke from his nap, Mother snatched him off the bed and squeezed him to her shoulder. He tolerated this unusual attention for a few moments, but once the sleepiness fell from his eyes, he pushed his limbs against her, whining to be set free. And it wasn't long before Amalthea was having a difficult time keeping him entertained in this tiny space that wasn't meant for children.

He ignored the toys she used to entice him with and constantly tried to escape through the opening.

He was a happy baby, normally nothing but smiles and giggles. But now, after being told "no" a dozen times, he opened his little mouth and wailed, his tiny white teeth appearing to glow against the gloomy light.

In desperation, I pulled my little statuette from the pouch at my waist and held her toward my little brother. He toddled over to me, intrigued by this new toy that glowed a creamy white, even in this light. I scooped him onto my lap and let him play with the tiny Artemis.

After a new peace had settled inside our tent, I realized the camp noises had taken on a new quality. A buzz filled the air, as if the soldiers had become a swarm of wasps instead of men. The buzz grew into a clamor outside our tent.

Finally! Father had come, as he said he would. His men were gathering round our tent to show him the honor he was due as the Lord of Men.

But, inexplicably, Aegisthus and Mother's guards barricaded the tent opening with their bodies, blocking our view outside.

Voices grew louder and closer until a man's voice cut above the rest. "I have come to see the queen."

He spoke in the formal tones of royalty, but his voice was unfamiliar and his heavy accent betrayed his northern roots.

"Who asks?" Aegisthus's deep voice was familiar, and Mother stood when he spoke.

The other man didn't hide the sharp edge in his voice when he replied. "I am Achilles of Phthia, son of Peleus."

Could it be true? Had my betrothed come to meet me, his young bride?

I set Orestes on the floor and rose so I could greet my husband with dignity, but Mother pressed me down by my shoulder, her grasp tighter than necessary. With her other hand, she motioned Ampelos to go outside.

Mother's fingers dug into my tender flesh, and I squirmed. "You're hurting me," I whispered through my teeth.

She looked at me as if only then realizing I was even there and released her grasp.

I didn't catch the next words, but Ampelos returned, cheeks blazing pink and a scowl pressed across her normally cheerful features.

Mother stood. As she stepped toward the opening, she threw a look back at me. There was no mistaking her meaning: *Do not move.*

But I did move. Of course I did. I stood and fumed. How dare she take my first opportunity to meet my husband away from me? He might not come back before our wedding. I might not have another chance to see him until then.

All at once, the strain of these last many days—the unexpected news, abandoning Elektra and Ismene, Father's cold welcome—flooded my every sense, my entire body.

I picked up the closest object in my reach—a polished bronze mirror—and threw it to the hard-packed earth. It bounced and flipped upside down, revealing a satisfying dent in the geometric design on the back. I grabbed a sandal and a delicate ivory comb, hurling them both to the ground with all my strength. Then I snatched a ceramic cup, and that smashed with a gratifying shatter. I smiled, pulling hot air through my nose and into my heaving lungs.

When I reached for the heavy jug of wine, a cool hand covered mine. Damalis's soft brown eyes pleaded for me to stop.

My shoulders slumped and every bit of strength drained from me as suddenly as it had washed over me.

"Come, lie down for a bit." Damalis led me to the free pallet. It was piled with woolen blankets that seemed unnecessary in this heat. "Let me get you a cool cloth."

Orestes, his eyes round and his bottom lip trembling, came to me, and I pulled him down to lie beside me.

Damalis sat on the edge of the pallet and dabbed my feverish forehead with a damp cloth.

Ampelos and Amalthea started cleaning my mess. Without looking up from her work, Ampelos said, brightness returning to her voice, "You'll meet him soon. When you are old and you look back at this moment, it will seem like nothing. This is just a brief flash in your long life."

I almost fell for it. My body eased, relaxing into the soft pile of blankets. But if I didn't move soon, I'd fall asleep. And then who knew what I'd miss?

I popped up and swept past Damalis before she could say a word. If I wanted to learn anything about my husband before my wedding, I had only one choice.

I had to spy.

Someone had closed the tent flaps. Sweat trailed down my back as I gently lifted one edge, shot Damalis and Amalthea a warning look, and peeked out. Aegisthus and another guard flanked the doorway. A tiny grin touched Aegisthus's lips. He saw me, but he didn't turn to scold me.

I scanned the part of the camp I could see until I spotted them. Mother stood with her back toward me, Father's Spartan slave hunched beside her. And before the two of them stood my husband. Achilles. Mother was tall for her sex and was nearly of a height with him. But he didn't shrink away from her, as other shorter men tended to do. He held his body as if he towered over men and women alike, and his boldness bordered on arrogance.

He wasn't brawny, as I'd imagined. Instead, he was lean, sinewy. My betrothed wore a clean tunic of fine white wool. Who kept his clothes so shining white in this filthy camp?

Achilles was trim and fit, almost wiry, and his golden curls hung below his shoulders, unbound. He was indeed attractive, as Odysseus had said, but he wasn't the gleaming half-god I'd been expecting.

He and Mother spoke for a long time, the old slave answering their questions when asked. Achilles stood tense, and even from this distance, I could see his jaw tighten each time Mother spoke.

Did they quarrel with one another, or did they stand together against an absent enemy?

Neither was happy. That much was obvious.

Eventually, Achilles spun on his booted heel and marched away. Mother stood for a moment, her back still toward our tent, whispering one last comment to the slave, before she turned to come back. But I was swift with practice and, throwing a warning look at the three servants in there with me, had lain on the blanket-piled pallet before she whisked into the gray tent.

I stood, rubbing feigned sleep from my bright eyes. I opened my mouth to speak, but Mother raised a hand to stop me.

"You will marry at dusk," she said. Orestes stood next to her, and she patted his head absently. Her eyes searched the tent for who knows what, but they didn't meet mine. The color had drained from her face and she held her pale lips in a tight line.

Why wasn't she overcome with joy with this quick settling of affairs? Her eldest daughter would be safely married to a powerful prince before the moon even revealed her broad face in the night sky.

I didn't understand what was going on, so I behaved the way I behaved whenever Ismene defied me. I pouted.

"Why didn't you introduce me to my husband? Why did you speak with him in secret, ignoring your daughter's only wish?" I folded my arms across my chest.

Mother looked at me then. Her eyes shone in the filtered light, but I couldn't read her expression. She stepped toward me.

"Iphigenia," she said, her voice thin. "You're no longer a girl."

I wanted to tell her I already knew this. That's why I was going to be married, wasn't it? But something in her face convinced me to keep my mouth shut.

"As women, we're expected to behave as our men want us to behave—our fathers, our husbands, and eventually our sons. We must do things we don't want to do, or refrain from doing things we want to do."

She sighed and sat on the edge of the pallet, patting the blankets beside her. I sat.

"My husband, your father, killed my first husband. He murdered my beautiful firstborn son, dashing him against a hard stone wall." Her voice wavered, and she swallowed, closing her eyes against the memory.

"He forced me to become his wife." Her voice was stronger now, but she kept her eyes closed.

I stared at her in wide-eyed horror, my body numb. So, the long-ago story from the girl in the storeroom was true. Aside from the appalling detail of how Father had killed Mother's baby, it had all been true.

"You must be brave, my sweet daughter." She opened her dry eyes, touched my cheek with her warm hand.

Ampelos snipped and Orestes whined to Amalthea until she picked him up. Damalis stood stiff, looking at the packed dirt floor.

"We women must endure, but that doesn't mean we must be weak. You love your betrothed now. You think he's beautiful and glorious and brave. But all is rarely as it seems, Iphigenia. You must prepare yourself for what lies ahead."

Foolish girl that I was, I refused to note the ominous tones Mother so clearly spelled out for me. Instead, I whined and complained that I wouldn't meet Achilles before he became my husband. I pitied myself and moaned that nobody listened to me, a mere girl, even when the most important moment of my life was within arm's length.

Mother cleared her throat, ignoring my childish complaints. She stood, plucked Orestes from Amalthea's skinny arms, and said,

"Ampelos. Damalis. Come with me." And in a heartbeat, they disappeared into the crowd outside, leaving me alone with a sulking Amalthea.

Amalthea was all sharp edges and hard surfaces. Her too-big eyes floated above sunken cheeks and I'd never understood why Mother had chosen this haunted woman to raise her only son.

I glanced at my dress spread across the other pallet. A palace slave had woven it from the most exquisitely fine wool, bleached the purest white. If we'd had the proper time to prepare, I might have begged Mother to embroider a delicate pattern along the hem.

I still remember what I was thinking: *I will make the most beautiful bride since Hera.*

I'm ashamed to remember it now, but there it is. Hubris.

The voices of the soldiers that had, not long before, sounded so urgent and so excited, died away. A constant hum of voices now rumbled from far off. They'd moved to a new place, congregated somewhere far from our tent.

I hadn't expected these soldiers to look forward to the wedding of their king's daughter. Weddings were women's work, women's joy. Men took part only as much as they had to—as the groom or the father of the bride or the many revelers to drink the wine and eat the feast afterward. Maybe they were bored with this place and any diversion would do.

Amalthea and I fidgeted in awkward silence for too long. Finally, I decided it was up to me to take charge. Sitting on the edge of the pallet, I closed my eyes and counted to one hundred. If, I decided, Mother wasn't back before I finished, I'd direct Amalthea to help me dress.

When I reached one hundred, I sighed, then pulled my shoulders back and stood.

"I need to start dressing," I said in my most commanding voice. The look she shot me was unmistakable. She was Orestes's nurse, not my maid.

"Help me wash again." I peeled my tunic off and tossed it across my closed wedding chest. Even though we'd washed only a couple of hours ago, I'd already sweated through my dry tunic.

Amalthea poured rose oil into the basin of water that sat on the table between the two pallets. I thought she poured too much oil, but I said nothing because I couldn't be sure. She dipped a cloth into the water, then began scrubbing every bit of skin on my body.

"Don't scrub so hard!" I jumped away from my brother's angry nurse and swiped the dripping cloth from her hand. "I'll do it myself."

Once I'd gently passed the cloth over my skin, I knew Amalthea had indeed used too much rose oil. It's true, roses were the favorite flower of Aphrodite, the goddess whose protection I would officially pass into in less than an hour, but I thought even the goddess of love might agree that sometimes there is too much of a good thing.

Relief washed over me when Mother peeled back the tent flap and burst inside, followed by Ampelos.

When he saw Amalthea, Orestes reached for her, his pudgy fingers opening and closing. Mother handed her son off to his nurse, instructing her to take the boy out to go look at the great war horses, hobbled and scattered around the camp's perimeter.

Together, Mother and Ampelos wrapped the white dress around my naked body, taking care to drape the folds so that my small breasts and hips appeared more womanly than they were. Mother reached her hand to Ampelos for the gleaming pin that would hold my dress in place, a fine piece of gold and rubies from her own collection.

Ampelos led me to a stool wedged between our travel chests. Mother started unwinding my braids while Ampelos painted my face, reminding me that we didn't have enough time for complete wedding preparations.

They draped my brilliant saffron mantle so the rich folds wrapped around my arms, leaving my pure white dress exposed, and then they draped the thick fabric over my elaborate hair. I was now transformed into the virtuous bride that every groom longed for.

Mother held the now-dented mirror before me, and I saw I had, for once, truly become beautiful.

Damalis slipped into the tent, and only then did I realize she'd been missing. Mother nodded to my maid and then stepped before me.

She took both my hands and pulled me up from the stool. We stood facing one another and her eyes filled with tears that didn't fall. I sensed my face beaming as bright as morning sunshine, and I couldn't keep a smile from touching my lips.

The filtered sunlight inside the tent had shifted. Now coming from the west, the sun burned low and orange. My breath quickened when I realized my time was almost here.

Mother handed me a cup of unpainted fired clay, chipped in three places and brimming with dark liquid.

Her unshed tears overflowed, leaving wet trails down her unpainted cheeks.

Unpainted cheeks!

"Mother, why haven't you dressed? It's almost time!" My panicked heartbeat thumped.

She cleared her throat. "This is your day, Iphigenia. All eyes will be on you and nobody else. Drink." She clasped her hands around mine, the cup gripped between us.

I lifted it to my lips and tasted the dark red wine. I nearly spit it out. "It's bitter! What's in it?"

"Just a few herbs to help calm your nerves."

"But my nerves don't need to be calmed." I moved to set the cup on the stool, but Mother caught my hand in hers.

"You'll have plenty of nerves after the wedding. This will help you endure what happens then."

After the wedding. Of course! In the chaos of traveling and wedding preparations, I'd forgotten about the terrors inflicted on girls after they married. It was no secret Achilles wanted to leave me with child, so there would be no way of talking him out of it tonight. I lowered my right hand to my side, feeling the weight of my ivory statuette hiding in her little flaxen pouch tied at my waist.

I drained the wine in four foul swallows, praying to both Artemis and Aphrodite that the herbs might keep me comfortable tonight.

A great uproar spilled from the direction of the sea. Shouts turned to unintelligible chants, and before long it sounded as if the entire camp of soldiers roared as one.

A man's all-too-familiar voice sounded outside the tent opening, and when Aegisthus popped his head inside, Mother motioned for him to enter.

"Odysseus has come for the princess."

Mother moved to the open tent doorway, her voice decisive. "My man will take my daughter to the altar, along with our two trusted maids."

"My queen, the king has commanded me to bring the princess to him."

"You do not listen, Odysseus of Ithaca. Tell my husband whatever you wish, but I will not send my daughter with you."

Mother left Odysseus to complain to Aegisthus and turned back to me.

"You'll walk with Ampelos and Damalis," she repeated. "Aegisthus will follow. Keep you safe. They'll all lead you to the great altar your father built for you today."

Mother reached toward her maid. Ampelos carried over a small wooden box carved with intricate sea creatures intertwined with delicate whirls and circles. Centered on the lid of the box was a great octopus, its many legs arranged in graceful arcs and its eyes inlaid with shining rubies.

I felt dazed, overwhelmed by the beauty and kindness that surrounded me. Mother placed a steadying hand on my bare arm. She motioned for Ampelos to hand me the box.

"Here are your sacrificial offerings to Artemis on your momentous day. Spread these herbs and barley onto the altar. Pray to the great goddess to watch over and protect you, her faithful servant."

Taking the box in both hands, I pressed it gently against my body. I nodded, finding that speech had abandoned me. I'd hold the sacred gifts safe until I reached the fire, where I'd offer them to the goddess. Those were instructions I could follow.

Tears caught in my throat. Somehow, it felt as if Mother and I were saying goodbye. But surely we'd see one another at Aulis after tonight. Surely she planned to stay here in camp, with me nearby, until the men sailed off to Troy. Then we'd return home to Mycenae together.

Our goodbye was only temporary. So why did it feel permanent?

Amalthea lit oil lamps around the inside of the tent, drawing my attention to the dim light that no longer brightened the canvas.

"It's time, isn't it, Mother?" My voice sounded distant, a faraway echo of someone else.

Mother nodded. Grasping my shoulders a little too tightly, she stared at me for a long time, her eyes red, her lips trembling. She pulled me close. I squeezed my eyes shut, taking in her warmth, her familiar jasmine perfume, her safe arms.

She kissed both my cheeks and then turned me to face the tent opening. I glanced over my shoulder.

I looked at Mother one last time. Then with a deep breath, I stepped into the silent dusk.

CHAPTER 11

Helios drove his bright chariot toward the horizon behind us, lighting the cloudless sky a blazing orange and sharpening the hovering hill as he began his westward descent.

Ampelos and Damalis stood on either side of me, and together we took our first steps toward the shore, the three of us. Odysseus kept a few paces before us, and Aegisthus walked close behind, as if I were being guarded, not led ceremoniously to my husband.

I saw nothing but canvas tents, the hills rising to the right and left, and the sky softening to a pale violet as dusk spread eastward toward the sea. The men had gone to the shore, I assumed, to witness my fateful marriage. I still didn't understand why all these men would be so interested in a wedding, but my mind whirled when I tried to think about it.

They continued chanting, but the words were still too muffled to understand.

As we wove our way between tents, around carts, and over paths beaten by weeks of booted feet, I noticed a thick, black smoke rising above the tops of the tents. Was this the sacrificial altar to Artemis Father's men had built for my wedding? What could be burning in the flames? I'd never seen such thick smoke on an altar before.

Was the goddess angry? Did she disapprove of my upcoming marriage?

My sandaled foot kicked a large rock, and I stumbled. I kept hold of the delicate box in my hands, but Ampelos and Damalis steadied me by my elbows. My vision blurred for a heartbeat, then focused once again.

I must have been more nervous than I realized.

As we neared the shore, the tang of the thick smoke filled my lungs and brought tears to my eyes. I tried to think if I recognized the scent, to imagine what was burning on the altar, but my mind had become as thick as the smoke.

The chanting grew louder, even more frenzied, and I thought I could finally understand the words.

Bring the wind! Bring the wind!

What kind of chant was this on a girl's sacred wedding day?

My eyes and nose burned as we drew closer to the edge of the tents. I coughed into my shoulder, the strange motion sending me off balance for a step. Damalis's grip tightened around my elbow.

When we stepped out of the mass of tents, I saw nothing but a wall of men, all facing away from us. Chanting.

Bring the wind!

The sun disappeared behind the hills to our backs, its rosy-fingered rays dying in the darkening sky.

Odysseus shouted commands, and the sea of men parted before us and then reformed behind us, the way a stream diverts around a stone, only to swallow it again in its watery path.

As I passed before the men, their chants slowed and then faded, leaving nothing but a deadly silence in my wake. Their faces blurred before my eyes. My vision doubled, then tripled, then focused once again. Damalis and Ampelos released my elbows and gripped me round my waist.

The smoke was almost intolerable by the time we emerged from the crowd and onto the open, still beach.

My knees buckled at the sight before me, and Ampelos and Damalis lifted me upright before I could fall to the ground. Somehow, I kept a tight grasp on my precious box.

The altar to our great goddess Artemis was the tallest and brightest I'd ever seen. Though there was no wind, the heat of the licking flames stirred my loose hair and the folds of my golden mantle.

Tears now streamed from my burning eyes, and I couldn't help but cough over and over again. I wished for a breeze to carry the smoke out to sea, but none came.

Glancing around for my husband, I desperately searched through the smoke, hoping to glimpse the man I was going to marry in only a few moments.

But Odysseus and two of his men stood before me. There was no one else.

Odysseus nodded. I didn't understand what he wanted me to do. His face was blurry in the smoke, and my head spun in confusion.

Ampelos and Damalis led me forward, their arms still firmly round my waist.

Together, we walked to Artemis's altar. The mass of men behind me had grown silent and still, as if they had disappeared altogether.

The flames burned so hot, I feared my face paint might melt and run. What would Achilles think of his new bride if she had makeup and tears pouring down her smooth cheeks?

With her free hand, Damalis lifted the wooden lid from the box, the octopus's ruby eyes glimmering in the firelight.

Where had this box come from? I couldn't remember.

I reached my right hand inside and tossed the contents onto the licking flames. The herbs popped in tiny, starry bursts that disappeared almost as soon as they came. I thought I recognized the scent, but I couldn't place it.

My head spun once again. I must have muttered a prayer, but I no longer remember the words.

Damalis gently removed the empty box from my trembling fingers and dropped it into the flames. Deep in my mind, I protested. I wanted to keep that beautiful remembrance of this day. But I couldn't speak. My mouth formed words that made no sound.

On legs weakened with smoke and nerves, I was led behind the altar to a narrow strip of dry land before the still waters of the bay.

One man stood at the sea's edge, watching my approach. For a joyous moment, I thought this man was Achilles, that I was meeting my husband at last, and we would clasp hands. He would hold me steady in his strong arms, and I would finally be his wife.

His figure swam in my vision, as if I were underwater, looking up at him through the rippling surface.

Then my knees turned liquid, and this time, Ampelos and Damalis allowed me to fall gently to the sand, kneeling before my husband, my back to the flaming altar.

When the figure stepped toward me, I saw it wasn't Achilles at all.

My mouth formed the word *Father,* but no sound escaped my

trembling lips.

I didn't understand.

Another man materialized from the thick smoke. I didn't recognize him, but I saw from his red-trimmed tunic and his long, twisted beard he was a seer. He held a golden basket toward Father, and still Achilles didn't appear.

Father's face wavered above me, and I feared I would faint. His eyes glowed, and a glimmering tear traced its way into his dark beard. He pulled his hand from inside the golden basket and a long blade glinted in the light of the flames.

He spoke words I couldn't understand and raised the blade above his head.

A scream fractured the still night air, splintering my mind, otherworldly and deafening in my ears. It came from nowhere and everywhere at once, both endless and abrupt. The shriek of a girl, of a woman, of a goddess.

And then: Nothing.

Part Two

CHAPTER 12

T he girl who hovered over me wore a mass of frizzy curls that stood in outline against the feeble light.

"Good! You're awake." Her voice was high and musical. "I'll send a message to Grandmother. She'll want to know." The girl whisked herself through a door, her colorless shawl billowing behind her.

My body began to awaken: my fingers tingled, my toes spread, my arms reached. My weary lungs filled with stale air. My head ached.

With limbs heavy with long sleep, I rolled onto my side, the side facing the pale doorway. In case someone other than the little girl came in through it. The movement made my temples throb, and I gasped with the pain.

Where was I? I knew nothing. One god or another had draped a heavy black shroud over my mind, filled my skull with thick, dark smoke. I could think of nothing but my aching head and the girl who had vanished through the door.

Where had she said she was going? I couldn't remember if she seemed threatening. I didn't know if I should worry about her return, if I should find a shadow to sink into and prepare to pounce when she came back. But my head allowed no such thing. No sudden movements. No movement at all.

I was at the mercy of that small girl, the one who had breezed through the door. How long ago had that been? How many times had pain pulsed through the burning veins in my head since she left?

Ten times? Ten thousand?

When she slipped back into the room, she carried a small dark urn in one hand and a bowl in the other. She'd tucked a cloth under an arm and a two-handled cup dangled from a finger. She kneeled beside me, beside the soft mattress my stiff body was curled onto.

"I've sent Heliko to fetch Grandmother. I don't know how long it will be before she comes to see you." These words meant nothing to me. I closed my eyes.

The sound of liquid pouring into the cup. The sensation of the girl's hand behind my heavy head, lifting, and the cup pressing to my closed lips.

"Honeyed water. Drink," the girl commanded softly.

I obeyed. What else could I do?

The water was sweet, as promised. The cool liquid slid past my cracked lips and flowed down my parched throat. I took the cup into both of my greedy hands and gulped.

Shameless.

My closed eyes squeezed tight. The girl filled the cup again, and again I swallowed each grateful drop, savoring none of it.

"Enough for now," she whispered, and I felt the damp cloth gently pressed to my depleted face, my closed eyes, my aching temples. Did the gods feel this cool delight when we poured our libations in their names?

"Can you sit?"

I didn't know. I tried.

I pushed myself up with shaking arms and held my body upright until a sudden wave of dizziness passed. It felt as if my stiffened legs were buried beneath piles of heavy blankets, but I dragged them around until I was sitting cross-legged on the low bed, facing the girl who still kneeled on the floor.

"Good!" she praised. "That's very good. Do you think you can stand?"

I didn't know. I tried.

Unfolding my crossed legs, I pushed myself forward until my feet touched the hard floor. My arms no longer shook and when I pressed my weight onto my feet, I felt solid enough. The girl stood close, prepared to steady me if I faltered.

I trembled, but I didn't fall.

With a gentle hold on my elbow, the girl guided me, shuffling, across the room. Through the door. She whispered as she guided me down a set of narrow stairs, "We need to get you outside. Zobia said we need to get you moving as soon as you wake so your legs don't shrink from not being used. She said you need to spend as much time outside as you can . . ."

The girl's words faded as I focused on my feet, picking my way down one step at a time. Blinking, I followed her outside. My blurred vision slowly focused, settling on the packed dirt floor at my feet.

We stood in a small open courtyard filled only with a scattering of stools and an insignificant cooking fire. The girl helped me lower my stiff body onto a stool, my back to the doorway. I closed my eyes against the whirling, shooting pains in my head.

An early morning storm brewed, threatening to pour rain onto our heads at any moment. Helios tucked his faint yellow disc deep inside the low clouds, and still my eyes burned in the dim sunlight. I squeezed my eyes closed and my head pounded.

The girl fluttered around the space, somehow managing to sound efficient and quick, and gently placed something in both of my trembling hands. When I opened my eyes, I saw an unpainted bowl of fired clay, brimming with a clear amber liquid. I brought the bowl to my lips and tasted a thin broth. I swallowed gratefully.

Through the haze of my aching vision, I guessed the girl was about nine or ten years old. She sat on a stool across from the cold fire pit, sipping from her own unpainted bowl. "I'm Melissa."

I said nothing, but that didn't stop Melissa from rolling right along.

"I have a story to tell you." The girl Melissa sat statue still, her liquid black eyes begging me to give her permission to share the story she so clearly wanted to tell. "Do you want to hear it?"

I stared at her blankly.

"The man came in the middle of the night—I don't know who he was—and he pounded on the door so loud Grandmother and I both jumped right out of our beds." Her eyes darted here and there as she told her story, as if she were finding bits and pieces of it hidden throughout the tiny courtyard.

"I put my ear against my bedroom door but I couldn't hear what the man was telling Grandmother downstairs. When she came back upstairs, she was in a real hurry, but she wouldn't answer any of my questions. She put on her mantle and her shoes so fast I could barely keep up. But she didn't tell me no when I started putting on my shoes too. So I followed her right out the door without even asking." She pushed her chin forward.

I rubbed my temples and focused my eyes on the dirt at my feet.

"We followed the man all the way through town and down to the shore. He was dressed like a Greek and he looked pretty old. Grandmother was out of breath by the time we got to the shore, but I wasn't." She paused. Was she waiting for me to praise her?

"But when we got to the shore, we had to keep going. The man took us around some big rocks far away from the harbor, and our shoes stuck in the sand because it was so wet." The girl's words were quick, light as air. Even if a midnight walk down to the shore didn't leave her breathless, this story seemed like it was going to.

"The man told us to wait in this little cave that was damp and had water dripping from the ceiling. The moon was half full, and it was light enough that we could see a boat in the water by the cave. I stood on my toes, but I couldn't see what was in the boat because it was too tall. But we didn't have to wait long."

Melissa sipped the last drops from her cup, setting it on the ground beside her. "The man who came to get us went out to the boat—he had to walk in water up to his waist to get there—and then two more men jumped out of the boat and waited beside him."

I closed my eyes and felt my mind trying to wander. Why was she telling me this story? And did I need all these details?

But she continued, unasked. "Some more men who were still on the ship handed something big down to the three men who were standing in the water. It was hard to see with only a half-moon, so I couldn't tell what it was yet. But the three men in the water took the bundle and walked as fast as they could—which wasn't very fast because the water was so deep—and they laid the bundle on the floor of the cave. Can you guess what the bundle was?"

I didn't respond, didn't even move a muscle. But Melissa was silent so long I eventually pried my eyes open far enough to peek at her. She sat on the edge of her stool, leaning toward me, eyes shining. She didn't wait for me to ask what the bundle was. My opened eyes must have been the only permission she needed to keep going. "It was you!"

My eyes popped wide open then. She clapped her hands together once, as if she were telling her tale to a delighted child.

I opened my mouth to ask the multitude of questions that flooded my mind, but no sound escaped my throat. Instead, my vision filled with flashing stars and the world spun around my head. Bile rose in my throat. My mouth snapped closed, and the world settled around me once again.

Melissa didn't seem to notice my failed questions. She moved right along. "You were wrapped in a yellow blanket, and when they laid you down, they put your head on a pretty blue cushion. They were so gentle with you."

She dropped her voice to a conspiratorial whisper, leaning even closer to me. "I think they were soldiers," she said. "I've never seen a Greek soldier before, but they were dressed like they sound in the poems."

Her eyes bored into mine and she held her breath as if the presence of soldiers in the story might be the detail that caught my full attention.

I stared back at the little girl, still speechless. After the silence had drawn out uncomfortably, she picked up the story's thread. Still whispering and with eyes as big and round as a doe's, she said, "Your yellow blanket was soaked in blood. I saw it as clear as if it was daylight."

I swallowed, but this time I didn't take my eyes off the girl. Now I wanted to hear everything.

"You were soaked in blood," she repeated. "But it wasn't your blood. I didn't know it then, but I know it now because I'm the one who bathed you when we got here. It was *not* your blood." She patted my hand the way Ismene used to pat my hand when I was little, reassuring and understanding.

I swayed on my stool, eyes squeezed against the pale sunlight, the throbbing pain, the paralyzing chaos of my thoughts.

Suddenly, I wanted nothing more than to go back to sleep.

"Grandmother and the man—the one who came to our house in the first place—they went off and talked in low voices. I knew Grandmother was angry by the way she was standing and waving her hands around like this." Melissa stood to demonstrate.

"By then, some of the other men from the ship were with us in the cave and they were all talking in regular voices, so there was no way I could hear Grandmother even though I wanted to. So I asked who you were. They all wanted to talk at once and it was very confusing, but I think these are the things they said."

She took in a deep breath, as if preparing herself for a very long tale. "The tallest of them said you were the bride of Achilles, but the one wearing all black said you were the sister of Odysseus." She stood to take both of our empty bowls to a place behind me. "Another sailor, the smallest one, said you were the wedded wife of the great Ajax. But the man with the big ears said that wasn't true. He said you were the cursed daughter of Agamemnon. The small sailor said your father, whoever he was, had slit your throat, but the one with big ears got angry and said you'd been stabbed in your beating heart by your uncle."

Melissa gasped, shocked at her own story. I closed my eyes again. This was too much. Of course, this wasn't true. Surely I'd remember if my uncle Menelaus had stabbed me. Or worse, if my own father had tried to murder me.

"But I knew you couldn't have been stabbed and your throat couldn't have been cut. Because you were still alive. I know because I checked right after they laid you down in the sand. You were breathing and everything."

She'd come back around and now stood before me. She leaned close to my ear to whisper: "And I know who you really are."

Chapter 13

A h, Iphianassa."

The woman's words came from my left. Her voice was raspy, and her Greek was heavy with a Spartan lilt, just like Melissa's. Just like Mother's.

"You are Iphianassa from Tiryns, second daughter of Daimenes, an ivory merchant of great fortune."

Iphianassa. From Tiryns. But where was I now? In which distant land did I wake, head throbbing and body aching?

My throat went dry.

The woman didn't answer my unasked questions. Instead, she answered a new question that hadn't yet entered my mind: "You slept for three days. You never opened your eyes. You never moved at all."

To Melissa, the woman said, "Has she eaten?"

Melissa said that, yes, I'd eaten broth. I'd drunk honeyed water and walked without stumbling.

Good, good. The king will be glad to hear this news.

The woman rested her heavy hand on my head. I winced with fresh pain, but I didn't open my eyes.

I must bathe, she told Melissa. A quick bath with an urn of

saltwater would do for now. I could have a proper bath on the appointed bathing day.

I must also be put into a clean tunic. I must be prepared to meet the king at his convenience.

The woman moved before me, lifted my chin with her calloused fingers. "Can you open your eyes, Iphianassa?"

Iphianassa.

But my name was not Iphianassa. I was Iphigenia, daughter of the beautiful Queen Clytemnestra and the mighty King . . . but I couldn't think of that now.

Slowly, my eyes opened, pried by the unwanted hand of an unseen goddess.

The woman was old.

Now that I, too, am an old woman, I realize she was only in her upper forties on the day we first met. But to my inexperienced eyes then, she looked as ancient as the hideous Graeae sisters from Ismene's stories. She wore a white tunic covered by a fine blue mantle and a simple white band kept her gray-streaked hair away from her face. She wore a necklace of glossy black beads with a drooping garnet pendant, marking her as a priestess of Artemis. Fine wrinkles framed her dark eyes, which may have been caused by years of laughing or a lifetime spent questioning and doubting. Judging by the way she was frowning at me, my guess was the latter.

"You've suffered a great deal, Iphianassa, but you're safe here. If you follow my rules."

Suffered?

"You must forget all that has come before. You must think only of what's happening now. Artemis has preserved you and given you to me so you might serve her faithfully for the rest of your days."

The woman stood and held both of my trembling hands in her steady grip. "Stand up, Iphianassa. It's time for your healing to begin."

I rose slowly from my stool. Fresh dizziness swept over my weakened body, my overwhelmed mind. The woman didn't let go of my hands until the spell passed.

"I'm Maia, High Priestess of Artemis here in Tauris."

Tauris. Who had ever heard of such a place?

A bowl of water sat on the floor in the kitchen. Melissa gave me privacy to wash, and I obeyed. I peeled away the coarse tunic that hung from my sore limbs. Only now did I notice the fabric was stiff with grime, pungent with an odor that must have been mine. Had this tunic been on my body for the three days that I slept, dreamless?

I let it fall gracelessly to the floor.

Sitting on a low stool, I used a cloth to clean my stripped body, to scrub the filth from my tender skin. If Melissa bathed me when I'd arrived, as she said she had, she didn't do very thorough work. I couldn't see much in the meager light that slipped through the small, high windows, but I could see that there was a pale film on my pale skin. The film slid from my skin to the wet cloth, rinsed easily from the cloth to the cloudy saltwater in the bowl.

Deep scrapes that were tender to the touch covered my knees and elbows. My fingertips stung as if burned but showed no signs of injury.

A thin, deep cut sliced the palm of my left hand from the base of my longest finger to the top of my wrist. It had not fully sealed itself closed.

A dark crust caked the soles of my feet, and it didn't come off easily. Blood. Mud and blood. The scrubbing cloth stung, reopening wounds that had scabbed over but hadn't yet healed. My delicate feet were shredded, ruined.

What perilous and polluted place had the gods—had Artemis—dragged me through to bring me to this faraway land? I felt and I looked as if I'd been carried through the underworld and back again.

Had I?

Melissa returned through that door, a young woman following behind. "This is Heliko," she said.

Heliko held a bundle toward me, a clean white tunic and a pair of low leather boots. I dressed myself slowly, my arms and legs still not willing to do exactly as I wanted them to do.

The boots pressed against my wounded soles, and I didn't like the feeling. But I didn't complain. If I were to complain, where would I start and how would I finish?

Melissa led me back into the cloudy courtyard. She handed me another cup of broth. For the first time, foul thoughts popped into my mind when I eyed the brimming cup. Had Maia slipped a tasteless powder into the liquid when nobody was looking, maybe wanting to rid herself of the burden that had been thrust upon her in the middle of the night?

I sniffed the broth and eyed Melissa as she busied herself around the courtyard. It smelled just as it had earlier in the day, and the little girl seemed so open, so earnest, and so honest. It was impossible she'd poison another living being. I couldn't even imagine her smashing a spider underfoot.

But her grandmother was a different story. Maia was sharpened to a point. She might be willing to ease her own burdens in any way necessary.

In the end, my stomach decided for me. After three days of swallowing nothing more than a few sips of broth and water, my awakening belly protested. After the third or fourth loud rumble, I gave in and gulped the latest serving in three big swallows. If there was poison in it after all, then I may as well get it over with.

Melissa walked by my side, ready to catch me if I stumbled as we paced round and round the courtyard. I wanted to lie down again, to close my eyes, to drift back into merciful sleep. But each time we passed the door to the kitchen, Melissa gently guided me away.

"Grandmother says you must rebuild your strength. You slept for three days," she reminded me.

Melissa chattered happily as we walked. Artemis was the king's personal goddess, she said. Artemis offered the king special protection, special preference, special promises. That was why he insisted he meet and approve each new priestess of his favorite goddess when he didn't do the same for Aphrodite's priestesses or Apollo's priests.

The king was especially eager to meet me, specifically me. Melissa didn't say why, but she did hint that it had to do with the way I arrived here, in this foreign city in this foreign land.

She passed along instructions for meeting the king: I was to drop to my knees, rest my forehead on the floor before his feet. I was to remain in that position until I felt the tap of his staff on my right shoulder. If the tap came to my left shoulder, the king's guards would haul me away and I'd never be seen again. I was not to speak unless he asked me a question. In that case, I was to answer directly, using the fewest words necessary. The king had no patience for frivolous talk, even from priestesses.

And I was not to look him in the eye.

The clouds finally made good on their promise, splashing fat drops onto our heads and hands. Only then did Melissa allow me back inside the house and let me sit on a bench in the kitchen.

"I don't think the king will call for you today," she said, and I breathed a silent sigh of relief.

ΦΦΦ

The king didn't call for me the next day, or the next.

Those days passed much like the first: pacing the sunny courtyard on sore feet, swallowing thin broth, drinking sweet water. I ate tiny bites of soft cheese and cured olives, sipped watered wine, but tasted none of it. Artemis didn't clear the black shroud that hid the memories in my mind, but she granted my body more strength each day. My muscles no longer ached and the world no longer spun when I stood.

Still, I did not speak.

The second morning, I sat on my stool beside Melissa, sipping some liquid or another, my eyes wandering aimlessly around the courtyard. A low wall of uneven gray stone surrounded the packed-dirt yard, which backed against the courtyard of another home. A gnarled tree grew against the back wall, perfectly centered, as if purposefully planted. Even though the branches still stood naked in these early spring days, I recognized the rough gray bark of an oak. Herb beds lined the outer two stone walls, tiny pops of purple and white peeking through the limp-looking plants.

Movement caught my attention, and I turned my head to the left slowly, to avoid the dizziness I was sure would sweep through me if I wasn't careful.

A squirrel sat on the stone wall, its fur just as gray as the stones it sat on. The animal froze at my slight movement, and its shining black eyes stared unblinking at me. After a few heartbeats, it scurried over the top of the wall and jumped onto the trunk of the bare oak. It wound its way around the thick trunk, where it froze again for a few seconds, evaluating me once more. Then, the squirrel climbed its way to the nest I now noticed in the highest branches.

Melissa stood abruptly, and for a moment, I worried she wanted to scare the squirrel away.

"Let me fix your hair." She disappeared into the house, returning with a bowl, a cloth, and a comb.

"It would be best if we could wash it, but we don't bathe for two more days." She dipped the comb into the bowl of water, and an unfamiliar earthy scent filled my nose. "I'll try not to hurt you."

As she combed and dipped, combed and dipped, the clear water in the bowl slowly thickened with gray clouds, and there were a few times Melissa had to use her fingers to wipe the clotted mess off the comb's white bone teeth. I couldn't tell what filth was in my hair, and in truth, I didn't even want to know.

Melissa tried to be gentle. Each time she pulled too hard, she gasped, as if she felt the tugging pain in her own scalp.

Even with the comb pulling, I allowed my eyelids to fall and tried to relax my shoulders. Gradually, my heavy mind drifted, perhaps guided by the gentle hand of Artemis.

An old memory played behind my eyelids: Mother was combing my soft hair with jasmine-scented water as I sat in a different courtyard, the bright blue sky painted with wispy white clouds. As she pulled the creamy ivory comb through my straight strands, Mother murmured the familiar story of Persephone, whose scheming husband Hades tricked her into tasting the food of the underworld, forever binding the goddess to return to his realm each autumn and forbidding her to return to the world of men until spring each year.

Four-year-old Elektra sat cross-legged on a bright yellow cushion in the shade of an awning, black curls already combed and bouncing, listening unblinkingly to Mother's tale. And to her familiar warning at the end: *Never trust a man who wants you more than you want him.*

"This is the best I can do until we can wash it." Melissa's words startled me back to the harsh present.

She pinned my hair on top of my head, stabbing me more than once, and then covered the mess with a square of white linen. She moved around to face me, frowned when she saw the results of her work, and let out a dramatic sigh. "You'll look better soon."

CHAPTER 14

On the third evening, as Maia, Melissa, and I sat on our stools around the hearth fire eating our barley porridge and boiled broad beans, someone burst through the front door and a wave of panic washed over me. Melissa jumped from her seat and stood bouncing on her toes by the entrance to the main room.

I glanced at Maia, who sat eating her meal as if nothing were amiss. I tried to peek around Melissa from my seat to see if I could glimpse the newcomer, but she kept moving, so I saw nothing.

A man's voice came from the vestibule, too quiet for me to understand the words. I heard rustling and imagined this man might be removing a cloak or boots. Moments later, he appeared in our doorway. Melissa ambushed him as soon as she saw him.

"Uncle!" she squealed into his shoulder as he bent to embrace her. "You've been gone a long time!"

Melissa's uncle planted a kiss on his niece's head, gave her a last squeeze, then extricated himself from her grasp. He fixed his eyes on me as he took a step into the room. "This must be the famous Iphianassa," he said, and the corners of his dark eyes crinkled. "I've heard all about you. I just came from the king's side, and you're the talk of the palace."

He stepped toward me, and I instinctively leaned away from him.

Maia cleared her throat but said nothing, continuing to pop beans into her mouth one at a time.

"This is my uncle," Melissa said. "His name is Lastratos."

Lastratos nodded toward me as if I were an ordinary girl and not a princess. Heat rose from my neck to my face and I tried to imagine what Mother would do if a stranger addressed her with nothing more than a slight nod of the head.

"She doesn't speak." Maia's voice startled me, and I flinched on my stool. "She hasn't said a word since she woke three days ago."

Heliko, who'd been hovering in a corner while we ate, handed the man a cup, and I noticed it shining in the firelight. Where Maia, Melissa, and I had been drinking from plain ceramic cups, this man's cup was polished bronze and boasted two handles. He sipped slowly and moved his eyes from Maia back to me.

"She'll speak when she has something to say." He winked at me over the rim of his cup.

"She should have plenty to say," Maia huffed, thrusting her empty bowl toward Heliko. "*Thank you* would be a good place to start."

Melissa came to stand next to me and in her innocence broke the tension that had started to brew. "I tried to fix her hair," she said, patting the linen that still covered the tangled mess on top of my head. "I didn't do very good work. But the king hasn't called for her yet, anyway, so it doesn't matter."

Lastratos smiled at his niece. "I'm sure you did fine work. Now, you girls go on up to bed. I need to speak with your grandmother."

You girls. Had this man really just lumped me together with Melissa? Had he really just referred to me, the princess of Mycenae, as nothing more than a nobody girl? I stood, thrusting my empty cup and bowl toward Heliko.

Melissa hugged the man one last time on her way out the door, but I brushed past him as if he weren't even there.

"Ungrateful," Maia muttered as I swept out of the room, my head held as high as I could manage.

"I need you to figure out why she won't speak." Maia's voice came from downstairs, her irritation ringing clear even from a distance.

I stretched in the bed, my still-stiff arms reaching above my head, my shredded toes pointing in the opposite direction. A narrow sliver of pale yellow painted itself across Melissa's sleeping face on the other side of the room.

A woman's voice answered Maia's question. "Send her down. I'll see what I can find out."

Moments later, soft footsteps sounded on the stairs, and Heliko popped her head into the bedroom. "The High Priestess has called for you," she said, the words sounding thick in her odd accent. "She wants you downstairs right away."

Melissa stirred under her blankets, then sat up as if stung by a scorpion hiding under her mattress. She didn't even have to rub her eyes awake or stretch her limbs. "What's going on?"

"Zobia wants to see Iphianassa," Heliko said, holding my tunic toward me.

"Zobia?" Melissa looked at me, alarm in her eyes. "What's wrong?"

I shrugged my tunic over my shoulders, shaking my head. Nothing was wrong. Aside from all the obvious things, of course.

Melissa threw her tunic on and the two of us followed Heliko down the stairs, the chill in each wooden tread soothing my burning bare feet.

The woman who stood in the kitchen with Maia was short and thin. The mantle she'd wrapped around her shoulders looked as if it may once have been red, but it was now the pale pink of a faded rose petal. She'd wrapped her hair in a thick band of brown linen, a few silver strands peeking from the edges around her face.

She gestured for me to sit on a stool, and I obeyed, eying the new woman as I passed in front of her. "I am glad to see you have awakened." Her voice was strong, but her accent was a mystery to me, her words slanting, tilting at the ends.

Was no one here from Mycenae?

"Maia says you will not speak. Is this true?" She didn't introduce herself to me, and I wanted to feel angry at her disrespect. But I said nothing, my eyes flitting to the floor. When I refused to speak to Maia, a tiny surge of power coursed through my veins. But defying this new woman, this stranger, felt more like disappointment.

She sat on a stool before me so we were sitting eye to eye. "Open your mouth then." Her voice sounded calm, but she was one of those people whose very demeanor demanded to be obeyed.

I lifted my chin and popped my mouth open, tossing a glance at Melissa standing in the corner. If she wasn't alarmed, should I be?

The woman peered into my throat, holding a tiny burning brazier to light the way. Then she tapped my chin, letting me know I could close my mouth. She poked around my neck and my jaw. I squirmed under her touch but forced myself to stay seated. When she'd completed her task, she sat back on her stool. Her eyes met mine, and she held my gaze until my face burned. It felt as if she were reading my mind and I wanted to dart from the kitchen.

"Well? What do you see?" Impatience dripped from Maia's words.

Zobia didn't respond to Maia. "Give me your hand," she said to me, and I held my right hand toward her.

"Not that one. The other."

I looked at my lap, where my left hand curved into a loose fist. Zobia gently turned it palm-up. My fingers still curled protectively over the tender flesh, and the woman peeled them away one at a time until my palm was exposed.

She blew her breath from her teeth in a noise that almost sounded like a hiss. The wound was an angry red, swollen and tender. She poked with her finger, and I flinched.

"I should have sewn this when she arrived," she said over her shoulder. Maia peered to look at my wound and mumbled her agreement. "But it's too late now. The edges are beginning to knit together. Stretch your fingers as far as they will go."

I stretched, and she nodded. "Good. That is good. I believe you will keep your function."

She moved her stool a little further from me and patted her knees. "Give me one of your feet."

The healer examined the bottoms of each of my feet in silence, gently poking as she'd done with my hand, letting each foot drop to the floor when she was done. Then she stood without warning, picked her large leather bag off the floor, and moved toward the door.

She looked at Maia. "The hand is not putrid yet, but it will be soon if you don't take care of it. Send your girl to me this evening. I will make an ointment for the hand, and the feet as well."

She stepped from the kitchen and Maia followed her to the vestibule. From my stool, I heard Maia ask, "What of her voice? Why won't she speak?"

The front door creaked open, and the healer said, "She will speak when she has something to say."

Maia huffed. "That's what Lastratos said."

Chapter 15

The king called for me on the fourth day. I was once again pacing the perimeter of the now familiar courtyard with Melissa by my side. The afternoon sun sat high in the clear sky, radiating a welcomed warmth that soaked through my thick shawl and into my very bones.

Melissa had just wrapped up a long-winded congratulations on my pretty cheeks, which were finally pinkening in the rays, when Heliko stepped outside and bent her head.

"Zotikos has delivered a message for Iphianassa," she said, allowing her eyes to flit to me before returning to the ground. "He says the king wishes to see you."

"When?" Melissa asked.

"Now. As soon as she can get there. Maia is already waiting at the palace."

"Now?" Alarm rang through Melissa's voice. She took my elbow and turned me toward the house. "Come with me. I have to get you ready."

Heliko cleared her throat. "Zotikos says not to delay. He says the king wants to see her now."

Melissa rolled her eyes and sighed. "But she looks like . . ." The girl trailed off, scanning me from my toes to my hair. She didn't finish her sentence. "I guess we have to hurry."

In our bedroom, we wrapped our mantles around us—Melissa's a vibrant green, mine an undyed off-white. As I tied the worn leather belt around my waist, I wondered for the first time where my clothing had come from. Compared to Melissa's and Maia's, and even Heliko's, my tunic and mantle were drab. They were clean, but they had been mended in several places, and my belt was fraying.

Melissa pointed to my boots. "Hurry!"

I sat on my bed and slid the leather boots over my feet, wincing at the pain. These boots, at least, were something I was happy to have second-hand. I couldn't imagine forcing my tender soles into stiff new leather.

Melissa and I burst through the front door like a pair of rabbits flushed from their burrow. I swiveled my head side to side, taking in my new view. A narrow, unpaved path snaked between humble, unpainted buildings of two or three stories. The only color seemed to come from the blue sky above and the colorfully clad people hustling up the street in both directions.

We turned to our left, toward the sea I could hear in the distance, and snaked our way down the path. We turned onto a street, still unpaved but much wider, and walked deeper into town. Here, people crowded the street, but the air of hurried business was replaced with an unhurried idleness.

Most people ignored us, but a few stared at me with unashamed curiosity that brought heat to my cheeks.

In one spot, the street was forced to curve around an enormous boulder, splashed with dry white droppings from the white sea birds that swarmed this place. The boulder must have been too heavy to be moved by the men who built this citadel, so they built around it.

I wasn't sure how I felt about that. A part of my mind insisted that no Mycenaean—no true Greek, for that matter—would be satisfied building a road around a mere rock, no matter the size; anything can be moved if enough men want to move it. But another part of my mind whispered: *Why not?*

On the other side of the boulder, I at last saw what could only be the palace. Stony and squat like all the other buildings, the only evidence that this was a palace instead of a home was its sprawl. Even from the front, it was clear that the building had been expanded least three times, jutting from itself here and angled into itself there.

Five great columns stood, unpainted and supporting nothing but the weightless air that hovered above them. My steps slowed as I pondered the reasoning behind this bizarre spectacle. Who had ever seen columns standing with no burden to bear? And these were no minor columns, either. They were as tall as any in Mycenae, taller by a third than the squat building they stood in front of. Even if their wood was unpainted, it was at least polished so that each column shone deep brown in the afternoon rays.

I shook my head to dislodge the confusion and followed Melissa between two of these tall mysteries and through an open gateway.

Two guards stood inside the unimpressive gate, dressed in clean red tunics, daggers prominently displayed in their leather belts. They eyed us as we passed.

Inside, the palace was somewhat more interesting than its haphazard, dull exterior suggested. The vestibule was two stories high, and this time the three columns spanning the narrow space were actually put to work, holding the wooden ceiling beams and the roof.

The floor was made only of slabs of gray stone, but soft tapestries featuring every color in the rainbow hung from the walls. Melissa rushed through the room, so I didn't have time to examine the tapestries, but they seemed to feature stories of long-ago gods, the same as our tapestries at home.

We swept our way through a wide opening and found ourselves in the throne room. My pulse raced when I noticed it was a miniature replica of the throne room in Mycenae.

The walls were plastered and painted, a hunting scene following a seascape, following a chariot race. This room was also two stories high, and the hearth fire that blazed in the middle sent its gray smoke up through a square hole in the ceiling, leaving the unlit corners in deep shadows. Four narrow columns surrounded this high opening, holding the square in place, as if it might slide one way or the other.

Maia stood in one of the shadowy corners, hands folded before her, motionless.

Flanked by great griffins painted in shining red, the king stood before his throne, a plain wooden chair set against the far wall. We'd had more elaborate chairs scattered throughout the rooms of the palace back home, and a tickle of a laugh wanted to escape at this pitiful spectacle.

He wore flowing black robes, so thickly embroidered in clashing colors, they must have hung heavy from his shoulders. His fair hair hung in plaits that reached his chin, and he'd tied a black sash around his forehead, as if he planned to haul heavy crates in the shipyard and needed to keep the sweat from dripping into his eyes.

He looked absurd. If I were at home and this man had dared to set one foot in the palace, I'd have stolen a glance at Elektra and we would have giggled behind our hands until our bellies ached. But I wasn't at home and Elektra didn't stand beside me, and I had no way to know if the man who stood before me was a friend or an enemy. So, any impulse to giggle sat wedged in my throat.

The carved staff he held in his right hand reminded me of another king's staff, and his attire—ridiculous as it was—held some semblance to another king's dress. Bile burned in my throat. I couldn't think of Father now.

Remembering Melissa's instructions, I bowed low, pressing my forehead into the cold stones before his booted feet. I don't know how long he made me crouch prostrate before him, but eventually I felt the light tap of his staff on my right shoulder.

I rose and didn't look him in the eye.

His voice was a high, nasal wheeze, long vowels, each abrupt word lopped at the end. Greek was not his mother's tongue.

"At last, our famous new stranger. You are smaller than I imagined," he said, peering down his long nose at me. He coughed. "And younger."

I stood motionless, fighting the rising anger in my heart, trying to ignore the immense disrespect this foreigner was showing me.

"When we hear such fantastic stories, we build images in our minds." He waved his hand beside his head. "Sometimes the reality does not live up to the imagination." Another quick cough.

King Thoas shifted his weight from his left foot to his right, shifted his staff from his right hand to his left, and an unfamiliar herbal scent wafted from his robes with each movement. I kept my head pointed toward his feet but allowed my eyes to scan the king.

I focused on the pendant that rested on his chest: a disc with what may have been a bear pressed into the metal—bronze, not gold—and dotted with green and blue beads—glass paste, not enamel. It hung clumsily from a thin leather strap instead of a glittering chain.

He stepped toward me, and I forced my feet to remain planted. He slid a long finger under my chin, lifted my face. I couldn't help but meet his pale eyes then, flat and blue as the washed-out sky above. "I trust Maia is treating you kindly. Has the High Priestess provided everything you need for your comfort?"

I said nothing.

"Have the gods frozen your tongue?" He took his hand away from me and twirled his fingers in his oiled brown beard.

Maia cleared her throat. The king flicked his gaze to her. "My king," she ventured, speaking to the man's feet. "The good goddess has granted our Iphianassa much of her strength back, but she hasn't yet chosen to return her voice."

The king shifted his weight from his right foot to his left, shifted his staff from his left hand to his right. He coughed.

"How old is she? Why does she not speak?"

"I'm told she's barely fourteen years old, my king. She will come to speak in time, when it pleases Artemis that Iphianassa is ready to serve in her honor."

He stared at me until my cheeks burned. "I see." Another cough.

"At least her color is good."

My cheeks grew hotter and my pulse thrummed in my ears. I wanted to spit on this man's boots, to kick his ankles until he kneeled before me instead of the other way around. I wanted to heave his cheap, wooden staff and his dull bronze pendant deep into the sea that I could hear nearby, an ungrateful offering to earth-shaking Poseidon.

"Keep up your work, Priestess," the king said to Maia. "Make sure this girl does not anger our great goddess. Call for me when she has returned to herself in full. I do not wish to entertain a mute child."

"Of course, my king," Maia said to the king's boots.

A final cough from King Thoas and then his man Zotikos ushered me away.

CHAPTER 16

One evening, Maia burst through the door in a foul mood, rain dripping from her mantle, boots soaked through to the skin. She started speaking before Heliko could come help remove her drenched head scarf. "I need you to start coming with me," she said to Melissa. "The end of spring is coming, and we need to get ready for the Daughters of Artemis."

Melissa opened her mouth, but Maia cut her off. "You know they don't all earn their way through. I need you to help with the ones who do, so I can tend to those who don't."

"But what about Iphianassa?"

When Maia responded, it was obvious she was struggling to keep her voice calm. "She'll sit with Theano and Aëdon."

"But—"

"I've already made the arrangements." Maia's tone took on a dangerous edge, and even Melissa knew better than to press further.

I sat in silence, hands folded on my trembling lap, breath coming in bursts.

Who were Theano and Aëdon?

I didn't sleep that night. My mind danced with images of these mysterious women. At one point, I pictured two white-haired hags driving me to work and forbidding even the smallest moments of leisure. In another image, they appeared as demanding, diseased creatures whose sores needed tending to all hours of the day. None of the pictures conjured in my brain were pleasant.

By the time the birds outside the high windows began to announce the coming of the day, my eyes felt puffy with lack of sleep and my blankets were wrapped around my legs like a thick cocoon.

We ate our breakfast in silence, Maia still in a dark mood, Melissa pouting.

All at once, the urge to speak threatened to burst from me, an overwhelming need to demand answers to my many questions.

The old questions: where was I and how did I get here?

The new question: who were Theano and Aëdon?

And the most important question: when could I go home?

More than that, I needed to remind this woman—this Maia—who I truly was. She needed to hear me say, "I'm not Iphianassa!"

And then, "I'm no priestess! I'm a princess. Bow down and press your forehead in the dust before me."

And finally, "I'm the daughter of Queen Clytemnestra of Mycenae. I am Iphigenia. I am strong-born!"

My eyes darted to Maia, sitting on her stool, glaring at me. For the first time, I met her sharp gaze head-on.

All those powerful words and many more bubbled from my hot belly and into my dry throat.

I leaned forward and opened my mouth. Maia and Melissa sat frozen on their stools, seeming to hold a collective breath. The world stood still for an endless moment.

My heart lurched once and lurched again; my breath heaved in my tightening chest. The world around me vibrated with the rhythm of my pounding pulse. Lights flashed along the edges of my vision; all sounds congealed into a deafening ring that filled the world. The room spun impossibly around my head.

I fell from my stool, landing hard on my knees. What happened next was a chaos that I don't remember. In the end, I found myself lying on my bed with a cool cloth on my forehead. Melissa sat beside me, holding my hot, trembling hand in hers.

I sobbed, gasping and shuddering, and couldn't stop until Artemis and Melissa together lulled me into a precious sleep.

ဪ ဪ ဪ

Rain had poured from the starless sky all night, fat drops slapping the wooden roof and keeping us awake. The three of us trudged the cold, muddy streets after daybreak. Maia stormed ahead of Melissa and me, ignoring the women and men who scrambled to let her pass, their right palms pressed to their foreheads in deference to the high priestess.

Our destination rested only twenty-six steps from Maia's house. I know because I counted.

The house was a three-story version of Maia's: narrow and brown and flat-roofed. A few wood-shuttered windows pierced the walls here and there.

An elderly slave greeted us in the entryway. This space would have been called a vestibule in Mycenae, even in a private home like this. It would have brandished painted murals and painted floors, blazing bowls of oil set on tripods to light the deep corners. I didn't know what a space like this should be called. Nothing but bare plastered walls, a plain stone floor, a low timber ceiling. A single lamp, carried by the slave, sent our long shadows dancing on the walls.

The old man nodded when Maia asked to see Theano, and we followed his shuffling steps through a short corridor and up a set of steep wooden stairs. He led us to an interior room on the second story.

My mouth went dry when I realized I was about to meet the mysterious Theano and Aëdon.

We stepped through the door and into a small, windowless room stuffed with a large floor loom, baskets, and cushions. Four women turned on their stools to stare at me, the newcomer, the stranger. White smoke from the cheap oil lamps clung to the low ceiling. When Melissa, Maia, and I entered the room, our bodies made the already cramped space unbearable.

My chest squeezed, and I felt the dizziness coming, bitter panic filling my mouth. I couldn't allow myself to faint again, in front of these strangers, to lose another day sleeping in bed. Anyone could do anything to me when I was sleeping.

I had to fight through this. Pressing my hands into fists under my damp mantle, I tucked my thumbs under and squeezed, one finger at a time. I counted each time my nails bit into the tender flesh of my palms. *One, two, three, four, five* on my right hand; *five, four, three, two, one* on my left, the raw wound stinging. Over and over again until my breath passed easily through my lungs.

"Iphianassa?" I realized someone had been saying my name. No, not my name, but the name Maia insisted on calling me.

Where was Maia? Where was Melissa? They were gone. They'd left me alone with these four women. No, five. I saw now, as my eyes darted around the room, an old slave woman sitting on a cushion in a corner, a basket of wool on the floor beside her. She, at least, wasn't staring at me.

"Iphianassa? Can you hear me?" The woman standing before me was tall and slender, somewhere around Mother's age. She'd pinned her dark hair into an immaculate style at direct odds with the simplicity of the house we stood in. Concern filled her soft brown eyes, and she gestured to the stool she had been sitting on only moments before.

She laid her hand gently on my elbow to guide me toward a stool. I twisted away from her touch, cringing as if she were diseased, but I took the offered seat.

"Water," the woman said, tossing a look over her shoulder.

The slave in the corner jumped off her cushion, defying everything I now know about stiff old joints, and poured a cup of water from a pitcher by the door. I sipped carefully, not because I was thirsty, but because I wanted to peek around the room above the ceramic rim.

The woman took the empty cup from my trembling hand. "I'm Theano, wife of Eumedes, the king's chief adviser." She paused for a second, and I got the sense she expected me to respond. When I said nothing, she continued, her smile never faltering. "This is my daughter, Aëdon." She held out her hand and a girl stood, moving next to her mother.

Aëdon's wide smile was a mirror image of her mother's, but

that's where the similarities ended. Where Theano's eyes were brown, Aëdon's were the blue of the deepest sea. Where Theano's hair shone midnight black in the lamplight, Aëdon's loose ringlets glimmered gold. And where Theano stood tall and slim, her daughter appeared to be growing into a plump young woman, the top of her head barely reaching her mother's chin.

"You must be around the same age," Theano added. "Aëdon turned fifteen last winter. How old are you, Iphianassa?"

Of course, I didn't respond.

The silence grew awkward, and Theano continued. "You and my daughter will become great friends, I'm sure of it."

Aëdon nodded, her smile still wide, and I looked down at my hands.

"This is Melantho and Koronis." Theano gestured toward each of the other two women. They both smiled at me. Identical smiles. Twins.

This, at least, was good news. Everyone knows twins are lucky.

We spent our day at work. I made the fifth woman in the room—the sixth if you counted the slave—and you really only need two or three to work a loom.

"Why don't you sit here and work on some mending?" Theano gestured to a cushion on the floor near the slave. She pointed to a basket overflowing with garments that needed mending.

I glanced at the cushion, then the basket, then Theano. The blood boiled in my veins. That was slave work, and I was a princess. A princess!

I wanted to shout at these women, scream to the gods. But I couldn't. I plopped down beside the old woman, my teeth clenched so tight they ached. I crossed my arms over my chest, and I understood at once that I must have looked just as Orestes looked each time his nurse tried to convince him to do something he didn't want to do.

But I didn't care. Theano might force me to sit next to this slave, but I refused to do her work.

I glared at the four women as they worked the loom, tying the weights, then untying them when it was time to roll up the warp. They were working on a travel cloak, which Melantho said was for her brother, who was constantly ruining his clothes like a child.

Back home in Mycenae, Mother and I never would have had to make something so simple as a cloak, unless we wanted to make a special gift for Father. We had slaves for that kind of everyday work. We spent our time weaving beautiful patterns for our rich dresses or embroidering scenes on simple cloth to soften the walls. Our tapestries were intricate and delicate, stories strategically sewn into the fabric in every brilliant color imaginable.

Muse, before you accuse me of weaving tales of my own, let me clarify: Mother's tapestries were intricate and delicate, and it was looking as if Elektra would develop the same skilled fingers as Mother's. My fingers, as you may have guessed, weren't so skilled and my tapestries were never comparable to Mother's. But at least I never had to make my own everyday clothing.

The four women chatted the entire day.

Melantho and Koronis came from Pylos. They'd been living in Tauris with their brother for nearly five of their twenty years. They'd each been married back in Pylos, but they offered no more information about their husbands to me.

Their brother was one of the king's favorite guards.

"Zotikos," one of them said. "Maybe you've met him already?" Her voice rose into a question, but I had the idea she already knew that I had.

The twins were short, their faces unremarkable. Flat brown hair, and dull, mud-colored eyes that were too large, even for their wide faces.

The four women made a lively group, happily sharing harmless gossip, speculating on the gender of coming babies, deciding what to serve for the evening meal in their separate homes.

I sat in the corner with the slave Doris, pouting like a toddler.

The second day, I came prepared. I brought one of Maia's sharp bronze needles and a ball of fine flax thread, and when I sat next to old Doris, I set to work embroidering a clumsy red pattern along the hem of my rough, undyed mantle.

Both Melantho and Koronis eyed me but said nothing. Theano pretended not to notice my blatant disregard for her authority as both my elder and the female head of her home.

They all tried to draw words from my mouth with their questions. Where was I from? Who was my father? Who had taught me to embroider? This last came from Koronis and I imagined hearing a tinge of irony in her question. Who in her right mind could teach a girl to embroider so poorly?

Their questions went unanswered. I didn't even try to show any responses with nods or gestures. I simply sat on my cushion next to Doris, my eyes never leaving my work.

What shame fills my heart when I look back on those days now. And what amazement that these women continued to treat me with respect when I deserved nothing less than a sharp tongue, along with a reminder that, even if I used to be somebody important, I'd now become nobody from nowhere.

These thoughts never entered my mind at the time. Embarrassment never washed over me for acting like a child, for disrespecting the order of authority, for ignoring the kindness that spilled from these women's hearts.

CHAPTER 17

Every sixth afternoon, we rested. Even Maia rested, but she always insisted on staying home alone, kicking Melissa and me out of the house.

The rest of us cherished our afternoons off. Occasionally, Melantho and Koronis would ask me to join them, but I spent most of these precious afternoons with Aëdon and Melissa. We each took turns choosing our activity, and we were all predictable. Melissa always chose the market, and Aëdon chose to wander through the apple orchard outside of town.

And my choice was simple. I always wanted to visit the harbor.

These were my favorite days, the only days when I allowed hope to rise in my breast and swell in my throat.

Most days, there were Greek ships anchored in the bay, sleek and black and mighty. Each ship that sailed to this faraway place, each ship whose captain dropped his heavy anchor into the bay, could be the one to carry me back home, back to Greece where I belonged. I expected that, any day now, a man would come off one of those ships, a man Mother sent to fetch me. He'd stride into the palace and demand King Thoas release me back to my family. Would it be Aegisthus, or would she send another of her trusted men?

Even now, tears burn behind my eyes when I think of the hopeful girl I was still in those days.

ꙮ

As the spring days lengthened, Melissa, Aëdon, and I started spending more of our free time down in the harbor. We sat on a large rock against the steep Taurian cliffs, our faces lifted to the bright south sun, listening to the bustle around us.

This was a busy harbor. Ships sailed from Miletus and Ephesus and Lesbos. An occasional merchant from distant Egypt sometimes carried baskets heaped with sharp lumps of pink alabaster or crates packed with blue-glazed pottery that Melissa and I would admire in the market, but could never purchase.

Now that the Trojans were busy fighting, their harbors were unguarded. And an unguarded harbor meant any sailor could pass without paying expensive harbor dues. So, more ships came than before—according to Melissa—though few of them were Greek and none of them were Trojan.

Through half-closed eyes, I'd watch the painted vessels bob lazily on the calm waters and imagine myself stowed in the belly of one of the majestic Greek merchant ships that came only in my imagination.

But I couldn't just jump onboard and demand to sail straight back to Greece, could I? I couldn't march up to the nearest captain, hold my head high, and say, "I am Iphigenia, princess of Mycenae, daughter of King Agamemnon, and the future wife of Achilles. Take me home with the next tide!"

No. These weren't things a girl—a woman—could do. We were expected to be seen and not heard. Mute, mellow, and obedient.

Even now that I was a sacred priestess to Artemis, I wasn't supposed to have opinions or hopes. I was expected to do as Maia commanded, as King Thoas insisted, and as the great goddess desired. I was supposed to happily stay put, right here in this barbaric land so far from Greece, without uttering so much as one syllable about going home.

These thoughts made me feel trapped, and I'd always push them from my mind. I knew in my heart that Mother would send for me as soon as it was safe. All I could do was wait.

On one of these lazy afternoons, as we sat on our rock listening to the chatter and shouts and laughter of the men in the bay, a boy shuffled toward us, his eyes fixed on his feet. Melissa's chatter trailed into silence and the three of us stared at him as if a dolphin had sprouted legs and was now walking toward us.

He cleared his throat. "H-hello." His halting word was barely audible among the clatter of the men and the lapping waves around us. "I . . . I have seen you here before. Are . . . are you the priestesses of Artemis?"

The three of us glanced at each other. Should we speak to this boy when we had no adult chaperone?

It was Aëdon who decided. "Yes, we serve Artemis Taurica."

"I . . . I was wondering if you'd help me. If you'd be willing to give an offering for my family." The boy dug in his pouch, eventually pulling out a small wooden token, a crude image of Artemis scratched on its surface.

He held the humble disc in his palm, his eyes downcast. "This is all we can afford. It's for my sister. She delivered a son and by the kindness of the goddess, she and the baby are both safe."

Melissa took the bit of wood and nodded.

The boy should have left us then, but he didn't. He continued shuffling his feet and looking everywhere but at the group of women before him.

"I'm glad of your sister's safety, and that of her son," Aëdon offered awkwardly.

The boy bobbed his head, sending his long sandy hair bouncing.

Aëdon and Melissa exchanged glances, seeming unsure what to say next.

When the silence threatened to become unbearable, it was Melissa who broke it. "My name is Melissa. This is Aëdon and Iphianassa." She tilted her head toward us, each in our turn. "What's your name?"

The boy stood taller now and held his chin high with pride. "I am Nikandros. Our family are fishers and have been fishers since the beginning of time."

Nikandros the fisher boy stayed with us far too long on that day. He and Melissa talked and talked as if the rest of us weren't sitting right there beside them. As if it were natural for the granddaughter of the high priestess to befriend the son of a poor fisherman.

On another of our free afternoons, when it was Melissa's turn to choose, we went to the marketplace as expected. It was an unusually pleasant day. The sun burned in a cloudless sky, warming our skin and raising our spirits. We rolled our long sleeves above our elbows, earning sidelong glances from the Taurian women, who never wore their sleeves above their wrists.

The modest Taurians, whose ancestors had lived in these lands since time began, mostly stayed clear of our little Greek city built on the dangerous cliffs above the sea. But some chose to live among us, to prosper in our thriving commerce.

"They'd faint with shame if they saw our clothes back home!" Koronis whispered, stifling a laugh at her own joke.

"Or they'd collapse from the heat," Melantho added, a little more seriously.

I wanted to ask if it ever got hot here in Tauris, but of course I couldn't. It had been early spring when I first woke in this place. Now summer was near, and the air still held a chill in the mornings and evenings.

I longed for the hot, humid days back home—the very same endless summer days that most of us complained about as sweat rolled down our backs and glistened on our temples.

But this day was warm enough and I still remember it clearly. The four of us wandered the crowded lanes, Melissa bouncing ahead, able to act the carefree young girl that she was still in her heart. She stopped at nearly every booth, savoring with her eyes the fine bolts of cloth, the shining silver brooches, the rich-smelling cakes packed with mouth-watering flavors. She touched nothing but eyed everything.

Before we left, Theano pressed a small pouch into my hand. "In case you see something you'd like to buy," she said, her gentle eyes smiling. "Until you have items of your own to trade."

I nodded my thanks. As I pulled the drawstring open, the contents clinked softly inside. I poured them into my left palm, on top of my angry scar. A handful of glass beads sparkled in my hand, tiny spheres in almost every color. I plucked a blue bead from the small pile and rolled the smooth surface between my thumb and finger. In truth, I wanted to keep these, to sew them to the plain clothing I'd been given. But, looking at Theano, I understood these were for trading, not keeping, so I smiled again and tucked the pouch safely inside my tunic.

The sash caught my eye from afar, as if a playful nymph fluttered the folds just when I looked in its direction. The bold yellow-orange stood out from the other items, which looked dull and colorless in comparison, and the fine wool was woven so expertly that it flowed in the breeze instead of hanging heavy and stiff, as something I wove would have done.

I reached a hesitant hand toward the sash, unsure if the Taurian shopkeeper might swat me away like a pesky fly. But he didn't. The deep creases in his face softened when he said, "My daughter wove that fine piece." Aëdon translated the man's words into Greek for me.

I inclined my head, letting him know I understood. Aëdon spoke a few words in the Taurian language, her speech slow and uncertain.

The man continued speaking directly to me, pausing every few words for Aëdon to translate. "My daughter is about your age, I would guess, and she has been weaving since she was about your age." He gestured to Melissa with his hand. "Yellow is her favorite color, so when I can buy yellow dyes, she uses them up before I even know what has happened!" He laughed. "This is a fine shade of golden yellow that will complement your complexion."

I knew this already. Yellow was my best color.

Butterflies fluttered in my stomach when I thought of wrapping this beautiful sash around my waist or throwing it over my shoulders, brightening the drab, mended garments I'd been forced to wear every day since I woke.

Images of long sashes, fine mantles, and bright headbands flashed in my mind, memories of home. My own wooden chest had once been filled to the brim with exquisite fabrics like this yellow sash.

Since I'd never been allowed to go to the markets of Mycenae, I'd never bought anything before. But from Ismene's stories, and from watching the people around me make purchases here, I felt I could manage the transaction.

I carefully pulled three beads from the pouch Theano had given me, making sure the others didn't shift and make noise. Holding them toward the man with my right hand, I reached for the sash with my left.

The man took the beads, but a chuckle rumbled in his throat. His eyes were still soft, but the lines around his mouth had deepened again. "Ah, my child, this is quite generous! My daughter would be grateful to learn that you value her work. But, I am so sad to say, this is not nearly enough." He tilted his hand so the three small beads rolled and bumped into one another.

I was confused. Based on the dealings I'd witnessed with Melissa and Aëdon, this payment seemed like plenty for a single sash. I wanted to tell this man I had twenty such sashes in my maiden chamber at home, and in a rainbow of colors. That his daughter wasn't the only skilled weaver in the world.

But I could say no such thing. Instead, I reached into my purse and pulled out another bead. The man took this as well, but he shook his head. "This flawless item is so beautiful," he said, running the wool slowly between his first two fingers. "It took my daughter a very, very long time to weave this. She dyed the wool herself, you understand, and then made this sash with her nimble hands. I cannot take less than double this amount."

After translating the man's words, Aëdon said to me, "It's time to walk away now, Iphianassa. Take your beads back. You should pay no more than you've already offered."

The man acted as if he hadn't heard Aëdon's words, but the new glint in his blue eyes made me think he understood Greek much better than he let on.

"But, you see, my wife has recently died," the man continued, speaking to me. Aëdon translated reluctantly. "It is only my daughter and me now. We are alone in this world, and must make the best of what the gods provide. The girl can only work so many hours in a day, and so we must receive full value for all of her exquisite work." He rattled the beads in his closed hand.

I was torn. In my heart, I knew Aëdon was right, that this man was trying to take advantage of my ignorance. I couldn't even know if he had a daughter at all.

But I wanted this sash like I had wanted nothing since I was a little girl. I began reaching toward my purse again, when Aëdon took my hand in hers. "Come this way, Iphianassa. I have something I want to show you." She tugged me gently away from the stall with the old man and the saffron-colored sash.

As I backed away, Aëdon still tugging at my right hand, I held my left out to the man. He scowled as he dropped my four beads into my heated palm, all traces of kindness erased from his face.

I pulled my hand from Aëdon's, and we wove through the crowd until we found a low awning to shade us from the sun. Melissa plopped her small body onto the ground and began drawing meaningless designs into the dirt with the end of a small stick.

"You were too eager." Koronis's voice was quiet among the loud throngs of people, and I had to strain to hear. "He could sense how much you wanted that sash."

Melantho continued, "These merchants have been selling their wares for most of their lives. They can sniff ignorance like a dog can smell a dead rat on the other side of town."

Aëdon sighed. "He probably spotted us in the crowd before you even saw the sash. We are no more than dim-witted women, when it comes to these things. Men prey on our innocence."

"You must learn to pretend as if you don't care about the things you wish to buy, no matter how much you want them," Koronis said. "You must be always prepared to walk away at any moment, empty-handed."

"And you must learn to be convincing," Aëdon added. "The wisest of the merchants will guess when you're bluffing."

Aëdon held her hand to Melissa and pulled the little girl to her feet. "Let's try again. This time, Iphianassa, try to buy something you truly care nothing about, and walk away if you don't get your price."

I was willing to try, so I followed the rest out of the cool shade of the awning and back into the jostling crowd.

We passed stall after stall, most of which were full of rich-smelling foods. Then we neared a table I had seen on our outings before. I can't say I truly didn't want an object in this stall, but at least I didn't want it as badly as I'd wanted that saffron sash.

I tugged on Aëdon's mantle and gestured. She whispered, "Give no more than one bead."

I wove my way to the stall with my heart beating furiously in my chest. Why was I nervous to buy this small token when I hadn't been nervous to buy a fine piece of woven wool?

The woman behind the table was in her middle years, her fair hair beginning to turn gray at the temples. She acknowledged me with a nod but said nothing. I pointed to a small wooden trinket on the table, and she gestured permission for me to pick it up.

The small piece of wood was carved into the shape of a fawn, its tiny legs tucked delicately beneath its smooth body. The figure rested perfectly in my rounded palm, warmed by the rays of the morning sun.

This sweet little fawn was no longer an item I didn't want. But I felt the gaze of the woman on me, judging and assessing me, so I arranged my face into an expressionless mask and hoped my eyes looked dull and uninterested. My unspent beads still sat in the heat of my left hand, and with what I hoped was an expert move, I pushed one bead between my thumb and forefinger and held it toward the woman.

In halting Greek, she said, "This is a fine piece. The details are exquisite. Did you notice the spots carved into the fawn's back?"

Of course I'd noticed.

"I must have at least three."

I took a deep breath, afterward hoping she hadn't seen. Gently, I placed the tiny fawn onto the table and, with a heavy heart, turned to walk away.

"Wait." The woman's voice was quieter now, as if she didn't want others to notice she was willing to bargain. "I must feed my children, but I will let you have her for only two."

I looked at the figure once again, and I'm not ashamed to admit that I would have paid two for that precious little deer. But Aëdon's advice rang in my ears, and I suddenly felt the need to do this on my own.

So I turned, once again, to walk away.

This time I barely heard the woman when she said once again, "Wait."

In the end, I walked away with the beautifully crafted wooden fawn in my right hand and one less bead in my left.

My heart soars even now, remembering the swelling triumph of that moment.

Chapter 18

The days lengthened slowly until the promise of summer rested just around the corner. One afternoon, Melissa came to pick me up from Theano's house and, instead of walking to Maia's house, she led me in the opposite direction, eyes sparkling. "Come this way. I have something to show you!"

We picked our way down the steep stone stairs to the shore, but instead of turning left toward the harbor, we turned right. The beach curved itself away from the harbor until, when I looked over my shoulder, I saw nothing but the rocky face of the cliffs and an endless expanse of sea sparkling in the sun. If I listened for it, I could hear the muffled commotion of the busy harbor in the distance.

We walked side by side along the sandy beach, our sandals dangling from our fingertips. Melissa refused to tell me where we were going, but the pink in her cheeks made me smile in anticipation.

Eventually, she stopped and faced the black cliffs. "Here," she said, stepping around a rock that punched its way out of the sand like a black fang. I followed and found myself inside a small cave, barely tall enough to stand in and only as wide as my outstretched arms. A flat, damp stone rested in the sandy middle, nearly filling the space.

"This is where they brought you. The men on the ship. When Grandmother and I came to get you in the middle of the night." Melissa watched me, clearly anticipating a dramatic reaction.

But I felt nothing.

Muse, you know that's not entirely true. I did feel something, but it wasn't the horror or shock or sadness Melissa seemed to expect.

Instead, a lightness filled me from my toes up. Almost at once, my mind stilled, as if the moisture that leaked from the walls and dripped from the ceiling was, in fact, a kind of calming liquid.

I sat on a smooth rock and peered at the sliver of sea that was visible through the narrow opening.

Melissa sat beside me. "You aren't afraid?"

I shook my head. Within moments of arriving, I began thinking of this as my place of solitude. My *erêmia*.

෧෧෧෧

I sought my *erêmia* more and more, always with Melissa in tow. Nestled within the sharp walls, I'd close my eyes, inhale the salted air, and listen to the waves slap the sand. When I'd open my eyes, I'd watch white sea birds perch atop the small black peaks that punched through Poseidon's foamy surface offshore, calling to one another in a tongue only they and the gods could understand.

When my mind stilled, visions of Mother and Elektra and Ismene filled my head. Scenes from long-ago childhood days played in my memory, and when tears began to form behind my eyes, I forced them away.

I was done with tears.

The moments that led me to this place, so far from home, so far from my family, still hid from my memories. But maybe it wasn't a matter of remembering or forgetting. Was it possible that Artemis kept my memory shrouded for a reason?

Gods don't always have good logic behind the inflictions they rain down on us. Many times, it's just a whim that compels them to pursue us. But sometimes the gods do shield us from harm, and I wondered if Artemis was protecting me now.

I knew I was Iphigenia, princess of Mycenae, the golden seat of mighty Argos. I was the daughter of Queen Clytemnestra, wise above some men. Elektra and Orestes, my sister and brother, I cherished above all others. My nurse, Ismene, loved me as if I came from her own body. My mind still held my childhood memories and played them freely in my imagination.

There are times even now when I wish the gods had left the dark shroud in place, times I wish they allowed the shadows of those dreadful moments to molder in some black corner of my mind.

As it turned out, the gods had a terrible trick in mind.

෨෨෨

Flower buds began to peel their outer petals, promising to unfurl themselves into the blooms they'd become in the coming days of summer. The backyard squirrel appeared one day with two replicas of herself, the three of them looking identical in their soft brown coats. They must have been her kits, and their playful tricks would bring a smile to my lips.

The mornings still held on to their chill, but the afternoons when the sun chose to show his blazing face brought a warmth that began to thaw the icy layer from my skin.

It was one of these late-spring mornings when Maia accosted me as I came down the wooden stairs, eyes still crusted with the night's restless sleep, a shawl wrapped around my shoulders against the morning chill.

"Go get dressed," she said before my bare foot even touched the cold stones of the kitchen floor. Her waxy skin looked almost translucent in the pale yellow light that leaked through the high windows, and I wanted to turn back and bury my face in my blanket upstairs.

I stared at her, hoping my eyes conveyed the question my lips couldn't ask: What for?

But she turned back to the table where a drink steamed in its ceramic cup, her narrow shoulders sharp under her wrapped robe.

I spun around and retreated up the stairs, my bare feet stamping their blazing anger onto each tread. By the time I'd pulled my tunic over my head and wrapped myself in my plain mantle, Melissa's chirping tones floated up the staircase and worked to calm the storm brewing in my head.

When I made my way down the stairs for the second time that morning, I found Heliko sloshing the water she must have just drawn into the basin for the day. I dipped my cup under the cool surface and relished the smooth liquid as it coated my throat.

"Hurry. We're running late."

Maia and Melissa had already dressed and combed their hair for the day, and I wondered how I'd slept through their bustle. I ran my fingers through my tangled hair and hoped Melissa might offer to twist in a few quick braids for me.

"Leave it down. Go get your comb." Maia pointed her chin toward the stairs as she swallowed the last drops of her drink.

I obeyed with, as you can guess by now, graceless stomps and huffed sighs. I'm sure I sounded like an agitated horse.

Maia snatched the comb from my fingers before Melissa could reach for it. She pulled the tangles from my straight locks. My head jerked on my neck with each stroke, but I refused to whimper or even to frown. Instead, I set my face into a smooth mask and settled my gaze on the unpainted wall ahead of me.

The newly healed scar on my left palm flamed.

Maia stepped outside and motioned for me to follow. Behind us, Melissa closed the door with a quiet thump and it was only then that I realized she wouldn't be coming along. I swallowed the panic that threatened to spread through me. Surely, being alone with Maia couldn't be anything worse than unpleasant.

By the time the two of us set our booted feet onto the path outside the house, the pale rays of dawn had melted into cloudless morning skies. The air still smelled fresh, the multitude of hearth fires, cooking food, and latrine use not yet permeating the day. We turned our steps toward the palace. My belly flipped at the thought of meeting the king again. His narrow face loomed in my imagination, his fidgeting and his whining voice filling me with disgust.

Maia ignored the two guards at the palace gates, breezing past as they touched their foreheads in her presence.

The throne was empty. My shoulders relaxed.

In the king's absence, I noticed two alcoves set into the walls on either side of the painted griffins. Each housed a single carved statue. To my right stood a crude Poseidon, his wooden pose stiff and unforgiving. He was almost unrecognizable, but for the small dolphin who rested on its nose beside the god's foot.

Artemis stood in the alcove to my left, snake-coiled arms raised in a gesture that might be welcoming or dismissive. I supposed it depended on the mood of the viewer. The man who had carved Artemis's flowing curves had done so with more care and more skill than the man who had carved Poseidon's rigid form.

If standing on the floor, each statue would have reached only to my hip, a far cry from the life-sized images displayed in Mycenae. Poseidon's painted face and limbs were chipped and faded, but the colors that covered Artemis looked fresh and shining, her white arms gleaming in the torchlight.

Both statues were draped in miniature robes that appeared to be newly woven for the purpose. Poseidon wore a rich blue, and Artemis donned a pure white robe, trimmed in deep red and brilliant gold.

Both gods stared back at me, Artemis with dark eyes that gleamed with lifelike intelligence, and Poseidon with exhausted blue irises, faded and indifferent.

And I wondered. Where were the others? No one had painted them on the walls or hung tapestries full of their stories. Did the people of Tauris not beg favors from Apollo or Athena, Demeter or Zeus? Was this king so foolishly self-assured as to think he needed no help from any other undying god?

Maia and I stood alone in the middle of this high-ceilinged room for several minutes, my unasked questions remaining unanswered.

I couldn't tear my eyes away from those of the carved goddess. I thought she whispered silent phrases to me, unintelligible, and my skin tingled.

A second set of footsteps approached behind me and my heart skipped a beat. A woman stepped toward us, holding a round silver casket in both hands. Later, I learned this was Koronis. But at the time, I still couldn't tell the twins apart.

Without a word between them, Koronis and Maia stepped toward Artemis. And not knowing what was happening or what I was supposed to do, I followed.

As Maia faced the goddess and muttered a prayer under her breath, Koronis handed the silver casket to me. It sat heavy in my hands, and a part of me wanted to believe the goddess had warmed the cool metal just for me.

Then, Koronis stepped to the blazing hearth fire in the center of the room and, with long tongs, pulled a glowing coal from the flames. Step by slow step, she made her way back to Maia and me, and that's when I noticed a shallow bronze bowl sitting on the floor beneath the goddess's feet. With a quick prayer, Koronis laid the coal in the dish, and the kindling that had been lying lifeless at the bottom burst into living, smokeless flames.

I stood dumbly, holding the silver casket and wondering what was happening. Maia and Koronis both seemed to understand what to do and when to do it, but I had no way of understanding anything at all.

Maia turned to me, her pale brown eyes swimming in unshed tears, and placed her hands on the top of the silver casket. She gazed at me for a long time, and I didn't tear my eyes from hers. Within a few moments, our slow breaths matched, and any turmoil left in my mind seemed to have fled.

Now I understood our purpose in this room on this morning. And, moving my lips in a silent repeat of Maia's words, I offered this prayer:

Come close to me, I pray,
Artemis of the golden arrows,
and may your protective form appear.
You, who watch over children and maidens alike,
and who guide us into our final sleep.
I, Iphianassa of Tauris, promise to keep your image before me always
and to protect and guide as you desire
the cherished daughters of this land,
until your ringing call fades from my ears.

Maia nodded, the tiniest movement of her head. I squeezed the casket tight as she pried the lid off. Then, balancing it in my left hand, my right hand dipped inside. Grasping a fistful, I tossed the sacred herbs into the small flame and watched as they popped and sparked for one beautiful heartbeat. The scent filled my nose, and I closed my eyes.

Maia reached both hands around my neck and fastened a necklace there. When I looked down, I saw that I now wore the black-beaded garnet pendant that would mark me as a sacred priestess of Artemis all the days that it rested above my pulsing throat.

⟡⟡⟡

"*Now* can I tell her, Grandmother?" Melissa ambushed us at the door the moment we returned.

Maia stepped past her granddaughter, heading for the stairs, and Melissa took her lack of response as the permission she'd been waiting for.

"Tomorrow is the Daughters of Artemis ceremony!"

When I failed to display appropriate excitement, she continued. "You know. When the Daughters of Artemis are passed over to Aphrodite."

Of course I knew. I'd completed my final year of this rite only last spring, giving myself willingly over to Aphrodite and gladly leaving the protection of Artemis. Or so I'd thought at the time.

"This will be my second year making the cakes," Melissa said, her enthusiasm dimmed. "I keep praying to Artemis to send my blood so I can pass through. But she hasn't heard me yet, so I guess I'll be making cakes again this year."

I wanted to tell her she shouldn't be so eager to pass through to Aphrodite, that she should pray to remain a Daughter of Artemis forever. That nothing good came from the promises of marriage and of men.

But even if I'd had the voice to say these things, she wouldn't have listened. I wouldn't have listened either, at her age.

Melissa kept chattering. "At least I'm not carrying the jars anymore. That's for the babies, and Grandmother says I should be grateful to have made it to the cake-making stage."

Melissa's talk of cakes made my stomach grumble. Maia had swished me to the palace so fast that morning that I hadn't had my breakfast. I piled slices of white cheese and a handful of dried figs onto a slab of yesterday's herbed bread and sat on my stool to eat.

As I chewed, I let my mind travel back to Mycenae and wondered if Elektra might be preparing to play her role in the Daughters of Artemis. It was, after all, the right time, with the new moon hiding her face from us, holding the promise of a fresh silver crescent the next night.

At eight years old, Elektra would be in her second year carrying the jars. The job of babies, as Melissa had put it. Girls aged seven to nine served this important role of transporting jars and urns and pitchers filled with water, wine, oil, and honey. Last spring, during my final year of the ceremony and Elektra's first year, my little sister had been charged with carrying a ceramic jar filled with aromatic dried dates. And she'd carried her jar so carefully, taking the priestess's instructions so seriously, that she'd held up the line by stepping too slowly and the girl who walked behind her whispered a surly "Hurry up!" that we heard all the way at the back of the line.

A smile touched the corners of my mouth at the memory. I hoped she might have more confidence this year, keeping up with the girl in front of her as she carried whatever vessel was in her charge.

"Right, Iphianassa?"

I pried my eyes open, not ready to leave behind the soft memories of home. Melissa stared at me from the table, knife in hand, ready to stab at the onion that lay helpless on the board.

"I said tomorrow will be exciting, right?"

My head nodded a silent lie.

CHAPTER 19

I didn't have the opportunity to discover whether or not the Daughters of Artemis was exciting, and neither did Melissa. She woke in the middle of the night, moaning and tossing in her bed. I lit a lamp and froze when the light illuminated the girl. She lay on her back, sodden sheets kicked down around her feet. Her skin glimmered in a sweaty sheen, plastering her hair to her cheeks, and her throat was so swollen, her neck puffed noticeably above her collarbones.

She looked toward me unseeing, eyes glassy with fever.

With my free hand, I dragged the stool beneath the high window and tore the shutter open. True, the cold night air poured into the room, but I had to give the sickness a way out of the house before it caught up to all of us.

Still holding the lamp in one hand, I tore the damp sheets from Melissa's bed and threw them to the floor. Then, gently, I laid my own blanket over her shivering body.

Before I had time to think, I wrapped my shawl around my shoulders, threw open the door to our bedroom and walked the few steps down the hall. And then my thoughts caught up to my actions. My fist hesitated in front of the door to Maia's room. I wanted to spin on my heel and run from this house, run down those steep stairs to the harbor, dive into the frigid waters and swim home to Mother.

But, Melissa. How could I leave such a sweet little girl alone with her angry grandmother like this? She needed me.

So, I knocked.

I heard rustling behind that door immediately, as if Maia had been lying in her bed waiting for that very knock, ready to spring into action. We both held lamps in our left hands, and the dueling lights fought across our faces. Her long hair fell down her back and the glow somehow softened the wrinkles around her eyes and mouth. For a heartbeat, I could see the young woman she'd once been. But then I caught the hardness in her brown eyes and remembered who she was now.

My expression must have spoken the truth. She clutched her shawl around her throat and pushed past me.

The room was chilly by now, and I hoped the dark night air was doing its job chasing the black miasma out of the space.

Melissa had thrown my blanket to the floor and a fresh layer of sweat coated her skin from toes to scalp. Maia laid her palm on her granddaughter's forehead, as if anyone with eyes couldn't see she was feverish.

"Send Heliko to me." Maia's voice was steady and low, but dark fear danced in her eyes. "Then get water and towels."

I didn't hesitate, pounding on Heliko's door and then rushing off to the kitchen before she even had time to answer. She'd figure it out easily enough.

By the time I'd started up the stairs with a pitcher, basin, and an armful of towels, Heliko was breezing out the front door, her narrow shoulders wrapped in my mantle, which she must have snatched from its peg on her way out of my room.

Iphigenia, princess of Mycenae, would have fumed at this blatant disrespect. But Iphianassa, nobody from nowhere, had more important things to worry about.

I set the empty basin on the floor beside Maia's knees.

"Get dressed."

Silently, I obeyed. I even slipped my boots onto my icy feet.

Maia stood slowly, a knee objecting with an angry pop, and handed me a dripping towel. "Keep her cool." Then she disappeared.

I pulled a cushion next to the bed and started mopping Melissa's little face. She thrashed every few minutes but was mostly still, her breath coming in ragged bursts. The light that crept through the window wove a soft blue shroud across the floor, the walls, the bed.

I extinguished the lamp. I'd seen everything I needed to see, and I didn't like the sickly yellow pallor the flames cast onto Melissa's face.

In the near darkness, I pictured the roles reversed, little Melissa hovering over my pale, prone body in the bed across the room. How many hours had she watched over me all those weeks ago, cooled my forehead, whispered soothing songs into my unhearing ears?

Dabbing sweat from her swollen neck, I opened my lips to whisper the song Ismene used to sing to me when I was sick.

But no sound came. Only a breath of silent air.

∽∽∽∽

Zobia arrived. We filled the room, four women and one sick girl. I sat on my bed, my feet tucked underneath me, making myself as small as I could. Heliko stood beside my bed, shifting from one foot to the other, arms crossed tight around her chest. She'd removed my mantle as soon as she returned and now stood almost naked in the cool dawn air. I patted my mattress. She hesitated, then stepped closer and sat beside me, shivering. I pulled a corner of my shawl around her and we sat shoulder to shoulder, statue still.

Zobia worked quickly. With practiced hands she poked at Melissa's throat, earning hoarse groans from the little girl. She peeled her eyelids open, shining lamplight into her pupils. She prodded under her armpits, and Melissa twisted away from the woman's fingers.

Finally, she pried Melissa's jaw open and peeked into her mouth.

"She has an infection in her throat that has polluted her entire body." She stepped toward the door. "I'll need help in the kitchen."

The woman had picked up the large leather bag she'd brought with her and was out the door before Heliko realized she was the one who was supposed to help in the kitchen. She jumped from my bed and scurried downstairs.

Maia stood, staring down at the girl. The woman looked tiny, almost as frail as Melissa. Her shoulders sagged and her cheeks were sallow in the brightening light. Eventually, she forced her shoulders back and stepped toward the door, a mask of false bravery slapped across her tired face.

"I'll tell Lastratos," she said, not turning to look at me. "You stay here."

I don't know how long Zobia and Heliko were in the kitchen. I barely heard the banging and bashing sounds that came from below as they undoubtedly chopped and ground and pulverized herbs. But Maia was back in the room by the time their footsteps sounded on the stairs.

Zobia kneeled once again beside Melissa, showing us what to do. She spread a thick gray paste over the girl's chest and throat. "Four times a day," she said. "Dawn, mid-day, sunset, and midnight."

Then she pointed to a cup of steaming liquid she'd set on the floor. "Three times a day. It's bitter and she won't like it, but she needs to drink it." Zobia shifted so she could hold Melissa's head in the crook of her arm. "It's for the fever and the pain. Dawn, mid-day, and sunset."

Melissa choked on the fluid and most of it dribbled from her lips. But her terrible throat bobbed a time or two, and I hoped that would be better than nothing.

"I showed your girl how to steep it."

Heliko nodded, maybe a little too enthusiastically.

Then the healer reached for the tray Heliko had been holding. As she took the tray, a dozen little yellowish lozenges rolled and bumped into one another. They were about the thickness and length of the first joint of my little finger.

"Once a day," she said, holding a lozenge between her finger and thumb. "Each dawn, she must swallow one until they're gone. But until she can swallow . . ."

Her eyes dropped to Melissa's lower half, and the woman didn't need to finish her thought. We all stared at the helpless girl, and I felt a pang of helplessness myself.

With her left hand, Zobia rolled Melissa onto her side, and before any of us knew what was happening, the lozenge had disappeared into the wrong end of Melissa's body. She groaned and twisted weakly, but it was over almost before it began.

I glanced at Heliko, knowing this would be her job, and saw her wiping her palms over her tunic. She knew it too.

Zobia peeked into her leather bag, nodded, then pulled the drawstring closed. "I'll visit each day to check her progress."

As the woman's footsteps retreated down the stairs, Maia, Heliko, and I looked at one another. Shock and confusion spread across the two women's faces, and I'm sure mine as well.

It was Maia who broke the spell. She sighed, glancing at the morning light that was now pouring through the open window. She flipped her eyes to me. "I have to perform the Daughters of Artemis today and tonight."

She was right. There was no substitute for the high priestess of any goddess, especially our Artemis.

"You heard the instructions. Do as Zobia said." Her eyes switched back to their usual hardened glare, but in the heartbeat before she could raise her shield, I saw.

Pleading. Fear.

In the weeks since I'd awakened in this very room, I'd already formed a habit. In this moment, that habit reared itself in my heart. I balled my fingers into fists and set my feet and my jaw firm. My breath thickened. But the moment before I shook my head and stormed from the room, some god or other softened my heart, my fists, my jaw.

I nodded. I would obey.

All that first day, I sat at Melissa's side, my new wooden deer clasped in my hand for luck. My back ached and my eyes drooped, but I sat beside the girl as she alternated between thrashing like a landed fish and lying corpse-still. Countless times, I held my finger under her nose, checking for breath.

Every once in a while, when the wind gusted just right, the sounds of the Daughters of Artemis ceremony drifted into the room. Beating drums, trilling flutes, high-pitched squeals.

And I'm a little ashamed to admit this, but there was a small tug at my heart each time these cheerful sounds drifted into my lonely ears. As Melissa had predicted only the day before, the festival may have indeed been exciting.

Heliko brought the medications at the right times of the day, and we worked together to spread the paste and dribble what little liquid we could down Melissa's throat.

Of course, Lastratos couldn't come into our maiden room to visit his niece, but Heliko updated the man each time he asked. At one point, he called for me.

When I met him in the hall, he pressed something into my hand. When I looked, an idol rested perfectly in my cupped palm, a goddess carved in white stone. Artemis.

Over the next few days, we prayed. Maia and I threw handfuls of herbs into the hearth flames, begging the goddess to spare her faithful little follower. We laid sweet cakes beside the hearthstones in case the goddess was in the mood for something edible.

The next few days passed in an exhausted fog.

Lastratos brought in a priest of Apollo, who stepped barefoot through the house in the deep of night, a smoking bundle of incense held before his skinny body. He waved the incense in the air, blowing the smoke into every corner of the home, chanting deadly Apollo's healing hymn over and over again until the sacred words burned themselves into my memory.

Apollo. The distant, deadly archer.

Melissa was only his first victim. The terrible god struck, night-like, again and again, his poisoned arrows clattering across his shoulders, the terrible clang of his bow ringing through the dark streets of Tauris.

In our house, Maia was next. Then Heliko and Elazar and Lastratos. When Zobia visited each day, she brought terrible news. Aëdon and Theano, Koronis and Melantho. Entire households stricken.

Praise the gods, the healer said. Apollo's arrows have not touched King Thoas.

And then she fell ill, and I was left alone to nurse a house that brimmed with pollution. I swam in the miasma of sickness with no guidance, no help.

I couldn't keep my mind from wandering to Mycenae. The little girl with damp hair spread limp on her bedding reminded me too much of my little Elektra. Had Apollo turned his lethal gaze on the palace, on my family back home? Did Elektra, even now, lie sometimes restless, sometimes still as death, with a swollen throat?

The sickness burned through Tauris in four feverish weeks, leaving only a small number of lifeless corpses in its wake.

Relief washed over me when Theano's old slave, Doris, came to collect Melissa and me. Theano, she said, was feeling well enough to resume our daily work. I was eager to see my friends again, to see with my own eyes that they were well. And, I must admit, I'd also grown bored stuck inside Maia's house for the past three weeks and I looked forward to hearing a little gossip again. For once, I was the one who nearly skipped up the street, leaving Melissa to shuffle behind me.

My optimism faded when I saw the women sitting in their usual places in Theano's weaving room. They were pale and thin and a little sluggish. But they were all there, and I sent my silent gratitude to Artemis.

We worked in near silence for about an hour before the household below stirred. With a tilt of her head, Theano sent Doris downstairs to investigate. Moments later, the old woman returned, her long face arranged in the blank mask all slaves wore when hiding their true feelings.

"The king's guard has come for the priestess, Iphianassa." She spoke to the floor at my feet, her tone bland.

A moment passed before I realized she was speaking about me, Iphianassa still a name that belonged to someone other than me. I glanced at Theano, my eyes asking the question my voice couldn't manage.

"I don't know, Iphianassa. My husband didn't mention the king wishing to speak with you."

Theano stood and motioned for me to come to her. She tucked my stray locks back into their pins before covering my hair with my white scarf. Her thin fingers were cold on my scalp, but her eyes still held their warmth. "Aëdon will go with you."

Aëdon stood obediently, wrapping her own scarf around her hair and stepping toward the door.

My heart filled with dread, memories of my first meeting with the king flickering in my mind. I never wanted to see that fidgety, small man again. But what choice did I have?

Theano nodded toward me, a gesture of comfort and dismissal at the same time.

Zotikos waited in the vestibule. Like most of the others, he'd grown thinner during his illness. Though he was still in his twenties, his depleted cheeks sagged like those of an old man, and his belted tunic hung loose on his wasted limbs.

But his dark eyes still glimmered, even in the dim light of the windowless room. If Mother described Odysseus as *slippery*, then I'd describe Zotikos as *slithery*.

"No, not you." He looked at Aëdon as if maggots crawled over her face. "One of my sisters. Send Koronis down."

He eyed me then, and his features changed. I tried to keep my gaze on the floor, but I couldn't help but steal glimpses of the shrunken man. The skin on my arms crawled. I truly could not decide if he looked like he wanted to strip me naked or to throttle me. Or maybe both.

I breathed a sigh of relief when I heard Koronis's steps behind me. "Brother! You look well."

Was she lying, or was she blind?

Zotikos answered his sister with nothing more than a grunt, then spun on his heel and marched out the door. I followed behind the pair as we made our way toward the palace. They walked quickly, heads together, muttering words I couldn't hear.

By the time we reached the entrance to the throne room, the dread that had filled me earlier returned. I looked around and saw only guards and advisers, some staring openly at me, others ignoring me completely. I saw not one friendly face, other than Koronis.

"You know what to do," Zotikos said to his sister before taking up his post near the open door.

She nodded, then gripped my elbow, leading me into the smoky throne room. The king wore the same ridiculous costume he'd worn the first time I'd met him, and I wondered if these were his only clothes. But what king would have only one robe?

Koronis and I kneeled on the floor before the seated king, pressing our foreheads into the cold gray stone. When we felt the tap of his staff on our right shoulders, we rose. We stood side by side, eyes cast on the floor, as King Thoas assessed us. To this day, I will swear to Artemis that I could feel his eyes travel from my head to my feet and back up again, the way you can feel a spider and all its legs on your skin.

Silence seemed to fill the room, and my pulse thundered in my veins. Finally, he cleared his throat, and it was as if the air itself shattered into tiny slivers.

"It seems, Iphianassa of Tiryns, that you and I are sculpted from the same stone."

Bile rose in my throat, and I swallowed hard.

"We alone escaped Apollo's dark arrows. We alone have been untouched by the terrible illness that swept through Tauris." He shifted his staff from one hand to the other. "And who do you think protected the two of us?"

I focused on a hairline crack in the stone at my feet, willing my breath to fill my lungs and my head to remain clear. Under my mantle, I squeezed my fingernails into my palms. *One, two, three, four, five. Five, four, three, two, one.* My scar screamed.

How could this man compare himself to me? I, of old royal blood; he, of new imposter stock. I was a princess by birth, the eldest daughter of the rightful king and queen of golden Mycenae. And he was who? Son of an upstart Athenian who ran to this barbaric land, escaping his own insubstantial life?

"It was Artemis, of course." His high voice cut through my thoughts. "She chose us. You and me. Above all others, she protected us against her brother's black disease."

Silence and stillness, then. I sensed him waiting for my response, and when I did nothing but stare at that crack in the stone floor, he rose from his seat. He stood so quickly that he was forced to fumble to keep his staff from clanging to the floor.

He cleared his throat. "She still does not speak?"

"No, my king." Koronis's voice was surprisingly high and cheerful, and I peeked at her suspiciously from the corner of my eye. She kept her eyes dutifully on the floor, her cheeks flushed a youthful pink. At that moment, I never would have guessed she was twenty-five years old. "Artemis has saved our Iphianassa from illness, but she has not yet returned her voice."

King Thoas grumbled incoherent words, then swept between us, forcing Koronis and me to step aside for him. He didn't bother to turn back to us, but his next words were quite clear. "I said I will not entertain a mute child."

CHAPTER 20

Our shadows moved before us in the slanted autumn daylight as Aëdon and I climbed the steep steps back to town. I'd spent an hour in my *erêmia*, Aëdon sitting silently outside the cave entrance.

When we reached the top of the steps and turned the corner toward the citadel, we nearly collided with Melissa. The three of us stopped in our tracks, Melissa and Aëdon laughing off the near-crash, earning an irritated scowl from a servant headed down the steps, probably sent on a last-minute errand to buy fish for supper.

Melissa snatched Aëdon's hand and led her up the path toward town. "I'm glad I found you two! I have big news!"

When Melissa said nothing more for several steps, Aëdon finally asked, "What's the news?"

But Melissa made us wait until we reached the flat road at the top of the cliff before stopping. She pulled Aëdon against the side of a house that sat on the edge of the road, out of the way of the stream of people coming to and from the harbor, and beckoned for me to follow.

Melissa's cheeks glowed, and she was breathless, making me

think she'd run from home to look for us. Surely Maia didn't know Melissa was here, did she? I couldn't imagine Maia allowing Melissa to run about town alone like a servant.

But that didn't matter. I wanted to hear Melissa's news just as badly as Aëdon must have. The two of us stood staring at the little girl as she caught her breath.

"Well, what is it?" Aëdon asked again. Her eyes danced with curiosity, and I wondered if mine did too.

Melissa finally spilled her news in one long breath. "A bard has come and the king called everyone to listen to him sing on the cliffs tomorrow and there will be a feast and dancing!"

Aëdon clapped her plump hands together in a gesture I'd seen from Melissa a hundred times, but never from Aëdon. "A bard! It's been so long since a singer has come! I can't even remember the last time!"

"It was when King Agamemnon called all the men to fight the Trojans. There was a bard that came after the messenger told King Thoas the news. He came to sing about Helen and how she ran off with that boy Paris and made her husband so angry he wanted to start a war."

I felt my eyes widen. Had the story of my beautiful aunt Helen reached this distant corner too?

The next morning, we tried to complete our daily chores, but even I was too excited to concentrate. Between the two of us, we were up and down off our stools, inside and outside the house, upstairs and downstairs on trivial errands.

It was a good thing Maia had left early that morning, or she would have been commanding us to sit still, to finish one task before starting another, to pick a spot and stay there. She might even have told Melissa, with an exaggerated sigh, to stop her chattering for one second, just one second.

Aëdon's visit was a welcome distraction. Melissa met her at the door with a squealed greeting fit for long-lost friends, not neighbors who'd just seen one another the day before.

"I brought this for you," Aëdon said, setting a bundle on the table beside the dates I'd been chopping. Her smile was sweet as usual, but her dancing eyes betrayed her excitement.

I dipped my fingers in a bowl of water, wiping sticky pieces of date onto a towel. Aëdon had tied the bundle with twine, and I had to pick at it with my nails to loosen the knot. Melissa hovered by my elbow, and I could sense her impatience growing with each second that passed. Part of me wanted to draw this out, to play with her anticipation, to make her wait even longer. Iphigenia might have enjoyed such a game with Elektra, but Iphianassa had no interest in that kind of nonsense.

"Sorry," Aëdon said. "I didn't mean to tie it so tight. You can cut it."

She reached for the knife I'd been using for the dates, but the twine finally came loose. I peeled back the corners of the white linen bundle revealing thick, fine wool neatly folded inside. I held up the mantle, pure red with white ribbon trim.

Under the folded mantle, there was a white ribbon headband, long enough to wrap around my hair at least twice, maybe even three times.

"I thought you might like to borrow it, since you don't have your own yet."

I wasn't sure—I'm still not sure—if the tears that filled my eyes were because of Aëdon's kindness, or because the mantle reminded me of Elektra, whose best color had always been red.

Through my watery eyes, I saw Aëdon move toward me as if to embrace me. I stepped backward and immediately felt guilty. I held the mantle to my chest, to my heart, hoping to show my gratitude that way.

If I'd offended Aëdon, she never showed it. I took the mantle upstairs and when I was alone, I collapsed on my bed and allowed my eyes to release the hot, built-up tears. My shoulders heaved with the first silent sobs since Mycenae, and my mind flooded with images of my family there. It was Elektra's little round face that took hold in my tortured imagination; it was her dark eyes that pierced through the clouds in my mind, pleading with fiery ferocity before fading away to nothing.

The eyes of a shade.

I lay on my bed, throat raw, face wet, body spent. Staring at the beams above me, I blinked away the last lingering tears, still gripping the red mantle to my chest.

I must have slept. When I pulled myself up to sit cross-legged on my bed, Maia's voice drifted up the stairs. She'd returned home for the mid-day meal.

Her clipped words floated up the stairs, asking where I was. I sighed, wiped the crusted tears from my cheeks, and laid my bundle on my bed.

After our meal, Heliko pinned my hair up and wrapped the fine white ribbon around my hair. When I gazed at myself in the polished bronze mirror, I thought I almost looked pretty. I might have even seen a smile in my eyes, but I looked away before I could know for sure.

Maia raised an eyebrow when I came down the stairs wearing the red mantle, but she didn't ask questions.

The three of us left together and headed down the street in a direction I hadn't been before. After we passed the last house on the road, we switched back and the path began to climb. My stomach flipped when I dared to peek into the gap to my left, a yawning chasm of deadly, black rock that plunged to the sparkling blue waters of the sea. I moved to the other side of the path to give myself a little distance and tried not to look again.

"This is called the People's Way," Melissa explained. "It's called that because . . ."

I glanced at her when her pause drew out longer than normal, and she was squeezing her brows together in thought.

"Well, I forget why it's called that. Grandmother, why is this called the People's Way?"

Maia was walking a few steps ahead of us, but she turned her head toward Melissa, and she used the soft tones she reserved only for her granddaughter. "Because it leads to the only space large enough to hold all the people of Tauris at once. This is the road the people of Tauris walk when we need to gather together at the Heights of Artemis."

"You'll see when we get there," Melissa said to me.

Sea birds circled high above us, their *kaw-kaw-kaws* sounding more like squeaks and shrieks than birdsong. Mycenae was too far inland for gulls, and the few times I'd ever seen the white creatures were when we made our annual pilgrimage to the sea to honor

Poseidon.

Here, they were plentiful.

A few birds perched on the precipice of the cliffs, unafraid of the steady stream of people who passed before them. Their glassy yellow eyes with their tiny black pupils sent shivers down my spine. It wouldn't have surprised me to learn these beasts were, in fact, inhabited by gods. Was there such a thing as a gull nymph?

At last, we stepped out of the constricted path and into a flat space that was wide open to the sky above and the sea below. As I looked around, I realized we were now on an outcropping directly across from the outcropping where the citadel of Tauris stood. From here, I could see the wisdom of the men who'd chosen the spot to build the palace. It would have been impossible for an enemy to launch an attack from this distant peninsula, with that deadly chasm between.

The afternoon sky was empty of clouds and the high sun felt more like the summer we'd already left behind than the autumn we'd just entered. As we headed back out toward the sea, a breeze lifted the edges of my red mantle, and I knew my hair must have escaped Aëdon's white headband, even if it was wrapped three times.

Greeks and Taurians alike packed the Heights of Artemis. They mingled and laughed and gossiped. The wide-open space that must have seemed so enormous when it was empty was now ready to burst. When I looked back the way we'd come, I felt we were being very foolish. Unless there was another way off this high peninsula, any enemy could easily trap us where we stood. All they'd have to do was block that terrible passage we'd just walked, and we'd have nowhere to flee.

"Come on! Let's find Aëdon!" Melissa pulled at my sleeve, and I followed her into the crowd, trying my best to dodge the bodies that swelled around me.

We found Theano and Aëdon along the far side of the open space, where most of the women had gathered. Theano wore her veil against the bright sun, and I regretted I had no veil of my own to wear on sunny days like this, even if I was unmarried.

The aroma of roasting meat and spiced vegetables drifted on the breezy gusts every once in a while, and my mouth watered even though I'd eaten my mid-day meal less than an hour before.

Somehow, someone had brought the king's throne up to this place, a makeshift dais arranged near the sea edge of the cliff. I couldn't guess how that feat had been managed. But there it was, planted against the blue sky as if it had always been there. Maia took her seat in the small chair beside the king, and his advisers and generals and friends sat on their stools or cushions around their king. They watched the rest of us in silence, not joining in the laughter or the joy. They simply sat and watched.

I turned my back to that depressing dais and tried to forget they were there at all.

The afternoon passed too quickly, laughter and chatter filling the vast open space around us. We women kept to our side of the space and the men kept to their side, leaving a small emptiness in the middle for children to run and squeal, bridging the gap between our two groups. Across the ever-moving heads of the playing children, we were easy targets for the gazes of the opposite sex, and my cheeks flushed each time I caught a boy's eyes on me.

As a fourteen-year-old princess who wasn't allowed to choose a husband, the idea of flirting had never entered my young mind. The combined protective shields of Mother and Ismene meant I'd never been so exposed in my life. I should have felt embarrassed. But my heart soared with the freedom, the choice to be seen.

We mingled like this for a long time, sometimes standing in small groups, sometimes sitting on our cushions. Slaves wound their way through the crowds, serving cool water and weak wine. Melissa and Aëdon introduced me as Iphianassa a dozen times, but the thrill of this day's freedoms overpowered any anger I might have felt at hearing my false name.

When at last the sun began to lower itself toward the surface of the sea, I started to notice a new quality to the people's postures, their voices. Men lit three great fires across the open space. Mothers called to their children and we scattered ourselves around the fires, each of us facing the dais.

I sat on my soft cushion between Melissa and Aëdon, our backs to the flames against the damp autumn chill that fell around us as dusk blanketed the sky. I was sure the crowd would never settle, and I looked around impatiently. But eventually a still hush filled the space.

The final murmurs dropped away when the singer arrived. He came from behind us, walking around the crowd. He grasped his wooden lyre tight against his body and took his seat on a high stool placed between the dais and the crowd.

He was maybe twenty. Seeing him perched on his stool, an old memory flooded my mind, quick and bright. Kadmos. He was old, even then, his hair more gray than black, deep creases crossing his face. And he was Father's favorite, so he visited the palace many times each year. Father paid him well, so he dressed well, always draped in fine robes with new sandals on his feet. He loved us, too, always bringing sweet treats to Elektra, Orestes, and me, pressing them into our little hands with a wink and a warning: "Don't tell your nurse."

Kadmos liked to sing the old songs. He'd sometimes bring tales from other parts of Greece that he picked up in his wide travels, but he preferred to sing harmless tales of brave heroes who saved their villages, or unlucky girls who caught the lustful eye of Zeus.

Sometimes, after Father had just returned from an expedition, Kadmos would sing of King Agamemnon's bravery, his boldness, his honor. We'd hear tales of our glorious father defeating monstrous kings, fearsome pirates, and armies of weak soldiers.

I'd be much older than I was on this night in Tauris before I'd realize that Kadmos's songs held meaning much deeper than the words that came from his lips. Long years would pass before I'd see it was my father who was the monstrous king, and his was the band of fearsome pirates, and he was the man who led the army of weak soldiers.

But as a young girl growing up in a sheltered palace, such thoughts didn't even exist. And on this night, as a fourteen-year-old exiled princess, truths like these merely loomed out of sight in the ether surrounding me.

When this fresh-faced singer struck the strings of his lyre—before, Muse, he sent his plea to you and your sisters into the crisp air—my body sat light on its cushion. My unblinking eyes followed his fingers as they ran up and down the instrument. I felt almost happy.

Sing to me, Muse. His first words were harmless and ordinary, and I heard them with lightness still in my heart.

Sing to me, Muse. The powerless beginning of familiar songs, the phrase we'd all heard since our earliest days.

But when the rest of the words came, their heaviness tore through the invisible air between us, their heavy syllables rolling, unhurried, toward me.

Sing to me, Muse, of the blameless Iphigenia,
whose royal father, driven by the rage of Artemis,
drew a bloody knife across her white throat
and butchered her with his own hand.

Those words pummeled me, one after the other. The silent crowd surrounding me wavered and then disappeared. King Thoas on his throne shattered, the thousand pieces of him slamming noiselessly against the rocky cliff. The dusk sky sucked each of the fresh stars into itself, leaving nothing more than a smudged darkness behind, a blur of pale light against a purple sky.

And then, vast emptiness.

Memories flooded the void: the promise of a blessed marriage, a hostile welcome in a camp of warriors, a smoke-thick altar, and a haunted father with a gleaming knife.

These images screamed in my ears and blinded my eyes. The truth of the memories was enormous. My neck failed to carry the weight of the scenes, and my head bowed. A great stone rested on my chest, constricting my lungs until they could barely heave air into my trembling body. My eyes squeezed closed and refused to pry themselves open.

But I couldn't allow these scenes to master me. With eyes still clamped tight, I forced one breath through my nose, and then another. My fists squeezed and my nails bit into flesh. I counted each bite on my right palm, and then my scarred left.

By the time the singer had finished his long tale—*my* tale—I'd reclaimed my body once again. And though I could stand on my own steady legs, breathe un-ragged air into my calm chest and open my eyes to the star-filled sky, I must have looked alarming.

Without questions, Melissa and Aëdon walked me home, hearing from a distance the music and dancing and laughter they chose to forfeit so they could see me safely to bed.

෧෨෪෨

Muse, you know already the story of the cursed house of Atreus. It is you and your sisters who have spread the tale throughout the generations and throughout the world. You already sing, Melpomene, of tormented Atreus and the unfortunate offspring who call him Father.

And the young singer from that chilly autumn night recounted the curse to all the people of faraway Tauris. Melpomene, the words you planted in that singer's mouth were already well-known. He told of those born under the ancient cloud which hovers over all who bear the ancient blood of my family.

But I, strong-born Iphigenia, have survived this curse. And so all you Muses, all you daughters of Zeus, what other falsehoods have you spread through your singers and your painters and your dancers? Why should we believe any story you tell when you don't care for truth at all?

Chapter 21

Achilles.

I whispered his name, and the syllables felt soft on my lips.

Aëdon peeked into the alcove, her eyes big and round. "Did you say something?"

I shook my head, closed my eyes.

Moisture from my *erêmia* soaked through my mantle and my dress, dampening my skin, but I barely noticed. I sat with my back to the cave walls, my eyes unfocused on the waves that still lapped the sandy beach. I ran my thumbs over the carved surface of my little deer, tracing the delicate spots etched into her small back.

Achilles.

His features formed in my mind, replaying the only time I had seen him: speaking heatedly with Mother in the bustling camp of soldiers on the deadly shores of Aulis. The scene played in my mind's eye, as if I were a goddess seeing it happen both from my own perspective and from afar.

When I was at that camp, all those months ago, spying on my mother and my betrothed, I didn't understand what was happening. But now, with full knowledge of the terrible thing Father had planned, the scene took on a different meaning.

Achilles and Mother were not spitting hateful words at one another, but at someone else. They couldn't understand Father's plans to murder his own daughter, and they were both furious. Mother's anger made sense, but I didn't understand why Achilles was so angry.

As I stared, unseeing, at the receding waves before me, a truth slowly unveiled itself. He was angry that Father wished to take away his bride even before he had the chance to wed her. A justifiable rage. A rage of honor.

Had he offered, before storming away from Mother, to save me from Father's sharp knife? And if he was so fuming with anger then, would he not still be furious at losing his wife before we could marry?

Another thought crept in, threatening to overtake all others: If Mother knew of Father's plans, why did she not stop all of it from happening?

But I couldn't think of that now. I forced my thoughts back to Achilles.

Wouldn't he feel a painful sense of betrayal for having his future children, his legacy and his happiness, torn from him before first bloom? Maybe he thought I was dead. Maybe he, even now, grieved his young bride.

I didn't know the answers to these questions. I didn't know whether he knew I still lived or considered me a burned sacrifice.

Still, hope flowered in my breast. If he thought me dead, he'd be happy beyond words to learn that I lived. Or, if he knew of my fate, he'd feel honor-bound to help me, his betrothed, return to my beloved family and avenge the man who stole my everything.

If he was an honorable young man, he'd come to Tauris himself to whisk me back home to Greece. Warmth rose in my breast as I realized I'd finally discovered my way out of this hated place and back home, back to the hot Mycenaean sun and back into Mother's soft arms again.

How would I send a message to Achilles, son of Peleus? I needed to find a messenger to carry my plea and pay him so well that he wouldn't be tempted to betray me if an enemy captured him. These were, after all, war days.

Who could I trust to carry such a delicate message, and to relay the words with just the right emotion to convince Achilles that rescuing me carried more honor and fame than raiding tiny villages near Troy and capturing slaves?

My mind went straight to Nikandros. But he never left Taurian waters. He kept his fishing boats always within sight of the familiar black cliffs.

Would he know of a man willing to carry such a message? Of all the sailors he dealt with each day, arranging business deals with trading ships, would there be one sailor among them trustworthy enough to keep me safe?

My heart swelled with the relief of having discovered a way home at last. But it sank again at the realization that I had no way to ask for this favor. I still had no voice in my throat. It had been four months since I'd spoken to anyone.

ဏဿဏဿ

I held Achilles in my mind as Aëdon and I meandered back in that early morning hour just after sunrise. When we reached the top of the stairs, Aëdon pressed my hand between hers. This time I didn't pull away from her touch. Her soft eyes seemed to absorb the sadness that must have been plain on my face. She sighed, then turned to walk to her home.

I longed to tell her then, to reveal my true identity, to tell her the awful thing that had happened to me. I wanted to confess my newly hatched plan to reach Achilles and to see her round cheeks glow with happiness for me.

But I couldn't. With a deep breath, I turned away from Aëdon and walked the few steps to Maia's house. As I rounded the corner to the front of the house, my feet froze mid-step. Voices leaked from inside, near-whispers that seeped from the windows.

I recognized Maia's raspy tones, but the second voice belonged to a man who wasn't Lastratos or Elazar. I felt my eyes widen. A man was in Maia's house at this quiet hour before the day's normal business began.

I wasn't sure if I should walk past and come back later, or burst into the house to interrupt whatever secret meeting Maia was holding. Instead, I squeezed behind a wooden cask that sat next to the exterior wall. The familiar movement of it—the darting out of sight, the crouching and holding of breath—swept me back to earlier days, sneaking around the palace with Elektra, eavesdropping on whoever happened to be nearby.

Maia and her companion spoke in urgent whispers.

"He must be . . ." The man spoke in a heavy accent and his syllables faded to muted mumbles.

"Yes . . ." I couldn't hear Maia's next few words. Then, ". . . full moon . . . has to be tonight . . . can't wait a month."

"It must be kept quiet until . . ." He trailed off again.

". . . swear my priestesses to silence."

". . . your newest priestess? The princess—"

Maia cut him off, her voice suddenly clear. "There's no princess here."

Shuffling. Murmurs. The door creaked on its hinges, and I pressed myself flat against the building. A bead of sweat rolled down my forehead and into my eye, but I didn't dare move to swipe it away.

I itched to peek around the corner, as Elektra and I would have done back when the worst that could happen was a scolding from Ismene. But those days were gone, and I wasn't ready to find out the worst that might happen to me here.

So, I waited behind the cask until the man's shuffling footsteps faded into the still air.

I could have gone up the street and doubled back, giving Maia time to hide any evidence of her visitor, to compose herself, to keep her dignity.

But I didn't. I walked straight into the house and tried to arrange my face into something of a knowing smirk. I wanted Maia to think I overheard every word, that I saw the man leaving her house and knew who he was.

It didn't work.

Maia hustled around the kitchen, gathering things into her reed basket, absolutely ignoring me. But I didn't see what she was packing because my eye had snapped to Melissa, who sat combing her hair in a beam of yellow sunshine, as if no man had just been in this room, whispering secret plans to her grandmother.

The man's scent lingered, an earthy, waxy smell that was becoming familiar to me here in this wild, faraway place.

Maia wrapped herself in her heaviest blue mantle, even though the morning was already quite warm, and fastened it in place with her simplest bronze pin. She, apparently, needed no ornaments wherever she was going.

"I'll be back in time for the evening meal," she said to Melissa and then swept past me, as if I wasn't even there.

∾∾∾

As promised, Maia returned in time for the evening meal. She carried a cloth-wrapped bundle which she laid delicately on the table, as if it were a bundle of fragile eggs.

She eyed me, daring me to ask.

Heliko served the simple meal of spiced barley porridge, boiled broad beans, and bits of soft cheese. We ate in silence. I peeked at Maia as I sipped my weak wine and she seemed just as she always was: quiet, observant, hurried.

The one thing that was out of the ordinary was Melissa's silence. In the hour before Maia's return, Melissa's chatter had dwindled until, as we ate, she was utterly speechless. I never, in the entire time I'd been in this place, dreamed this was even possible.

When Maia swallowed her last bite, she finally spoke. "Girls, dress in your ceremonial gowns. Paint your faces and put on your jewels. We leave just as the moon starts to rise."

Was this to be my first ceremony as a sacred priestess? And what ceremonial gown would I wear? I barely had everyday clothes for myself, let alone a gown fit for a ceremony.

I didn't know what to do. Nobody had taught me. Was I to be the basket bearer, or would Maia ask me to light the sacred herbs? Would I carry a torch or raise my plaintive hands to the darkened heavens?

I was terrified into stillness. I didn't want to further anger the powerful goddess who was already so angry with me she'd stolen my home, my family, my voice. One misstep, one false move, and what would she take from me next?

Melissa nudged me, and I saw Maia was staring at me. "Do you have questions for me?"

Of course I had questions. I couldn't count them. But I also couldn't ask them, so I shook my head.

Maia rolled her eyes and pointed to the table. "Your dress is there. It's new-made for you. I picked it up from the palace this afternoon. The king's women have been working on this dress almost since you arrived. But you will need to start taking care of your own business soon. I can't tend to you like a child."

I wanted nothing more than to tend to my own business, to buy my passage away from this place, to escape unnoticed back to Greece. If the first step toward freedom was to pick up my own dress from the palace women, then I would have rushed to do so. But I couldn't tend to business that I wasn't aware needed to be done. I wanted to spit these words into Maia's wrinkled face, but instead, I bit the insides of my cheeks and gathered up the bundle.

We dressed, the three of us, in Maia's room. The flames from the oil lamps danced on our faces and cast us in long shadows on the walls. How much simpler it would have been to dress in daylight. What ceremony did Artemis demand we perform by moonlight?

Heliko and Melissa helped Maia into her gown, its crimson fabric draping in elegant folds from the old woman's bony shoulders. I wondered who'd stitched the complicated blue and white flowers around the borders. I'd never seen Maia lift a needle and thread, and Melissa couldn't yet have enough skill to sew such fine work. The dress was open in the front in the usual style for the high priestess, exposing her drooping breasts to the goddess who honored woman's fertile womb, and the embroidery around the open front was intricate. Shining glass beads were sewn into the design and I could imagine the bright light of the full moon glimmering off their surfaces.

She stood tall as Melissa fastened around her throat a long necklace of gold links that hung below her humble black-beaded garnet pendant.

For the first time, I saw that she'd once been beautiful. And then, that evening when I was only fourteen years old, I felt a maddening disgust toward the woman for allowing herself to succumb to savage time. For allowing her hair to fade from shining black to dull gray, for allowing her skin to crinkle and sag, for allowing all but her bright brown eyes to shrivel and shrink.

What a heartless fool I was.

When Maia was dressed and Melissa had started to paint her face, I sat on the edge of Maia's bed next to the mysterious bundle.

I touched the corner of the coarse linen cloth, its fibers scratching my fingertips. Then I peeled back the edges and gasped at what lay beside me: a gown of the finest wool, carefully folded in a smooth bundle. On top of the gown sat more golden jewelry than I'd seen since my arrival. More, even, than Mother—the queen of Mycenae herself—ever wore at any one given time. I traced the gold with my fingertip: a pair of dangling earrings tipped with red rubies; a large brooch, the gold pounded thin as a blade of grass into the shapes of two winged bees facing one another above a bountiful honeycomb; two bronze chains with dangling bronze bells to wear around my ankles; and two golden armlets of coiled snakes, each with one onyx eye, to wear coiled round my arms. Five large pins, enameled in white.

Where had these treasures come from? Who had purchased them, and why did Maia give them to me?

I looked up at the old woman, tears blurring my vision, my questions plain on my face.

She shrugged. "The king insisted you have them. He commissioned them for you. I don't understand why, but there they are."

This drained some of the wind from my sails. I didn't want such rich gifts from King Thoas. But I couldn't send them away. They were too beautiful and their shining weight reminded me so much of home that I was willing to wear them and forget who they came from.

I spread each piece across Maia's bed, and the precious metal glimmered in the lamplight. Then I lifted the dress with trembling fingers. I looked at Maia again.

She nodded. Yes, this was also a gift from the king.

The soft fabric was dyed the darkest of blue, the hem embroidered in intricate swirls of azure and black—water and wind.

Long strips of saffron ribbons were affixed down the length of the skirt in even intervals all around. The bodice was woven with matching saffron threads, the edges trimmed in white ribbon. The dress was open in the front, but unlike Maia's, it was designed to be fastened closed with the five enameled pins.

I blew out my breath and sat heavily on the bed, my new jewelry tinkling with the movement.

Even as a princess of the mighty kingdom of Mycenae, even as the eldest daughter of powerful Agamemnon and noble Clytemnestra, I'd never worn such a fine dress.

This was a strange land, indeed, where a priestess wore finer clothing than royalty.

And that night, as we stood fully dressed in our ceremonial attire, the three of us were more than royal. We were divine.

Chapter 22

Single file, we twelve priestesses moved slowly down the street, the silver moon lighting our way. Melissa led the procession, her head wreathed in the season's last leaves from a walnut tree, and Theano followed, carrying a golden basket covered in a fine white cloth. I pulled up the rear, dutifully taking the place at the end of the line behind Melantho.

Only a handful of people lined the street, silent as the grave. They kept their eyes downcast as we passed before them, but I was certain I could feel their gazes on my back as we wound our way out of town.

Maia came behind Theano, bearing a white-painted box patterned with jewels in red, blue, and black, chanting so low that I couldn't understand the words.

We passed out of the city and made that sharp turn toward the dreaded People's Way.

The rest of the priestesses took up Maia's chant, already knowing the sacred prayer, and their volume rose as our footsteps fell into a rhythm. I tried to hum, to take part in my own way, but my throat remained stubbornly silent. Even now, as I walked piously in a procession honoring no one but her, the goddess refused to return my voice to me.

Cool breezes blew in from the sea, lifting the hem of my heavy dress and pulling strands of my hair from its jeweled pins. The townspeople packed the Heights of Artemis, standing in communal silent solemnity.

We walked toward the cliff's edge, townspeople creating a passage for us to step through, the moon's silvery light casting long shadows on the rocky earth at our feet. The sharp tang of smoke filled the air, but I saw no fire.

In fact, I could see very little beyond Melantho before me, and the double line of townspeople on either side of me. Our procession came to a stop, and that was when I realized the few people who'd lined the streets in town had followed us out to the cliff. They were gathered behind me now.

I suddenly felt penned in, like an animal prepared for sacrifice. I forced long gulps of cool sea air into my lungs, squeezed my fists until my nails pinched the meat of my palms and my scar screamed.

Please don't let me faint. Please, goddess, hold me upright.

Our line moved again, and my breaths came more easily. My racing heart slowed and my eyes drooped closed in gratitude.

Artemis had heard me.

When our procession poured out of the tight crowd of townspeople, I finally saw the source of the smoke. A burning altar stood at the cliff's edge where the king's dais had been that night the singer came. Bile rose in my throat, and for a sickening moment, the two golden snakes that were twisted around my arms seemed to shift, to slither toward my bare throat. But our procession moved past the spot, and I pressed these deadly images down into my roiling belly.

As we passed, I saw King Thoas standing next to the altar, flanked by his men.

But we wound on, and I forced my mind to concentrate on my feet as they stepped over the narrow, rock-strewn path. We traced our way along the edge of the cliff, and if I allowed myself to look to my left, I knew I'd see the dark waves foaming white against the unmoving rocky cliff.

We walked until I could no longer hear the murmur of the crowd. When we stopped at Artemis's sacred stone altar, I peeked at my new surroundings. The modest fire we'd passed was no longer in sight, but its smoke swirled in the silver light.

I followed Melantho's lead, and we twelve priestesses formed a ring around the goddess's flat stone. The moon was nearing her zenith and her beams seemed to focus on the stone's charred surface.

Melantho and Koronis stepped forward. Koronis pulled open a small bag she'd carried through the procession and, stooping, stacked a few thin twigs onto the middle of the stone. Melantho removed the lid from the small ceramic bowl she'd carried and, with a pair of tongs, pressed an ember into the kindling.

Another priestess stepped forward and sprinkled the contents of her small box over the flames. Incense released its sweet, earthy scent, biting into the salty, fresh air around us. The breeze seemed to die on cue and the new smoke hung around us like a gray shroud.

The altar and the flame were both humble, and I understood we wouldn't be giving Artemis an animal sacrifice tonight. I breathed a sigh and sent a silent thanks to the goddess.

We carefully laid the items we'd carried through the procession at our feet. In our circle, I stood between Melantho and Koronis and was surprised when they each took one of my wrists in their hands. I resisted the urge to pull my arms away.

We stood motionless, grasping one another's wrists, silent. Each priestess had closed her eyes, so I did the same and we leaned toward the smoke, breathing the rich incense into our lungs.

Little by little, Artemis filled my body with ease, loosened my limbs, relaxed my face, settled my mind.

When Maia began to whisper a new prayer, my skin tingled from my scalp to my fingers to my toes, as if the goddess herself filled my body with her sacred breath.

We stood in the silence following Maia's prayer, breathing as one, existing as one with the goddess.

When I finally opened my eyes, the moon's rays had shifted from the flaming center of the altar. Maia opened her wooden box and presented it to each of us in turn, chanting a new prayer. When she came to me, I did as the others had done and reached my two hands inside, pulling out fistfuls of dried mixed herbs. One by one, we stepped to the altar and sprinkled our herbs into the jumping flames, adding new scents to the thick smoke. Others whispered their personal prayers, but I remained prayerless.

I felt dizzy, my skin coated in sudden sweat. Koronis touched my elbow with her dry hand, and I didn't faint.

Aëdon lifted her drum from the ground by her feet. Had she brought it with her, or had it been placed here by another?

The rest of us clasped wrists once again, and this time I didn't cringe. We swayed to Aëdon's slow rhythm; the staccato beats absorbed into the heavy air, and the priestesses sang a last prayer to the arrow-pouring goddess.

Aëdon's hands flew faster over the taut skin of the drum, and the priestesses' words grew louder, almost frenzied.

When they all fell silent as one, cut off in the middle of their communal prayer, I didn't understand how they knew when to stop. My skin prickled.

To fill the silent void, the sound of waves so far below filled my head, deafening and complete, leaving no room for anything else. Then Theano broke free from our circle, lifted her basket from the ground, and began a new chant. The other priestesses joined, and the crashing waves receded into a space in the back of my head.

Aëdon carried her drum with her and beat a slow rhythm as we trailed back the way we'd come.

I drew the night air deep into my grateful lungs, but the fog that had settled in my mind refused to budge. My knees trembled as we wound our way back toward the waiting crowd and the bright-black sky tilted first this way, and then that with each slow step I took.

But my relaxed muscles tensed, as if a bucket of icy water had splashed over my head, when I saw the fiery cliffside altar once again, the flames reaching toward the black sky, orange and red and blue. Thin black smoke pulled inland, and my eyes burned.

My mind darted back to the clear vision of another altar on a deathly still night not long ago, thick with angry flames and heavy with bitter smoke.

This altar that burned before me no longer appeared insignificant, and I worried that I was wrong in assuming there would be no animal sacrifice on that night.

I wondered for a moment what ill-fated beast these strange people would give to her. Ewe? Boar? Goat?

Aëdon never stopped her drumming, and we stepped in time to the cadence until we'd formed a long line facing the altar, clasping wrists once again, standing so near one another our shoulders touched. It felt as if we'd formed a wall of women. But for what purpose? Were we meant to keep something inside or outside?

King Thoas had moved so that he now stood alone before the flames. A cool breeze swirled for a second, touching the back of my neck, hot from the incense-guided walk, and sending a shiver down my spine.

Two girls about my age and dressed in acolyte robes tended the great flames on top of the altar, feeding dried sticks into the fire to keep it exactly the prescribed height.

A thought flashed unbidden through my mind, sent by some spiteful god or other: the dried sticks were so very unlike the wet wood that must have been used to build that other faraway pyre on the shores of Aulis.

My knees threatened to melt beneath me. Biting the insides of my cheeks until the metallic taste of blood filled my mouth, I willed myself to stay upright, my mind to clear. I was not in dreaded Aulis now. I was here, in Tauris, witnessing nothing more than a standard sacrifice to appease an easily angered goddess. These ceremonies happened all the time across the world. This night brought nothing ominous, nothing out of the ordinary, nothing to fear.

Aëdon's unceasing drumbeat grew louder, faster. Still we stood, facing the burning altar and the vast sea below the cliff.

We didn't sway; we didn't speak. Even the children in the

crowds seemed instinctively to understand and were silent. The solo staccato filled the night air so completely that I felt the beat must be coursing through my veins, my pulse thumping in time with Aëdon's pounding hands.

Beneath the thundering drumbeat, the very air around us seemed to ripple, to stir.

Melantho, standing shoulder to shoulder to my left, tensed and then shivered, her palm slick around my wrist.

A disturbance behind us grew close, as if an invisible god crept near, and at any moment I expected a touch on my shoulder. A reminder that I didn't belong here and must now leave.

Then behind me, shuffling. Low, desperate moans that sounded almost human. This must be the sacrificial beast, being led blindfolded to its sacred end.

What animal made such a sound, such a constant moan? This must be a creature of Tauris, something known only in this foreign place.

Beside me, Melantho stood stiff and still. I wanted—almost needed—to turn my head and see this chosen creature. But I forced my head forward, my eyes fixed on the dancing flames.

From the corner of my eye, I saw Maia and Theano break from our line and turn to stand next to King Thoas, facing the sacrificial beast that had been led up the path behind us.

Melantho still didn't move, so I didn't either.

My heart thrummed in my ears, and I didn't think I could stand still for one moment longer.

And then.

And then.

And then.

In my memories, what happened next is at once a blur in my mind's eye and as clear as the glowing moon. I feel, Muse, as if I can tell you with exact clarity what happened next, while at the same time, I wonder if what I'm about to say is the fabrication of a tortured mind—a memory formed from years of nightmares and haunted visions.

Maia and Theano led the sacrifice to the head of the altar.

But the victim was not an animal at all.

He was around twenty years old, wispy-bearded and short-haired. He wore a clean Greek tunic, but I knew that he wasn't Greek—the high set of his cheekbones, the round-tipped nose, the fair hair and fair skin.

I don't know the color of his eyes. I only know that, after Theano removed the blindfold, he stared straight at me. His eyes caught the light of the flames, and with that glowing gaze, he pierced my heart.

And then his eyes darted down the line of priestesses before him, begging each of us in turn to free him from his obvious fate.

He muttered and moaned, whisper-quiet, in his foreign tongue. He clasped his unbound hands before him, wringing them together and squeezing so tightly I thought he might crack his own bones.

King Thoas moved to stand on the other side of the trembling man, this man who was now flanked by the High Priestess of Artemis and the king of the Taurians.

Theano stepped forward, bearing that covered basket before her, and Maia peeled away the protective white cloth. She reached inside.

Muse, I already knew what she was about to pull from that golden basket. I knew it would be long and deadly sharp. I knew it would glint in the moonlight and the firelight at once, and I knew the victim would see it with terror in his beating heart.

She held the knife in both palms, spoke a prayer, and then brought the bronze to her lips.

Then she presented the blade to the king. Aëdon's drumbeats saturated the air, sending vibrations through the ether and filling our minds.

The man uttered a choking sob, then lifted his chin high, baring his naked throat to the goddess. When the blade flashed in the firelight, he uttered one final plea, recognizable in any language: *Mother!*

Then the women in the crowd and the priestesses' voices rose together in ululations, an enormous, plaintive wail that permeated the world.

A woman screamed.

The world shimmered and churned. A terrible ringing filled my ears, and the packed earth lurched to meet me where I stood.

Sometimes, I still long for the blackness that followed. The emptiness. The peace.

Chapter 23

The next morning, Maia insisted I'd been the one who screamed. She refused to allow me to deny her with vigorous shakes of my head.

"Do you doubt my hearing? My memory? My eyes?" she asked as we sat down to our breakfast around the warm hearth in the kitchen.

Once again, I shook my head.

"It really was you," Melissa tried, patting my hand as if I needed soothing. "You screamed loud enough to wake the dead, and then you fainted. I thought you might have died too, but Melantho said you were still breathing."

"If you can make that ungodly sound, then you can speak," Maia said, her unblinking eyes daring me to disobey. "Speak."

My fingertips grazed my throat. Was there a new rawness there? A rough soreness that hadn't been there before?

But I shook my head. Just the idea of speaking sent the room spinning around me.

"No." Maia's harsh word forced the spinning to stop, and I looked at her long, pale face. Her eyes now held a gentleness that I'd only seen when she gazed at her granddaughter, but her voice still carried a menacing edge. "No more fainting. You're stronger than that, Iphianassa."

I shook my head again, and my heart pounded behind my ribs. I was not Iphianassa.

"Should I send a message to the king that his newest priestess still fails his favorite goddess? That he should send his precious Iphianassa back to Tiryns where she belongs?"

No. My breath flowed through my nose as if I were a bull ready to charge. I clenched my jaw and shook my head again.

"Heliko," Maia threw over her shoulder. "Go fetch Lastratos. Have him tell the king Iphianassa wishes to return to Tiryns."

"I am *not* Iphianassa!" The words squeaked from my unused throat, my voice unfamiliar even to my own ears. I gripped the edges of my stool, waiting for the rush, the sickening whirl, the darkness.

But it didn't come. The world remained upright, the figures sitting around me focused and solid. I glared at Maia. She popped a morsel into her mouth and chewed, an unfamiliar grin spread across her face.

I felt naked without my silent shield. Maia no longer allowed me to ignore her demands, and Melissa peppered me with more questions than I ever knew existed. Theano and Aëdon encouraged me to use my new voice, having me order Doris to fetch refreshments and baskets of yarn.

It was like a performance, as if I were a slave in a troupe of traveling entertainers, required to entertain on a whim.

Koronis and Melantho sidled next to me in the market, listening wide-eyed as I ordered the day's wine delivery.

"You have a pleasant voice," Melantho said. "Good and clear. I was afraid you'd sound froggy like that kitchen girl we used to have. What was her name? Koronis!"

Koronis had wandered over to the next stall to admire the shining silver pieces there. "What?"

"What was our old kitchen girl's name back home? The little one with the froggy voice and those crazy eyes?"

Koronis didn't take her eyes off the silver. "Hekatonyma." She touched a glittering piece with a fingertip as the seller eyed her, ready to pounce at the first wrong move.

There was no going back. Now that everyone knew I could indeed speak—now that I knew I could speak without panic rising in my belly—there was no going back.

∽∂∽∂∽

The sun refused to peek around the heavy gray clouds, but the wind wasn't so shy. It came from the south, pushing us up the street, blowing our clothes against our backs and sending chills through me. Maia stalked ahead of me and Zotikos followed behind. It was as if they expected me to turn and run away.

Maybe I should have.

Now, I understand the dangers lurking beneath an imposter's facade. The ghosts scrambling to escape into the open air. Imposters have so much more to lose than those of us who were born into our proper places.

But on this day, I was still just a girl with so much to learn, and I marched to my destiny with no care to the outcome.

King Thoas sat on his sad little throne draped in a red mantle, fidgeting with the jewels on his ringed fingers. His carved staff lay lifeless across his lap. Like the first time we met, I bowed low before him, pressing my forehead and my knees into the cold gray stones.

He tapped my right shoulder with his staff, and I rose, sighing. What a tiresome ritual that was. He must have tapped Maia's shoulder too. She rose beside me, and the two of us stood before him.

My eyes snapped to his before I remembered he hated eye contact. We stared at one another, assessing. He looked away to scan me from my boot-clad toes to the beads in my braided hair, keeping his face unreadable in the heavy silence.

Finally, he said in his little nasally voice, "I'm told Artemis has shown you favor once again. She has returned your voice?"

"Yes." I made sure my tone was clear and unmistakably Mycenaean. No lilts, no speaking from my nose, no mumbles.

He twisted his fingers in his beard. "Call me *my king*."

I forced my face into a smooth, unreadable mask. *You aren't my king. I had a king once and he was my father and he tried to murder me with his own hand. I don't want another king.* The words sped through my mind, swift arrows flying in the darkness.

I stood with my empty hands clasped loosely before me, and my mind rested on the small weight hanging at my left side. Hidden under my tunic, safe in her soft pouch, my little deer rested in silence. Her legs may have been tucked under her body in a frozen pose, but I felt her power seeping from her.

I said, "Of course, my king," and the words tasted bitter on my tongue.

King Thoas stared at me until I wanted to squirm. I clenched my jaw and stared at his sad little pendant, forcing my legs to keep still, my hands to relax. I refused to fidget before this man.

When he spoke, his words were soft. "Your strength failed you. You allowed your weakness to show." He leaned forward and his next words came out as a hiss and spittle flew from his mouth when he said, "I will not tolerate a weak priestess."

He leaned back on his throne and seemed to struggle to calm himself. Though he spoke his next words quietly enough, I sensed a darkness stirring under the surface. "Artemis chose you. She told me you are special; you are her favorite." He paused again, breathing heavily through his nose. "I expect you to behave like a chosen priestess."

Then he grasped his staff in his fist and stood. With his left hand, he waved me away, as if flicking at a pesky fly.

The guards behind me shifted, and with a fiery face and clenched jaw, I spun on my heel. I stormed out of the palace and down the street. Maia followed behind me, her footsteps heavy, but I didn't slow until I reached the house.

When I walked through the door, I turned to spit angry words at Maia. But she wasn't there. Instead, Lastratos stood facing me, and it turned out that he had been the one who followed me home.

"Come with me." He brushed past me and went into the kitchen.

Heliko hurried down the stairs. "Oh! You're home early. Do you want food?" She pulled a platter from the wall shelf along with a jar of figs.

"Not now, Heliko," Lastratos said. "Just wine."

I stormed into the courtyard, pacing the perimeter in a fast-paced imitation of the many, many laps Melissa and I had walked in the early days. My fingers pulled at the end of my leather belt and I felt my hair fluttering around my hot face.

"Sit," Lastratos said, nodding to a stool in the dappled shade of the oak tree. I paced the courtyard once more before accepting the cup of wine he held toward me.

I gulped the wine, draining it like a barbarian and wiping my mouth with the back of my hand. Then I sat on the hard stool, fixing my eyes on the dancing shadows of the yellowing leaves. My racing heart slowed, my face cooled, and the sounds of a squirrel rustling above my head soothed my nerves.

Lastratos stood near Maia's herb bed, watching me. "You can't let the king upset you like this," he started, sipping his own wine. "He may be the king of Tauris by birth, but his people don't love him. He lashes out when he thinks someone is powerless because it reminds him of his own weakness. Intimidating vulnerable people makes him feel strong. You must make sure you're never one of those people."

He moved so that he was standing before me, then kneeled so we were of a height. "You must remember who you are. You're a priestess, the favorite of Artemis. Born in strength."

I'd been staring at my hands, but at this my gaze snapped to his. Born in strength. Strong-born.

He winked.

Lastratos knew who I was.

Later, I waited until Maia and I were alone in the kitchen before I said, "I remember."

She looked up from her sewing, her face a smooth mask.

"I want to go home to my sister."

"This is your home now."

"It isn't. Not a place like this." I threw my arms in the air, indicating the unpainted walls, the hard stone floors, the windswept sky. "My home is—"

"Your home is *here*, Iphianassa." She thrust her long finger toward the ground. "Not one more word about it."

I stamped my bare foot on the floor. "I'm not Iph—"

"You are who I say you are, Iphianassa of Tiryns." Her words were cold and sharp, but her face was still blank. How many years of practice had it taken to learn to keep her eyes so expressionless? To hide her thoughts so thoroughly from the world?

Without my permission, my eyes filled with tears and my voice trembled when I said, "These people are barbarians."

Those tears insisted on falling down my cheeks, even as I swallowed hard, trying to force them back like I'd done so many times before. I wiped them from my chin and bit the insides of my cheeks to slow the sobs.

"Barbarians, Iphianassa?" Maia lowered her voice to a whisper, even though we were alone in the house. "King Thoas has taken you into his care at his own grave risk. If your father—if any Greek warrior—finds out you still live, they will blame you for anything and everything that goes wrong with their petty little war. Plenty will go wrong, and they'll look for anyone other than themselves to blame for it. You can bet they'd whisk you straight to Troy and make sure the deed gets done right the second time."

"But last night. What kind of king murders men like that?" I swallowed fresh tears. "What about the sacred laws of hospitality? What about *xenia*? No Greek would ever dream of such cruelty!"

Maia snorted. "Do you hear what you're saying? You said you remember everything." When I didn't respond, she said, "Your own father!"

I stood before the old woman, my mouth open, my tears suddenly dry.

No, of course I hadn't forgotten.

My Greek father and his Greek men—every general, every soldier, every chieftain among them—were more barbaric than Thoas and the thousands of Taurian people who called him King.

Her eyes softened, and she sat me on a stool, handed me a cup. "Drink and forget everything. Never speak of this again. Do you understand, Iphianassa?"

I nodded, gulping the undiluted wine and feeling it harden like bronze in my pulsing veins.

෨෩෨෩

The next time we saw Nikandros, he brought us news.

News from Troy.

He shaded his eyes from the late-morning sun with his hand, and I realized that, to him, the three of us must have appeared as dark silhouettes against the white sun at our backs. But he came toward us with a lively step and a grin spread across his face. When he reached us, he didn't bother with any greetings. "I've just heard news from Troy!"

A wintry gust lifted my hood, and a chill fingered its way through my mantle. I squeezed the fabric tight against my throat. This was the first time I'd heard the word *Troy* spoken in months. Thoughts clamored in my mind, each striving to overpower the next.

Troy. The reason I was here now, in Tauris, so far from home.

Troy. The reason Father had tried to murder me, his own precious daughter.

Troy. The location of Achilles, my betrothed and my only savior.

As I wrestled with my thoughts, I missed most of Nikandros's news. I only caught the last of it: The Trojan warriors, famed through the world for their fierce strength, were easily keeping the rag-tag Greek army at a safe distance from their high citadel walls. The Greeks outnumbered the Trojans, but the Trojans had the advantage of fighting from behind their strong fortress and returning each night to their own homes, their own beds, their own wives.

So the frustrated Greek soldiers, determined to release their pent-up aggressions and to take some of the prizes they'd been lured to battle with, resorted to shameful raiding. They raided small, unsuspecting villages, looting and destroying. Bringing with them to their new camp on the plains of Troy anything of value they could find: golden cups, shining jewelry, great jars of wine.

And, of course, the greatest prize of all: women.

This war wasn't the grand war the bards insist on singing—the honorable battle Father himself had claimed he was bound to fight. This new thought, quieter than the rest, loomed black and large in my mind and my cheeks burned, despite the cool air.

We'd all thought this expedition would last only a few weeks. We'd been expecting to hear that the powerful Greeks sailed onto the beaches of Ilium, fought the fierce Trojans for a week, maybe two, breached their walls, and captured the city.

Nobody expected to hear such sorry news of pitiful Greeks, overpowered and unable to reach the citadel walls, reduced to raiding vulnerable local villages.

There was no honor in that.

I wondered where Achilles was in all of this. Surely he wasn't taking part in something so shameless as stealthy raids. Surely he was above behavior like that.

But Nikandros mentioned no one by name. Not Achilles, not Odysseus, Menelaus, or Ajax. Not even Agamemnon, Lord of Men.

Those stories would come much later, as you know, Muse, since your greatest joy is to plant seeds of heroic tales into the mouths of men.

The three of us sat on our perch, listening in silence as Nikandros told us the news, and Melissa's eyes grew wide when he spoke of the heaping treasures the Greeks were finding in their raids.

When he finished, she asked, "But what about Helen? Haven't they rescued her yet?"

Ah, Helen. To Melissa, rescuing the kidnapped woman was the noble goal of this dishonorable attack. But this was just a child's version of the ugly truth. A myth.

It's true, people wielded Helen's name as the reason to wage war.

How many times had I heard her name tossed around the halls in those long days the noisy chieftains stayed in our palace?

But *rescue* was a word no one ever used in the same breath as *Helen*.

CHAPTER 24

Late that winter, Nikandros brought us a sailor, a white-bearded, sun-hardened man who looked out of place in his brand-new white tunic.

"This man came straight from the battlefields of Troy!" Nikandros was winded, as if the very idea of presenting this sailor to us was exhausting. "He has news that I thought you should hear straight from him."

I wasn't sure why Nikandros thought the three of us wanted battle news so badly. But we humored him and listened to the sailor, eyes cast discreetly to the sand, mouths clamped against any words that might spill out.

"The war isn't going great. At least not for the Greeks," the man said. His accent was that of the sailor, bits and pieces from all over the Greek-speaking world, making it impossible to determine the region he was born to. "Just came from there. They need provisions, you know. Who am I to deny soldiers their wine and grain? I was there when this happened. Didn't see it, but heard all about it afterward. Soldiers do talk, you know."

The man leaned against a stack of casks next to us, settling himself in for a long story. "Old King Priam offers the woman Helen back to her husband. Doesn't even demand payment. Just says he'll give her back if the Greeks pack up and sail back home. But King Menelaus is petty, as we all know, and he spits on the ground at Priam's feet. A big old wad of . . . um, forgive me, ladies."

He cleared his throat. "Says his wife is ruined by the nobody shepherd prince. Says Paris broke the sacred laws of *xenia* when he was staying at Sparta, in Menelaus's own palace no less, and he—Menelaus, that is—is doing the gods' work by punishing the entire Trojan race for Paris's bad behavior. He stole Helen and ruined her and no honorable man would want a woman like that in his bed."

Now in my old age, I understand this was nothing but nonsense. Of course any honorable man would want his wife back, if only to kill her himself.

"Priam tries and tries. He wants rid of the nasty woman. Nothing but a curse since the day Paris brought her to Troy."

I bristled. Helen was my aunt, my mother's beloved sister. I'd only met her once when I was very small, and I remembered nothing of the meeting, but I loved her and I hated hearing men talk of her like that.

"But Menelaus and his bull-headed brother Agamemnon—who claims he's the king of all Greeks, you know—they stand firm. They say no. It's too late and they want revenge. Gold is what they want, if you ask me. All they've ever been after, if you ask me. Heaps and heaps of jewels and silver and ivory. That's what's in the storerooms of Troy, they say. Piles taller than the tallest of men. So much gold . . ."

I wasn't listening, an idea forming. Could this sailor take a message to Achilles? Was this wind-burned man the messenger I'd been waiting to meet? Eyes still on the ground, I interrupted. "What of Achilles?"

"Who?"

"Achilles," I repeated. "Commander of the Myrmidons, prince of Phthia. Son of Peleus and Thetis."

"Oh, yes! They're all sons of gods, aren't they? Until they die like any other man. And then how do you explain that?" The sailor laughed, a long bellow that rose from his belly and made other men turn to look.

I swallowed my response and switched topics. "What of the wives?"

The sailor wiped tears from the corners of his eyes. "Whose wives?"

"Of the soldiers. Of the kings."

The man laughed again. "Who cares about the wives?" Then he seemed to remember he was talking to a group of young women, and he put on airs of embarrassment. "Apologies, ladies. I only mean that no one talks of the wives, you know. People only want to hear about the fighting and the spoils."

ೲೲೲ

"Why not?" Melissa sat beside me on my bed, her feet swinging above the floor. She was eleven years old now, as she'd reminded me over and over toward the end of summer, when the grains in the fields had begun to yellow on their stalks. But she was still just a little girl, swinging feet and pudgy cheeks.

"You're the granddaughter of the High Priestess of Artemis, and niece of Lastratos, the king's most trusted adviser," Maia said. "You can't be seen with sailors and fishermen. You're above them."

"But they're nice people! They never hurt us. Nikandros gives us gifts every time he sees us, and his sister has a little baby and . . ." Melissa sounded petulant, despite her advanced age.

Disappointment mixed with panic in my belly. Nikandros was my only possible contact with Mycenae. He was the only person I knew who might someday bring someone to me who could give me news from home. Someone who could send a message to Achilles at Troy. Someone who could even offer to take me back, if the gods would allow it.

"What about me? I'm nobody from nowhere." I spat the words at her and she glared back at me.

"You're Iphianassa of Tiryns, not nobody from nowhere. You're obviously of high birth, or you wouldn't have been chosen as a priestess." Her head tilted to one side, daring me to argue with that.

I allowed a smirk to touch my lips. "Nobody cares who I am."

Maia started to argue, but this time I was the one who interrupted her. "Nobody cares if an eleven-year-old girl, no matter who her grandmother is, takes gifts from a harmless fisher boy who isn't even a grown man." This was the longest string of words I'd managed to utter since Artemis had returned my voice, and my heart thrummed in my ears with the effort.

Maia's thin face flamed red and her jaw tightened. She took three deep breaths before she said, between gritted teeth, "You will do as I say. It's my duty to keep my granddaughter safe, and to keep you safe." She waved her hand toward me. "I didn't ask for this, but the goddess has chosen me for the role. No more arguing. And I'd better not hear that you've disobeyed me."

She spun on her heel and left the two of us scolded children behind. As she stepped out of the house, I heard her mutter, "What did I do to deserve this?"

ᔑᔑᔑ

The three of us ambled through the apple orchard, abandoned by all but a few roosting blackbirds this time of year. The sprawling trees reached their bare branches toward us, creaking in the wind.

We draped our mantles over our heads and squeezed the fabric tight against our throats.

"Can we trust Heliko?" Aëdon asked.

We continued several steps in silence, no sound but rime-crusted grass crunching under our boots.

Finally, Melissa said, "Yes. I think so."

"What about the other end of it, then? Who will Heliko work with?"

We walked in silence again, and this time I was the one who broke it. "Nikandros."

"Nikandros!" Melissa stopped in her tracks, and the three of us turned to face one another. "But Grandmother said—"

"She says *we* can't go to the harbor anymore," I reminded her. "She never said anything about Heliko."

Aëdon's pink cheeks glowed against the heavy white clouds. "We know we can trust Nikandros."

And so we had a plan. If we couldn't get news directly from

Nikandros anymore, we'd get it through Heliko. She visited the harbor on business almost every day anyway, so it would be nothing for her to stop and chat with our friend for a few minutes every once in a while.

Hope swelled in my heart. Not only could I get raw news before the bards got hold of it, but I could finally send my message to Achilles.

But first, I'd send word to Mother, to tell her that her daughter was alive and wanted to return home.

"I still don't understand why you're so desperate for news, though," Aëdon said.

Melissa stooped to pluck a stick off the ground. "We just want to know what's happening, that's all."

I'd been in Tauris ten months now, and Maia had done excellent work terrifying both Melissa and me into silence about my true identity. If word were to spread that Agamemnon's daughter, the slain Iphigenia, still lived, any priest or seer or chieftain could use the fact of my survival as the excuse for any Greek failure in Troy. And the consequences would be deadly.

Melissa swung her new stick, tapping the sprawling, low branches of the naked apple trees as we passed.

It was difficult keeping my secret from Aëdon. Harmless, happy Aëdon. I'd wanted to tell her almost since my voice returned to me, but I always hesitated. I didn't truly know who I could trust in this place.

"Bards twist their words," I said. "They spin their songs until the truth is woven with so many lies we can't tell one from the other."

"Yes, of course. But that's what makes their songs so much more interesting than the truth alone. Why does it matter?"

Melissa threw her stick with all her strength, sending it flying high against the heavy white sky. It fell into a nearby tree, clattering through the branches, never reaching the ground.

"I just want to know the truth. I have family in . . . Tiryns. That's all."

ᴓᴓᴓ

I couldn't wait to use my new system. I had to send word to Mother. The words I asked Nikandros to repeat to his trusted merchant were something like this: *Now in exile, a strong-born daughter of Artemis awaits her return home, to feel the embrace of her beloved mother once more.*

As the phrase sailed south to Queen Clytemnestra, I waited. A full month passed before I got a response. Heliko waited until Maia left the room before whispering her news.

An early spring downpour meant we couldn't conspire in the courtyard, so Melissa, Heliko, and I huddled in the corner of the main room, heads together like three mischievous children.

"Nikandros has news of the war," Heliko whispered, her eyes dancing in the gray light.

I wanted to scream, but I forced my voice into a strained whisper. "Of the war?" Where was Mother's response? "I don't care about the stupid war!"

Heliko blinked.

Melissa tried, her tone softer than mine. "Did he hear any news about the wives and the children? The people the bards never sing about?"

Heliko rolled her eyes to the ceiling, as if her memories had scrawled themselves across the wooden beams and she could read them there like omens.

"No," she finally said. "I don't think so. All he talked about were the soldiers and the Trojans. He said the Greeks are losing even though it's been almost a year, and they were supposed to win in a few weeks."

My shoulders drooped and I took a step out of our little conspiratorial circle. I may as well get on with my day before Maia found some odd job for me to do.

"Wait!" Heliko's voice was a little too loud, and Melissa put her finger to her lips.

Heliko dropped back to a whisper. "I just remembered. He did say something about someone. Who was it?" She looked at the ceiling again. "What's Helen's daughter's name? I forget."

"Hermione," Melissa said.

"Yes, that's right! Hermione. Nikandros said Hermione tried to run away, even though she's very little. She wanted to go find her mother, but a butcher found her wandering in the streets of Sparta and he took her back to her nurse in the palace. Just think how bad that could have been for the little princess!"

I clenched my jaw and closed my eyes. I should have been relieved my system was actually working, that I was able to get the kind of news I'd asked for, even if it wasn't directly about my family. But the frustration was hard to swallow.

Heliko looked at Melissa and then at me. Her cheeks glowed pink, and she seemed to be waiting for one of us to dismiss her.

When we both stared at her, speechless, she shrugged and turned to leave.

"I guess there was one more thing," she added as she stepped toward the stairs. "Something about Agamemnon's daughter. The one he didn't kill."

"Elektra," Melissa said, squeezing my hand.

"They say she's been cursed. Her mother keeps her locked in the palace." And she climbed the stairs, leaving me clutching Melissa's hand, the scar across my palm pulsing.

෴෴෴

That's when the nightmares began. They were always the same.

Elektra stretched her arms toward me as a man hauled her away, her beautiful little face contorted into a silent scream. I couldn't see the man's features, but I turned to look into the face of the person who held me back, the one who prevented me from rescuing my little sister. It was Maia who pinned my arms behind me, her gaunt features neutral, unfeeling. A fire burned in the distance, tall and hot, and I knew it was a funeral pyre. I struggled and fought until Maia morphed into Mother, whose grasp tightened and bit into my skin.

I'd wake in a puddle of sweat-soaked blankets, Melissa by my side to soothe me.

The need to go home overwhelmed me. I refused to believe my mother had imprisoned her only remaining daughter. I couldn't make my mind twist what I knew about Mother into the kind of monster who could be cruel to any of her beloved children.

But I still needed to go home. I needed to see for myself that Elektra and Orestes were both safe, and that Mother hadn't transformed into a jailer.

It had been a year since that horrific night in the bay of Aulis. Since that night Agamemnon—I never thought of him as Father anymore—tried with all his power to murder me, his first-born daughter.

And a year was a long time. I didn't deny that people can change a great deal in a short time. All I had to do was take one look at myself to know this was true. But it was impossible for me to believe Mother to be capable of morphing into a version of herself that was the exact opposite of the version she'd been my entire life.

But Muse, as hard as I tried to remember Mother's soft hazel eyes and her tight embrace, cold fingers of doubt snaked through my heart. When I'd sit alone in my *erêmia*, with nothing but distant shouts of men in the harbor and the nearby cries of the gulls to fill my ears, I'd wonder.

Even when I tried to push the thought away, I couldn't completely forget Mother's behavior on that night of my fateful wedding. Her distance from me, her silent conversation with Agamemnon in his pavilion. Her argument with Achilles, and her absence from my wedding preparations.

And there was that cup of bitter wine she insisted I drink. That draught which was surely responsible for the fog that filled my head as I wandered toward the altar, my weak knees, my confused, stumbling steps.

When I replayed those painful memories, I couldn't help but think her guilty. She knew of Agamemnon's plan to slaughter me and was complicit in the scheme. Wasn't she? Was there another explanation to excuse her behavior that night?

I could think of none.

When my mind was in this awful place, I knew something more. If she was willing to help Agamemnon butcher me, then she'd be capable of imprisoning Elektra.

And maybe worse.

Chapter 25

Warm summer breezes replaced chilly spring winds, and I finally sent my message to Achilles. The words didn't come easily. I composed short sentences in my mind, working them over and over, worrying and teasing them into the perfect phrase. I had to be clear to Achilles while hiding my true identity from the people who would relay the message.

In the end, I whispered this phrase to Heliko: *Grandsons of Thetis, yet to be born, await you among the people north of the Euxine Sea.*

She was to pass this message, along with instructions to speak this to Achilles, son of Peleus, commander of the Myrmidon troops. I hoped this would be enough for him to understand. With well-placed questions and well-paid scouts, I felt he could easily find his rightful bride and claim his future heirs.

And, surely, he would want nothing more than to collect what was rightfully his.

The Daughters of Artemis ceremony ushered in the early summer days, and this year, Melissa and I were both able to attend.

In the weeks leading to the ceremony, Maia taught the little girls how to tame their wild ambitions, how to settle their minds, how to quiet their questions. She taught them how to become good wives, to honor their husbands. To obey.

And she insisted I join her as she taught the girls. She insisted I learn the ways of the teacher, to help guide these little ones from girlhood to womanhood. When Maia worked with the girls, she was patient. She was kind and gentle. She spoke in a soft voice I'd only heard her use with Melissa, and I wondered why she saved all her harsh words for me.

In Mycenae, Elektra would be nine years old now. Did Mother allow her to participate in the ritual this year? Was she allowed to carry a jar in the procession?

The thought forced itself into my mind again and again as Maia and I worked with the little girls. Achilles hadn't responded to my message, though three months seemed like plenty of time for a reply to reach me. I held on to the hope that, instead of sending me a response, he was working to gather his loyal men to come find me and take me home. Once under his protection, I'd beg him to take me back to Mycenae so I could look after my sister. Maybe we'd even take her with us to his home in Phthia, where I'd soon be queen.

All I could do was wait. And I tried to push terrible thoughts of my little sister from my mind, to focus on my work.

On the day of the ceremony, we twelve priestesses gathered for an afternoon of festivities and an evening of solemn ritual. The girls who were passing from the protection of virgin Artemis and into the care of passionate Aphrodite wound their way down a special set of stairs that led from Artemis's stone altar to a similar altar for Aphrodite. Their nervous titters floated up to us as they stepped carefully down, their individual torches lighting the way.

The next morning, as she tied weights to thick twists of flax, Aëdon made an announcement.

"I am to be married." She didn't look away from her work, but her cheeks flushed and a smile spread across her plump face.

Melissa dropped the tunic she was mending and leaped to hug Aëdon around the neck. Aëdon winced when Melissa squealed into her ear, and she gently pushed her away, still smiling.

"That's wonderful news!" Koronis said from the corner of the room where she sat at her own work. She cleared her throat. "Isn't it wonderful, Melantho?"

Melantho didn't respond immediately, and when she finally muttered, "Yes. Congratulations," a dark shadow fell across her face.

Theano beamed. I leaned forward and took Aëdon's hand. "I'm happy for you," I said.

"Who is the lucky man?" Koronis asked, her voice an unusual high chirp.

"Daaxios, eldest son of Boethos."

"Yes, we know who he is," Melantho snapped. Of course we all knew that Daaxios was son of Boethos, one of the king's advisers, but why would this news anger Melantho? When she saw our eyes on her, she smoothed her scowl and smiled, forcing her voice into happier tones. "You will be so happy."

Melantho's cheerless reaction was surprising, but my own thoughts wound to a dark place.

If Aëdon disappeared on her wedding day, would Daaxios search for her? Or would he forget about her entirely, as if she never existed? Would he allow her to live her remaining years among strangers, or would he travel to the far corners of the world in search of his missing bride?

ၜ௦ௐ

The new moon came, and Aëdon was married.

After that, another moon came, this one full and low and heavy.

Four days earlier, a visitor knocked at the door. I recognized his voice right away. This was the man whose whispers I'd heard at daybreak nearly one year before.

This time I was inside the house, so I saw the man when he arrived. It was Zotikos, King Thoas's head guard, his broad shoulders draped in the red cloak his twin sisters had only recently made for him.

The black beads of his eyes glinted in the dim morning light. He flicked his gaze to me as he followed Heliko through the main room and out into the courtyard, and the blood froze in my veins.

He and Maia spoke in urgent whispers, but I heard every word. It wasn't difficult to find the perfect place to stand in the silent room, Heliko pretending not to notice as she crept up the stairs to her room.

Another man had had the misfortune of washing ashore on the Taurian beach, his wrecked boat shattered by the sharp teeth Poseidon hid beneath the calm surface of the sea. The king's men captured him and he was being held in the palace's prison.

When Zotikos left, Maia stood alone in the courtyard, staring up at the green oak leaves and running her fingers over the beaded necklace at her throat—the chain that bound her to Artemis.

I turned toward the stairs, hoping to creep into the shadows. But she must have sensed movement, and she turned just as I was crossing the doorway.

"Come here, Iphianassa." Her voice sounded small, almost choked.

I hesitated, regretting that I'd drawn attention to myself, then stepped out into the courtyard, my chin held high. I squinted against the morning sun. Standing before Maia in that moment, I somehow felt tall and straight and noble against her thin, rounded shoulders.

"Have you eaten?" she asked, her eyes studying my face.

I nodded.

"Good. You're coming with me."

We carried small baskets of bread and fruit up the street to the palace, nodding at the few people who were beginning their daily chores in the warm, clear morning.

The palace doors were already open, but we didn't pass through. Instead, we skirted the walls, following a narrow stone path toward the back of the building. Smaller structures clustered behind the palace, backed against the open nothingness of the steep black cliff. Two of the smallest buildings stood so close to the cliff's edge it looked as if it would take no more than a good shove with both hands to send them tumbling into the sea.

Maia led me to one of these structures. Unlike the stone palace, this was a wooden building, no bigger than the maiden room I shared with Melissa. A short door punctured the front wall, but I could see no windows from where I stood.

A guard lounged to the side of the door, his red cloak pulled behind his hip so his sword hilt glinted. When he saw us, he scrambled to stand upright. His eyes darted to the ground, and he touched his right hand to his forehead.

"High Priestess," he mumbled. "Priestess."

This was the first time I'd been addressed as priestess. The pride of my status as Priestess of Artemis mixed in my belly with anger at not being addressed as princess instead.

But I didn't have time to dwell on the conflict of the two thoughts. Maia whisked past the guard, ducking into the open doorway. I followed.

An odor hung thick in the dark room, and my hand flew to cover my nose. I didn't know it then, but over the years I understood the smell to be fear and sweat, and it had seeped into the wooden beams and the packed-dirt floor. Terror had permanently lodged its stench in the cracks and corners and would never leave this room, even when no prisoner cowered in its shadows.

My eyes needed several moments to adjust to the darkness. Then I noticed the gray-haired man crouched in the dim corner, hands and feet bound with thick rope. He was naked, and I blushed at the sight.

"I am High Priestess to Artemis." Maia's clear voice cut through the heavy air, but her words hinted at a softness that sounded almost foreign to my ears.

The man didn't move. He fixed his eyes on the floor at his feet, and he didn't even blink when Maia spoke.

"Do you understand?"

The man made no response, but Maia continued, and invisible, icy fingers crawled up my neck. "Artemis has given you to our king. And in thanks for her generosity, our king wishes to return you to her. With the full moon, we will sacrifice your body to our great goddess. You will give your life in glory and honor. Do you understand?"

Still, no movement.

Maia set her basket near the man's feet and motioned for me to do the same. We left the prisoner, alone, naked, and ignorant of his fate.

"See that he eats. I will send priestesses to bathe and dress him." Maia threw these words over her shoulder as we walked away from that hideous room on the cliff's edge.

Looming silence followed us as we walked back home. When we were only a few steps from the door, she finally spoke. "They are usually foreign," she said. "And they don't understand their true fate until the last moment, when it's too late."

ℓⱺℓⱺℓⱺ

"No." Instead of the defiance-filled note that seemed to underscore every word I'd uttered in this wild place called Tauris, this sound squeaked from my throat with plaintive edges.

I shook my head and repeated, "No."

"It's as Artemis wishes," Maia said. "It's as King Thoas wishes."

"Theano did it last time."

Leaves rustled above my head, and I didn't need to look up to know that the squirrel sat somewhere in the green canopy. I imagined her gazing down on me with her shining black eyes, and my pulse slowed.

Maia pulled a stool into the shade, sitting across from me so we were eye to eye. "The king and the goddess both want you to bear the basket. It's an honor and you should be proud."

She leaned toward me, and for a panicked heartbeat, I thought she might take my hands into hers, the way Mother or Ismene might have done in better days. I tucked my fists into the folds of my tunic.

"But Theano knows what to do. She can do it again." My voice cracked on the last syllable and I cleared my throat.

Maia sighed, and the lines around her eyes hardened. "You will carry the basket."

She stood and stepped toward the house, then stopped and turned back to me. "And you will stop arguing like a spoiled child."

As she walked away, I thought I heard her mutter: *Just like her mother.*

ꙮꙮꙮ

I carried the basket, its deadly burden hidden under a pure white cloth. Each time an image formed in my mind, each time I saw Agamemnon's blade flash in red flames, I squeezed my eyes tight and shoved the memory away.

We walked our slow steps to and from Artemis's secluded altar. We sang, we chanted, and we prayed. We inhaled precious incense, and we clasped wrists and swayed to the beat of the goddess's undying heart.

The prisoner stepped toward us with his head held high. And when King Thoas grasped the knife in his right hand, the prisoner did not cry for his mother.

243

Chapter 26

Chronos is relentless if he's nothing else. At once, he gives the appearance of speeding by, as an arrow on the wind, while also ambling onward, like a turtle in the mud.

Four years passed. Just like that, they passed and were gone, and I remained in Tauris. Nobody came to fetch me, nobody sent word promising to bring me home, nobody from Mycenae uttered a single syllable to me.

Six unfortunate men washed onto the Taurian shores during those years, and they all died in the name of Artemis. I remember each as if I'd met them only yesterday—the old ones and the young ones, those who wept and those who raised their chins to meet their death with brave faces.

Maia insisted I always carried the weapon, that I was the one to pass the blade over to her. And so each time, it was my trembling hand that initiated the sequence that would end in the death of an innocent man.

Even today, I still feel as if I drew the knife across their bobbing throats myself. In my dreams, I still watch, helpless, as thick black blood flows down my arm and drips in a puddle at my bare feet.

I still must push those images from my mind.

I never heard from Achilles. If he sent a response to my message, I didn't receive it, and he never set sail to retrieve me.

Overall, my message system worked perfectly, as far as I knew. But I learned that sometimes we need to be careful what we wish for. Through Heliko and Nikandros, I found out that Mother was ruling Mycenae in Agamemnon's absence. My heart soared at that news, but plummeted at the next part: she was living in dishonorable union with Agamemnon's cousin Aegisthus. And worse, they had a child together, a little girl they called Helen. A tiny sister I may never meet.

It was my fourth summer when I finally received the message from Mother.

Melissa, Maia, and I had been gathering the offerings from Artemis's shrine on the cliffs as part of our weekly duty. We each carried baskets heavy with figurines, clothing, and jewelry. Normally, we would have taken these offerings straight to the secure storeroom in the palace, but Heliko had run to fetch us, breathless.

Lastratos met us in the vestibule. "You have a visitor," he said to me, his calm face refusing to betray whether this visitor brought good news or bad.

We set our bundles on a table and followed him through the kitchen and into the courtyard.

My heart soared when I saw Aegisthus pacing before the great oak tree. I resisted the childish urge to run to him, to grasp his tunic, to glue myself to his side until we boarded the ship that would take me home at last. Instead, I forced my feet to freeze in place as I stared at the man.

Disappointed as I was that he'd stolen my mother for himself, that he'd sired a daughter who was my half-sister, nothing but joy filled my breast in this moment. His familiar Mycenaean features melted my heart. His bronzed skin, his dark eyes, his oiled black beard. He wore a travel cloak over his simple tunic, the rich folds of blue fabric so fine and so familiar. I noticed the purple ribbon and wondered that Mother would allow him to wear the royal color, even if it was just a narrow trace along the edges.

But that didn't matter. What mattered was that Mother had finally sent for me. After keeping me away four years, Mother finally thought it was safe for me to return to Mycenae. In no time at all, I could hold Elektra in my arms, inhale the spice of Mother's jasmine perfume, allow Ismene to squeeze the breath from my lungs. I would lift Orestes to the sky and laugh at his joyous squeals. I would even embrace Damalis if she would let me.

This scene flashed before my eyes, and I felt an unfamiliar smile touch my lips. I was only eighteen. There was still plenty of time for me to marry and fulfill the royal duties I'd been born for.

But when Aegisthus finally spoke, his voice was edged in ice. He greeted Maia formally, bowing to the high priestess and touching his forehead with his right hand. I couldn't tell if they'd ever met before. Both wore blank masks.

Aegisthus simply nodded in acknowledgment of my presence, as if I were nothing more than a girl. Not a princess, not a priestess. Nobody.

When he spoke, his familiar voice came to me in unfamiliar stiff and formal tones. He directed his question to Maia. "Is this the girl Iphianassa?"

Iphianassa! Even Aegisthus? How had Maia's ridiculous rule spread so far as Mycenae?

Familiar panic squeezed my belly, its black fingers stretching to squeeze my chest. But I shoved the darkness down until it was no more than a hard ball sitting in my belly.

"This is the girl Iphianassa." She shot me a fiery look, a flash that warned me to keep quiet.

Aegisthus turned to me, his face still blank. No sign of recognition, no hints that he'd watched me grow from an infant in my nurse's arms into the young woman who was stolen from her home. "Clytemnestra, the queen of Mycenae and of all Greece, sends you a message, Iphianassa of Tiryns."

He bored his cold eyes into mine, and I refused to look away. "The queen forbids you from sending her messages. Her daughter, whom you so cruelly claim to be, is dead. The queen placed her body on the pyre with her own hands and has buried her bones in the royal tombs in Mycenae. In her grief, she does not wish to be made the fool."

My face felt numb. I stared at the man before me, the man I'd seen nearly every day of my first fourteen years. This man—this cousin—had been Agamemnon's trusted adviser, and then my mother's. He was part of my family. And he was standing here in my courtyard, under my oak tree, the Taurian breeze lifting his purple-trimmed cloak, daring to deny me my name, and looking me in the eye while doing it.

I said nothing. I locked my gaze to his, and I hoped he saw Mother's hazel eyes glaring back at him. After many seconds, he looked away, toward Lastratos. My breath came easy, steady and slow. My fists didn't clench, and my scar didn't scream.

Slowly, I turned and stepped through the door into the kitchen. I didn't acknowledge the man's message, didn't respect his rank with a nod, didn't speak my mother's name, nor did I call this man "cousin." Instead, I allowed my feet to trace the familiar path down the steep stairs to the beach, watching as my sandals stepped through the thick sand that led me to my *erêmia*.

It's true, I'd been a foolish girl. And I would be foolish again and again, even after this. But I was learning.

CHAPTER 27

I was surprised, even if I shouldn't have been, when Heliko came to Melissa and me at Theano's house on a day in early autumn. Maia had sent for us, she said, and we were to come home at once. Both of us.

We weaved our way through the citadel streets, crowded even in the cold autumn rain, and then through the quiet lanes to the house.

Maia lay in her bed, blankets pulled to her chin and a fire blazing in a pot near her feet. Her white hair spilled over her pillow, so long it brushed the floor. Each wrinkle on her face seemed deeper in the soft gray light that crept through the high windows.

Why were the windows open when it was so cold outside? I pulled up the stool and started to draw the shutter closed, but Maia spoke. "Leave it open."

Her voice was ancient, a hundred years older than she'd sounded earlier that morning. When I came to her side, I saw what I'd missed from the doorway. The entire left side of her face drooped and sagged like melted wax.

"Artemis comes for me," she mumbled, droplets of spittle coating her lips. Melissa wiped her grandmother's mouth with the corner of her blanket.

"What do you mean, Grandmother? You were fine at breakfast." Melissa's tears dropped onto Maia's blanket.

"She will take me soon."

I had to lean close to understand her slurred words. Her breath smelled sickly sweet, and I tried not to gag.

"No one will take you." Melissa's voice trembled, and she squeezed her grandmother's limp hand.

Maia's eyes darted round the room, then settled on mine. She swallowed several times before she was able to whisper her next words.

"I owed her."

"Who?" I was confused.

Though her left eyelid drooped to cover the iris, her right eye brightened. She strained to say her final words to me. "Your mother. I owed her."

I shook my head, not understanding, not wanting to think of Mother. But Maia could say no more, and she sank back into her bed, right eyelid fluttering closed.

She lived for three more days, refusing to eat or drink. Melissa cared for her grandmother, wiping her face with a soft cloth, fanning her sweaty body, and tucking her into her blankets in turns.

And what did I do during those three long days? I'm ashamed to admit it now, Muse, but I need to tell you the truth.

I plotted and daydreamed about leaving this place once Maia was gone. I concocted elaborate schemes to finally stow myself away on a Greek ship, to sneak back to Mycenae.

And then what would I do? With a mother and a father who both wanted me dead—no, *thought* I was dead—with no husband and a brother who was far too young to take me under his protection? But I didn't dwell on these details. I would land on Greek soil and then let Artemis guide me.

That's all I thought about in those three days. At eighteen years old, I still thought only of myself, like a selfish child.

But I suppose I shouldn't be so hard on myself. There was one moment when decency shined through my stubborn gloom. It was one fleeting second, but there it was, and it's all I have now to console myself in my final years.

Clutching my little deer, I was the only one at her bedside when Maia breathed her last breath, when her heart thumped its last thump, when the light in her dark eyes faded and blinked out forever. In that moment, after her final breath seeped from her lips, her shining eyes met mine.

And I saw fear.

She was afraid to die, and I took her bony hand in mine and squeezed. And then she was gone.

Maia's funeral was a spectacle fit for a queen.

The day she died, we carried her body to a sunny room in the palace in what should have been a queen's quarters. We washed her and rubbed scented oils into her skin. Melissa and Aëdon wept, but my eyes remained dry.

We took turns muttering prayers over the prone body as we all worked, so there was a constant stream of supplications rising to the gods. They prayed to Artemis, of course, reminding the great goddess of the lifetime Maia had given to her honor. And we prayed to white-armed Hera, the queen of the gods, in thanks for Maia's long life, and to Hades and his wife Persephone, begging their protection as Maia's shade entered the underworld.

Theano purified Maia's body with thick smoke from a burning bundle of herbs, and then we wound her in a long white cloth of fine linen.

She lay on her table, lifeless, for three days.

Those three days, we ate nothing but thin barley porridge and drank nothing but water. We were allowed no meat, no fruits, no wine. But I, selfish girl that I was, tucked little bits of dried fruit and handfuls of nuts under my mantle, sneaking bites when no one was looking, wondering if any of the others were doing the same.

Her funeral procession was on the fourth day. Streaks of white clouds painted the sky, and yellow rays of sunshine warmed our skin as we stepped, slow as a line of snails, out of the town and into the distant rocky cemetery.

King Thoas hired fifty funeral mourners, a huge number considering Tauris's tiny population. I recognized many of the women, but some looked unfamiliar to me and I wondered where they'd come from.

When Maia's body finally rested in its shallow grave, we all cried our grief into the skies.

Next to me, Melissa whimpered instead of wailed. She didn't tear at her hair or scratch at her face like the rest of us. She stood motionless and dry-eyed, staring at her grandmother's shrouded body lying in its stony grave.

CHAPTER 28

Nearly three full months passed before Artemis had a new high priestess to oversee her sacred rites in Tauris. Theano performed Maia's role during the regular ceremonies, but everyone knew that was temporary.

It was the king's duty to appoint the new high priestess, but he repeatedly said he was waiting for a sign from the goddess before making his choice. Everyone knew Koronis wanted the position, and I didn't understand why he wouldn't just appoint her immediately. Really, what difference did it make who wore the ceremonial gown and carried the sacred herbs and sang the prayers? I found it impossible to believe Artemis truly favored one mere human over another, as long as she was getting the terrible honors she demanded.

The day he finally made his choice is one I'll never forget. I still remember the low sky, heavy with threats of rain, and the gusts of cold spring wind that tore through my mantle and my dress to bite my skin.

The king called all priestesses and our families to his throne room. The roughly three dozen of us filled the room from wall to wall, uncomfortably squeezed shoulder to shoulder.

His slaves must have lit poor oil in the braziers and torches because a blanket of thick smoke hovered beneath the ceiling, threatening to drop at any moment like a woolen blanket and smother us all.

We stood coughing and wiping our watering eyes until someone finally had the idea to pull back the shutters on the tiny, high windows.

King Thoas was forced to shove his way through the crowd of mostly women to reach his throne. I smirked under my hand. He obviously hadn't thought that through.

When he finally sat, resting his staff across his lap, we slowly stilled and quieted.

He cleared his throat. "I have chosen the new high priestess who will fill the void left by our beloved Maia. The fearsome goddess sent her wishes to me in a beautiful dream. She made her desires clear and left no room for doubt."

Whispers rippled through the gathered priestesses, some eager to be chosen, others eager to remain hidden.

"Moreover . . ." His voice squeaked, and he cleared this throat again. "Moreover, I have received a second important message." He gestured to someone on his left, and I stood on tiptoe to see the person who sidled up to his throne.

My heart stopped beating.

I swallowed the cry that rose in my throat and clasped my hand to my mouth.

Aegisthus. Mother had sent him here to Tauris once again. Had he come to ignore me again, to treat me as if I were nothing more than a squashed worm stuck to the bottom of his booted foot?

"Come, Aegisthus of Mycenae. Give the priestesses your news."

Aegisthus stared above our heads at a spot on the wall behind us, carefully avoiding eye contact with anyone. "The great Queen of Mycenae and the Queen of all Greece, Clytemnestra, daughter of Tyndareus and mother of Orestes, has seen a vision. She has seen the woman whom Artemis has chosen to be her closest companion here in the land of the Taurians."

We stood still as stone.

"The one Artemis has chosen is the honest Iphianassa of Tiryns."

The blood drained from my face and the room lurched. I clenched my jaw and dug my nails into my palms. I couldn't collapse now.

The king continued. His words pulsed in and out of my consciousness, and I only picked up a few: ". . . my own dream . . . Mycenae . . . our protector . . . anger fearsome Artemis . . . keep her happy."

I blinked. Fingers bit into my elbow, and I saw Aëdon standing by my side, her brown eyes pleading with me. But what was I supposed to do?

The room settled once again, and my heartbeat thumped its regular rhythm behind my ribs. I breathed the heavy air through my nose and twisted my elbow from Aëdon's grasp.

Thoas rose from his throne and the murmuring crowd fell silent. We parted before him so he didn't have to shove his way out of his throne room. He didn't look in my direction as he passed.

Women congratulated me in soft voices, as if they could sense my unease and didn't want to speak too loudly. Some of them touched my shoulders, my arms, my hands, and I wanted to run, screaming, from this close room that seemed to be always full of bad news.

I wanted to go straight to my alcove, my *erémia*, to pull my mantle tight under my chin, to turn myself invisible to all human eyes.

෦෫෦෫

"How do I get out of this?" My words sounded more plaintive than I wanted.

Theano sat silent for many moments, her hands resting motionless in her lap. We were sitting in my *erêmia*; it was the first time I'd ever invited her to join me there.

"I don't think there's a way out, Iphianassa. The king has made his wishes clear. And so has the Queen of Mycenae, who holds special influence over King Thoas." She peeked at me from the corners of her eyes, then focused her gaze on the lapping blue waves.

Eventually, my words came out in a whisper. "I can't do it. I can't be responsible for those men when they wash up on shore."

She patted my arm. "It's a horrific task. I didn't envy Maia that responsibility, and I don't envy you. But Artemis demands the sacrifices. She craves them."

"You know that's not true." My fingers twisted the fabric of my mantle. "It's only to please the king's ego. Nothing more."

Theano looked at me, her soft eyes full of pity. "You have no choice," she eventually said. "You have to obey the king. Don't let yourself think he wouldn't sell you into slavery. Or worse."

"I could run away," I said, my pulse quickening.

She took my cold hand in hers, and I let it rest in her soothing warmth. In that moment, I envied Aëdon for still having a kind mother. "Where would you go?"

I wanted to say *home*. But the word stuck in my throat. Four years of Maia insisting that I had to keep my identity secret had set deep roots in my mind.

When I didn't respond, Theano continued, releasing my hand back into my cold lap. She murmured, as if there were danger of being overheard, even though that wasn't possible. "High priestess is a very prominent role. Yes, it comes with many difficulties, but it also comes with power."

She paused, letting the idea settle in my mind.

"The king is a superstitious man, Iphianassa. You may have noticed he's very afraid of Artemis."

It was true, though I hadn't thought about it before. When the king spoke of Artemis, he always used words like *fierce* and *terrible* and *fearsome,* but he didn't choose those words for Aphrodite, Poseidon, or Apollo. Could Theano be right? Did King Thoas fear Artemis above all other gods?

Then my mind jumped to an entirely new idea: if I could use Thoas's fear of Artemis against him, could I finally find a way home?

When we left my alcove, Theano and I were shocked to see Koronis and Melantho wandering the beach on the other side of the sharp stone that hid access to my spot.

"Oh! There you are," Melantho said, reaching to tuck a strand of hair behind my ear.

"We've been looking for you." Koronis squeezed my hand. "We need to talk about your initiation ceremony. The king has granted you such a high honor, Iphianassa!"

"We're so happy for you! We want to make sure your ceremony is perfect."

And, even though Theano stiffened beside me, I chose to believe them. Sometimes my youthful ignorance amuses me, now that I have the wisdom of hindsight.

The four of us walked back to town, the twins chattering about fabrics, jewels, and sandals. But my mind was far off, processing my new understanding of King Thoas, wondering how I could use him to get back home.

Chapter 29

W hy Callisto?"

"Oh, don't pucker your brows like that, Iphianassa." Koronis pressed her thumb between my eyebrows, and I took a step backward. "You don't want your face to freeze in a scowl. We can't have you looking like a Gorgon."

"But why Callisto?" I repeated, leaning toward a cluster of pink blossoms to breathe in the sweet scent of future apples. We wandered the straight lines of the orchard, bees buzzing around us as they gathered their pollen.

"It's a beautiful story," Melantho offered. "Artemis's most beautiful hunting companion, preserved forever in the night skies, her stars shining bright and looking down on us forever."

A wistful sigh slipped from Koronis's lips.

"But—" I started.

"The details don't matter," Melantho interrupted.

We walked in silence for a long time. The story of Callisto could be seen as beautiful, I supposed. At least hers was a happy ending. But who could forget all the dreadful things that happened to the poor girl, landing her in her heavenly spot in the first place? True, she was the most beautiful—that's what her name meant, after all.

And yes, Artemis loved her dearly, as she loved all her hunting partners and nymphs and companions. But did Artemis not perform a great injustice to her favorite friend? Did the goddess not, in punishment for a deed that was utterly out of Callisto's power to prevent, punish the wrong one?

Ismene had told Elektra and me the story many times. It had been one of my favorites as a young girl, when I, too, glorified the ending and ignored the rest.

Being the most beautiful, as she certainly was, Callisto, of course, caught the eye of Zeus, that most ravenous of gods.

And Callisto tried to say no. Of course she did. What girl wouldn't? But, ignoring her desperate pleas and thinking only of his own pleasure, Zeus took what he wanted from her.

Then, when she understood the terrible reality of her new condition, she draped loose robes over her body to hide her shame. But the day came, as it was sure to do, when it was impossible to hide her secret any longer.

And then, anger. Fury. Wrath.

Artemis couldn't contain her rage. This girl, this most beautiful Callisto, had sworn to protect her purity on behalf of the goddess. She'd offered this part of herself to the virgin goddess as a gift, a truly wonderful gift. But then she'd allowed this offering to be torn from her own body, and at the same time, torn from Artemis.

In an instant, the furious goddess transformed her favorite companion into a bear, destined to forever wander the forests alone.

But even the gods make mistakes. Artemis should have seen what was to come.

Now in the form of a bear, Callisto was still nourishing the child of Zeus in her womb. When the day came, the child burst forth, a dazzling half-god. Even though the boy took a human form, Zeus called him Arcus. Bear.

He whisked his boy away, giving him to the goddess Maia to raise into a great hunter. And when Arcus was grown, he went hunting one day. Even you can guess what was bound to happen then, though Artemis didn't seem to have seen it coming.

Yes, the son threw his javelin at the bear. He had no way of knowing she was his mother. And, one final time, a god intervened. Zeus, in the very last heartbeat before the javelin hit its target, transformed both mother and son into constellations and hung them together in the black night sky.

Callisto and Arcus. The Great Bear and the Little Bear.

I couldn't see how this story related to my initiation into my new role as high priestess. It seemed more like a bad omen than a good one.

Melantho must have been waiting for me to finish running through my thoughts, because as soon as I opened my mouth to speak, she interrupted. "In the end, Artemis is satisfied, isn't she? Her beloved Callisto is forever safe from harm, and her spirit has become a beautiful string of glowing stars." She waved her hand toward the clouded spring sky.

"And Artemis cherishes bears," Koronis said. "Above all animals, she loves bears."

I didn't think this was true. Surely she cherished her deer above bears, but that wasn't the point.

"But the violence," I started. "I want to please the goddess, not anger her."

Melissa spoke for the first time. "I agree. We don't want to give Artemis reason to punish Iphianassa."

Melantho ignored Melissa and aimed her response at me, looking me in the eye as she spoke. "Sometimes, it seems, our goddess punishes those she loves most dearly."

♾♾♾

The day of the ceremony, I woke at dawn with butterflies in my belly and thoughts speeding through my head. The amount of planning Melantho and Koronis had done was overwhelming. I was surprised they were so concerned about my rise to high priestess, but they'd put all their efforts into this day. And, if I was being honest, I was relieved I didn't have to think too much about the details.

As I tied my leather belt around my waist, the memory of the first time I wore this ceremonial gown bubbled to the surface. I tried to shove it away, but the boy's quiet plea to his mother just as the knife struck played over and over behind my eyes and in my ears.

When the two of us left for the palace, I asked Melissa question after question just to keep my mind distracted.

Festivities began at daybreak. The town came alive with the first rays of dawn and hadn't quieted since. The streets, normally busy with people running daily errands, now swarmed with Taurians and Greeks who rumbled with excitement. Children ran through the streets like wild animals, their shrieks echoing off the walls. Even the city's countless dogs joined their voices to the cacophony, sensing collective excitement in the air.

We eleven priestesses ate breakfast in the throne room, the king in attendance. The meal itself was nothing special, just leftovers from last night's palace dinner, but the priestesses were humming with excitement.

I felt like I was on display as I sat on my cushion, picking at my food. The priestesses—*my* priestesses—seemed happy enough chatting among themselves, and I caught no one staring at me, but I still felt exposed. And why? I'd been born for this kind of honor, to sit before all who were my subjects. I was born a princess, a future queen. But that all seemed impossibly long ago now. A lifetime.

After the meal, I glanced at Artemis's statue, the painted white of her face shining in the dancing flames of the great hearth. Her white dress rippled in the breeze that came in through the windows, and for an instant, she looked truly alive. Her dark eyes stared into mine, but I couldn't decide what she was trying to tell me.

If I was going to be her high priestess, I hoped she'd start sending clear signs to me soon. I didn't know how to interpret her cloaked messages.

Lingering in the throne room as long as I could, I paced the perimeter, my heart thumping behind my ribs. I hadn't wanted this day to come. I'd hoped, and even prayed, that Artemis would change her mind, in the way gods are famous for. Anyone could see Koronis longed to be high priestess. Surely any goddess would choose the one who wanted the duties so badly her face glowed with it.

But Artemis's ears remained deaf to my pleas, and the king's eyes remained blind to Koronis's obvious longing.

I paced and paced.

Aëdon walked with me for a few circuits. "It's a beautiful day," she tried.

I only nodded.

"You couldn't have asked for anything better. The sun is warm, and there are only a few clouds."

"Come sit by me." Melissa patted the cushion beside hers. I looked at the girl. At fourteen, she was the age I'd been when I was ripped out of my own life and dropped into another. Had I been as bright-eyed then as she was now? Had my face been so open, so innocent?

"What?" She fidgeted with her gown, her hair, her jewelry. "What's wrong?"

I smiled. "Nothing. You look perfect." And I resumed pacing.

"Come here, you're driving me mad." Melantho pulled me toward the front of the throne room by my elbow.

"It's almost time," Koronis said. "We should get ready."

We'd all discussed the way this would go. We'd walk in procession, our flautist leading the way. I'm sorry to say that my old memory no longer recalls the girl's name, but I do remember her clearly. She was a new priestess, chosen for her skill with the double *aulos.* Even my deaf old ears can still hear the girl's penetrating notes as her fingers flew over the openings in the flute like the wings of a moth and her breath flowed through the vibrating twin reeds.

Koronis would follow, carrying the sacred idol in her careful hands. I would come third with a box of saffron clutched to my breast. The box was painted a brilliant golden color and would look stunning against my rich blue mantle, Koronis assured me. And the beautiful color accented my skin tone and my hazel eyes beautifully, she said. But I already knew that.

Behind me, the remaining nine priestesses would fall in line, Aëdon taking up the end, beating her drum in rhythm to our slow steps as we walked the People's Way toward the Heights of Artemis.

We gathered near the statue, still standing in her little alcove beside the king's throne. The old prickle of panic fluttered in my belly, but I pushed it down before it could take root. The box of saffron threads sat heavy in my sweat-slick hands as we proceeded in our line out of the throne room and out of the palace.

I squinted at the sudden harshness of the glowing mid-day sun and wished I could shade my eyes with my hand. The few people who were still in town stepped aside as they heard the flutes approaching. We wound our way through town and then switched back to head out to the Heights of Artemis.

Our bare feet padded in the dust as the twelve of us made our slow procession up the People's Way, the tiny bronze bells around our ankles tinkling in time with the music.

Gentle gusts of wind puffed at our faces when we first started up the path, but as we neared the open space of the Heights of Artemis, the breeze faded into an eerie stillness and my mind shot back to the long-ago windless beach of Aulis. I squeezed my eyes tight for a breath, forcing the image as far from my mind as it would go. Surely, the Artemis who had made her deadly demand on that day was a different Artemis from the one who would certainly be satisfied with today's offerings.

The people of Tauris had gathered in the open space, mingled conversation and laughter tracing a path toward us. They had their music, too, but the notes faded respectfully when the musicians saw our flautist emerge from the path.

The crowd split into two silent halves as our single line crept toward the cliff's edge. The king had assembled his dais near the edge once again. He sat motionless on his throne, his heavily embroidered black robes draped over his narrow shoulders and his wooden staff lying lifeless across his lap.

As we neared, I saw the empty painted chair next to his. That had been Maia's seat and would now be mine. A tingle ran down my spine, and I bit the insides of my cheeks to keep the panic at bay.

A low altar was set before the king's throne, three long, flat stones stacked one atop the other. Melantho had told me they would set up a temporary altar for today, so all the people of Tauris could see the initiation of Artemis's new high priestess. For most of these people, this would be a once-in-a-lifetime experience.

Because I would be the high priestess for the rest of my life.

We formed a circle around the small altar, the flat stone empty save for a small pile of kindling. The flute trailed into silence until the only sound that was left was the tapping of Aëdon's drum. When Melissa bent to light the kindling, Aëdon's hands flew into a faster, louder rhythm, and our chanting intensified.

I stood behind the altar, facing the crowd, my box clutched in trembling hands. Koronis stood to my right, holding the idol before her. She began a new chant, but the ancient words sounded distant and foreign. Melissa stood directly across from me, her back to the crowd, and we locked eyes. An unusual glow shined through her dark pupils, unmistakable and unnatural. Not fear, but uncertainty, a look I wasn't sure I'd ever seen on Melissa's face before.

Despite the warm, still air, a chill crept through my thick ceremonial mantle, and I felt suddenly exposed. The garnet-eyed gold snakes that wound around my arms almost writhed against my skin. I was aware of my bare breasts and fought the urge to pull the edges of my dress together. Melissa didn't blink, and her look shifted from uncertain to unreadable.

From my left side, Melantho pulled the lid from the box in my hands. Koronis lifted the idol of Artemis into the air above her head, her words growing louder, the tempo of her chanting quickening in time with Aëdon's drumbeats.

I reached inside the box and plucked out the precious saffron. I stared at the red-orange threads pinched between my thumb and fingers, knowing they would stain my fingertips a dark yellow. A clear image rose into my mind then: these threads may have been poisoned, or instead may spring to life and wind their way around my throat. I dropped them onto the flame and a gust of wind swept in from the sea, lifting my hair and sending a chill all the way to my bones.

The atmosphere shifted, crackling with ancient energy.

I dared to look at Melissa again. Her gown rustled in the new breeze and the look in her eyes was clear terror.

And then the sound came. It was difficult to hear above Aëdon's drum, but when her hands suddenly froze in mid-air, we all heard it. A hoarse bellow came from the far end of the peninsula, a plaintive cry rising into the space above our heads. My first thought was this was the wail of the beast that had been chosen as a sacrifice on this day, and irritation at the beast's handler coursed through me.

The cries were wild and raw, unbroken for many moments. The crowd turned to look behind them, murmuring and then gasping and then screaming. People scattered in all directions, including forward toward us, and we priestesses clustered in front of the king's dais, unable to see beyond the crowd ahead of us.

The untamed cries stopped abruptly, and I dared to think that whatever beast had found its way to our Heights had been done away with. But then an earth-shaking roar froze my heart mid-beat.

I climbed into the chair next to the throne—my chair—and stood on my toes to see above the heads of the people. The king followed my lead, and together we watched in horror.

In the back of the Heights, nestled against the great stone wall that blocked all but the one entrance to the area—and the one exit—a yearling bear cub stood on his hind legs. He was bound to the earth with thick, twisted ropes, but even from a distance, I could see that one rope had already snapped.

And the brown cub's mother stood on the rocks above him. Her flesh swayed as she towered on her hind legs, her massive teeth dripping with saliva as she roared her deafening threat. When she landed on her front paws, her haunches rippled and her glossy coat shone in the sun.

She flung herself into the crowd.

The cub's cries pierced through the screams of the people, as if they were arrows shot straight into my ears. Sweat streamed down my back; my heart pounded. King Thoas took my hand in his, and I barely noticed.

People crushed against us as they tried to flee, and I made the mistake of turning my head. Behind us was nothing but fistfuls of open air, and below us only the waveless sea, glistening as the sun peeked from behind its heavy, gray clouds.

A breath froze in my chest and I turned to face forward again. Melissa had joined me on my chair, and I clenched her small hand in mine. The three of us—King Thoas, Melissa, and I—stood hand-clasped, staring with unblinking eyes at the horrors unfolding before us.

The king spoke, but his words fluttered into the chaos.

"What did you say?" I turned my head to him. He looked directly at me, all color drained from his face, pale eyes swimming in unshed tears. My mouth went dry.

"Can you make it stop?"

I was speechless. This king, ruler and protector of these very people who were being mauled by a great bear in the sacred Heights of Artemis, was powerless to help.

And he thought I held the power he lacked.

I blinked slowly, allowing the white lights to dance behind my dark eyelids for a few seconds, and I forced my breath to slow. I turned toward the madness once more, and in that instant, a woman's wail filled the entire world. Hers was not the scream of physical pain, but of emotional agony.

Then the bear cub's cries ended abruptly. Seconds later, I saw him clambering up the rock face, his great claws scrambling for purchase. Then the mother followed, nudging her son with her nose. Her overheated grunts floated across the invisible air toward me until I could hear nothing but the bear and her cub struggling for their lives. When the pair finally reached the top of the rock, they paused. And, looking back at us, the mother opened her mouth to unleash one final, deafening roar that rattled my very bones.

I will forever swear on the names of all the undying gods and goddesses known to mankind: the splendid mother bear looked directly at me. Her shining black eyes bored into mine for an entire heartbeat before she turned and led her cub away from the madness.

And I knew who they were. Callisto and her son Arcas.

The Great Bear and the Little Bear had come down from the midnight heavens to teach us who truly ruled our lives.

Chapter 30

The events of my initiation day came to be known as the Wrath of Callisto. I hated that. Why put more burden on a woman whose shoulders already carry a great weight, who forever hangs above our heads through no choice of her own?

In the shocked days that followed, King Thoas did nothing. He seemed paralyzed by the enormity of it. I was the one who arranged the elaborate funeral procession for the little boy who had the tragic misfortune of standing exactly where the mother bear landed when she jumped from her rocky perch. I was the one who arranged for my priestesses to pay daily visits to the homes of the dozens who were injured on that disastrous day, some grievously.

It was my idea to open the locked storeroom, allowing anyone in need to take their share of the gathered offerings from the altar of Artemis and all the gods who had altars in Tauris.

And while the king hid himself away in his rooms wondering what he'd done to anger Artemis, I was the one who sent a great hunting party to track down the two bears and bring their flesh to us, hoping to appease the terrified and furious people of Tauris. The five days the hunters fanned into the flats outside the city, I silently prayed they would never find the pair.

Those prayers, at least, were answered.

Perhaps most important of all, I was the one who launched a swift and thorough investigation into the weeks leading up to that horrific morning.

In the days that followed, I set Lastratos to the task of learning all he could from the noble families. I sent Heliko and Elazar out as ears among the slaves and servants, listening for any clue that might help me uncover what exactly happened. And I charged Nikandros with learning all he could from his fellow fishermen, merchants, and harbor workers.

It only took a few short days to learn the entire plot.

"No," King Thoas whispered. He sat on his throne, his staff across his lap as always. But unlike his usual habit, he sat perfectly still. His fingers didn't twirl his beard, his boots didn't tap the stone floor, his eyes didn't dart from one of us to the next.

"My king—" Lastratos started, standing solid before the throne.

"No! Zotikos is my best man." The king bolted from his seat and his staff clattered to the floor. The noise echoed off the plastered walls in the nearly empty room, and a thick crack traced into the carved wood that topped the staff.

He paced the small space, first right and then left and then right again. Lastratos and I stepped backward and forward to keep out of the king's frenzied path.

"I do not believe you. You have been fooled by liars. Bring them to me and I will have their tongues."

"King Thoas," I started, and he whirled on me so suddenly, I jumped backward.

"You." His blue eyes darkened to a shade I'd never seen before, and I couldn't tear my gaze from his. "She talked me into it, you know. She forced me to choose you."

I didn't know who the king was speaking of, but I swallowed my question.

He continued, his eyes still fixed on mine. "It is an omen. A bad one."

Sweat prickled my palms, and my old scar pulsed.

"It's not a bad omen," Lastratos said. "We're here to relieve you of that terrible thought."

The king's shoulders fell, his eyes returning to their normal pale blue. "I do not believe you. Zotikos is my best man."

But there was no longer venom behind his choked words. The fire had drained from his face, and he stooped to pick up his staff. If he noticed the new crack, he didn't dwell on it.

"My king, may we sit?" Lastratos didn't wait for a reply. He picked two low stools from those that lined the wall and set them before the king.

In low voices, Lastratos and I told the king everything we'd learned. We left nothing out, coated none of it in honey, added no embellishments.

Together with their brother Zotikos, Melantho and Koronis had come to Tauris for a distinct purpose. From their home in Athens, they'd heard of the city called Tauris in the north of the Euxine Sea. This new Greek city perched atop cliffs and sat among the Taurian people who'd lived in the area for generations. This Tauris was ruled by an unmarried young king who was said to be weak and impressionable.

The brother–sister trio saw opportunities.

For a long time, their plan seemed to work. Zotikos secured himself among the royal ranks as a palace guard. He quickly earned the confidence of the king, who honored him as his chief guard.

Melantho pinned her hopes on the king, dreaming of filling those forever-empty queen's rooms with her own beautiful items. While slow going, she thought she was making progress. Though she hadn't yet found herself in his bed, she was sure she could talk him into marrying her.

Then there was Koronis. When they arrived in Tauris five years earlier, Koronis's plan was to follow in her sister's footsteps, hoping to find a nobleman to marry. But as months and years wore on, her sights wandered to the gods. She saw that the High Priestess of Artemis was far older than the high priestesses of Aphrodite or Hera and thought she may have a chance at taking Maia's place when she died.

The siblings would someday make a formidable triad: queen, high priestess, chief of the royal guards.

But five years passed. Zotikos was secure in his place, but Melantho was still no queen.

And then, when Maia finally died, the king ignored Koronis and chose me.

The yearling bear seems to have been Melantho's idea initially, and Koronis opposed the scheme. But, as you know, Muse, Melantho won that argument. The idea was to have the bear tied down for the townspeople to view and admire before the ritual began. Then, at Zotikos's cue in the middle of the ceremony, the bear's handler was to remove the muzzle and jab at him with a sturdy stick. The bear would roar and fight against his tethers, and his bellow would be interpreted as Artemis's extreme disapproval.

But the hunters who captured the yearling failed to notice that he still had a protective mother. And the man they hired as the handler had never managed any animal more ferocious than a cow.

Even now, with all this new knowledge, King Thoas hesitated to punish his favored Zotikos. He insisted his man was faithful. And the twins? Well, they must also be honorable if they took any guidance at all from their brother.

Lastratos tried every angle. He reminded the king that rulers across the world would hear of this day—this so-called Wrath of Callisto. The terrible story was surely already sailing over the endless seas in the mouths of merchants and fishers and bards. What would the kings of faraway Egypt and Ephesus and Hattusa think to hear of a king so weak that he allowed known conspirators to live freely in his lands?

Would one of the various chieftains of the Greek lands, after they finally returned from their campaign against Troy, see his weakness as a prime opportunity to take Tauris for himself?

Then he tried to reach the king's heart. The very people who relied on the king's protection were injured in the catastrophe. Would these grieving people of Tauris not want to see justice done? Did they not wish to see the instigators of this hideous crime punished?

But the king's heart wouldn't budge. He insisted his beloved Zotikos could not harbor such betrayal in his breast, to use the king's good favor so he and his sisters could scramble to the highest power in Tauris.

He sat like a lump of stone on his small wooden throne, glazed eyes fixed on the floor, lips twitching with suppressed sobs.

Eventually, Lastratos's arguments ran dry. He had no more words to convince King Thoas that he must rid Tauris of these three siblings who plotted against him and against Artemis.

The three of us sat in silence for many moments, the only sound a sparrow spilling its impossibly bright notes into the gloom outside the palace. I touched Lastratos's elbow, keeping my eyes on the king's cracked staff. The two of us rose from our low stools, and I didn't know what I was going to say before the words poured from my mouth.

"My king, the decision is yours, of course. You must do as you wish. Artemis, in her grief and fury, will strike when she chooses. She will loose her deadly arrows without mercy. She will fling into the black underworld all who anger her, all who do not please her. Like her brother Apollo, she will stalk and hunt on silent feet; she will rain terrible blows on the heads of us all, of everyone who spoiled her sacred day, of all who dishonored her golden name. She will pursue us until her thirst for vengeance is slaked."

My eyes rested steadily on the king's bowed head. An unfamiliar warmth coursed through my veins, and I felt my pupils dilate. My scarred palm prickled with a new sensation as my own strength spilled from my body, expanding to fill the room.

I turned and stepped slowly toward the door, Lastratos behind me.

The sound that came from the throne behind us was more like a breath than a word: "Wait."

The king exiled Zotikos, Melantho, and Koronis from Tauris. He didn't care where they went—he didn't want to know—but he made one point very clear. If any of them returned to Tauris, they would become the next full moon sacrifice to Artemis of the golden arrows, who watched over us all.

PART THREE

Chapter 31

Achilles is dead.

The words echoed in my mind and bounced, feverish, in my hollow heart.

Achilles is dead.

The alcove walls wept, but I did not. I could never weep for a lost husband who had never truly been my husband, for a young man who'd ignored my pleas for help, for a man who refused to honor his betrothed.

King Thoas called me to his throne room, where he spilled the story in one long puff of breath, sounding eager to get the news into the world.

The thing about the story was this: regardless of how foolish it seemed on the surface, I believed every word. The way Agamemnon stole Achilles's war prize—the woman Briseis—and how Achilles's response to that theft was to sulk in his tent. His refusal to fight, to lend his brilliant strength to the war that had now been raging for nine years, would have been detrimental to Agamemnon's campaign.

For his part, Agamemnon would have been too stone-headed to back down. He'd have thought Achilles was playing a game for power. He'd have thought the petulant young warrior couldn't keep himself off the battlefield for very long. He'd have called Achilles's bluff. Or tried to.

And then for Achilles to rage over the death of his foolish friend, Patroclus. A rage so red he could no longer see the danger he put himself in, even as he slaughtered the mighty Trojan prince Hector.

Even the manner of Achilles's death—at the hands of the nobody Paris, who'd supposedly played an instrumental part in starting this war and who hadn't even fought until this moment—held the ring of truth.

Once the singers got hold of this tale, they would insert gods and goddesses, exaggerate vanities and vices. The story would grow into a living thing that would resemble lore more than truth, something outside the boundaries of belief. But in this moment, Muse, with nothing but the raw facts before me, I believed each word King Thoas spoke.

King Thoas. Wasn't it odd that the king wanted to tell me this tragic news himself?

It's true that the tale of the glorious boy-warrior would grow with time. Muse, it was you who spread his story to the corners of the wide world throughout generations.

But on this day, the day King Thoas told me of the boy's reckless death, almost nobody knew the name Achilles. He was yet to be glorified, honored, exaggerated into the shining hero he'd later become.

That's how I knew, with as much certainty as if Artemis had told me herself, that the king had intercepted the messages I'd sent each spring, begging Achilles to come collect his bride.

Later, Lastratos confirmed my guess.

On that bitter day five years earlier, after pretending I wasn't Iphigenia, daughter of Queen Clytemnestra, after scolding me for trying to contact my own mother, my treacherous cousin Aegisthus had gone straight to the king and betrayed me.

All these years, King Thoas had known of my desperation to escape Tauris, and he'd been the one to keep me here.

I now understood I was stranded in this distant, cold, backward place for the rest of my life. Forced to sacrifice innocent men in the name of the very goddess who wanted my own lifeblood spilled in her honor, to tear them from the living and rush their shades to the underworld.

I'd never see my mother again, my sister, my nurse. I couldn't go back to Mycenae, my rightful home, and help Mother and Elektra rid the palace of the usurper Aegisthus, help them dispel the curse of the house of Atreus forever.

☙❧☙

I woke with a scream in my throat for the first time in years. Melissa tried to soothe me, but I was inconsolable. Sobs wracked my body until my throat ached and my chest burned. Melissa asked and asked what the dream was about, but I couldn't tell her.

This was no dream that falters with the light of day; this was a nightmare that trailed me in the days and weeks to come.

Even now, it's difficult for me to recount the beasts who hunted my sister in shadowy woods, while I stood by, paralyzed and helpless. And so I'll leave it to you, Muse, to fill in the details, a task you'll most likely perform energetically.

As the days rolled by, I couldn't shake the feeling that my dream had been a vision. After all, had my sleeping mind not predicted Maia's death with terrible accuracy?

I sent prayers to Artemis and to Hera and Athena, begging them to send me a sign. I listened to the rustling leaves and the twittering birds, the humming insects and the lapping waves, hoping one of the goddesses might whisper to me, to assure me my sister was safe.

But no goddess murmured a secret message with her undying breath. Instead, one of them sent me a proper message. And it came in the form of Damalis.

She met me in my alcove one dawn, and to this day I don't know who told her where to wait for me. But when I arrived, there she was, sitting on the smooth rock in the middle, as real as you and I.

We embraced quickly, patting one another's backs two or three times before stepping apart. Like me, Damalis would have been around twenty-three years old, but she hadn't changed much at all. She was, it seemed, one of those women who would forever look like a child. Her nose was still too small and her ears too big. Her eyes still darted about, as if she expected a great snake to slither from the shadows at any time.

"It's good to see you," I said, and I meant it. In earlier days, I'd never have dreamed I'd be happy to see Damalis, but my heart swelled on this day.

"And you, Princess."

Princess. My heart froze mid-beat at the old title. It sounded foreign to me now, a word that no longer lived in my mind, no longer fit in my life. It was a word that used to wrap itself around me like a comforting blanket, but now it was no more than a scratchy, unwanted burden.

"I am a priestess, not a princess."

"Of course, Priestess." Pink rose into her cheeks, and I saw the young girl I used to laugh at, the girl who'd become my handmaid. But her voice wasn't the little squeak I remembered, and I wondered whether she'd outgrown her childish way of speaking, or if my memory had led me astray.

She wore the clean, well-made tunic of a servant and held her shoulders with a confidence she'd clearly grown into over the past nine years.

I gestured for her to sit on the rock again, the only comfort I could offer my guest in the small space of my *erêmia*.

She shook her head. "I don't have much time. I'm expected at my cousin's home for breakfast."

Cousin? How had I never known Damalis had a cousin in Tauris?

"Who sent you here?" I tried to keep my voice steady, to mask the hope and dread that clashed together in my heart.

Damalis's pause told me the words she was about to speak would be false. "Nobody, Priestess. I've come to collect my cousin, who will marry a carpenter in Mycenae."

The pause that came next was mine. I wasn't sure if I should press Damalis to tell me the truth, or if I should assume she had good reason to lie.

"What news, then, do you bring from Mycenae?"

Relief washed over her plain features. The girl she'd known, the princess Iphigenia, would certainly have insisted on hearing the truth. But the priestess Iphianassa stood before her now, a foreigner who let her continue without asking hard questions.

"The war has made life in Mycenae difficult," she started. "Everyone is angry that their men have been away these nine years. Honorable people have resorted to theft and dishonesty. Hunger and disease have haunted us all."

I remembered the illness that swept through Tauris my first year in this place and shuddered. Adding hunger and despair to a disease like that would surely have deadly results.

"Does the queen want something of me?"

"The queen?" For a heartbeat, Damalis seemed genuinely confused. "No. Not the queen."

"Who, then? Who sent you?" Certainly, whoever had sent her to Tauris wanted something from me. I could think of no other explanation for this visit.

Damalis took a step toward me, lowering her voice. "As I said, Priestess, nobody sent me here. My father and I have come to fetch my cousin for marriage."

She motioned toward the rock in the middle of my alcove, and even though I was a high priestess, I obeyed. We sat knee to knee, nearly nose to nose. "We've come to bring you home."

Her words were hurried, and the sudden rush of my pulse in my ears made me think I surely hadn't heard her clearly. I shook my head.

"Yes. You must come with us."

She clasped my hands in her cold fingers. She spoke with such urgency, such low whispers, I had to strain to understand her words. "Aegisthus has usurped the throne of Mycenae. With the aid of some god or other, he's bewitched Queen Clytemnestra, who rules beside him. They've had two children together, and Aegisthus insists his son, Aletes, will take the throne after he's gone."

Damalis paused for breath. I held mine.

"They've forbidden Princess Elektra to leave her rooms. She hasn't been allowed outside the palace walls for years, and she withers in loneliness."

I squeezed Damalis's hands and clenched my jaw. My nightmare seemed to hold an ugly truth.

"Prince Orestes, the rightful heir to King Agamemnon's throne, is in exile. The queen sent him away at the beginning of the war. For his own safety, she sent him to his uncle by marriage."

These last words barely reached my ears. I could think only of Elektra. I still pictured her as I'd last seen her: dark eyes dancing with questions, youthful face open, honest, and innocent.

"What can I do?" The words escaped my throat as a croak.

"You must come with us. Back to Mycenae. There are many of us who wish to see Aegisthus ruined. Even some elders want him gone. We'll bring your brother home. He's twelve now, old enough to claim his throne with guidance. You, Elektra, and Orestes are Agamemnon's true children. There are many who will stand behind you."

"But I'm dead," I said and immediately heard the foolishness of the words.

"What a miracle to bring you home, then! With Artemis's blessing, you're alive. And you'll bring the goddess with you. She'll stand behind you and all those you love. Aegisthus is superstitious."

All kings are superstitious, I thought, but I kept silent.

I stood. A new thought filled my mind. "Does my mother truly want me home? Even now, you're here without her knowledge."

Damalis rose to stand before me in my little *erêmia*. I saw the truth in the lines of her face, and the weeping walls closed in on us. "No," she whispered. "I don't think she wants you back."

My heart sat heavy in my chest and the old disappointment constricted my lungs. I sat down again, waiting for the dizziness to pass. So many years had gone by since panic filled my world. I remembered my old trick and squeezed my fingernails into my palms to keep the despair from crushing me.

Damalis sat beside me again, taking my fists into her hands. "You're safe here. Safer than you would be in Mycenae."

When the spinning world around me finally came to a stop, I pulled my hands from hers and fixed my gaze on the waves outside the alcove.

I didn't speak, so Damalis continued. "Even now that the war is over, you're still in danger. All three of you are. Aegisthus has the throne now and he holds it tight."

I pulled my eyes from the soothing blue sea. "But he knows I'm here. What makes you think he won't come for me?"

Damalis paused, her brows pulled together in thought. Finally, she said, "I don't know. I know only what my father tells me and what I hear from palace servants and slaves."

But of course the answer was obvious to me: King Thoas. The king who entertained Aegisthus in his own throne room here in Tauris. The king who'd intercepted my messages to Achilles and who'd convinced himself that I'd been sent to Tauris by Artemis herself. The king who wanted his favorite goddess's approval so desperately, he'd do anything she demanded of him.

And I wondered. For the first time, I wondered about that visit years ago, when Aegisthus stood in Maia's courtyard, wrapped in his purple-trimmed tunic, and chastised me like a disobedient child. He'd said Mother forbade me to send her messages. But had it truly been Mother who'd issued that command? Had she even heard my message at all?

Then I asked a question I didn't even know was in my mind. "Was it Aegisthus who poisoned me?"

"Poison?"

"In Aulis. Before . . . " I couldn't say the words.

"Before we led you to the altar?"

For a moment, I felt Damalis and Ampelos gripping my elbows as I wandered, dazed, toward the smoky pyre on that windless beach. And I tasted the bitter wine in my throat. I nodded.

A breath of a laugh slipped from Damalis's lips. "No, not Aegisthus. And not poison."

Anger rose from my belly then. "Yes, poison. Do you think I'd forget a thing like that?"

Damalis stood, her eyes hardening as she stared at me. "Do you truly believe . . . " She paused, then started again. "Do you truly believe you were poisoned that day? Do you really not understand?"

The sudden anger faded from my heart as quickly as it had come. "I don't know what I think."

Her voice softened, and I saw pity in her eyes when she described that awful night on the beach in Aulis.

"It was a calming draught. I bought it myself, from a woman in one of the red tents. It was meant to calm your nerves. To protect you from fear. To make sure you didn't panic and ruin the queen's plans."

I swallowed, remembering that Damalis returned late to the tent, a cracked cup in her hand. "Plans?"

"To keep you away from your father. From his seer and his knife. Plans to take you away from the soldiers who wanted to watch your blood soak into the sand."

The truth of Damalis's words was unmistakable. That bitter wine at Aulis wasn't meant to speed me to my death, but to slow my mind enough that I couldn't see what was really happening. To keep panic from my heart, to keep me from spoiling the very plans that would save my life.

When I agreed to return with Damalis, butterflies filled my belly. I was finally going back to Mycenae. Back to Elektra, to Mother, to Ismene. With Artemis at my back, I'd help pick up the shattered pieces of our lives, to glue us back together into some semblance of our early happiness. But would Artemis's approval be enough? Would the men who stood against Aegisthus also protect me once my feet touched Mycenaean soil?

I had to try. I had to play my part in standing against Aegisthus the usurper, and placing Orestes on his rightful throne. We would stand firm against Agamemnon when he returned from the long war, send him back to Sparta with his plotting brother, where his mind would replay his final moments with his eldest daughter, whom he tried to slaughter before an army of men.

We agreed to meet in my *erêmia* at dawn in three days. Together with her father, Damalis would smuggle me onto the merchant ship that had brought them to Tauris and brisk winds would sail me home at last.

Those three days were bittersweet. I suffered in silence, unable to shed goodbye tears with Melissa and Aëdon, Theano and Lastratos. I couldn't pass parting gifts to Aëdon's children, or nod farewell to Heliko and Elazar.

I had nothing but my little wooden deer to take with me. I didn't care about the shining jewels I'd be leaving behind. Instead, I was happy to think I'd never again wrap my ceremonial dress around my body, feel the golden snakes coiled around my arms, pass the deadly dagger to King Thoas before the eyes of sacrificial men.

I tried to behave as I normally did, tried to keep the happiness and sadness from my face as my heart flipped from one to the other. So, I was surprised to see tears sliding down Heliko's cheeks as she swept fallen leaves into a corner of the courtyard the afternoon before I was to sail away. I considered slipping into the shadows, leaving her to her sadness.

But she spotted me in the doorway. Wiping her nose with the back of her hand, she whispered, "Sorry," as if a slave was forbidden to feel sadness.

"What is it?" I stepped into the courtyard. I didn't really want to know, didn't want to find out that my plans had been discovered.

She sat on the edge of the courtyard wall, her broom clutched in her trembling hands. "I'm sad to hear that I've lost a friend."

My breath caught. I hadn't realized Heliko considered me a friend, and guilt flooded my heart because I didn't think of her with the same fondness.

"Heliko . . ." I started.

But she didn't seem to hear me. "My friend Elaphia has left."

I stood in the middle of the courtyard, confused. All I could say was, "Elaphia?"

Heliko nodded, dabbing her eyes with the edge of her tunic. "She was my dear friend. We spoke at the well each morning, and always at the market and harbor. We've known each other as long as I can remember."

So I hadn't given myself away after all. My shoulders relaxed, and I considered turning to leave Heliko to mourn in private. But I remembered all the favors she'd done for me—all the messages she'd sent with no gain for herself—and I settled on the wall beside her.

We sat shoulder to shoulder in silence. Heliko's sobs slowed, and I said, "Tell me what happened."

She swallowed. "She worked in a house across town, for a man and his daughter."

When she said nothing for many moments, I said, "And where has she gone, then?"

"Just this morning, she sailed away with her mistress! I didn't know what happened, so I asked around and found out her mistress is sailing to Greece to marry. And she took Elaphia with her."

I closed my eyes, forced my breath to remain steady.

"It was all so sudden! We didn't even get to say goodbye!"

My eyes peeled open, and my voice was surprisingly steady when I said, "Which ship did they board?"

Heliko paused with this unexpected question. She furrowed her brow. "I don't know. I suppose that merchant ship that's been anchored for the last few days. That's the only Greek ship I've seen in a while."

My legs reacted before my mind could catch up. I popped up from the edge of the wall and ran. I ran out of the house and to the top of the stairs leading to the harbor. I ran down those steep stairs and turned left. I ran in the sand toward the anchored ships, toward the very place Maia had forbidden us to visit all those years ago.

Shoving my way through the crowds of merchants, fishermen, and servants, my eyes darted from face to face, searching.

I finally found Nikandros near the end of the harbor, unloading the day's catch from his boat, his sand-colored hair matted with sweat. When I tugged at the back of his tunic, he whirled round. His blue eyes flashed in surprise before registering my face.

"Iphianassa?"

"Where's the . . . Greek . . . ship?" My words came between heaving breaths.

"Come with me," he said to me. And to his companions, he said, "I'll be back. Don't steal my catch!"

Nikandros led me to the great rock where Aëdon, Melissa, and I used to sit when we were girls, before Maia forbade us to return. We stepped into the shade around the back of the rock, and my heart fluttered for one beat.

"What happened?" The concern in his eyes was real, and I forced air through my nose to calm my breathing.

"Where's the Greek merchant ship? The one that leaves tomorrow morning?"

Nikandros stared at me a good long moment, eyes narrowed. "Why?"

I felt my face redden. I had no answer, and no energy to lie. "Just tell me."

He sighed and then confirmed what Heliko had already said. "There's only been one Greek merchant ship in weeks. As you know, they've been scarce as fish feathers since the war started."

My nails bit into the flesh of my palms in the old way, and the scar on my left hand flared.

"She left this morning. Ahead of the storm reported in the . . ."

I squeezed my eyes tight, and Nikandros's words faded to nothing.

CHAPTER 32

I sat, dry-eyed and shrunken-hearted, in my *erêmia*, staring into the frothy sea. Dusk was settling and the occasional shouts from the harbor had trailed into silence. The lapping waves sounded gentle at first, but as I sat, the sound seemed to grow until it filled the space of my alcove and thrummed in my ears.

I stood and the salt air filled my lungs. One breath, then two, then a third. I placed my right foot before my left, and then my left before my right. Slowly, I walked across the beach, the wet sand squeezing between my ten toes, my heels squelching as I pulled them gently from their sandy grasp. I walked through the brown scum the waves left behind, until frigid water covered my ankles. As I stepped further, the waters engulfed my calves and then my knees.

The sea reached the tops of my thighs, pressing my tunic against my skin, between my legs. A great wave rolled toward me, shining blue-green in the dying sun. It rolled and rolled and time slowed almost to a stop. I watched the water rise until it was a looming wall, now the blue-black of a bruise, edged with white foam. I thought I could see my reflection in the watery wall and my hollow eyes stared back at me, my mouth an empty maw.

When Poseidon finally took me, thundering over my body with possessive ferocity, I didn't fight. I allowed his salted waters to fill my open mouth, to slide down my dry throat, to trickle into my lungs. I welcomed him into my body and felt him fill me, burning, until I thought I might burst. But still I didn't struggle. Black and red and white filled my vision. I heard nothing but the crackling depths, the god himself speaking to me in the language of the gods.

I allowed my hands and my arms, my feet and my legs, to float limp beside my face-down body in the suddenly calm water.

In that timeless embrace, a whisper of doubt flickered within me. Was this truly my fate? To surrender to the ocean's greedy grasp, to let Poseidon tear me from Artemis and claim me as his own?

Old Chronos is both cruel and kind at once. He takes our everything and none can escape his final grasp. But he can also be gracious enough to grant us the blessings of wisdom, of experience, of hindsight. In this way, he's the wisest of all teachers.

Even now, when Poseidon drapes his depths in that particular shade of bruised purple, I remember that night with the clarity of youth.

I don't think I wanted to die. Truly. I think I wanted, at some level in my desperate mind, to wash myself clean of the horrors that had passed. To start new and move forward, instead of constantly struggling to move backward, always swimming against the current of time.

Don't get me wrong, Muse. This thought was almost certainly

not in the front of my mind. At twenty-three, I was still far too young and too naive to have formed a thought this complex in my hour of desperation. But I do like to think—to at least give myself a little credit—that Artemis or Poseidon or some other god had lodged a seed of the idea somewhere in my mind. To cleanse myself of the soiled past, to scrub myself raw, to purify.

I didn't want to die.

I wish I could say this with confidence.

Whatever my true motivations, I didn't die and I did feel cleansed. Melissa had been my companion that evening, and I can barely imagine the depths within herself she had to reach to gather the strength to drag me out of the water. My wool tunic and mantle were soaked through and heavy, but somehow she pulled me to safety and watched as fishy water spilled from my mouth. She held my head on her lap as I coughed and wept, clutching the dry fabric of her dress in my fists.

I have a flash of a memory from that night: my head rests in Melissa's lap, her face hovers over me and her mass of frizzy curls stands in outline against the fading light. And she whispers, "I'm here."

CHAPTER 33

This can't be what you want." I paced the courtyard, clutching my shawl beneath my chin against the late autumn chill.

Melissa sat near the fire, shelling the last of the season's beans. She looked completely serene, as if this was, indeed, exactly what she wanted.

"She will be queen," Lastratos said from his perch on the low stone wall.

I stopped mid-lap so I could look him in the eye when I said, "As queen, her jewels may rest lightly on her neck just as easily as they may squeeze her throat like a snake."

An image of Mother sitting tall on Father's throne rose in my mind. And it was followed by an image of that same woman, Queen of Mycenae, sitting on a low stool in her own room, shoulders slumped and eyes red with tears. Alone.

I thought of the children her husband, the king, stole from her only because she was his queen. The little boy he'd murdered so he could marry her in the first place, and then me, her eldest daughter. He'd also, in a way, forced her to give up her two remaining children for the sake of his royal ambitions.

My heart shattered at the thought of Melissa carrying the weight of the world on her narrow shoulders, at the thought of Melissa facing the tragic role of queen with nothing but a shield of innocent kindness to protect herself.

"I'm already twenty." Her voice was cheerful as always, but did she bow her head only for the work she was doing, or was she shielding her eyes from me? "Aëdon had three children by the time she was my age."

I pulled a stool next to hers and piled a handful of unshelled beans into my lap. We worked in a tense silence for many minutes, the only sound the plump beans dropping into the bowl at our feet.

It was Lastratos who spoke first. "I know, Iphianassa . . ." He paused, as if gathering his thoughts. "I know the Fates spin tragic threads for some queens. But Tauris is at peace, and King Thoas is . . . he's not unkind."

My eyes popped up to meet his. In them, I saw all the descriptions of the king that Lastratos left unspoken: paranoid, eccentric, selfish. How would a man like that make a good husband for sweet, happy, honest Melissa?

"The king is in his forties," I tried. "He's nearly twice your age."

The two of them gave me the *why-are-you-telling-me-this* look reserved for children who tattle on their siblings for stealing their favorite toys.

"There are many young men who would be lucky to marry you, Melissa. Men who would be kind to you."

She sighed, and her face softened. "As queen, I'll have power, Iphianassa. If I can give the king heirs, I'll be able to change things we don't like about Tauris."

I knew exactly what she was talking about. But could gentle

Melissa truly convince King Thoas to put an end to his beloved practice of sacrificing shipwrecked men to Artemis?

As if reading my mind, she said gently, "With your help, of course. Do you truly think he could stand against the mother of his sons and the high priestess to his precious goddess?"

I wasn't sure if I truly believed it was possible, but the idea was tempting.

Lastratos spoke gently. "I'm getting old."

I glared at him. Lastratos, with his long dark hair and long dark beard, untouched by silver strands, didn't look a day past twenty-five. But I knew he, too, was in his forties, and my gaze dropped to my lap.

He continued. "Where will Melissa live when I'm gone, if not with her own husband? Where will you live?"

Of course, he was right. Even if he still looked young, he wasn't. Maia hadn't been much older than him when she died.

I stood and resumed my pacing. Ignoring Lastratos, I tried a different tactic. "Don't you want to serve Artemis? To serve her in the purest sense?"

"I can still serve Artemis." Melissa looked at me as if she were explaining a simple concept to a foolish child. "Theano, Aëdon, all sorts of married women serve Artemis. You know that."

"But I mean to keep your purity. As the highest honor to the virgin goddess."

Melissa opened her mouth to respond, but Lastratos cleared his throat and stood from his spot on the wall. "It's arranged already," he said, stepping toward the door. "They will marry at the next new moon."

Six days, then. In six days, I'd lose my closest friend in Tauris, and she'd lose her carefree life, her happiness, her innocence.

಄಄಄

Winter temperatures and gusty winds forced us indoors more than any of us truly wanted. By now, I felt somewhat accustomed to the frigid winters in this place, and I no longer complained about wearing thick, long sleeves under my mantle.

I lived alone with Lastratos and Elazar now, but I spent most of my time in the palace. Theano, Aëdon, and I moved our weaving and mending into the queen's chambers. The space wasn't much larger, but at least there was a window to let out the smoke from the lamps.

In the evenings, after eating our meal in Melissa's own throne room, we'd join the king and his men in his.

It was one of these evenings as we sat on our cushions in one corner, the men on the opposite side of the room, when King Thoas tried to pierce my heart with his words.

As we sipped our watered wine, he cleared his throat and spoke in a volume that was clearly meant to carry to our side of the room. Melissa lowered her voice almost imperceptibly, maintaining her chatter, but I still heard every word that spilled from the king's mouth.

"King Agamemnon is dead. Murdered in cold blood." I felt his eyes on me and I struggled to keep my face blank, my breath steady.

I'd heard the dreadful news two days before. I'd made Aëdon repeat the story three times before, still not believing the words, I fetched the messenger boy who brought the report from Mycenae. The boy told me the story in its naked, unembellished truth. And still I didn't believe the truth of it. Surely the words he spoke were no more than a tale spun by hateful Eris, the goddess who loved nothing more than she loved sowing discord among gods and men alike.

So, I was forced to hide my devastation when King Thoas's version matched exactly the words I'd already heard.

"Murdered in cold blood," he repeated. "By his own wife."

My pulse throbbed in my throat, and I forced my breath to still, willed my coloring to stay neutral. Melissa and Aëdon chatted quietly beside me, speaking words I could no longer understand. Theano squeezed my hand under the cushion so no tears collected in my eyes. I gripped her fingers tight.

With his eyes still on my face, Thoas continued. "The queen has brought terrible shame to her children. With her own hands, she has created a son and a daughter of a murderess. But not just any murderess, a husband killer."

He paused a long moment, and I couldn't stop my gaze from sliding to him on the other side of the room. His blue eyes bored into mine, and without permission, my neck and then my cheeks and then my ears burned hot.

Mercifully, he looked away before he finished his thought. "It is fortunate that her eldest daughter has been dead these ten years. She, at least, will not be forced to live in this shame."

The singers came again, summoned by you, Muse. They came from all corners of the Greek world, from Pylos to Sparta to Athens.

Most of the singers came to Tauris on foot by heading north out of Greece, through Macedonia and Thrace, and braving the rough terrain all the way to Tauris. But some were wealthy enough to buy passage on black merchant ships.

And so, by land and by sea, they fell upon us like fleas on a dog's back.

And while they weaved their tales, I sat beside the king, my breath steady, my face blank, my hands limp in my lap, swallowing the spit that collected in my mouth. Like a good priestess should.

They sang of the brave King Agamemnon, returning to his shining palace on the cliffs of Mycenae after ten long years at war, clad in glittering gold, carrying glorious plunder, trailing a long string of women and girls—fresh new slaves to fill his painted halls. His dutiful wife greeted him at the gates with sweet kisses, having arranged a welcoming ceremony fit for a victorious king, and he ate like a king and drank like a king and sang like a king.

And then his doting wife poured him a refreshing bath in his splendid silver tub and coaxed him into the herb-scented water. She scrubbed the grime from his arms, his face, his back. She poured soothing water over his hair, singing softly all the while.

After cleaning the travel dust from his strong body, his evil wife smiled and slid a sharp blade between his ribs. Shocked, he looked into her hard, grinning face as he sputtered red blood into the cool water.

Some singers said that, in this moment, Clytemnestra whispered a name. My name. *Iphigenia.* But who can say for sure? These singers weren't there, and I wasn't either.

The songs continued. Behind Agamemnon's vicious wife, his beloved cousin Aegisthus stepped into view, silent as a stalking lion, and, leaning forward, opened the great king's throat from one ear to the other.

The beloved king's body slumped and then slid under the surface of the red bathwater, and by the time two of his trusted guards came to fish him out, his skin was stained pink with his own life blood.

But even that wasn't all. Some bards sang of another innocent who fell victim to Clytemnestra's black rage. They sang of Agamemnon's greatest war prize whose life was also cut short by the murderous queen. Some called her Kastalia, some said her name was Kassandra, and yet others used Chrysis. They said she was a priestess or a princess or both. Sometimes she was a maiden of sixteen, mute and timid and wide-eyed innocent. Sometimes she was a woman of eighteen, raving and wild and wide-eyed mad, spewing black curses in the lilting Trojan tongue. But all said she met her fate at the hands of my jealous mother.

My jealous mother.

And I had no choice but to sit there, in King Thoas's throne room or next to the great cliffside fire or in the middle of the marketplace, and listen to these vile words and pretend to have no feeling one way or the other. I had no choice but to hear these cursed tales and pretend to enjoy the men's entertaining songs, and act like they weren't inventing evil stories about my beloved mother.

My beloved mother.

With Agamemnon dead, Orestes was now king of Mycenae. My brother would be only thirteen years old and would need a trustworthy adviser, but he would still be the king. Should I send a message to Orestes, begging him to finally bring me back? Would he remember his eldest sister, gone these ten years?

Surely he'd heard my story, even living in Phocis. I wanted to think our aunt Anaxibia, our father's own sister who was now raising Orestes, would have told him of me, even if she'd never met me before.

But what did it matter? Orestes didn't really know me at all. He would have no reason to risk angering any man who remained loyal to Agamemnon and who might hold a grudge against me for having a heart that still beat in my chest.

And I had no way of knowing how Orestes felt about Agamemnon's death. Was he devastated to have lost his beloved father or relieved that the cursed man was gone from the world forever?

"You should send a boy," Melissa said one day as we were loading the loom with fresh yarn, alone for a few brief moments. "Find out the mood in the city. The status of your brother."

"The status of my brother? He has to be king now. There's nobody else, no other sons to inherit."

"There's always somebody else," she said quietly, and my skin prickled.

We worked in silence for long minutes. Of course she was right. There was always somebody else. Some men were greedy for power. Some men would go to unthinkable lengths for the opportunity to rule over others.

After all, Agamemnon himself had gone to great lengths to gain the Mycenaean throne almost twenty-five years before. Everyone knew the story.

Agamemnon, exiled from his rightful home in Mycenae, returned with anger in his heart. He and his brother Menelaus came from exile in Sparta, a band of strong warriors at their backs. Together, they drove out the father and son who had usurped the throne—Thyestes and his son Aegisthus.

Thyestes they sent back into exile—nobody knows where—for the crime of eating the flesh of his own sons long before. Even if that crime had been committed unknowingly and only by the trickery of his own twin brother. That didn't matter to Agamemnon and Menelaus.

They kept their cousin, Aegisthus, close in Mycenae. And now, that very cousin Aegisthus lived in the palace and ruled alongside Mother. At thirteen, Orestes was extremely vulnerable. Did Mother have the power to keep him safe?

I took Melissa's advice and sent a boy to Mycenae.

The news that came back wasn't clear. Now that Agamemnon was dead, rumors spread that Orestes was coming home to claim his throne. But Agamemnon had been in his grave almost four months, and still Orestes hadn't arrived.

People whispered that Queen Clytemnestra was keeping her son away, forbidding him to return. She'd developed a taste for ruling in the years her husband was away, they said. She and her lover Aegisthus, having murdered the great king together, now ruled Mycenae as one and refused to give that power away, even to the queen's own son and the rightful heir.

The couple, people said, wanted to secure the throne for their own young son, Aletes.

Some said my brother was on his way but had been distracted by the allure of competing in the famous Athenian games, and so postponed claiming his throne in order to participate in a chariot race. Of course, I didn't know my brother's heart and mind, but this tale was difficult for me to believe.

Another rumor circulated too. This one spoke of old Thyestes, the very man whom Agamemnon had shoved off the Mycenaean throne, making his way back from his exile in the far reaches of the world. Nobody seemed to know where Thyestes had been living these twenty-five years, but many seemed confident that he was surely on his way to take the palace and stand behind his son Aegisthus.

I didn't know which of these versions to believe, if any.

"What of Elektra?" Melissa asked after I repeated all of this to her. "Have you heard news of your sister?"

"I've heard nothing," I said. Nobody cared about the lost daughters of the house of Atreus.

"What will you do? About your brother, I mean."

We worked in silence a long time. My hands fumbled as I tied weights to the twisted yarn, the only job anyone allowed me to do at the loom.

True, the tumult of this chaotic time would make the perfect opportunity for me to beg my brother to bring me back, but the risk was too high. What if Orestes received my message and still chose to leave me in Tauris? What if my brother didn't want me either?

Finally, I said, "I will do nothing."

CHAPTER 34

King Thoas sent a boy to fetch me on a summer evening in my thirteenth year in Tauris. A singer was in town, the boy said. A new one. A man we hadn't heard before, and he promised a sensational story.

I was at home, sitting in the slanted rays of the dying evening light, sewing delicate ivory beads onto my new ceremonial gown, and I wanted to stay and finish my work. But the boy said the king insisted.

I sighed, threw my shawl over my shoulders, and followed the messenger to the palace. My mind wandered back to the unfinished gown at home, and I resented the king more with each step I took.

I was tired of singers. They streamed through Tauris almost non-stop since the end of the war, and I was sick of hearing their tales. I was sick of hearing about the glory of the Greek warriors, their bravery and unequaled might. I was sick of hearing what splendid kings Agamemnon and Menelaus were, and what a horrendous wife Helen was, and Clytemnestra. I was sick of it all.

And if this singer was new, then he was probably young. The young ones were the worst. The details they inserted were always uninspired, and they made mistakes. Once, one of the young ones mistook Elektra for me, saying my sister went to the flames in Aulis and I stayed back in Mycenae, weeping endless tears.

I followed the boy into King Thoas's cramped throne room and sat on my cushion next to the throne. Thoas scowled at me but didn't meet my eye.

As it turned out, this singer wasn't one of the young ones. When he hobbled into the room, my breath caught in my throat. The man was older than Maia had ever been, with deep creases across his face and a hunched back. His stringy gray hair fell to his waist, and his long beard was patchy. Gnarled fingers gripped the arm of a man who escorted him to a plump blue cushion on a painted chair so we could all see him from our places on the floor.

Despite the years that had passed since the tragic events that sent me to this distant land, I recognized Kadmos at once. Our palace singer, who had skillfully woven the old stories into rich tapestries of song as we sat, wide eyed and statue still, listening to each word the man sang. He painted pictures in our minds that were so vivid, glorious images of heroes and gods danced in our imaginations, brought to life by this skilled bard.

Kadmos took a long time to settle his old bones, and the small crowd around me carried on with their murmured conversations as if the world hadn't just flipped upside down. I sat silent, my eyes fixed on this man to keep the room from spinning.

When he was finally as comfortable as he ever would be, he scanned the crowd. A thin blue film coated his left eye, but his right was still as bright and as brown as I remembered. And that eye settled on me for many heartbeats. He kept his face expressionless, but he recognized me. Even now that I was twenty-seven, he recognized the fourteen-year-old girl that I'd been the last time he'd seen me. I was sure of it.

A boy entered the room, weaving his way through the seated guests, carrying a lyre. My mouth went dry. Kadmos always sang in the old style. He never played an instrument. He needed no music to augment his voice like the younger singers did.

So, when he took the smooth, wooden lyre into his trembling hands, my eyes filled with hot tears. The lyre could mean only one thing.

He drew a shaking breath, and the room fell silent as death when he sang his first words. He sent the usual prayer to the Muses, of course, but he didn't aim his plea to just any of those powerful goddesses.

He shot directly at you, Melpomene.

The Muse of tragedy.

The words you planted on his tongue, Melpomene, were cruel. You forced him to sing of another royal death, a second murder in Mycenae. You urged him to spin a tale of a daughter and a son who, broken-hearted over the death of their father, dared to seek deadly vengeance. A sibling duo who sought justice by killing their father's killer. A pair who, together, spilled the blood of their own mother.

My own mother.

I wanted to feel nothing, to numb my mind and my heart. I wanted my pulse to slow and my face to cool, the sweat on my palms and my neck to evaporate. But the tears that rolled down Kadmos's cheeks made my own tears flow, and sobs escaped my throat.

Aëdon and Melissa led me from the throne room, and I fell limp in their arms. Helpless.

They took me to the queen's rooms and made me drink cool water, dabbing my face with a damp cloth.

My sobs died away with time, and I sat on a stool, staring at the dancing flames of a torch in the corner. I don't know how long I sat like that.

Finally, I said in a flat voice, speaking into the flames, "Bring him to me."

"Who?" Aëdon whispered.

"The singer."

"The singer? But a man can't come here!" Melissa didn't bother keeping her voice soft.

I stared into the flames as Aëdon hushed Melissa's protests. "Just send for him."

I listened to Melissa leave the room, mumbling incoherently under her breath. Aëdon fell still behind me, and together we waited.

When Kadmos shuffled into the room, fresh tears flowed from both of our eyes. He sat on a stool next to mine and squeezed my hands painfully in his bony fingers. I clung to him as if I were drowning.

When we spoke, we stared at our intertwined hands, mine white and soft, his brown and streaked with blue veins.

"Who sent you?" I finally managed, turning my head to wipe my eyes on my shoulder like a barbarian.

Aëdon brought the old man a cup of water and he drank deeply, as if trying to swallow down the tears in his voice. Finally, he said,

"Your sister."

I felt the blood drain from my face, and I gripped his hands tighter. "Elektra knows I'm here?"

"She must know, my child. She sent me away . . . afterward . . . and told me to go to the land of the Taurians, to the far north of the Euxine Sea. Your sister told me to sing a new song to the priestesses of Artemis there. Here."

We sat a long time, then. His grasp had loosened, but he still clasped my hands in his. As if he didn't want to let me go again.

Finally, I looked into his eyes—both the good one and the bad—and asked the most difficult question I've ever asked in my life: "Is it true?"

He waited a long time to answer, and I could barely breathe in the silence. Then he swallowed, his lips quivered, and he nodded his gray head once.

"How do you know? You weren't there, so how do you know?" My voice rose with panic.

"She confessed it herself. With her own voice, she stood before the elders and confessed. I was there on that dreadful day. I heard Elektra's terrible speech with my own old ears."

"Did my brother also confess?"

Kadmos finished his water and held his cup to Aëdon for more. "Orestes fled. He slipped out immediately after, probably with blood still staining his hands, and hasn't been heard from since. Most of the elders think that's as good as a true confession."

My shoulders slumped, and for a moment, I felt as if I would fall from my stool. But Kadmos gripped my hands. He wouldn't let me fall.

Even after hearing the words of honorable Kadmos, even with the obvious truth behind his story, I couldn't believe this terrible tragedy. I refused to believe my brother had killed our mother. I refused to believe my sister had killed our mother.

I refused to believe my mother was dead.

⌒⌒⌒

Aëdon had many questions after that. I sat, mute as my earliest days in Tauris, and allowed Melissa to tell my story. I let her carry on with her embellishments and didn't correct her little mistakes. She would have been a good bard.

I watched as Aëdon's face drained of all color, flushed a furious pink, then faded again to a deadly pale as my history spilled from Melissa's lips. She'd heard the stories from years of singers, but knowing that these horrors had happened to me seemed to have broken her heart. When she embraced me and refused to let go, I worried she might squeeze the breath from my lungs. But I squeezed back.

Kadmos stayed in Tauris four days. "Take me with you," I whispered one evening when I was sure no one else was close enough to hear. "Take me home."

When he looked at me, I saw pity etched in every line on his face. "I can't take you with me, my child. You know I can't do that."

"But Mycenae has no king. No queen." My voice faltered on this last word, but I swallowed and continued before Kadmos could protest. "The prince has disappeared. Elektra will forever carry the stain of our mother's blood on her hands . . . if the story is true.

I'm the only one. The only heir to the house of Atreus. Any man who marries me will become king of Mycenae and maybe even king of all Greece. And I can still have sons. I'm only twenty-seven. Chieftains from all over Greece will line up to marry me, and pay a steep price for the honor."

My words trailed off. Kadmos was smiling now, and shaking his head.

"What?" I was breathless with the thought of finally going home. But even in the half-heartbeat between my final words and Kadmos's first, I knew all I'd said was false. I didn't want to marry some chieftain, to bear him sons. I didn't want the ties that bind wives and mothers to their husbands and homes. I'd grown used to the small freedoms King Thoas and Lastratos granted me here in Tauris, and I wondered if I even wanted to return to Mycenae at all.

"That's a pretty story, my child. But it can never be. First of all, I'm an old man and swift travel is no longer part of my life. King Thoas's men would catch us with no effort at all. And as for the rest, I'm afraid it's already too late. Even by the time I left, there was talk of men gathering forces in the name of Aletes to take the throne. No man would marry you now that you're the daughter of the cursed house of Atreus. Nobody would even believe that you're who you say you are. Iphigenia."

My heart fluttered. This was the first time since my arrival in Tauris that someone had called me by my true name.

"There's nothing left for you there."

"What about Elektra? Even if she truly killed my mother, I still want to see her again."

"Your sister is lost. You'd do best to forget about her."

I tried a different angle. "If you can't take me with you, surely you can bring her here to me. Someone can. Nobody wants her now that she's committed matricide. Send her to me."

Kadmos sighed, then looked me in the eye, and I felt like a child again. "Iphigenia, I will not return to Mycenae. And I will not return here either." He took my scarred left hand into his, and when he looked at me, his eyes swam in unshed tears. "I am old, and I've sung my last song. I couldn't bear to sing another note."

Chapter 35

*T*he hot flames have already eaten the furniture, swallowed the
tapestries, devoured the wooden crossbeams. Now the fire is so
blazing hot, such an inferno, the plastered walls yield and crumble.

*I perch high above the flaring palace and I'm not sure how I can see so
well from such a great distance. I watch my home burn—the very palace
in which I was born, my father's palace and my great-grandfather's—until
nothing is left but one tall column engulfed in deathly flames.*

*Impossibly, a figure emerges, and I see that it is my own baby brother,
now grown into a strong young man. He walks, untouched, from the
yellow flames beneath the thick column. He emerges casually, as if there is
no blaze surrounding him, as if his hair and tunic don't stir in the heated
air. His eyes are on me, high above. I see that he recognizes me, though
he was no more than a small boy when I was whisked away from home.*

*My brother walks toward me, the burning flames following but not
touching. He leaves fiery footprints on the earth. He extends his hand to
me, his right hand. I reach out to him but we are so far apart, we can't
hope to touch.*

*I see that my fingertips are dripping with water as I stretch toward him.
No, not water. Tears.*

And just as he is about to step close enough for our fingertips to touch—mine wet with fatal tears, his glowing an otherworldly red—the flames behind him blaze as if he walks in a potter's furnace. The final standing column slowly begins to topple. The very moment that the column begins to stir, I see that it is no column at all, but instead it is an image of Apollo, the life-like paint still intact despite the licking flames. He is an image bigger than life, an idol that has stood in this palace for generations. He holds his terrible bow in one hand while his other reaches for an arrow slung across his back.

The image teeters for an impossibly long moment. I open my mouth to warn my brother, but my screams are swallowed by the roar of the inferno. When the monument crashes, Apollo falls directly on top of my brother, crushing his mortal body under the thick-painted wood.

I sat up in my bed. At first, my eyes saw only blinding flames, but slowly my vision cleared and I saw the flames were nothing more than cool, white moonlight.

I slid from my bed and tiptoed from the room. I stepped down the stairs and into the shadowy courtyard, breathing in the dewy night air. I allowed myself to be soothed by the sounds of Poseidon's waves gently kissing the beach below the cliffs, closing my eyes as the cool breeze dried my sweat-soaked hair.

But even now, in my newly calm mood, I knew that I'd seen the truth. I'd had no dream or nightmare. I'd had a vision.

Orestes was dead.

CHAPTER 36

The prisoners sat side by side, backs against the windowless wall. They weren't bound by ankle or wrist, and only one guard was set to watch over the single door.

There was no chance they'd try to run. They were Greek, honor-bound to meet their god-given fates with dignity and bravery.

I recognized their race right away, even if I couldn't place their exact tribe. But the two boys—yes, they were only boys—displayed their Greek blood for all to see, even if they didn't realize it themselves.

They were dressed in simple undyed tunics, clean and new. Their own clothes probably washed off their bodies as they struggled in the sea.

I didn't see any obvious wounds on their skin, which was a miracle in these shores. Their dark curls had dried by the time I entered the prisoners' room, their wispy adolescent beards barely noticeable shadows on their still-plump faces.

My heart lurched, either from excitement or dread or both. These boys were the first Greek prisoners I'd seen in all my days in Tauris.

King Thoas always let Greek castaways go free, even

commanding his locals to help repair their ships, to feed and clothe them before sending them on their way home.

Why had he decided to keep these two? And why had he sent me to them? Surely there was some mistake. Surely he didn't expect me to play any part in murdering my own kind.

The boys watched from under their lashes as I entered the small room, a smoking brazier in my hand. I stood before them, wearing my best tunic, and they pretended not to notice me.

It wasn't until I spoke, my Greek tongue clearly registering as native to their ears, that they both looked up. One of the boys, the one who was short and stout, started to rise to his feet, but the other pulled him back to the floor by his tunic.

"What are your names?" I asked.

The boy with the long legs and lean arms looked me in the eye. In the dancing light of the brazier, his eyes glimmered, giving him a mischievous look. But his words were flat, tinged with no humor.

"I am a cursed man, and this is my companion." He nodded toward his friend, and I kept a smile from showing on my face. This boy considered himself a man, did he? When he could be no more than sixteen or seventeen years old?

"Does this . . . cursed man . . . have a name? A house?"

The second boy opened his mouth to answer, but the first boy nudged him, his smooth brow wrinkling into a scowl.

The hint of a knot formed in my chest. Dark clouds stirred in my mind as some long-lost memory tried to surface. That boy's scowl, the way a double line formed between his eyebrows, the way his bright eyes dimmed to black pools, seemed vaguely familiar. Was that Melissa's scowl? Aëdon's?

I shook the thought from my mind. "If you won't tell me your names, how will I speak of you to Artemis?"

"Oh! I'm nothing but a cursed man," he repeated, his face softening, his gaze far off, as he cocked his head to one side. "Chased by the unrelenting Erynies, who allow me no rest!"

So, this boy was full of drama then. A fool for the absurd. A natural-born story-teller, maybe, speaking in the style of a poet.

A bad poet, it would seem.

"Tell me your story then. I'm listening." I looked back toward the door. The guard stood out of sight, but I knew he was there.

The boy bowed his head so low his chin rested on his skinny chest, and I could barely understand the words he muttered. "I am but a wretched pawn of the gods. Both manipulated and chased by them. I have no control over my own actions. The dreaded Fates have spun my thread, and I can do nothing to change their desires."

I waited for more, but he was silent. I had no time for theatrics. If he didn't want to tell me who he was, that would be for Artemis to worry about.

"What about you then?" I nudged the other boy's bare foot with my boot. "What's your name?"

"I'm Pylades." The boy seemed eager to talk. "Son of Strophios."

Strophios. The name sounded familiar, but no faces came to mind. Surely Strophios was common enough. Maybe some of the traders who'd come and gone over the years carried the name.

I allowed impatience to fill my voice when I asked, "Who's your friend?"

Pylades looked toward the other boy, who was now slumped in the corner and seemed to have fallen asleep.

"He's my cousin, Priestess. We were raised as brothers since we were babies in our nurses' arms."

The first boy's head snapped up, and Pylades and I both flinched. The flame from my brazier danced in his eyes and he moaned, "Nurse! My poor nurse!"

"Is your cousin mad?"

Pylades paused, watching the boy as if he might pounce. Then, eyes bright with unshed tears: "Priestess, I don't know! Please help us! I don't know what's happening!"

My heart plummeted. How was I now, after this desperate and innocent plea, supposed to tell these two boys that, with the full moon in five nights, their throats were to be opened, their dark blood spilled onto the earth, and their lifeless bodies tossed over the cliffs as if they were nothing more than animal offal?

I moved toward the door and poked my head out to speak to the guard. "Send a boy to fetch me a stool," I said.

I had a feeling I was going to be there a long time.

ᥨᥩᥨᥩ

I poured the boys each a cup of water before sitting on my stool. Pylades drank gratefully, but the other boy's cup sat untouched beside his foot.

"Tell me everything, Pylades, son of Strophios. Start from the beginning."

"No! Say nothing, cousin!"

"Are you so important then? Is your name so famous you fear recognition in these far reaches of the world?" I forced more irony into my voice than I felt.

"No. Not famous, but hunted." The boy raised his head and his shadowed eyes seemed to clear for a moment when he moaned, "Haunted."

Pylades placed a soothing hand on his cousin's arm, but the boy couldn't be calmed. He raised himself from the floor, and I prepared to dart toward the door. But he only shifted onto his knees on the hard-packed dirt.

He raised his eyes toward the beamed ceiling and began to wail. Pylades wrapped his arms around his cousin's shoulders and whispered into his ear. This went on for too long, and I sat on my stool wondering if I should just leave these boys to their fate.

Surely the people of Greece wouldn't miss a mad boy and his one companion. Surely my gods would forgive me this one time.

Just when I was about to stand and walk out of the prisoners' room, the boy's wails turned to wracking sobs. I strained to understand the words he was saying.

"Apollo. Apollo! Pity me, as no other god will do!"

My nightmare flashed in my memory then. The dreadful, fiery sight of Apollo's likeness crashing down on my brother's head, shattering the house of Atreus forever.

"Pity me, as you have never done before! First you lied to me, then you tricked me. I trusted you and followed your commands, only to be forced to flee my own home with Erinyes screaming in my ears, in my head, in my dreams!"

"Shhh. Quiet now." Pylades tried soothing his cousin, but the boy was beyond consolation.

"With your godly hand, you forced me to kill, a deed I could never have dreamed of without your guidance. And now, I'm brought to die at the hand of this poor priestess."

His words fluttered to a soundless gasp, and I must say I did pity him then. He was mad, true, but he was also terrified when he should have been brave. When he should have accepted his fate with dignity and honor, he was wailing and sputtering pleas to a god who wasn't listening.

He slumped against the wall once more, chest heaving and sweat dripping from his brow.

I stood then, impatient to leave these pitiful boys behind. Eager to erase my stubborn nightmare from my mind.

"In five nights, the two of you will be given to Artemis. Your blood will pour onto the earth to slake her thirst. Some men go to their fate with their heads held high, courage coursing through their veins. Others must be dragged to the altar, crying and screaming for their mothers. Which will you be?"

Pylades swallowed, his throat bobbing under his wispy beard. "I'll be brave, Priestess. I will die with honor."

"And your cousin?" I nodded my head toward the sobbing boy in the corner.

"He'll be brave, too, Priestess. In the end, he'll do what will bring honor to his father's shade."

"I want to give you both the easiest death I can, Pylades. I won't hold the knife, but I do have the king's ear. If I tell him to be swift because you're Greek, he'll do it for my sake."

Pylades nodded, his eyes dull with fear. I felt a tenderness for him, for the weight that rested on his shoulders—the weight of his own fate along with that of his cousin's.

I sighed and sat on my stool once again.

"I'll ask once more, Pylades. What has happened? Tell me the entire story." I eyed the hunched boy. "I won't ask again."

"The entire story?"

I nodded.

The boy in the corner didn't stir. Pylades reached across him and grabbed his cousin's cup of water, downing it in two loud gulps.

Wiping droplets from his beard, he began.

"Like I said, we were raised as brothers since we were tiny babies. He was sent to us when his father was away at Troy, bravely fighting—"

"Skip the theatrics," I interrupted. "Almost every man fought at Troy. Just give me the details. I don't need to know who's brave and who's treacherous and who's the most beautiful and who's the strongest." I was so very sick of these things, these things that didn't matter. Had never mattered.

"Of course, Priestess." Pylades began fidgeting with the cup in his hands, tracing his finger over a hairline crack. "His father was at war, so his mother sent him to my father to raise him."

This was nothing unusual. Arrangements like this were made across the land and across generations.

"Why was your father not fighting at Troy then?"

"He was old when the war started. And he had a long-healed injury in his left leg that grieved him until the day he died. He would have been no good on the battlefield, Priestess."

"But he could have been a general," I said. Everyone knows generals do very little fighting. Why fight when you have hundreds of men who will do it for you?

"No, Priestess. He wasn't strong enough even to lead other men. His health was failing." He cleared his throat. This wasn't the entire truth, but these details didn't matter. He continued, "So we were like brothers."

"Yes, you said that already."

"Oh, sorry. We were happy. My father held lands all around, so we didn't have to work much ourselves. So, the two of us were trained to fight. My father hired the best instructor he could find—which was hard to do since all the fighters were at Troy, defending the—"

I must have scowled because he bit off the words of praise that were about to flow from his lips.

"And then, when we were about thirteen years old, the news came that the war was over. The honorable Greeks had finally beaten the . . . Oh, sorry. After the war ended, men started to straggle back home. We had a grand festival once we were sure everyone had made it back home . . . everyone that was going to be coming home, that is. My father had sent four ships with two hundred men to set sail from Aulis to Troy."

A shiver ran down my spine at the very name *Aulis*.

"But only half returned. Maybe even less." He paused, throwing a glance at his cousin. "I'm not sure how long it took, but after a while, a messenger came. He was a royal messenger from Mycenae, so we knew he had big news for us."

"Mycenae?" I tensed at the name.

Pylades didn't seem to notice. "Yes. My father let us stay in the room when the messenger delivered his news, but I'm sure he regretted it right away."

The boy in the corner moaned, but he didn't stir. Pylades glanced at him nervously and paused so long I worried that he might not finish his story.

"Well? What was the message?" I squeezed my hands into fists under my mantle. An impossible idea kept surfacing in my mind, and I shoved it away again and again as the boy told his tale.

Pylades sighed. "The messenger said my mother's brother was dead."

The boy moaned again, this time a long, drawn-out sob that teetered on the edge of a cry. Pylades's eyes glistened with tears.

"Were the two of you fond of your uncle? Did you know him well?"

"Did we know him?" Pylades seemed genuinely confused by my question. "Of course not! I mean, no, we didn't know him, Priestess. I'd never met the man, and he," he nodded toward his cousin, "well, he couldn't remember a man he'd only met when he was just a little boy in his nurse's arms."

A twinge ran through my stomach. The insistent idea had become impossible to ignore.

"What's your cousin's name?" I asked before I could think twice.

But Pylades seemed not to hear my question. He continued his story, his words rushed now, as if speaking them faster might make them disappear. "My uncle was dead, but that's not all. He was murdered. By his wife and his cousin. In his bathtub . . ."

I held my face as neutral as I could, willing my heart to remain calm, but my pulse throbbed in my ears and I didn't hear the rest of Pylades's words.

The boy in the corner sobbed uncontrollably now.

The boy in the corner.

I knew the truth in my heart, but my mind refused to believe.

"Just tell me his name!" The words flew from my lips before I could stop them.

Pylades glanced at me, surprise on his face, and then back to the boy in the corner. "Orestes. His name is Orestes, Priestess."

My jaw clenched, and I took a deep breath. My voice came out flat this time, even and toneless. "But Orestes is dead."

Pylades looked confused again, and I began to think this was a common look for him. "Dead? Why would you think he's dead?"

My dream had been no prophecy. It had been a lie, sent by some god to sow doubt in my tormented mind.

I swallowed. "Singers," I lied. "Bards have come with songs of Orestes's death on their lips. They sing of the cursed house of Atreus."

"Songs and lies," Orestes muttered, still unmoving. "Lies and songs."

We stared at the form in the corner. Pylades seemed to pity Orestes. But as I sat on my stool, staring at the brother I hadn't seen since he was a toddler, my heart slowly hardened, a thick and bitter crust that smothered any warmth I might have felt on seeing my own blood for the first time in fourteen years.

When I looked at him now, I saw nothing more than the boy who had killed my mother.

Silently, I stood and walked through the door, leaving the pitiful scene behind me. When I'd stepped outside into the night air, I spit on the ground beside my left foot.

Chapter 37

I visited the boys immediately after breakfast the next morning. There was no point in waiting. Better to get the job done and carry on with my day.

They'd been tied during the night so the guard's job would be easier, but by the time I arrived, their bonds had already been removed.

They sat on the floor in the same spots as the night before, but Orestes was alert now, no longer slumped in a heap in the corner. Hatred slithered through my veins when I saw that he was sharp and clear-eyed. Had he been this sane, this wakeful, this *present* when he schemed to kill our mother? When he held the blade in his steady right hand? When he stabbed and slashed and sliced? Had his mind been as calm as it seemed now when he stepped in our mother's warm blood, leaving a trail of foul red footprints as he fled her rooms?

For a flash, I thought I saw the Erinyes, dark shadows hovering in the vile stillness of the prison. I stood in the doorway, not daring to enter a space filled with such black horrors as those that hung over Orestes's head.

They both looked at me as if startled to see me there. As if they hadn't heard me approach, speak to the guard, and step through the doorway.

Pylades stood—his mother had taught him manners—but Orestes didn't move a muscle.

"In four nights, the two of you will give your lives to deathless Artemis, the divine huntress." My voice punctured the silent room, and Pylades flinched. "You will walk bravely to the altar and you will die with honor."

This was more than Orestes deserved, but I couldn't say as much. I looked at Pylades. "I will send a message to your mother so she can pour your funeral urn and put your shade to rest. Do you understand?"

Pylades nodded, keeping his eyes on the floor at my feet.

"But this won't work." Orestes still sat in his corner, but he looked directly at me.

"It's not for you to decide. The gods don't honor the wishes of men who kill their mothers." The words tasted bitter on my lips, sounded sharp in my ears, bit deep into my heart.

"No, Priestess, it's not for me to decide. You're right about that. But you're wrong about the gods. There's one god who, mercifully, has heard my desperate pleas and has taken pity on me. Apollo has shown me kindness. He's made a request of me, and in return for fulfilling his request, he will free me from the hateful Erinyes who poison my mind."

I wanted to laugh at this delusional boy's fantasies, this quest he imagined Apollo charged him with. This mythical errand that sounded an awful lot like the ancient stories nurses tell children at night. "I will come to you the morning before the full moon and prepare you for your meeting with Artemis—"

"But you can't ignore Apollo's demand," Orestes interrupted.

I clenched my jaw, took three deep breaths. "Apollo has no home here in these lands. But Artemis does, and she wishes to see your blood flow."

Pylades gasped, whether from my blasphemy toward Apollo or from my cold announcement of his coming death, I wasn't sure.

"But Apollo's demand is for the benefit of Artemis, his twin sister. It will benefit her for generations to come, not just one night of feasting on blood-soaked flames."

"I don't care what your god says—"

He interrupted again, and heat rose up my throat and into my face with the disrespect of it. "He has commanded me to come and retrieve his godly sister's likeness. The very idol that these barbarians stole decades ago when they took her from her beloved homeland and forced her to dwell here, among strangers in this foreign land all these long years. Apollo wants me to take Artemis home."

"I told you; Apollo's wishes mean nothing here." I spun on my heel and stepped toward the door.

"You're Greek." My feet froze. Orestes's words were nothing more than fact, but I sensed more meaning behind his simple statement. "I know by your words, your way of speaking with your hands as well as your voice. And a Greek is bound by the gods to help another Greek in peril, especially in a foreign land. Surely, you would never allow a fellow Greek to perish in this horrible place. Surely you would help if you could."

Behind me, I heard him stand, his young body rising from the floor with the ease of youthful joints. I wanted to call for the guard, but my lips remained sealed and my feet remained stuck in their spots on the ground. I turned toward him and he stood before me, his black curls nearly touching the ceiling beams, his hands spread toward me in a gesture of supplication.

He was tall, as Agamemnon had been. But where our father had been soft in the belly and arms, Orestes was lean and wiry. Where our father's face had sagged and jiggled, my brother's beamed with the freshness of youth, even within these prison walls. He carried our mother's straight nose, and as he moved into the light cast through the doorway, I saw his eyes clearly for the first time.

Mother's eyes. My eyes.

Ours were the darkest amber, peppered with specks of emerald and bronze and golden honey. Our eyes were unmistakable.

And in that heartbeat, I saw that Orestes noticed too.

He took my hand in both of his, and I instinctively tried to pull free of his grasp. But he held tight and stared at me for too long.

"Who are you?" he finally asked, letting my hand drop.

I swallowed. "I'm the one who will bring you to your fate."

Once again, I turned on my heel and this time I walked out. I didn't stop walking until I'd reached my *erêmia*, Heliko trailing silently behind.

CHAPTER 38

Y ou're quiet today, Iphianassa," Aëdon said as we meandered through the orchard the next morning, the sweet perfume of nearly ripe apples enveloping us.

Melissa walked between Aëdon and me, our linked arms creating an unbreakable chain of grown women.

"She's thinking of the prisoners," Melissa said with certainty.

Low gray clouds threatened an autumn rain, and I squeezed my mantle to my throat with my free hand. The children ran ahead, their nurses hustling behind them, muttering warnings that went ignored.

At thirteen, Aëdon's eldest son had left the protection of his nurse and was now under the instruction of his father, but her four younger children—three more sons and a cherished little daughter—squealed and giggled as they ran through the heavy-limbed trees.

I kept my protective eye on Princess Rhanis, as if her mother and nurse weren't doing the same. She was Melissa's first child, a plump three-year-old and a mirror image of her mother.

Melissa's infant son, whom King Thoas had insisted on naming after himself, slept in his nurse's arms, and so the three of us were at peace to wander and chat uninterrupted for the first time in a long time.

"It's difficult, I'm sure, to condemn men of our own race to the brutal whims of Artemis," Aëdon said. "It must weigh heavy on your mind."

"It always weighs heavy on my mind, even when they aren't Greek." My words sounded harsh on the breeze, and Aëdon didn't respond.

Melissa filled the silence that followed. "We'll give them the draught first, as we've done for years now. We'll make them as carefree as we can."

I pulled my arm from Melissa's and turned to walk back the way we'd come. Footsteps followed behind me.

"Where are you going? What's wrong?" Melissa was beside me, trying to link my arm with hers again. I pulled away and spun to pace the other direction again. My two friends watched as I paced back and forth between two rows of trees.

"Surely this can't be about the two castaways," Aëdon said, more to Melissa than to me. "Yes, it's shocking, but nothing truly new."

I froze. "They're not just any Greeks," I started, my voice barely more than a whisper. The children and their nurses were distant now, but like slaves, nurses seem to have powerful ears.

When I took too long to continue, Melissa asked, "Who are they?"

I took another lap between the trees, back and forth again, twisting the bronze bracelet around my wrist until my skin felt raw.

Dropping my hands, I stopped in my tracks, hoping stillness in my body might translate to stillness in my mind. I inhaled three times, blowing the breath from my lungs slowly each time, as Ismene had taught me when I was little.

"One of the prisoners is my brother." My voice sounded small and shaky, and not like my voice at all.

A breathless silence. Sparrows in the trees above our heads sounded as if they were leagues away; the children's laughter might have been on a distant island. The breeze seemed to die, and Helios may have halted his fiery trek across the clouded sky.

Melissa broke the silence with a terrible whisper. "Orestes."

"Are you sure?" Aëdon took my hand in hers.

I swallowed. "Yes."

I told them of the boy's mission to take the idol of Artemis back to Athens, of his belief that Apollo sent him on this mission, and how he believed the god was on his side. I wanted to tell them about the Erinyes, how he truly thought they were haunting him day and night. I wanted to tell them he was a madman. But those words wouldn't come.

"What do you mean to do?"

I bit the insides of my cheeks to keep the tears out of my voice. "I can't help but think . . ." I cleared my throat and started again. "I can't help but think he might finally be my key out of this place."

Aëdon flinched as if I'd slapped her across the face, and Melissa squeezed her eyes tight.

Out of this place.

Why had I said that? Why had I chosen words that turned Tauris into an evil, barbaric land when this was the land of Melissa and Aëdon?

"Hallanis!" Aëdon called for her children's nurse. "Hallanis! Bring the children home."

She pulled her mantle over her head and turned her blue eyes on me. "There's nothing left for you in Mycenae." Then she whirled and led her children away.

Melissa gathered her children then, taking the infant Thoas into her arms, kissing his fair hair. We walked back to town in silence, Melissa alongside the children's two nurses. I trailed behind, eyes focused on the rocky ground at my feet.

How could Aëdon say there was nothing left for me in Mycenae? Of course that wasn't true! I tried to imagine Elektra as she might look today, at twenty-two years old, as I'd done so many times before. In my mind, she always looked much like Mother, but with dark eyes instead of hazel. I saw a wealth of shining black curls and high cheekbones and smiling lips.

But today, her features seemed hazy, blurred at the edges, muted. Today I realized I truly had no way of knowing what my sister looked like after fourteen long years. After all she'd been through.

After killing our mother.

Bile rose in my throat and I swallowed it down.

Kadmos said she was a confessed matricide, having admitted her role before the elders. But were there not many reasons to give false confessions?

The singers told different stories of Elektra's role in our mother's murder. Some said she convinced our brother to hold the knife, others said she'd done it herself. And there were even a few who sang that Elektra was falsely accused, that she carried the blame for Orestes's crime so he might rise to the throne unimpeded.

I knew I'd never ask Orestes. Who could trust the tales of a madman? The only way I'd ever learn the truth—the only choice I had—was to ask Elektra herself. To judge the truth of her confession in my heart.

Melissa's voice broke through my thoughts, and I realized we'd reached the edge of town. "Stay with me tonight." It wasn't an invitation. It wasn't a question. It was a command.

That evening, as purple dusk painted the low horizon, Heliko walked with me to the palace. This wasn't the first time I'd spent a night with Melissa now that she was queen. We'd shared a maiden room for so many years before she married, and we both found comfort in the familiarity of one another's sleeping breaths on the other side of the room.

Now, we lay side by side in her wide bed, listening to the palace noises dwindle into midnight silence. When insect-song had become the only sound, Melissa took my hand in hers, and then she whispered, "The key is in the idol."

"What?" I wasn't sure I'd heard her correctly.

"To go home to your sister. The idol of Artemis is the key."

And we whispered into the dark night, unmoving, eyes fixed on the black ceiling above our heads until we each fell off to sleep. First Melissa and then me.

෴෴෴

We both woke before daybreak, and I crept home in the shadows. Heliko helped me dress in one of my newer tunics and my blue mantle. I wore no jewelry and covered my pinned hair with a scarf of colorless linen. I wanted to look well, but not formal. Subtlety was going to be my friend for the next couple of hours.

Heliko followed me back to the palace, speaking only to comment on the oranges and pinks of the blazing sunrise.

The palace gates were already open for the day, as I knew they would be, and the two of us marched into the atrium as if we belonged there.

Theano's husband, Eumedes, greeted me with a smile just outside the closed door to the throne room. "Priestesses. What brings you to the palace at this early hour?"

I raised my chin and drew my eyebrows together into a scowl my face wasn't accustomed to, hoping I wasn't overdoing it. "I need to speak with the king. Right away. It's very important."

Surprise flitted across Eumedes's face, but he erased it as quickly as it had appeared. "Of course, Priestess. Please wait here."

Heliko melted into the shadows, joining other slaves who were meant to be available, but not seen. Eumedes opened the door and stood aside. "The king will see you, Priestess."

King Thoas sat on his throne, dressed for the day in his ridiculous black robes, looking as if he'd been awake for hours already. Faint blue light crept in through the high windows, but it wasn't enough to dispel the morning gloom. Tall tripod lamps burned their stale oil in each of the four corners of the smoke-thickened room, and my eyes burned.

My bow wasn't much more than a shallow, quick bob of my knees and head. I wouldn't prostrate myself at his feet on this day.

"What brings you here at such an hour?" He didn't bother to mask his irritation.

"What in the name of the gods were you thinking?" I held my

breath, hoping I hadn't started too boldly.

He tilted his head to one side, genuinely surprised. I saw no trace of anger. "What are you talking about?"

I started pacing the throne room, my hurried footsteps echoing off the plastered walls. "How could you put us all in so much danger? Did you not know one of your prisoners is a matricide? He killed his mother with his own hands and now his dark pollution stains the lands of Tauris!"

King Thoas actually flinched, blinking several times. "I don't understand," he muttered, keeping his voice low.

But I didn't bother keeping my voice low. I needed his aides and slaves and guards to hear this. "Artemis came to me in a dream last night. She's furious, as she should be! This cursed creature has polluted her sacred temple, her chosen land."

"But I didn't know this prisoner was a matricide. How was I supposed to know that?"

I softened my stance, lowered my voice a fraction. "Of course not, King. You had no way of knowing then, but now you do. Artemis wants to forgive you. She told me in my dream. She doesn't want to harm you or her loyal Taurians."

The king grasped his staff in his right hand, his knuckles whitening. "What can we do to keep her happy?" His nasally voice rose an octave.

"We must honor her with a feast. She demands fifteen sheep and fifteen cows tomorrow night. The night of the full moon. But before we do that, she has a more important command."

I paused. The king tried not to squirm in his seat, whether from nervousness at angering his favorite goddess, or because of the enormity of preparing thirty animals for sacrifice in less than two days' time.

"Well?" I had a feeling I had only a few moments left before he would bolt from his chair and start shouting commands to make these arrangements. "What else, then? What does she want before this impossible feast?"

I stood tall and looked the king in the eye. "She insists the two prisoners—both the killer and his knowing companion—be sacrificed with great ceremony. She demands their stained bodies be wrapped in black cloth and thrown over the cliffs to the east, with none but the men who perform the act knowing where their corpses lie. She wants the entire area purified with her sacred herbs and her priestesses to sing until the deed is done." I wanted to look away from his blazing blue eyes, but I forced myself to keep my gaze steady.

He started to stand. "There's more, King," I said, and he sat down with a huff. "She wants her idol covered and taken away during the ceremony, to a secret and safe place. She does not want to risk the black miasma polluting her own likeness."

I nodded my head toward the statue standing innocently in her little nook to the king's right.

He shook his head and let out a sharp laugh. "The goddess's demands are immense," he said. "How am I, one humble man, to accomplish all of these commands before nightfall tomorrow? It's impossible."

What a predictable man he was.

"Of course, King. I will help you, naturally. And so will my priestesses. We will all work to rid this land of these two cursed men. We will remove the idol and hide her in a safe place, away from the evil that hangs around us now."

I held my breath.

He stilled on his chair, no longer squirming. Then he nodded, one quick bow of the head, and stood abruptly. "Eumedes!"

Eumedes opened the door almost immediately and, by the look on his face, I was sure he'd heard every word.

"Get my men. I want you and all my advisers here immediately. We have a feast to plan."

His eyes met mine then, and he nodded toward the door. My time was up.

CHAPTER 39

I didn't think you'd come." I stepped into the cool dimness of my *erêmia*. The stone walls seeped their perpetual tears, and for the first time I wondered if the cave's tears held the same saltiness as mine.

Aëdon sat on the rock in the middle, head bowed, hands motionless in her lap. In the morning, I'd sent Heliko to arrange this meeting at mid-day, and I truly expected to find the cave empty when I arrived.

"Thank you," I said when Aëdon didn't respond.

She looked at me then. This time of day, the light inside the space was a misted gray that had a way of softening edges and blunting points. In this light, she looked pale and delicate, almost frail. I wanted to reach out to her, to hold her, to pass along some of the strength that coursed through my veins since Melissa and I hatched our midnight plans.

But in her blanched face, her sapphire eyes shot me a bitter glare, and frosty fingers ran up my spine.

I wanted to run to the safety of my home, to ignore my friend's uncharacteristic coldness, to will it to disappear. But I forced myself to stand in the cave opening—this was my *erêmia*, my safety, my solitude. I inhaled the damp air and blew it out in a slow stream.

"I'm sorry—" I started.

Aëdon interrupted me, but I couldn't understand her mumbled words. "What?"

She stood, then. Her head only came to my nose, but in that moment, her body seemed to fill the space from wall to wall, from sandy floor to stone ceiling. I took a step backward.

Those icy eyes were frozen through, now, and I squeezed my fingernails into my palms to keep myself still.

"I said, *how dare you?*" Her voice shook at first, but as she continued, her words rose into a steady shout. "How can you even think of leaving?"

"Aëdon—"

"There's nothing for you in Mycenae. You know that."

Heat flowed through my body, and my voice rose to match Aëdon's shouts. "My sister is in Mycenae!"

"Your sister!" She laughed then, a single, humorless syllable. "Your sister who's never sent for you? Who's never come for you in all these years? Who only sent a singer to spread awful news when she should have come herself?"

A lump formed in my throat, and I swallowed hard. "She couldn't come for me any more than I could go back to her. We were both held against our wills."

Another of those ugly laughs that sounded so foreign coming from my sweet friend. "And what about after—"

"Don't say it."

My voice was a whisper now, and she finished her question with matching whispers. "After she killed your mother?"

I dropped my head into my hands.

"Where was your sister then? Why didn't she escape with Orestes? She could be here even now. She could be sitting right here in your precious little cave instead of me."

"I'm sure there's a good reason." I spoke into my hands that still shielded my face.

"I'm sure there isn't."

Her voice was rising again, and I dropped my hands, stepping toward her. "She needs me. She always needed me."

Then Aëdon sat back down on the damp rock, the color that had risen in her cheeks drained. Her shoulders slumped, and she gazed into the sand as she spoke her next words. "*We* need you. Melissa, me, our daughters. My mother."

Theano. She was old now, and a hard ball had grown in her belly over the past year. She could eat nothing solid, and her diet of broth and water had left her thin, weak, and confused.

Guilt wedged itself in my chest, and I tried to ignore its weight. "Melissa will lead the prayers when Artemis calls your mother."

"It's not about prayers or about Artemis. We need *you*."

I sighed and sat down next to Aëdon. The rock was barely large enough for the two of us, and my shoulder brushed hers when I sat. She pulled away, slid further from me.

"I do want to stay, Aëdon. I do." Tears burned the backs of my eyes, but I refused to allow them to fall. "I love you and Melissa and your mother. I love your children and Lastratos and Nikandros. You've all been like my family here in Tauris."

A sob squeaked from Aëdon's throat and she stood, looking down at me. "But?" she demanded.

"But I'm a princess, not a priestess. Yes, my mother is dead, but my sister still lives. And she needs my help to take our rightful home. If I marry well, I will be queen and my son will become king of Mycenae the moment he draws his first breath. Elektra and I will live our days in the security and happiness we, as princesses, are owed."

Muse, I assure you, as these words spilled from my mouth, I truly believed them. I told no lies on that day, neither to Aëdon nor to myself.

But Aëdon knew me for the foolish girl I could still be, even after fourteen years in Tauris. And she stepped toward the opening of my *erêmia*, then stepped out of it, then walked away without one look back, where I still sat on the cold, damp rock between the weeping walls.

CHAPTER 40

My eyes took a moment to adjust to the dim light of the prison. What little light crept through the door couldn't dispel the gloom from the edges of the room.

Both boys rose to their feet, and it was Orestes who greeted me. "Priestess. I thought you wouldn't come see us again until tomorrow morning, to give us our rites and prepare us to meet Artemis. Do I have my days wrong?" He seemed as clear-headed as he'd been the day before.

I'd left Heliko outside to distract the guard with gossip, and I paused to listen. She was doing her job nicely.

"Change of plans." I allowed impatience to color my voice. "And keep your voice down."

Orestes's confusion only seemed to grow, but Pylades's face lit up.

"Has the king changed his mind then?" His voice was high with excitement and his round eyes glowed in the dim light.

"No. Not exactly."

My cousin's shoulders sank, and I felt sorry for him. He seemed like an honest boy.

"But I have. I've changed my mind."

The two of them stared at me with brows drawn together, eyes narrowed.

"Before I spell your new fate, I have something to explain." I'd carried a stool in with me and I set it on the floor. I gestured for the boys to sit on the floor once again.

I looked at my brother, whose eyes were shadowed from this angle, and I regretted having him sit in that spot where I couldn't monitor his shifting moods.

"We don't have time for drama, so I'll get straight to the point," I said into those shadowy eyes. "I'm your sister."

Pylades shifted and opened his mouth to speak.

But I held up my hand and continued. "I'm your eldest sister. Iphigenia."

"But Iphigenia's dead!" Pylades squeaked.

I sighed. "This is no shade seated before you. I'm truly here."

When Orestes spoke, his voice remained clear, and I was grateful. "My father killed my sister with his own hand, before hundreds of men who saw the terrible thing happen. I've heard the story my entire life."

"Father . . ." I swallowed. This was the first time in years I'd referred to Agamemnon as my father, and the word felt oily on my tongue. "When Father's knife slashed down, it met the flesh of a bleating deer instead of the flesh of his eldest daughter. Our goddess filled his eyes with smoke, charmed his vision so he thought he saw my white throat instead of the pale throat of a deer."

My own heartbeat should have swallowed the silence that followed, should have filled my ears and drowned out the chirping birds and the gossiping Heliko outside the prison. But on this day, my heart pulsed calmly and silently in my chest, no sweat coated my palms, and my face remained neutral with no effort at all.

Orestes sat still as stone in his corner, and I worried he'd fallen into that same moaning, muttering, senseless state. Pylades whispered, "Tell us something only Iphigenia would know."

I thought for a moment. If Elektra sat before me instead of Orestes, I could speak a hundred memories she and I shared during our early years together. But for this boy, who was only three years old when I left Mycenae forever, there were no memories to share.

So, I began with our ancestry.

"Tyndareus was our mother's father, and our father's father was Atreus." I turned my gaze to Pylades then. "Your mother, Anaxibia, was my father's sister. You and I are cousins, though we've never met before."

I paused, and in the quiet seconds that passed, a sea bird squalled and a man shouted an unintelligible command from the distant shore.

Pylades's voice cracked when he spoke his next words. "You're right, Priestess. But many people know the ancestry of the cursed—" He cleared his throat. "I mean the royal family of Mycenae. Tell us something only Iphigenia would know."

I didn't know how long Orestes had been in Mycenae after his return from Phocis. Had he been there hours, days, weeks before deciding to murder our mother? How much time would he have had to explore the palace before embarking on the cursed journey that landed him here on these deadly shores?

"When you returned home from your childhood away, did you meet our sister? Did you spend time with Elektra?"

Orestes moaned, an ominous sound from deep in his chest, and I knew the madman had reappeared. When he spoke, his words came out as a croak. "Don't speak of that woman."

My breath caught. *That woman.* My beloved little sister was not—could never be—*that woman.*

I shoved away the dark thoughts that threatened to flood my mind and forced my voice into steadiness. "When you were home, did you see the tapestry of the golden lamb? The one that told the story of the fight between Atreus and Thyestes over the poor creature? When I left, it was hanging in the room I shared with . . . It was hanging in my maiden room. On the east wall, beneath the window."

Orestes leaned toward me, a tiny movement that would have been easy to miss. His fisted hands relaxed, and for a heartbeat, I wasn't sure if he wanted to jump up and embrace me or to slap my face with curses on his tongue. Instead, he sat before me in the dim prisoner's room and said in a monotone, "Go on."

"Does it still hang in my room, or has Mother moved it?"

His hands bunched into fists again, so I continued softly. "I made that tapestry when I was very young." I let a breath of a laugh escape my lips. "What clumsy work it was."

Orestes raised his chin, a silent agreement.

"Did you also see the tapestry of Helios changing his course? To deny Thyestes the Mycenaean throne, and instead grant it to Atreus?"

He nodded.

"I made that one too." I didn't mention that Elektra had helped, weaving the yellow threads into the blue wool with her chubby little fingers. "Does it still hang in the Queen's chamber?"

Orestes remained silent as the grave.

Pylades spoke when Orestes didn't. "We've seen these tapestries, Priestess. When we both came to Mycenae, we inspected every room of the palace, from the underground stores to the royal apartments. I remember these two tapestries, among others, of course."

Orestes cocked his head to one side, a gesture I was becoming familiar with, and the flesh at the nape of my neck prickled.

"I believe you, sister." His voice was flat, dead. I don't know what I was expecting, but it wasn't this blank-eyed stare from a side-cocked head and toneless words spilling from an unsmiling mouth.

Icy fingers ran down my spine. Was this figure the last that appeared before Mother's eyes? Was this demon-possessed face the final image she saw before her beautiful eyes closed forever?

Again, Pylades broke the silence, as if he was used to his role as mediator between his mad cousin and the rest of the world.

"It's good to see you, cousin." The words were bland enough, but somehow they brought my brother out of his spell.

Still crouched in the corner, Orestes raised his face toward me. His features crumpled into a frown, and for a moment, I saw the little boy I'd known in Mycenae, whose broad brow wrinkled into that very frown when he didn't get what he wanted.

Tears flowed down his cheeks now, into his short beard. His body heaved with sobs that rose to wails. He scrambled to his feet and stepped toward me, arms held wide as if to embrace me. His cries were almost unintelligible, but I think he said, over and over again, "For you! It was all for you!"

I stood abruptly, knocking the stool onto its side. Stepping backward, I forced myself not to lurch toward the door. I didn't want him to see the disgust that filled my heart.

"Please, brother," I started. "You must not touch the sacred robes of our great goddess."

His arms dropped slowly to his side, and his face drooped into sad lines, his cries fading into silence.

The guard popped his head through the doorway, and my heart froze in my breast. "Do you need help, Priestess?" His face was so close to mine I could smell his breath. He'd had fish for breakfast.

"The prisoner was confused for a moment, but I think he understands better now."

Pylades stood and rested his hand on Orestes's shoulder. Light returned to my brother's eyes, our cousin's touch acting as a soothing balm.

"I'm sorry, Priestess. In this light, you looked much like someone I once knew. But now I see I was mistaken."

I glanced at the guard. "I won't be long."

He hesitated, then stepped back outside, and I heard Heliko pick up the thread of a story where she'd left off.

I looked back to my brother and my cousin, standing in the dim room before me. I moved toward them and something in my face forced them to take a step backward. So, I stepped closer still, and again they both retreated.

When the two boys were backed into the dark corner, I spoke. My voice was so low, they had to lean forward to hear me. "I will get you both out of here alive, and I will let you take Artemis's sacred statue. But you must do exactly as I say."

Orestes's eyes glowed. "Give us weapons! We will fight with all our strength and honor!" His whispered vow sounded so childish, so ignorant.

Of course he'd want to fight. It's what every Greek boy was raised to do, from farmers to fisherman to craftsmen to princes. They were all trained from the moment they took their first tottering steps. They were given toy weapons to play with. Their bravery was praised with every swipe of the wooden sword, every jab of the blunted dagger. Our Greek boys were taught from the beginning that the best way—the only honorable way—out of a dangerous situation was to draw blood.

I bit my tongue to keep vile words from spilling from my lips.

"No fighting. If you fight, we all lose. You will both die and I'll be stuck here for the rest of my life." I looked at each of them, and they both shifted their eyes from mine. "Do you understand?"

Orestes nodded and Pylades muttered an almost imperceptible *Yes*.

They were clearly terrified of me now. Whatever they saw in my eyes, in my face, in my stance scared them more than the Erinyes or Apollo or Artemis ever could.

∾∾∾

By the slanted late afternoon light, Heliko helped me dress. I chose to wear my ceremonial gown. I'd rather have worn a simple tunic and mantle for travel, since I had a long journey ahead of me. But that would have raised questions.

350

Butterfly wings flitted in my stomach each time the thought of returning home crept into my mind. But I forced those thoughts away. I needed to focus on the false ceremony I was supposed to perform, and I must keep my mind clear of any distractions. I couldn't risk discovery. Not when escape back to Mycenae was finally within my reach after these fourteen long years.

Heliko pinned my golden brooch beneath my breasts, clasping my blue gown so that I was exposed, in the old way. This was to be a solemn ceremony, of course. A ceremony meant to appease an angry goddess, to rid her favored land of the miasma of matricide. And ceremonies of this kind required full preparations.

I slid the two golden snake armlets onto my arms, above the elbows, where their onyx eyes would gaze out to observe the processions and the prayers.

Would they report to Artemis, whispering in her ears the songs we sang in her honor? Would they read the plans that rested in my heart? Would Artemis approve of my leaving Tauris, at last returning to Mycenae, to the home she'd torn me from herself?

I belted my rich mantle over my gown, pinning it close to my throat. I would remove my mantle when I stood before the sacred idol of Artemis, displaying to her the richness of my gown and jewels that I wore in her honor.

Heliko arranged my long braids down my back and tucked some stray strands that had already fallen from their pins on the top of my head. She stepped back to look at me, and for half a heartbeat, I thought I saw sadness in her eyes. She wasn't supposed to know of my plans, so why would she be sad? But slaves had a way of understanding everything, even the things that lay hidden in our hearts.

Hints of purple touched the sky outside my open window. It was time.

I walked the sunset streets toward the palace, Heliko trailing behind me. A subdued air hung above our heads, and the few people who hadn't yet joined the crowd on the Heights of Artemis touched their foreheads in silent acknowledgment as I stepped past them, my eyes fixed straight ahead.

I tried to keep my mind from drifting into memories with little success. I remembered the first time I'd taken these same steps to the palace on feet that still stung from my ordeal in Aulis, hurrying to keep up with little Melissa's quick pace.

And as we passed Theano's home, tears burned at the thought of the woman inside. I'd gone the evening before to say my silent farewell. I couldn't tell her I was leaving, and I wasn't sure she'd understand with the painkilling draughts she drank constantly now. But I held her thin, cool hand and spoke of meaningless things, then planted a light kiss on her forehead and left her bundled in her chair by the hearth fire.

We entered the palace and wove our way straight to the empty throne room. Someone had added plenty of lavender to the lamps, and I was grateful that the sweet smell overpowered the stench of stale oil.

At the entrance to the room, Heliko removed my mantle. Crisp morning air slid through the small windows, brushing my exposed breasts. I imagined this to be the breath of Artemis, telling me she approved of my plans.

Alone, I stepped toward the goddess. She stood naked in her

alcove, her white gown removed ahead of today's ceremony, and I suddenly felt as exposed as she was. It was entirely possible King Thoas knew the plot Melissa and I had hatched in the darkness. If Heliko had guessed I planned to leave, then it would make sense that any one of the king's numerous slaves knew also.

But as I gazed at the goddess, lavender-scented air filling my lungs, I saw her painted eyes come to life. She stared back at me, a silent smile touching her lips. Her outstretched arms reached toward me, welcoming me into a divine embrace.

I closed my eyes and allowed Artemis to rise in me then. She entered through my nose and swelled, expanding herself until she filled my head and my heart, my fingers and my toes. The old scar on my left hand pulsed with her presence, and my scalp tingled.

My lips moved in a whispered version of the prayer Maia had led when she initiated me into Artemis's fold fourteen years before.

Come close to me, I pray,

Artemis of the golden arrows,

and may your protective form appear.

You, who watch over children and maidens alike,

and who guide us into our final sleep.

I, Iphianassa of Tauris, have kept your image before me always.

I have protected and guided the cherished daughters of this land,

And now I ask you to watch over me

And guide me in my new life to come.

The hushed shuffles of many feet sounded behind me, and I allowed my eyes to open slowly. The goddess still gazed at me, and I understood that she was with me now, and would remain with me until I was safely returned home, her stolen idol in my arms.

When I turned, eleven priestesses stood before me, dressed in their fine ceremonial gowns, jewels sparkling from their fingers and wrists and throats.

As their queen, Melissa stood in front. Her dark eyes glimmered with unshed tears, and I hoped she could keep herself composed. We'd said our goodbyes the night before, sitting together in her chamber, clasping hands and whispering remembered scenes from our time together.

"I understand," she'd said in the darkness. "I understand why you're leaving. Why you must return to your home. But I'll never like the idea. I'll never grow used to life without you by my side."

"Come with me," I'd begged. "Bring little Rhanis and Prince Thoas, and come with me. We'll settle in the palace of Mycenae with Elektra, and we'll be untouchable in the hills of Greece."

She'd shaken her head slowly, a motion I felt more than saw. "You know I can't do that."

And now she stood facing me, our priestesses gathered behind her, and I knew she would become the next high priestess when I was gone. I swallowed the tears that wanted to flow and set my jaw against them.

I scanned the women's faces and my heart swelled when I saw Aëdon in the back of the group, features set in hard lines that looked out of place on her round face. Our eyes met for a mere second before she averted her gaze. Her meaning was obvious. She was there, she would support me, but she refused to accept my choice.

CHAPTER 41

Our solemn procession streamed from the palace through the town. We snaked up the narrow People's Way, across the Heights of Artemis, and to the goddess's stone shrine. Like we always did the nights we killed castaways.

The moon's full brilliance was cold on this night, illuminating the stony landscape with an unnerving clarity. I swallowed. Only a few thin clouds were scattered across the starry black sky. We hadn't planned for the moon's revealing brightness. How could we have forgotten she would cast no shadows when she reached her highest perch, just as the sun cast no shadows when he sat at his peak each day?

A breeze whipped in from the sea, cooling the sweat that dampened my neck. I shuddered.

Melissa nudged me with her elbow, and I forced myself to focus on the ceremony. The moon would shine her light on us, whether we wanted her to or not, and I would have to find a way to weave myself invisibly through the crowds when the time came.

But for now, I must perform this ceremony as if no scheme burned in my breast. I must behave as I normally would, so none of my priestesses would suspect anything was amiss.

I'd ordered a great fire built on the Heights of Artemis in place of the modest altar fire we normally lit for these ominous rituals. I couldn't see the flames from where I stood, but the smoke swept toward us, a thick herbal aroma mixing with the woody tang of burning oak.

The herbal mixture was familiar, and I breathed a sigh of relief—my two young acolytes seemed to be following my instructions. Earlier, I'd explained to my priestesses the goddess's wishes for this night. She'd come to me in a dream, I'd said, telling me exactly how this ritual should progress—the ways it would be the same as usual, and the ways it would differ. She'd been very clear, I'd said, that we should not burn her special herbs on her stone altar. Instead, she wanted us to burn them in heaps on the great fire, to cleanse Tauris of the miasma the two prisoners brought with them.

The moon's cool fingers brushed the edge of the altar, slowly creeping toward the center, ready to pour her light onto the flat stone once she reached her zenith. We formed our ring around the altar, and two of my priestesses lit a humble fire in the center. I began the ceremony, singing and praying and chanting out of habit, my mind focused on the events that were to come.

We traced our way back along the cliff's edge, Aëdon's drumming nearly drowning the sounds of the dark waves crashing below. I focused on the sound of my friend's hands tapping the skin of her instrument.

The breeze sent gusts of herbal smoke toward us, and I prayed that enough of the air was hanging around the Heights of Artemis and not blowing away. How nice would it be, I thought, to have a heavy, windless night, like that long-ago night at Aulis.

By the time we returned to the Heights, I plainly saw the goddess had answered my prayer. The herbs were doing their work. This was the sign I needed, proof that she approved my plans, that she wasn't angry with the lies I'd told my priestesses, and that she wanted me to sail to Greece with her likeness in my arms.

The people of Tauris who had crowded close to the flames stood nearly motionless, nearly silent, their eyes lightly glazed and distant. They'd attribute this to the might of Artemis, the goddess hovering closer than usual, showing her delight in the dual sacrifice to come.

But I knew better.

We priestesses developed resistance against the goddess's incense. Over the years, we would have needed more and more of the sacred herbs if we wanted to still feel their tranquil effects. True, my newer priestesses, including my two acolytes, might feel the thick euphoric blanket cocoon their minds. Their hazy vision might provide them a blissful escape from the awful moments that were to come.

But I didn't need those priestesses this night. I needed only Melissa to keep her head as clear as mine.

We formed our line facing the fire, wrists clasped, Aëdon's drumming puncturing the near-silence. King Thoas stepped before the flames, facing us. I peered at him from the corner of my eye. Did his eyelids droop a little? Were the muscles in his face slack, his shoulders loose, his grip on his staff relaxed?

Melissa gave my right wrist a gentle squeeze, and I knew she'd seen what I saw. The herbs had worked on her husband as we'd hoped.

Like all the times we'd performed this gruesome rite, Aëdon's drumming stopped abruptly, sending a shiver up my back. Behind us, a slow shuffling, and I knew Lastratos led the victims toward their fate.

Melissa and I broke from our line and turned to stand beside the king. I was sure he swayed now, tiny motions side to side that would have been easy to miss.

Lastratos led Orestes and Pylades toward us, the lethargic crowd barely parting a path wide enough for the three of them to walk abreast. The boys wore clean white tunics and their wrists were bound with rope that was so loose it was almost comical.

So far, it was all as I'd instructed.

I scanned Orestes's face, his hands, his overall appearance. He seemed calm and present, and as the boys stepped closer, I met his eyes. My own eyes blinked closed for a heartbeat and I sent another grateful prayer to Artemis. My brother was sane. No trace of madness flickered behind dead pupils, no muscles twitched. His head sat straight on his neck, and not cocked to one side, birdlike and listening to his invisible god.

We began our chant, whisper-quiet at first, our voices rising with each passing moment. King Thoas moved so he and I flanked the two victims, his feet dragging in the rocky soil. He stumbled but righted himself, and my lips twitched in a fleeting smile.

Melissa held the covered golden basket toward me, and I lifted the linen cloth with trembling fingers. With both hands, I reached inside and pulled out the gleaming knife, its blade sharpened to a deadly point earlier that morning.

I gazed at the weapon resting across my palms for many

moments, the scar pulsing beneath the bronze. I muttered a prayer, then brought it to my lips, and the warm metal felt as if it moved at my touch, slithering in my hands.

Had the herbs gone to my head, after all?

But when I opened my eyes, I saw the blade was just a blade, resting motionless in my hands.

I moved as if my feet had sunk in mud, twisting toward King Thoas with exaggerated slowness, drawing out the moment so it would feel surreal in the king's dazed mind. My heart crashed behind my ribs as I held the knife toward him, and I forced my breathing into a slow rhythm.

The king reached with his right hand, missing the gilded hilt in his first attempt to take it. He reached again, this time grasping the hilt in loose fingers, and I thought he might drop it.

He looked at me then. Confusion mingled with bliss, and I whispered, "My king, has the goddess filled you?"

Chanting filled the air now, my priestesses nearing the height of the prayer, and Aëdon's thumping hands were nearly overpowered by the voices of my women.

The king stared at me with glassy eyes, as if he hadn't heard my question. He tightened his grip on the knife, turned toward Pylades, and raised the blade.

Pylades's eyes darted between the king and me, fear written across his face. He moved his hands, and I gave my head a tiny shake. His wrists may have been bound in loose loops, but he couldn't break free. Not now.

King Thoas lurched, and for a second, it looked as if Pylades might have to steady his killer on his feet. But the king managed to keep himself upright, and held the blade high once again, moving as if underwater.

A flash caught my eye, and I saw Orestes moving now, following our cousin's lead, and wriggling his wrists in their rope.

I looked at Melissa, standing next to my brother. She blinked, then moved next to me, our backs to my line of chanting priestesses.

"Husband," she started. When he didn't respond to her voice, she tried again. "My king, the goddess is showing her approval. She loves you and our people, and she wishes to banish the pollution these boys brought to your shores. Do you feel her inside you?"

He nodded, his eyes drifting from my face to hers. For a moment I saw the child he'd once been, vulnerable and innocent and ignorant. "She makes me weak," he muttered, his words slurred on his tongue.

"She has filled you with her infinite power." Gently, she touched the fingers that grasped the knife, and he didn't resist. "She wishes for her high priestess to complete the rites."

He moved his eyes back to my face, unfocused and distant, and nodded once. Melissa slid the blade from his hand and passed it to me.

Then, before I had time to reconsider, I did what I needed to do.

Chapter 42

I started with Pylades. I couldn't bring myself to look at his face, but I could see by the way he held his shoulders and squeezed his bound hands into fists that he was terrified. My hand trembled and my scar pulsed as I brought the blade to his throat, bright flames glowing on the polished point. He was half a head taller than me, and I had to hold the knife at an awkward angle to reach under the top hem of his tunic.

My priestesses' chanting reached its crescendo, high-pitched and pleading, and women in the crowd joined their voices until the sound filled the world around us.

The blade met resistance just under the fabric. The chanting behind me rose to sharp ululations. My breath escaped my lungs in a big puff as I thrust the point downward in one smooth, puncturing movement. Dark blood spurted once, then spread across the front of my cousin's tunic, clear and bright in the moonlight.

He crumpled in a heap at my feet, face down and motionless.

I stepped to the side and stood to face my brother. The women behind me maintained their piercing wails, drowning the rush of my own heartbeat, my own breath.

Again, I didn't dare to look into his face, but his shoulders were relaxed, his hands hanging limp before his body. I prayed his mind was still clear and then did the same to him as I'd just done to our cousin. When Orestes collapsed, I sent desperate prayers to Apollo and to Artemis, the twin gods who ruled over my brother and me, begging that the skin I'd punctured had been the tightly sewn sheep intestine, and that the blood spreading across the boys' clean, white tunics had been the blood of the sheep who'd been slaughtered for tonight's feast.

Through Lastratos, I'd sent very clear instructions that the boys were to tie these blood-filled pouches at their throats, under their tunics. But I had no way of knowing whether they'd received the message or if they'd followed my commands.

I forced my breath to steady and willed my pulse to slow as four men carried the limp bodies away. When we performed this grim ritual on other nights, the victims' corpses were thrown over the edge of the cliff. But the men who hauled away my brother and cousin were Lastratos's men, and I knew they wouldn't fly over the cliff tonight.

Melissa and I took our seats on either side of the king, who sat with drooping eyelids and hands held limp in his lap. He moved his head side to side, as if scanning the crowd with his glassy gaze.

An acolyte handed the three of us wine in bronze cups, and I remembered the cup of bitter wine my mother had forced me to drink fourteen years before. A smile touched my lips as I sipped the sweet liquid that filled my cup now. How much had changed in those years.

Musicians brought their instruments next to our dais, the cheerful flute and plucky lyre an almost whimsical clash with the woozy, lethargic crowd. I'd ordered my acolytes to stop feeding the herbs into the flames, but the hazy smoke still carried their soothing effects, and all those who stood nearest the great fire would feel detached and euphoric for a while.

We still had time.

Half of my priestesses continued to sing prayers to Artemis, begging her forgiveness and asking her to help us cleanse her home. They stood to our left, in a line facing us, and their loud voices clashed with the musicians to our right. It was an assault on our ears, and I hoped the confusion of music surrounding us roared chaotically in the king's unfocused mind—and in the minds of all the spectators who were still feeling the surreal effects of the herbs.

Slaves carried heavy platters of meat toward the flames, the blood of fifteen sheep and fifteen cows dripping down their arms. I sat and watched as the other half of my priestesses blessed each platter before shoving pieces onto spits that would hang above the burning altar until a black crust formed, leaving the middle pink with flavor.

People who'd been standing toward the inland portion of the Heights of Artemis began to move toward the roasting meat, their minds less clouded by the herbs. Some pushed their way forward, and I was glad to see a few scuffles break out among the spectators.

I sipped my wine, welcoming any distraction.

As a little tussle began to escalate into a brawl, a flicker of movement near the cliff's edge to my left caught my eye. I turned my head the tiniest bit and saw three figures emerge from behind the great pile of oak that was meant to fuel these celebrations until dawn.

I allowed my eyes to flick to Melissa, whose face told me she'd seen them too.

The men were recognizable, and I hoped it was only because I knew who to look for. Lastratos led the two boys, now wrapped in black cloaks, toward the back of the crowd. The moon seemed to shine directly on them, as if she wished to distinguish the three of them from the rest.

I dared a look at King Thoas and was relieved to see that he was focused—as much as he was able to focus—on a second brawl near the musicians.

The three men picked their way toward the back of the Heights, the moon's rays still seeming to bathe them in her midnight clarity. Lastratos stopped to help break up one of the fights. He'd aged the past few years, his hair peppered with silver and his face lined with deepening wrinkles, but he still moved as if he were twenty.

And as Lastratos held the two brawling men apart with both his hands, one of the few clouds drifted across the moon's bright face. Its edges were soft and wispy, like smoke dissolving into the night sky, but as it passed over the disc, the silver light dimmed, casting the scene in a faint, ghostly shadow. For a few moments, the crowd was lit only by the unreliable flicker of the great fire. Shadows deepened, and I closed my eyes for a heartbeat.

This, surely, was a sign from Artemis. She was happy. She approved.

The cloud passed along and the moon reappeared, but a heaviness I hadn't realized was there lifted from my shoulders. The boys were nowhere in sight, and Lastratos was moving toward the People's Way.

My stomach grumbled as the smell of roasting meat filled the space, but I would have no time to eat on this night. I would save my feasting celebrations for the moment I rested my feet on Greek soil.

I glanced at Aëdon, singing among the half of my priestesses lined to my left. She fixed her eyes on a spot above my head. Regret sat sour in my belly. I would never see her plump round face again, never feel her soothing hand on mine, never hear her calming words again.

We hadn't said goodbye. She'd avoided me the last day, the way she was avoiding me now. And I was going to leave in moments, keeping this unnecessary rift between us. I could only hope that, with time, she'd forgive me for leaving.

I turned toward Melissa. She tried to keep her face neutral, to show nothing in front of the king, but I saw the tears fill the corners of her eyes and her lips tremble. And mine did the same.

She nodded once. It was time for me to leave, to slip out of my seat on a contrived errand to speak with my acolytes about the height of the flames. I must move swiftly, work my way around the crowd and toward the People's Way.

I'd given strict instructions that Lastratos and the boys weren't to wait long. With all the people mingling about for the ceremony and the feast, the risk of discovery was too great. If I was too long in coming, they were to make their way through town without me.

I swallowed the last of my wine, took a deep breath, then rose from my seat. But before I had a chance to step away, one of my acolytes—a young daughter of a palace adviser—held a platter before me. She seemed to come from nowhere, and my heart skipped a beat with surprise. Of course, it was custom for the king, queen, and high priestess to enjoy the first tastes of the feast. How had I forgotten that?

Forcing myself to sit back down, I picked a tiny bite from the platter with my fingers. I didn't even taste the meat as I chewed and swallowed. Had it been mutton or beef?

The girl with the platter of meat was followed by a parade of girls bearing platters heaped with all manner of food. Slices of roasted roots and stewed apples passed before me, followed by dried figs and fresh nut cakes. When a girl tried handing me a bowl of steaming soup, I stood once again.

"Please excuse me, King," I muttered. "I drank too much water before the ceremony."

The king waved me away, focusing on the food before him. His movements seemed more fluid now, and I hoped enough fog still lingered in his mind that he might not notice the length of my absence for a good long while.

Pulling my blue cloak tight to cover my breasts, I picked my way through the crowd and toward the pots hidden behind a purpose-built wall of sawn logs. I wished I hadn't been reduced to using this as my excuse to step away, but there was no point lingering on the indignity of it.

I paused at the beginning of the People's Way. The crowd was thin this far from the fire, only a few slaves rushing in their duties to serve their masters. I glanced at the sky. The moon had started her descent, but her bright rays still illuminated the Heights of Artemis. There were still no shadows to creep into, and I felt exposed standing at the head of the path.

The single cloud that had passed across her face when Orestes and

Pylades made their escape only a few minutes before seemed to have been alone in the otherwise naked sky. Not a single companion floated above.

I sighed, then looked away from the unhelpful sky.

As my gaze slid downward, it met a pair of eyes staring straight at me. Icy fingers ran up my spine in the heartbeat before I recognized the face they sat in.

Heliko stood at the edge of the crowd, looking directly at me.

I froze, as deer are said to sometimes freeze at the sight of an arrow pointed directly at their hearts. My feet refused to step forward, my head refused to turn, my eyes refused to blink. The old scar across my palm throbbed.

Slaves have a way of knowing. They know their masters' every movement through the world, through time. They know all the plans we hatch in our breasts.

Of course, I'd enlisted her help distracting the guard as I spoke with the prisoners. And now I chided myself for involving her at all, for inviting her into even one moment of the plotting.

Chaos filled my panicked mind, and the only thought that came through clearly was this: I was running out of time. If Lastratos hadn't already given up on me, he would at any moment.

And then an unbidden thought: what would Maia do in this situation?

I hadn't thought of Maia in a long time, and her appearance in my memories now felt almost intrusive. But there she was, Muse, alive again in my mind.

And I knew, then, what to do. I pulled my spine straight, raised my chin, and clenched my jaw. Then I turned and walked down the People's Way, and I didn't look back.

Heliko was a slave. She couldn't speak to the king even if she wanted to. The best she could do would be to speak to Melissa. And what good would that do her?

⌀⌀⌀

My breath escaped in an involuntary sigh when I spotted the three men standing against an empty house. They'd squeezed into the lengthening shadow, but it failed to hide them completely.

Lastratos shot me a questioning look, but I brushed past him without explanation. I led Orestes and Pylades through the town like a pair of black-cloaked ducklings, weaving through streets and between buildings. We descended the steep stone stairs, the rush of my pulse drowning any joyous sounds from the festival above.

My bare toes sank into the cool sand, and I shivered. The moon's rays took on a bluish tint, but her white orb spread a glittering path across the rippled sea.

We hugged the black cliff side as we picked our way around the bend, toward my *erêmia*. My thrumming heart slowed bit by bit with each step that took me closer to my peaceful place. The thought that I'd never invited a man to my sacred cave—not even Lastratos—tried to bubble to the surface, but I shoved it away. It was too late to allow doubt to creep into my heart.

"I see the ship!" It was Pylades who broke the silence with his whispers, and it was Lastratos who uttered a low, "Shhh!"

Pylades had been right. The silhouette of a large vessel bobbed in the water ahead, the bulky hull identifying it as a slow merchant ship. Its sides were draped in black fabric, even though the wooden planks were most likely painted black already. Melissa had suggested that extra shield, and I saw the wisdom of cloaking the ship in non-reflective cloth.

A flickering orange glow seeped from the opening of my *erêmia*, and I quickened my steps. Orestes and Pylades tried to follow me into my cave, but I turned and held my hands against their entry, shaking my head. Brother or not, I refused to allow this mother-killer into my sacred space.

A small lamp burned inside the cave, the tiny flames flashing in Orestes's eyes. Mother's eyes. My eyes.

They glowed nearly bronze in this light, and I wondered if mine did too. For the first heartbeat after our eyes met in the dancing light, Orestes gazed back at me. His mind seemed to be clear and he seemed to recognize me. But even as we stood there, even as my chest tightened and my jaw clenched, he transformed.

He tilted his head to the side, listening to that voice in his head, and all light drained from behind his eyes. The blood froze in my veins, but my scar still throbbed.

In that moment, I wanted only one thing. I wanted those dead hazel eyes to vanish from the world forever. I wanted the unblinking boy who stood before me to meet the same fate he'd delivered to my mother. I wanted to send his shade to the underworld with my own hands.

Lastratos cleared his throat, and I blinked. Forcing a shaky breath deep into my lungs, I turned my back to the two black-clad boys who stood far closer to my *erêmia* than I liked. Shuffles behind me, murmurs and movements. I felt the emptiness that now filled the cave opening, a thick, calming blanket that enveloped me. My shoulders and my fists relaxed, and my breaths came easily.

Artemis lay on the stone in the center of the cave, wrapped in pure white cloth and set atop a bed of yellow straw. A single oil lamp burned against the back wall of the cave, far from the flammable object on the stone. The oil burned clean, a good quality that spread a scented white smoke into the small space.

It took a moment for me to place the aroma, a sweet floral scent that seemed both familiar and brand-new at once. My mind reeled, speeding back in time. I was a girl again, wrapped in perfumed arms, my face resting against perfumed robes, a secure smile touching my childish lips.

The girl recognized the jasmine oil in the perfume. Mother's favorite. An aroma I hadn't encountered for fourteen long years.

Through the blur of tears, Artemis seemed to shift in her white shroud and jasmine filled the entirety of my *erêmia*, the whole of my heart.

And I knew.

EPILOGUE

More than forty years have passed and I am nearing my seventieth spring. My ears, as I have said, have failed, and so have my knees. And the gods have stolen all of the memories of the past many years.

But those long-ago days still live in my mind, ripe and raw and real.

You know, Muse, that I did not sail to Greece with Orestes. I did not restore the statue of Artemis to Athens, where men say she originated and where they say she belongs. I did not set my feet on Greek soil again.

It was Aëdon who had lovingly wrapped Artemis and laid her wooden figure on a soft bed of straw. It was Aëdon, with anger still brewing in her breast, who filled the lamp with jasmine-scented oil and lit the tiny flame that would fill my heart with courage. And so it was Aëdon who convinced me to stay in Tauris, even if she did not realize it.

It would be easy now, Melpomene, to set you aside and beg you to focus your attention on another poor soul. You, who are the Muse of tragedy, should be finished with me now. How pleasant would it be to call on one of your many sisters instead of you, to beg her to sing of happiness and joy, simplicity and peace?

How easy for me now, Melpomene, to ignore any evil that followed these events. What pain I could spare myself and all who are listening if I passed by the drawn-out death of gentle Theano, or the sudden illness that struck Lastratos and his faithful Elazar, sending their shades to wander the underworld together. Or if I forgot to mention King Thoas's reckless attack on a band of Taurians to the east that ended in nothing but catastrophe for so, so many.

I would beg your sister to sing of Melissa's third and last child, a little girl who clung to my mantle as a toddler and grew to love me as a second mother. A girl who, now, has accepted a gift which I have gladly given: the sacred role of High Priestess to Artemis.

I would ask your sister to tell of the happy day when, in his new role as King of Tauris, Melissa's only son banished the gruesome ritual his father had refused to abandon. Under the bright young King Thoas, no men were sacrificed to our goddess. With her approval, we replaced these killings with a ceremonial, harmless puncture on the willing victim's neck.

Bards have come with long tales of Orestes. I believe only that he and our cousin Pylades arrived safely in Mycenae and that he reclaimed the throne of the house of Atreus.

They also weave tales of my precious sister. They say it was Elektra who held the blade that stole my mother, the beautiful Queen Clytemnestra, from the world and from me. They lay the guilt in her hands, and hers alone. But I have refused to listen to these stories since the beginning. I refuse to believe even one syllable.

The men who spread these lies have no honor in their hearts. They have no courage. It is far easier to blame a princess than it is to blame a king.

I have told you my story now, Muse, and it is for you to pass along the truths of those distant days. The truth of my father's betrayal and my mother's murder, my lost sister and my mad brother. It is for you to tell of Melissa who became Queen of Tauris and Aëdon who stood by my side, even when I tried to betray her devotion. You can even sing of Maia if you wish. Maia who pointed my stubborn heart in the right direction, though I was too foolish to see it.

I cannot say I did not forget a few moments or misremember small details. But I can say with certainty in my heart that I purposefully left out nothing and embellished nothing and fabricated nothing.

Sing, Muse, not of the princess Iphigenia who was sent to her death on the windless shores of Aulis, but of the priestess Iphianassa, who rose from the smoking ash of a pyre that was lit by kings and by gods and by men.

MORE BY J. SUSANNE WILSON

Thanks for reading! More books are coming soon. You can sign up to be notified of new releases, giveaways, and specials—plus, get a free short story from the Songs and Lies world.

www.jsusannewilson.com

I hope you enjoyed this book and would really appreciate a short review on the page where you bought the book. Reviews are important in helping readers find new authors and in helping authors find new readers.
Thank you!

Author's Note

As with most Greek myths, many versions of Iphigenia's story come down to us from antiquity. This work is based primarily on the play *Iphigenia in Tauris* by Euripides (c. 414-413 BCE) with some hints of the same author's *Iphigenia in Aulis* (c. 405 BCE). Of course, it was necessary to expand on his work and to fill in some missing pieces.

One of the chief areas I chose to stray from Euripides's play was by removing divine intervention. In *Iphigenia in Tauris*, our heroine is whisked away from her father's blade by Artemis and magically transported to the land of the Taurians.

Because I wanted my version to sit firmly in the historical fiction genre, it was essential to remove all elements of fantasy and magic. In this example, it is Clytemnestra, and not the goddess, who orchestrates Iphigenia's rescue from sacrifice and removal to a faraway land.

Another area in which I stray from the play is in the ending. Euripides ends his play like this: Orestes and Pylades are shipwrecked and slated for sacrifice, an unhappy Iphigenia tends to them, brother and sister recognize one another and hatch a plan to escape Tauris. It is Iphigenia who sketches the plot to deceive

King Thoas and the brother-sister-cousin trio escapes with the statuette of Artemis in tow. They eventually return to Greece where Iphigenia goes on to establish anew cult of Artemis outside Athens. The end.

I originally mimicked this ending for my book. And I didn't like it. I felt like I was removing Iphigenia from one unhappy position on foreign soil and placing her directly into an equally unhappy position in her homeland. But I wanted my Iphigenia to exert her own power, to make her own decisions, to craft her own ending. And so, I gave her the freedom she deserved and let her take the reins.

Regarding the land of the Taurians, I must point out a glaring fact: there was never a place called Tauris. During the Late Bronze Age, when this story is set, the people who we call Greek had not yet colonized outside the Mediterranean.

The people referred to as Taurians were, indeed, real people who lived in the north of the Black Sea region in modern-day Crimea. Greeks didn't colonize the peninsula until the fifth century BCE—more than 800 years after the events of *The Death and Life of Iphigenia.*

For a long time, I wasn't sure how to handle this massive time discrepancy. Because Euripides was writing in the fifth century BCE, it made sense for him to place Iphigenia among the Taurians after her failed sacrifice. But I wanted to write a story that was historically plausible, so this was a challenge.

I toyed with a couple options: I could invent a purely fictional location, or I could send Iphigenia to another real Greek city, like Athens. I didn't like the first option because I didn't want to confuse historical accuracy with fantasy. And the second option wasn't ideal because I really wanted to place Iphigenia into a purely foreign land and remove any chance of her returning home to Mycenae. In the end, I decided to use the location that would be familiar to many readers, even if the timing doesn't line up.

This is all, I suppose, what they call creative license.

Acknowledgements

Every story has its hidden heroes. These are mine.

My heartfelt thanks go to Mary Depew, Associate Professor Emerita of Classics at the University of Iowa, whose encyclopedic knowledge of ancient Greek culture and religion proved invaluable. I appreciate the time you took to discuss the importance of priestesses in Bronze Age Greece and to check the words I included in Greek.

I'm grateful to my wonderful editors who helped sculpt this story into its final version, polished each line, and added all the missing commas. Pippa Brush Chappell, Hailey Peterson, and Naomi Munts, thank you for lending me your expertise.

And Jessica Bell, you somehow captured Iphigenia's entire world in a single cover design, and I don't know how you did it.

Thank you to my earliest readers—Howard, Jerry, Kathy, and Tom—who helped guide Iphigenia's journey in the right direction.

A huge thank you to my family for your heartfelt encouragement and endless curiosity. Special gratitude goes to my husband for your patience and for tolerating an absent-minded wife for the nearly three years this book filled my mental space.

My humble thanks go to you, my reader, for taking a chance on a new voice.

Any mistakes are, naturally, my own.

ABOUT THE AUTHOR

J. Susanne Wilson is a historical fiction writer focusing on myths set in Bronze Age Greece. She earned her B.A. in Ancient Civilizations from the University of Iowa. Her concentration was on Greek and Roman art, religion, history, and languages. She lives in the Midwest United States with her husband and their cat.

www.ingramcontent.com/pod-product-compliance
Lightning Source LLC
Chambersburg PA
CBHW020349010826
48973CB00005B/1333